Praise for the slightly twisted and wholly terrifying thrillers of Thomas William Simpson

THE CARETAKER

"A clever thriller with an original plot and twists that will keep fans of suspense fiction turning pages until the end."
—*Phillip Margolin*

"An elaborate and sinister con game . . . genuinely surprising."
—*Chicago Tribune*

"The ultimate revenge novel."
—*Roanoke Times & World News*

"A page-turner that will grab even those not addicted to them."
—*Booknews from The Poisoned Pen*

THE HANCOCK BOYS

"An imagin

Bantam Books by Thomas William Simpson

THE CARETAKER

THE HANCOCK BOYS

THE EDITOR

THE
EDITOR

Thomas William Simpson

BANTAM BOOKS
New York   Toronto   London   Sydney   Auckland

THE EDITOR

A Bantam Book / September 2000

ISBN: 0-553-57396-9

Published simultaneously in the United States and Canada

Bantam Books are published by Bantam Books, a division of Random
House, Inc. Its trademark, consisting of the words "Bantam Books"
and the portrayal of a rooster, is Registered in U.S. Patent and Trademark Office and in other countries. Marca Registrada. Bantam Books,
1540 Broadway, New York, New York 10036.

PRINTED IN THE UNITED STATES OF AMERICA
OPM   10   9   8   7   6   5   4   3   2   1

If life had a second edition,
how would I correct the proofs?

—JOHN CLARE

DECEMBER 29.

Yesterday the judge sentenced the man who murdered my wife and son. I sat in the courtroom and held my breath. The judge ordered the creature to serve two consecutive life terms for his ruthless acts of brutal and random violence.

I felt only a few fleeting moments of satisfaction. Secretly, I had hoped the court would deem it appropriate to take the creature's life. Yes, me, Sam Adams, a man fully and firmly against the death penalty even in the most grisly cases, wanted an eye for an eye.

Amazing how emotional vengeance can so completely swallow up intellectual commitment.

But now I face the most difficult and daunting challenge of all: getting on with it. My own life, I mean.

DECEMBER 30.

A cold, dreary day. Damp and gray. Like my mood.

I stayed in bed until almost noon. No need to get up and go to work. Jackson, Jones & Reynolds always closes up shop between Christmas and New Year's. A gift from the boss for a job well done.

In the past I always looked forward to this extra week off. It was a time to relax and rejuvenate, to spend time with the family, with my wife and my son. But this year I wish the office was open. I would prefer the hustle and bustle of my coworkers to all this silence and solitude.

JANUARY 1.

I drove into the city last night to celebrate New Year's Eve with a few friends who live on the Upper West Side, our old neighborhood. I might not have been the life of the party, but I managed to have a good time. It felt good just to be among people enjoying their lives.

I even joked around and danced with a young woman, recently divorced, who had surely been invited for my benefit. Or I for hers. She was sweet and amusing, but I sensed something tragic about her. I felt quite certain she had some terrible secret hidden beneath her pretty eyes and her engaging smile. Probably it had to do with her ex-husband. Had he abused her, either physically or emotionally? Or had he simply made off with the house and kids after an expensive and exhausting legal battle?

I decided I could not bear to hear the details. Nor could I share with her, over several quiet dinners in mediocre restaurants, the intimate details of my own tragedy. So after a round of cheers at the midnight hour, followed by a quick kiss and one last glass of champagne, I made my escape after thanking my hosts for a very pleasant evening.

They, of course, wanted me to stay, had expected me to stay, to spend the night. A bed had been made up for just that contingency. But I begged off, claiming many things to do, what with a new year suddenly and relentlessly upon us.

JANUARY 2.

I live now, at least for the time being, in a small cottage on a small estate on the outskirts of a small town. I did not used to live here. I used to live about an hour from here. In a larger town closer to New York City. In a house. A house that Ellen and I bought and lived in together with our son.

I loved that house: three bedrooms, two-car garage, white picket fence, chair rail in the dining room. I put that chair rail in myself one rainy afternoon four years ago. Painted it Williamsburg blue.

I felt safe in that house.

But I could not stay there. Not after what happened. So I moved out here a week or so ago, the day after Christmas.

JANUARY 4.

I had a dream last night about Nicky. A nightmare really. I woke up in a cold sweat, wet and shivering.

Yes, I had to remind myself, it is true: I have lost my son.

But I am still a young man, still over a year away from forty. I am plenty young enough to have another child. Another son. I could watch him grow up. Love and nurture him so that he will take care of me when I am old and decrepit.

JANUARY 6.

I possess the most vivid memories of the first time I ever laid eyes on the young woman who would eventually become my wife. It was early summer, maybe even the very first day of summer. Fourteen and a half years ago. Up on Cape Cod. Out on Nauset Beach.

I had the night off from work. Early in the evening I went out for a walk. I wound up, as usual, at the beach. I loved to walk in the wet sand, the waves washing up around my ankles. The water was still cold that early in the season, but the chilly sensation felt fine, especially the occasional wave that broke late and soaked the bottom of my shorts.

I saw them coming from a long way off: a girl and her dog. The dog raced in and out of the surf, utterly impervious to the temperature of the water. The girl flipped a bright orange Frisbee out beyond the waves. With tireless enthusiasm, the dog battled the breakers to make the retrieval.

As they drew closer, I could see the dog was a large,

splendid-looking golden retriever with an impressive head and a rich reddish coat. Absolutely my favorite kind of canine.

We had owned several goldens during my youth. Although, my mother often claimed that it sometimes seemed as though they owned us. Especially old Dolly Madison. Dolly lived to the ripe old age of seventeen. She was my father's faithful companion, rarely leaving his side. She used to accompany him to many of his lectures. That old dog knew more about American literature than most Dartmouth graduates.

As the girl and her dog neared, I could see this was not a girl at all, but a young woman with the physical presence of an adolescent. She was tall and thin and loose limbed. Her long legs carried her easily though the wash. She pulled that bright orange Frisbee from her dog's mouth and casually flipped it out into the cold Atlantic. And when a hearty wave got the best of her beast, tossing that golden back up onto the beach, she just laughed and patted the dog's head.

"Come on, Reggie," she encouraged him. "Go out and get it, boy! Go on now and get it!"

She had long, reddish brown hair, loosely braided and reaching practically to her waist. Her eyes were blue, I was sure, though I could not tell just how blue in that dull, dusky light. She had beautiful skin, clear and creamy with just a faint hint of the sun's color.

I took a quick look up and down the beach. Except for a couple walking arm in arm off to the north, we had that open stretch of sand all to ourselves. I tried to think of something clever to say. Something witty.

As the distance between us diminished to just a few feet, I settled for the obvious. "That's a good-looking dog you have there."

She gave me only the briefest glance, preferring to keep her gaze fixed on her furry friend. But her rejoinder held hope. "Don't tell him that. His ego's big enough as it is."

I laughed, probably with a bit more vim and vigor than necessary. She threw me another glance, this one slightly more curious than the first.

Reggie came bounding out of the surf, his Frisbee held firmly between his jaws. He headed straight for me, gave me a sniff, then shook quite a puddle of salt water from his coat.

I did my best to slide back out of range.

"Reggie!" shouted his mistress, in a not very authoritative voice. "That's an ugly display of manners."

I assured her the soaking was quite all right while at the same time stepping forward to extract the Frisbee from Reggie's mouth. Reggie, however, did not know me. He had no intention whatsoever of giving up his precious plastic disk to some total stranger.

I gave a tug or two, then found myself uncertain as to how to proceed. I could give up and assume a stance of utter disinterest. Or I could make a concerted effort to gain possession of the Frisbee, either through force or cajolery. I took a moment to wonder which scenario would play better in the eyes of the pretty young lady standing now almost close enough to touch.

Before I could make up my mind, she commanded, her voice somewhat more forceful than before, "Give it up, Reggie!"

Reggie glanced sideways at her, then relaxed his powerful jaws. I grabbed the disk and prepared to give it a ride. I had passed a few college hours playing Frisbee on old Dartmouth Green.

But Reggie, tense with anticipation, suddenly redirected his energy. His head turned, his ears sprang forward, and his eyes focused on something farther down the beach. I took a look myself. It was the couple, still walking arm in arm, now coming closer. And then I saw they had a dog with them.

Reggie saw the dog also. He took off. He went from standing still to a full sprint in about a second and a half.

"Reggie!" his mistress hollered. "No!"

But Reggie had no intention of turning back.

She grabbed the Frisbee from me and started off after him. "I have to go," she shouted over her shoulder. "Reggie drives that dog absolutely crazy."

I tried to think fast. I did not want this pretty girl just running out of my life. "Hey, wait!"

"What?"

I thought as fast as I could. "Do you really think," I shouted, "that dogs have egos?"

I could hear her laughing, even as she continued to run in the hard wet sand.

I tried to think of something else. "Why do you call him Reggie?"

She turned around and smiled at me, but she kept running, backward. "For Reggie Jackson. Right fielder for the New York Yankees!"

I shouted another question or two. But she didn't answer. Or maybe she couldn't hear me. And a moment later she was gone, in hot pursuit of her four-legged friend.

JANUARY 7.

I had moved out to the Cape earlier that year. At first I had lived up in Wellfleet with an old college buddy. After a month or two I'd rented a small apartment on the second floor of an old house halfway between Orleans and East Orleans. If the wind blew out of the east and I had my windows open, I could sometimes hear the waves crashing out on Nauset Beach.

I had settled on the Cape after a lengthy global ramble in the hopes of writing my first novel. I was twenty-four, three full years out of Dartmouth College. Much to my father's disappointment, I had not done much in those years to advance my vocational standing in the world. I'd worked at a wide variety of menial jobs; I'd traveled wherever the wind blew me. I came to the Cape prepared to buckle down and make something of my life.

Throughout our youth, our father had drummed into us the absolute necessity of striving for success and achievement. We were, after all, descended from men who had signed the Declaration of Independence and served in the highest levels of government, including the office of president of the United States. So yes, I felt a certain obligation to pursue my ambitions. Since just a boy I had wanted to become a great writer of powerful novels. Our father had read aloud to us from the works of Hawthorne and Melville and Cooper and Twain. These men, he told us, had helped shape a nation's destiny with their pens.

I wanted to do the same.

Potent stuff, but along the way I had to support myself. So in my other life I had a job on the Cape as a waiter at the Orleans Bar & Grill. We served burgers and steaks and wine and beer and a wide variety of homemade ice cream. I worked lunch three days a week and dinner three days a week. It paid the bills. And I still had plenty of free time to pursue my literary ambitions. And to stay in shape. I played in two basketball leagues and a lacrosse league. Plus I ran on the beach and rode my bike everywhere since I didn't own a car.

Anyway, a day or two after our brief meeting on the beach, Reggie's mistress walked into the restaurant. I had been hoping she would. I spotted her immediately from back in the kitchen. She came in with three of her friends. The four girls were clowning around, laughing at some joke I couldn't hear. I just stood there and watched as they sat in a booth along the front window. I remember she had on a New York Yankees baseball cap. Her long reddish brown braid hung out through the hole in the back.

Carla, the hostess and day manager, bustled into the kitchen. I made myself look busy. "You have a booth up front, Sam. A bunch of gigglers."

They were in my station, but I did not want to wait on them. I did not want her to see me as a lowly waiter. So I hung back and tried to plot my next move. I tried to get one of the other servers to take my table, but no one was available.

Carla, an efficiency nut, made another pass. "That window booth still doesn't have menus, Sam."

Okay. So I scooped up some menus, took a deep breath, and headed out to take my lumps. By the time I reached the booth, they had all made tepees out of their napkins. And they were laughing, uncontrollably. I mean they were laughing so hard that tears streamed down their faces.

I gave them a smile and started handing out the menus. This bit of business caused them to laugh even harder. And when I asked, "Can I offer you ladies something to drink?" they almost fell on the floor from the sheer hilarity of my question.

"Hey," said Reggie's mistress, bringing herself back

under control for a few seconds, "I know you. You're the guy from the beach."

I nodded in acknowledgment.

"God," she added, "I thought you were a lawyer or something. You looked so serious out there."

This caused a new round of laughter to gush from their mouths. I felt insulted and started immediately to no longer like her.

They did not look at their menus. They knew what they wanted: chocolate malts with lots of extra malt. I filled their order and kept my distance. They left without leaving a tip. In fact, their bill came to something like eleven dollars and thirty cents, but they only left a little more than ten.

I covered the difference.

JANUARY 10.

Here is how I wound up living in this cottage.

One Sunday afternoon this past December, I was out driving around in the minivan, killing time, more or less waiting to go back to work Monday morning. I took this turn and that turn, not really paying much attention to my route or to my destination. I eventually stopped to buy a sandwich and something to drink. The town looked familiar. Ellen and Nicky and I had definitely stopped here before. I even remembered the small café down by the Delaware River.

I sat at a table overlooking the river and asked the waitress if she might have something I could read. A newspaper or a magazine. She brought me the menu and a well-thumbed copy of the local paper, a weekly rag featuring the best places in the area to buy Christmas trees. I did not want to think about Christmas, so I turned the page.

There was not much of interest: a deadly car crash out on Route 31, rabies discovered in local raccoon population, angry words exchanged at planning board meeting between residents and developer, high school basketball scores. Having been both a high school and a college cager, I read these scores over with at least some momentary interest.

The waitress brought me an enormous whole-wheat pita sandwich stuffed with turkey and cheese and an assortment of vegetables. I dug in and turned to the classified section in the back of the paper. There was a drum set for sale. I'd been wanting to buy a drum set for years. Not because I knew how to play the drums, but just because I thought it might be nice to have something to bang on. I've always considered the beating of drums one of man's most basic primal urges.

I browsed through the classified until I reached the For Rent section. There were a few apartments for rent, one or two houses, but the final listing immediately caught my eye. For months I had been thinking about moving, at least temporarily, out of our house, the house where Ellen and Nicky and I had lived together for almost six years. I often felt sad and lonely and gloomy in that house. At least once or twice a week I felt an almost desperate need to escape that house, to abandon my grief.

So I sat there eating my sandwich and reading that listing over and over:

ONE BEDROOM COTTAGE AVAILABLE ON SMALL COUNTRY ESTATE. PARTIALLY FURNISHED. CLEAN AND QUIET.

Soon thereafter I found myself searching out a pay
phone, shoving some coins into the slot, dialing the
number at the end of the listing. A boy answered, perhaps a young man. I told him I was interested in the
cottage. He said fine, but that I had to come see it immediately or else wait until the end of the week. I
wanted to tell him I would wait until the end of the
week, but instead, I heard myself asking for directions.

It was not far. Just a few minutes outside of town. A
wooden sign hung at the end of the drive: BLIND PASS.
I turned in, my instincts telling me to retreat even as I
pushed forward. The driveway was lined on both
sides with old and gnarled sycamores. Dead ahead
stood the main residence, a huge and ancient Tudor
with a slate roof and ivy-shrouded walls. A long black
Mercedes-Benz sedan sat outside the detached garage.

I could see the cottage out back and off to the side.
It stood in a clearing, beyond a clump of evergreens. It
looked quiet back there all right. Quiet and peaceful. I
thought it looked like an excellent place to pull myself
back together, to work and read and maybe even do
some writing again.

I parked, combed my hair, took a deep breath, and
headed for the front door. A cold wind blew, reminding me that winter would soon be rapping on the windows, rattling the glass.

I rang the bell, waited. A minute or two passed. I
rang again, then knocked on the door.

A young man, somewhere between sixteen and
twenty, finally answered my knock. He stood about
my height, right around six feet. He wore gray wool
slacks and a navy blazer. He looked like a young Tony
Perkins, of *Psycho* fame, with his wandering eyes and

his sweep of wavy brown hair, held in place by some kind of shiny hair gel.

He threw me a smile, a slight hint of condescension in the curl of his upper lip. "You called about the cottage?"

"Yes," I said. I reached out to shake his hand. "I'm Sam Adams."

He glanced at my hand but did not take it. "Roger Richmond," he told me, his eyes darting all over the place. Then, "Listen, Sam, Mother and I are on our way out, so we'll have to make this fast."

Roger Richmond did not invite me inside. Instead, he stepped outside, and together we made our way along the brick sidewalk and across the driveway to the cottage. Roger took the lead. He walked quickly. I fell in behind him, almost at a march. There was no time for small talk. Roger marched up to the cottage, pushed open the door (it was not locked), and beckoned for me to enter. It was a simple, one-story dwelling, clean and spare. I felt attracted to it immediately. I knew right away that I could live there.

An entrance foyer opened up into a large space that served as living room, dining room, and kitchen. The entire room had a high, vaulted ceiling. Off the back was a bedroom and a remodeled bathroom. Everything had recently been painted, and the wall-to-wall carpeting looked brand-new. There was not much in the way of furniture, but I saw virtually everything I would need, at least in the short haul: bed, dresser, sofa, table, chairs.

"The rent," Roger Richmond informed me, his eyes still roaming, never quite meeting mine, "is eight fifty a month. Plus utilities: heat and electric. Mother likes a month's security and ninety days' notice before you move out."

"Do you allow pets?"

He smirked. "Mother likes dogs, but she hates cats. Too damn quiet and sneaky for her taste."

"I have two golden retrievers."

"I don't see a problem."

I had a few more questions, but Roger was in a hurry. He more or less shooed me out of the cottage and dragged me back to the big house.

"Now listen, Sam," he said, suddenly very chummy, hand on my shoulder, as we went through the front door, "before I take you inside to meet Mother, I should warn you: she's blind. Blind as a bat. But don't let on. She hates when people make a thing about it. Absolutely cannot stand anyone feeling sorry for her. Pride and ego and all that shit."

I gave Roger a glance, then assured him I would give nothing away. I followed him down a long, dimly lit hallway. Dark paneling covered the walls. We went through a set of solid cherry doors into a large oval room. Floor-to-ceiling double-hung windows most of the way around the oval. Not much furniture in the room, but a magnificent Oriental carpet covered the middle of the hardwood floor. A cello lay upon the carpet.

JANUARY 11.

I knew the instrument lying on that Oriental carpet was a cello, and not, say, a double bass or a viol, because Karin Dodd, the first true love of my life, had been a cellist. Seeing that cello lying upon that Oriental carpet brought back an instant array of erotic memories. Karin and I had more than once made love in the presence of that musical instrument.

But the memories faded the moment I lifted my eyes and glanced across the large, oval room. There, perched upon a love seat upholstered with bright red flowers and yellow songbirds, was my would-be landlady, Roger's mother, Mrs. Richmond. She sat with her legs curled up under her behind, her arms resting on her lap. She looked tranquil and serene, almost Buddha-like. The sun streamed through the window over her right shoulder. She had her neck cocked slightly and her face tilted toward the sun, like a plant seeking nourishment.

As Roger and I came across the hardwood floor, the heels of our shoes *tap tap tapping*, Mrs. Richmond casually turned our way. A pair of small dark glasses in gold frames covered her eyes. I could not tell her age; no longer young but far from old: forty, maybe forty-five. I remember thinking she must have had her son as a rather young woman.

"Mother," said Roger, "the man is here about the cottage."

She took several moments to consider this announcement.

It might have been my imagination, but I could have sworn I saw her sniff the air.

"Is he white?" she asked.

My eyes opened wide at that one. I threw a glance Roger's way. He did not so much as bat an eye.

"Yup, white as the moon."

"Any unusual physical characteristics?"

"Nope."

"Over twenty and under forty?"

This time Roger tossed off another smirk. "Closer to the latter, but within that range."

"What kind of car?"

"Late model minivan."

"Domestic?"

"Plymouth."

I was surprised Roger had noticed these innocuous details. I would have figured him for someone indifferent to the outside world.

The thought of Roger checking me out, sizing me up, made me only slightly uncomfortable. I was actually mildly amused, an emotion I had not experienced much in months.

"A domestic minivan," said Mrs. Richmond, her voice resonating with depth and clarity, each word perfectly enunciated. "What does that tell us? Perhaps that you are a family man, Mr. . . ." She waited, I realized, belatedly, for me to offer my name.

"Adams," I said. "Sam Adams."

"Ah. Like the patriot?"

"Yes," I answered. And added, "Another in a long line."

"A fine American epithet. Short and to the point."

I smiled, then remembered she was blind. "Yes."

"Come over here, Sam Adams, and let me get a feel for you."

I took a few hesitant steps in her direction. She scared me. Perhaps scared is too strong a word. Let us say she unsettled me. I did not know exactly why. Her blindness? Her bluntness? Her beauty? Probably a combination of all three. Evelyn Richmond was certainly beautiful: small and slight and angular with smooth, pale skin and short, jet black hair, cut like a boy's.

"Closer," she said, as though issuing a command. "Close enough so I can touch your face. It will help me know who I am dealing with."

I stepped up to that love seat with some amount of

trepidation and bent until my eyes were level with her dark glasses. She must have felt my breath upon her lips, for she reached out with her right hand and very gently began to touch my face with her fingertips.

"Are you nervous, Mr. Adams?"

"No," I lied.

"Of course you are. That's all right. This is not something you subject yourself to every day." She worked her fingertips over my chin and up my cheeks, across my nose and around my eyes. She moved out to my right ear, then along my forehead to the left ear.

"You have excellent skin, Mr. Adams. You must come from good stock."

"My mother," I assured her, partly in jest, but also in an effort to make a good impression, "is active in the DAR."

Mrs. Richmond seemed both pleased and amused by this bit of news. She continued to stroke my cheek. "I would say you are between thirty-six and thirty-nine years old. You are carrying quite a lot of tension in your facial muscles. I suspect it is more than just my request to touch you.

"Mrs. Richmond," I told her, "your assessment of my age is both accurate and remarkable. But as for the tension in my facial muscles, I think you underestimate the power of your touch."

This gave her a moment's pause. Then the hint of a smile crossed her face. "I see you are a talker, Mr. Adams. 'Beware of the smooth talkers,' my dear and now departed mother used to tell me."

I smiled back, then, once again remembering her blindness, I let out a small chuckle for her benefit. "Let me assure you, Mrs. Richmond, I am perfectly harmless."

This caused Mrs. Richmond to lean back in that love seat and laugh. "No man is perfectly harmless, Mr. Adams. Although, experience has taught me that men who have dogs are sometimes less harmful. Especially if they are connected with one of the more congenial and gregarious breeds. What kind of dog do you live with, Mr. Adams?"

"Actually," I answered, "I have two dogs. I suppose their scent lingers?"

Mrs. Richmond nodded. "Yes. But not in an unpleasant way." Then, "Longhaired dogs would be my guess. Retrievers, perhaps, who have recently gotten wet."

I was impressed. "Exactly right," I told her. "Golden retrievers. A mother and her daughter. They had a long run and a swim just yesterday. In water so cold it turned my fingertips blue."

All this news brought a genuine smile to Mrs. Richmond's beautiful face. I could see the cottage was mine, if I so chose. The pros and cons flashed through my brain. It would be both scary and troublesome to move out of our house, the house Ellen and Nicky and I had made our home. On the other hand, I desperately needed a change of venue, someplace removed from all the memories and daily reminders.

"Tell me, Mr. Adams," Mrs. Richmond asked, "are you gainfully employed?"

"I like to think so," I told her.

"What do you do?"

"I am an editor at Jackson, Jones and Reynolds in New York City."

"The book publisher?"

"Yes."

"Then I may assume you can afford to pay the rent?"

"Absolutely. On time and in full."

She leaned back into that love seat and took a few moments to think things over. I glanced over my shoulder at Roger. Was that a scowl I spotted on his face? Tough to tell; he wiped it off the instant he caught my gaze.

"I suppose, Mr. Adams," said Mrs. Richmond, finally, "I should ask you some personal questions. Such as who are you, where do you presently reside, why do you wish to move, do you possess any unpleasant habits, have you ever been convicted of a crime? But you will certainly hide any unpleasantries from me, so I, for the time being, will forgo any interrogations. I will simply trust my instincts. If you can afford to give my son a check for the first month's rent, plus a month's security, the cottage is yours anytime after Christmas."

Before I left the Richmonds' house, I wrote Roger a check for seventeen hundred dollars. He snatched it from my grasp.

JANUARY 12.

Who am I? Where did I used to live? How do I make a living? Have I ever been convicted of a crime?

What is more important in life? To ask questions? Or provide answers? To confess our sins? Or to commit no sins at all?

What is a sin anyway? Something that offends God? How do we know what offends God? Isn't it rather presumptuous of us to conjecture as to what may or may not offend the Almighty? Maybe nothing offends Him. Maybe He is actually a She. And maybe She is merely amused by all we do here on earth. Maybe She enjoys watching us love and slander and slaughter one another. Maybe She gets off on the whole tempestuous cycle of life and death and rebirth.

All I know for sure is that Mrs. Richmond has nothing to fear from me. I have a good job and have never been convicted of a crime. My worst offense would be going the wrong way on a one-way street. And even that was just an accident. It happened up in Boston one night many years ago when Ellen and I were trying to find the Boston Garden for a game between the Celtics and the Knicks. Ellen, map in hand, was the navigator. I told the policeman that he should be giving her the ticket. He laughed, ripped the ticket off his pad, and said, "People from out of town go the wrong way on these streets all the time. Handing out tickets is how we fill the city coffers."

JANUARY 13.

I have been living in the cottage now for almost three weeks. I did not bring much with me. I brought the dogs, of course, Sunshine and Moxie, and whatever else I could pack into the van. Mostly I brought clothes and a few personal items, including pictures of Ellen and Nicky. I also brought a TV set, a radio, some books, and my cross-country skis.

I have not even unpacked the TV or the radio yet. I have had no use for either one.

When I moved in, I had no idea how long I might stay here. I felt strange about leaving our home, as if I was somehow abandoning Ellen and Nicky. I thought I might just stay here on weekends. I had no definite plans. My life, I must say, has been very much up in the air for some time now, really since the terrible events of last Easter, more than eight and a half months ago, two hundred and fifty-three days. I eat. I sleep. I go to work. And I often stay at work long after everyone else has gone home. I read. I write in my journal. I try to get a little exercise each day. But mostly, if I'm honest about it, I feel sad and lonely, adrift.

When I arrived at the cottage, that first day, a few weeks ago, I found the door unlocked. I pushed it open and entered. Everything was clean and tidy, just as it had been on the day of my initial visit. On the kitchen counter I found a note:

> Dear Mr. Adams,
>
> Your check cleared. The cottage is yours.
> You are responsible for any and all damage.
> I hope everything is satisfactory.
>
>   Roger Richmond

And that was it. Nothing more. Not another word. So while the dogs raced around, sniffing everything in sight, I carried my gear in from the minivan and busied myself putting things away.

JANUARY 14.

Since my arrival here, I have seen zero activity over at the main house. No one comes or goes. No lights switch on at dusk. No smoke rises from the three massive chimneys. No cars venture up the drive. The sound of Mrs. Richmond's cello has not echoed through the still winter air as I had hoped it would.

I have been feeling kind of blue. Depressed might better describe my mood. I know all the reasons why. It is not some great mystery. My life has been turned upside down and inside out, and some days it is all I can do to haul myself out of bed and splash some cool water on my face.

JANUARY 15.

Early this morning, in that vague light just before dawn, I had a terrible scare. I was sound asleep when suddenly both the dogs began to bark. My eyes snapped open. I came wide awake.

And there, outside the window, staring in at me, baseball bat in hand, stood the creature. I screamed, then scrambled out of bed. He raised that bat high over his head and brought it crashing down against my bedroom window. The glass shattered.

That glass shattering shook me from my dream. Yes, just a dream, a very bad dream. A nightmare. The creature cannot hurt me. He has been locked away, incarcerated for his heinous crimes.

JANUARY 17.

This morning, while out with the dogs, I met the people who live across and down the street. Except for Mrs. Richmond, they are my closest neighbors. Frank and Carol Karr. Frank has a construction business: Karr Construction. I am not quite sure what he constructs. Carol stays home and takes care of the kids. Three of them, two girls and a boy. The youngest is

Kathleen, age nine and a half. She could not get enough of Sunshine and Moxie. They licked her from head to toe while she giggled and begged for more.

I told Kathleen that she could come over and play with Sunshine and Moxie whenever she wanted. Then I told her I would pay her if she would occasionally walk the dogs for me when I had to work late. She thought getting paid to do something she wanted to do anyway sounded like the best job in the whole world.

JANUARY 21.

I have not written in the journal for a few days. Too busy at work. I have half a dozen projects going at once: four novels, a biography, and a nonfiction book on fly fishing. I am not a fly fisherman, but the author's style mesmerizes. He makes what I always considered a fairly dull sport both entertaining and exhilarating. He puts me right out there on the water with him. As his editor, all I have to do is keep him from going off in too many different directions. He wants to explore every minor tributary. I want him to stick to the main river.

It has not been difficult for me to wield my editorial sword. This young man bends at the first sound of praise.

With all these projects vying for my attention, my mind sometimes feels like a jumble of disconnected prose. Still, I press on. I would rather have too much work than not enough. Or, God forbid, none at all.

A couple nights ago I actually slept at the office. Just curled up under my desk and nodded off. But before I did, I called Carol Karr and asked her if Kathleen could feed, water, and walk the dogs. In the background I could hear Kathleen giving a very positive response. I found out later that she actually brought Sunshine and Moxie home so they would not have to spend the night alone.

Nevertheless, my assistant does not think I should be sleeping on the floor under my desk. Mitchell has been my assistant since September. He graduated from the University of Pennsylvania last June. This is his first job. He worries about me all the time, insists I eat healthy things for lunch and drink these herbal tea concoctions instead of coffee. When he found me the other morning, fast asleep under my desk in this twisted and contorted position, he said, "This is not a good thing, Sam. You're going to drive yourself to an early grave."

I hope not. I have too much I still want to accomplish. Of course, other days I wish it would all be over. Quickly and painlessly.

JANUARY 22.

My commute from here to the office is considerably longer than the one I had from our house. From the house it took me just over an hour door to door. I drove the car to the station, took the train into the city, and walked or took the subway to the offices of Jackson, Jones & Reynolds up at Rockefeller Center.

But from the cottage my commute takes closer to an hour and three-quarters each way. But all this extra commuting time does not bother me. In fact, I enjoy it. The drive takes me through some beautiful rolling countryside. And I have always loved trains. As a young man, fresh out of college, I traveled all over Europe and parts of South America by train. It is an excellent way to travel. You just sit back, settle into the rhythm of the rails, and let your thoughts wander.

During my new commute to the office, I stare out the window, watch the scenery slide by, maybe work on a manuscript. I always have a manuscript within reach. Never travel without one. But some days I want nothing more than to just ride the train back and forth, back and forth. The gentle rocking motion is soothing, like being a baby again in my mother's arms.

Of course, I occasionally fall into a funk on the train if I think too hard or too long about Ellen and Nicky. This, I know now from experience, is not healthy. So I do not allow myself to grieve or feel sorry for myself for more than a few minutes each day. Half an hour at the very most. I learned early on in my period of mourning that days and even weeks can be consumed by grief and self-pity. So I developed the mental fortitude to tough it out, to keep my mind and body focused on more positive rewards.

In bed at night is still the roughest time. During those quiet, dark hours I sometimes miss my wife and son so badly that it hurts. I can actually feel the pain. Both physically and emotionally.

So I turn on the light and read. I gobble up entire novels before dawn finally reaches through my windows.

JANUARY 24.

I have been here now for about a month. Perhaps the strangest thing that has happened is what has not happened. I have not mentioned the cottage to anyone; not my family, friends, or coworkers. I have not notified a soul about my change of address. I keep meaning to make some calls, write some notes, take care of this bit of business. But I also keep making excuses, putting it off, telling myself I will do it tomorrow or next week.

I am not sure why I have kept the cottage a secret. I suppose it is one of two things, probably a combination of both.

In perfectly logical terms, I see no need to notify people of a move that might prove meaningless at any moment. At least once a day I consider returning to our house. My loneliness has not really dissipated here, as I had hoped it might. And in some ways, the solitude that surrounds me on this secluded estate has made my feelings of isolation even greater. I would have to say the cottage is a day-to-day proposition.

But also, on a far more emotional level, I think I have kept the cottage a secret because I enjoy my hideaway. Ever since the terrible events of last Easter Sunday, I have been receiving calls and visitors almost daily inquiring about my condition and my state of mind. I know family and friends mean well, that their hearts are in the right place, but it grows tiresome reassuring people that you are doing just fine, that everything is all right. By having my secret cottage in another town, where no one knows my tragic story, I can mind my own business.

It is not like I have run off to Bali or Timbuktu, suddenly vanished from the face of the earth. My mother or my brother or my sister can leave me a message on the answering machine at the house. I go over there to check on things at least once a week. Or they can call me at work. After all, I spend most of my waking hours at the office, crouched over my desk, editing with my precious red pencil.

I understand their concern, but I am tired of being

treated like a victim. So in the evening and on week-ends, I escape here for some peace and quiet.

JANUARY 25.

The name I gave the novel I wrote that year out on Cape Cod was *Inside Out*. Whatever that meant. It had some-thing to do with an outsider suddenly being thrust into a situation he could not possibly hope to control. I thought the title sounded hip, coy, puzzling, sophisticated. The first few lines went something like this: *I knew there'd be trouble in that foreign capital. But I went anyway. I had to. A matter of pride. A matter of honor.*

The story centered around this young American guy who gets mixed up with these rebel types down in some unnamed Central American country in the middle of a bloody civil war. Too bad I knew next to nothing about pride or honor or war or rebellion or the complexities of political and social life down in Central America. I'd spent a couple months traveling through Costa Rica and Belize. The trip did not ex-actly make me an authority on local customs.

Still, my ambitions and intentions for the novel were first-class all the way. I had a blend of Graham Greene and Ernie Hemingway all figured out in the back of my mind. Unfortunately, I did not possess the maturity or the prose style to pull it off. I had no prose style. So I wound up with a wordy, rambling 450-page manuscript spattered with displays of rough sex, non-chalant violence, and stereotypical melodrama.

Of course, at the time I thought I had created a mod-ern literary masterpiece. I felt sure the book would bring me fame and fortune.

I must have been about three-quarters of the way through the manuscript when the pretty girl with the long reddish brown hair stepped into my life. It didn't take me but a day or two to find out that her name was Ellen Reynolds and that she lived out on Lighthouse Road in a big old summer house overlooking Nauset Beach. She had spent every summer of her life in that house.

Ellen Reynolds came into the Orleans Bar & Grill three or four times a week all through that summer. She never came alone, always in a group. I quickly forgave her for that crack she'd made about me looking like a lawyer. I was much too attracted to her beauty and her laughter and her carefree manner to walk around with a chip on my shoulder.

I always waited on her table whenever she came into the restaurant. But I did not just take the order and disappear into the kitchen, only to return a few minutes later with a tray filled with victuals. No, I made a show of it. I took on the role of a different waiter each time she came in to eat. I might play the part of a pompous Parisian waiter with excellent manners but an incredibly condescending attitude toward loud and overbearing Americans. I knew only a few French phrases, but I have always possessed a fine ear for languages and accents. Ellen and her pals loved my shtick. They laughed and laughed.

So each time they came in for a meal or a chocolate malt, I played a different part. I could be a French waiter, an Italian waiter, an Australian waiter, a New York waiter, an L.A. waiter. Whatever they wanted. Whatever Ellen wanted. I just wanted to see her smile, watch her laugh.

And secretly I wanted to touch the smooth skin on

her cheek with the back of my hand. I wanted to run my fingers through her long, lovely hair. I wanted to gently kiss her lovely lips with my own.

For weeks and weeks I longed to ask her out on a date. I had it bad, as bad as I had ever had it in my whole life.

But even though she got a kick out of my role-playing, I had the distinct feeling that Ellen Reynolds would not have recognized me outside the confines of the Orleans Bar & Grill. We ran, I suppose, with different crowds. Ellen hung out with the yacht club set: well-heeled summer folks who owned the big places near the beach. She sailed and played tennis and went to cocktail parties. She did not have a summer job.

As for me, well, I worked and wrote and played hoops and went out at night to the local dives to drink beer and shoot pool and throw darts. Our paths did not cross except when she craved a hamburger or an ice cream soda.

I wanted to tell her in the worst way that I was not really a waiter. I was an Ivy League graduate, a world traveler, a novelist on the rise.

Unfortunately, appearances can indeed be deceiving. June and most of July slipped away, and in the eyes of Ellen Reynolds, I remained the goofy waiter with the funny accents down at the Orleans Bar & Grill.

I longed to play a more personal role in her presence.

JANUARY 26.

I finally got my opportunity one rainy morning in late July. And by that time I had learned a few more details about Ms. Reynolds. She might have acted like a silly rich girl, but she too was Ivy League educated. She had done her undergraduate work at Brown University in Providence, Rhode Island. And she had just earned a master's degree in business administration from Columbia. This was her final summer in the sun before beginning her career. One of the other waiters at the restaurant told me Ms. Reynolds was going to work for one of the large publishing houses in New York City.

My ears grew to twice their size at the sound of that news. Not only was she smart and pretty and fun, but she was going into the book business. The Book Business!

<hr>

JANUARY 27.

I was spending quite a lot of time on my own book in those days in an effort to finish the first draft. On a cool, foggy, drizzly morning, laboring away at my desk, I hit a snag. I simply reached a point in the narrative where I just could not figure out what my protagonist should do next. So what did I do? I did what I had been doing all spring and summer whenever that happened: I headed for the beach to walk and clear my thoughts.

I did not see a soul as I crossed the dunes wearing a slicker and a canvas hat. People stayed away from the beach on days like that; I never understood why. I loved watching the fog dance along the tops of the breakers, loved listening to the gulls squawking invisibly overhead. The low sky and the obscured ocean gave me a sense of intimacy amidst all that vastness. On a morning such as that I could easily imagine walking in the sandy footprints of Thoreau. When the beach was full of swimmers and sunbathers, I never felt that kinship.

And then, suddenly, after I had been walking on the beach for maybe twenty minutes, a bright orange Frisbee came flying out of the fog, followed immediately by big Reggie in hot pursuit. He pulled up fast the second he caught sight of me. I must have spooked him. He began to bark. But the bark sounded confused, as though he was not sure if he wanted to defend his turf or turn and retreat.

"What is it, Reggie? What's the matter?"

I could hear the voice of Ellen Reynolds, but I could not yet see her through the fog. Reggie continued to bark, but his tail was wagging now. He took a few cautious steps in my direction.

"Is someone there, Reggie? Who's there?"

"It's just me," I answered quickly, not wanting to scare her. "Sam. From the restaurant."

She came then, like some ghostly apparition, out of the gloom. "Oh, yes," she said, recognizing my face if not my name, "so it is. How are you this morning?"

"I'm excellent," I assured her. "I love this kind of weather."

"Me, too," she agreed. "The beach feels so private when it's like this."

She had on a green rain jacket and her New York Yankees baseball cap. The brim of the hat was all wet from the mist. Her blue eyes sparkled. I tried not to stare.

"All those meals you've served me," she said, smiling, "and we still haven't been formally introduced."

"Oh," I told her, without thinking, "I know who you are."

"You do?"

I nodded.

She put her hand on her hip, stuck her pretty little

nose up in the air, and said, "Well then, I know who you are, too."

"You do?"

She raised her eyebrows and winked at me.

"So who am I?"

"You tell me who I am first."

"You're Ellen Reynolds," I announced, as Reggie circled us, Frisbee between his teeth. "B.A. from Brown. M.B.A. from Columbia."

"Very impressive," she said, after giving it some thought. "Although, I should probably be horrified that my personal bio could be so easily obtained. Did you at least have to pay dearly for it?"

I shrugged. "Not really. A couple free chocolate malts is all."

Ellen Reynolds laughed. That beautiful laugh.

"Well?" I asked.

"Well what?"

"Who am I?"

"Oh. You're Sam Adams. I have no idea where or if you went to school. Lots of rumors about where you come from, some quite mysterious. You are supposedly descended from our second commander-in-chief, and the grapevine claims you are writing a novel."

"My God! And I thought I was just going along minding my own business."

She laughed again. "It's a small town, Sam. No one gets to mind their own business. Especially someone with the guts to write a novel."

She leaned over, grabbed the Frisbee out of Reggie's mouth, and tossed it down the beach. It disappeared into the fog. Reggie bounded off after it. "Come on," Ellen invited, "let's walk this way."

So we did. For miles. At least a few miles. For over

an hour. Through the rain and the fog. Our first date. We talked about all kinds of things, argued about a few of them, laughed about the rest. Once or twice I held her hand. She did not seem to mind.

And before we parted company (me back to my novel and Ellen back to the family beach house to help her mother hang some pictures), I made a bold move. I made it out of fear and hunger. Fear that if I did not grasp this opportunity, another one might never present itself. And a hunger that had been gnawing at me since the first time I had encountered Ms. Ellen Reynolds on that beach several weeks earlier. Walking side by side, I moved around in front of her, put my arms around her waist, and kissed her full on the mouth. For just a moment, she resisted, but her resistance soon gave way. We shared several long kisses while the rain fell and the tide rose and the gentle waves of the Atlantic lapped onto the beach and washed over our bare ankles.

JANUARY 20

The first real winter storm of the season hit last night. The snow fell silently while I slept. I awoke this morning to nearly a foot of fresh powder. I decided at once not to brave the roads in some misguided effort to reach the office. Instead, I would work at home. I had more than enough to keep me busy. But before settling down to my labors, I decided to venture outside with Sunshine and Moxie for some fresh air and exercise.

I strapped on my cross-country skis and set off across the snow-draped countryside. Only the main roads had been plowed, so I skied for miles on virgin powder. The two goldens led the way, the younger one, Moxie, cutting the trail with her boundless energy.

We made a wide loop, then skied into town on the old canal path running alongside the river. The town looked deserted. None of the antique stores or art galleries had bothered to open. The only eatery in town with its lights on was Rosie's Breakfast Nook, a small place on River Street with pink porcelain walls and chrome tables and chairs. I stopped in for sustenance. Rosie, a rather plump woman with gray hair, though still in her thirties, welcomed my furry friends. She gave them a bowl of water and a handful of oatmeal raisin cookies. The two dogs settled down in a corner and licked their frozen pads while I ate a towering stack of buttermilk pancakes and sipped my piping hot coffee laced with sugar and plenty of cream. Mitchell, I felt sure, would never know.

It was nearly noon by the time we returned to Blind Pass. Quite a number of changes had taken place during our brief absence. The driveway had been plowed. The sidewalks had been shoveled. And the main house was aglow with light. I even saw smoke rising from two of the three chimneys.

I put the dogs in the cottage, then headed straight over to the back door of the big house. I knocked on the glass. No one answered. I knocked again. Still no answer. So I turned the knob and pushed open the door. "Hello!" I called. "Is anyone home?"

No reply. But I heard the vacuum cleaner running somewhere deep inside the house. So I stepped inside, into a small sitting room just off the kitchen. I waited for the vacuum to stop, then called again. "Hello?"

A few moments later a young lady, maybe eighteen or twenty, appeared in the hallway. "Yes," she asked, "may I help you?"

"Good morning. My name's Adams."

"Yes?"

"Sam Adams. I live out back."

She seemed momentarily doubtful. As though I might be an intruder.

"In the cottage," I added.

"Oh yes. They told me someone new had moved in."

"And you are?"

"Julie. I work for Mrs. Richmond." Julie had a strong English accent, working-class London, rather thick and wormy, tough to understand. She spoke rapidly to cover her insecurity.

I asked after Mrs. Richmond.

"She's not home," Julie answered curtly.

"Well, do you know when she will be home?"

"Not until the end of the week."

"I see." Before this fountain of information dried up, I decided to give it one more go. "I haven't seen her since I moved in last month. Do you know where she's been?"

Julie sighed. "Dallas. Houston. Phoenix. Los Angeles. San Francisco. Some other cities."

"Sounds like quite a trip for a blind woman."

This time Julie frowned. "She's on tour."

"On tour?"

"Yes, her winter concert tour."

"Winter concert tour?"

"Didn't you know? Mrs. Richmond is quite a well-known cellist."

"Really?"

"Yes, really."

"As well-known as Yo Yo Ma?"

She frowned again. "I don't know Yo Yo Ma."

I smiled at her. Julie did not smile back. Maybe she

thought I was making fun of her. Maybe I was. But not maliciously.

Then the telephone rang. Julie answered it. I waved good-bye, turned, and left the house. It might not have been the most agreeable encounter of my life, but I nevertheless feel better now, not quite so lonely, knowing there is someone next door.

JANUARY 29.

I spoke to my mother this morning. I finally broke down and told her about the cottage. She took the news in stride, then asked if I planned on selling the house. I told her I didn't know yet, that I would have to wait and see.

She asked for my new telephone number. I somewhat reluctantly passed it along; the first crack in my fortress.

We spoke for a few minutes about this and that: work, the weather, my father, my brother, my sister. Then, near the end of the conversation, I told her my landlady was a famous cellist.

"Who is it?" she wanted to know.

"Evelyn Richmond," I told her.

"Yes," she said at once, "I'm quite sure I've heard of her."

I was not surprised. My my mother is a classical music aficionado. She owns thousands of recordings and goes to concerts in Boston and New York several times a year.

"I believe," she added, "that she used to play with the Philharmonic."

I told her I didn't know, but that I would certainly find out.

JANUARY 30.

I slept at the office again last night. I worked until almost one A.M., then I just crawled under the desk and dozed till dawn. By noon I was exhausted, so I packed up the manuscript-in-progress and told Mitchell I would return in a day or two. I retreated here to the cottage for a fresh start. I need to polish these pages. The author has been waiting for my edit for weeks.

It is an excellent novel. Or it will be after I correct its thematic flaws. But right now I seem not up to the task. My concentration is poor. I can see the flaws, they stare me right in the face, but I am powerless to exert my control over them. It takes too great an effort. I am presently preoccupied with my own stories.

In the past, before the events of last Easter, I would have buried myself in this novel. Literally taken root within its pages. This total immersion is why I have been considered a first-rate editor for almost a decade now. Sometimes I think I prefer a well-executed fictional world to the real world. With my red pencil I can rearrange events, fix problems, give hope to hopeless situations. I can solve the problems of the world.

In the real world we have so little control over even our own lives. We think we have control, but then something happens and we are reminded just how tenuous our lifeline really is.

This novel is the author's third. He has been with me, has trusted me, since the beginning of his career. This is his finest and most ambitious work yet. But he has overstepped his abilities. He needs my assistance. Ponderous themes of jealousy, rage, revenge, and manipulation have overwhelmed his somewhat naive sensibilities. Only I stand between him and public ridicule.

I will sleep now, and in the morning I will take another shot at it.

Sunshine and Moxie are up on the bed. I think I will let them stay.

FEBRUARY 1.

I have been editing almost nonstop now for the past forty-eight hours. Slowly and laboriously I have gone through the manuscript thought by thought, word by word, sentence by sentence. I have revised, shifted, and erased.

Of course, I must be extremely careful. The author must see my work not as intervention but as mere reflection. Delicate egos are at risk here.

Cautiously I clear a path through the muddle. It has taken a tremendous leap of faith, but I have finally come to grips with the protagonist. He is a man who has faced both rejection and deception. He has had enough. He wants to even the score.

I think I have helped him get his wish. And along the way I have come up with the perfect title: *The Seduction*.

We shall see.

FEBRUARY 2.

Mrs. Richmond returned home late last evening. Sunshine and Moxie heard the car first. They went from sound asleep to wide awake in about the time it takes me to blink an eye. First they began barking, then they made a mad scramble for the door, as though they would do anything more vicious than wag their tails and lick the hand of even the most grisly assassin.

I left my editing station here at the dining room table and crossed to the front window. I saw a limousine pull up to the back of the big house. The outdoor lights had all been turned on, no doubt in anticipation of Mrs. Richmond's arrival. Not that she could make use of those lights.

But her driver could. In black suit and cap, he stepped out from behind the wheel and hurried back to open the door for Mrs. Richmond. He helped her out of the limousine and along the shoveled brick walk to the back door where I could see Miss Julie waiting, a heavy frown draped across her face.

Mrs. Richmond looked tired. Exhausted even. And quite helpless. I thought perhaps I should go out there and see if I might be of some help. It would be the neighborly thing to do. Besides, I wanted to go out there and see if I could help. I had this mystifying desire to run out there and sweep Mrs. Richmond up into my arms and carry her into the house.

But before I could make my move, Mrs. Richmond slipped through the back door of her home. In no time at all the door was closed, the limousine driver pulled away, and those outdoor lights went dark.

I stood there for a long time watching that limousine's bright red brake lights as it neared the end of the driveway, then I sighed and went back to work.

FEBRUARY 4.

The second storm of the year hit last night: six inches of fresh powder. I found it when I woke up this morning. I never hear the weather. My television is still stuffed into the hall closet. So is my radio. I have been here over a month, but I have not gotten around to setting them up yet. I am afraid of the news, scared to death of all the violence and chaos, all the murder and mayhem.

Before last Easter I was a news junkie: radio news, TV news, weekly news magazines, newspapers. But then, out of the blue, I found out that news can happen to me too. Misfortune suddenly came a-calling at my door.

"How do you do?" the creature asked. "Mind if I come in and play?"

So now I have become an isolationist. I no longer want to know what is going on out there. I want to live here, away from the madness, behind closed doors. I have my books, my manuscripts, and my collection of classical music on compact discs.

FEBRUARY 5.

I should go over and see Mrs. Richmond. Welcome her home. Let her know I am available if she needs any help.

But I cannot do it today. Today I need to get to the office. We have our weekly editorial meeting this morning. It is not a good idea to miss that.

FEBRUARY 7.

I must have waited too long to contact Mrs. Richmond. Yesterday I arrived home late in the afternoon, and practically before I could put down my briefcase, there was a knock on my door. After calming down the dogs, I pulled open the door and found Miss Julie standing there in a heavy wool sweater. She did not bother to say hello but instead went straight to the crux of her visit.

"Mrs. Richmond wants to see you." Her voice sounded harsh, her tone like a general issuing a command.

I told her I would be over in a few minutes.

After washing up and taking the dogs for a quick walk, I headed across the driveway to the big house. Julie waited for me at the back door. She did not say a word as she led me through the kitchen and down the long hallway to the oval music room where I had first encountered Mrs. Richmond back in December. The room, I noted once again, contained almost nothing but the Oriental carpet, the love seat, and Mrs. Richmond's smooth and sensuous cello.

And, of course, Mrs. Richmond. She sat curled up on that love seat wearing a long black silk kimono. A thin gold necklace hung around her neck. She ran the thumb and index finger of her right hand slowly up and down the necklace. Her eyes lay hidden behind tiny dark glasses.

"Good evening, Mr. Adams."

"Good evening, Mrs. Richmond."

"Can we get you something? Coffee? Tea?"

I hesitated. "Well, yes, thank you. Tea might be nice."

Mrs. Richmond smiled. "Tea for two, Julie."

Julie left the music room, closing the double doors behind her with, I thought, a bit too much force.

"A lovely girl, Julie. English, you know. She's been with me now, oh, it must be close to two years. She told me you'd met."

"Yes, we did. Just a few days ago. She told me you were quite a well-known cellist."

Mrs. Richmond gave her response with what I thought looked like a practiced moment of modesty. "I suppose I have a certain style."

"I would love to hear you play sometime."

"Yes," she said, "but not just now." Mrs. Richmond patted the cushion of the love seat. "Come over here, Mr. Adams. Sit beside me."

I crossed to the love seat with somewhat more confidence than I had the first time I'd been in that room. My confidence, however, fell off markedly when I caught the scent of Mrs. Richmond's perfume. It smelled vaguely of jasmine and rose petals. At least that was my initial impression. I do not have the most reliable sense of smell. But I know for certain the impact that scent had on me: one of pure sexuality. It was a fragrance that radiated carnal desire. I wondered if Mrs. Richmond recognized the power of her perfume. I felt sure she did. Cautiously, I sat down.

She placed her hand gently on my thigh. "So, Mr. Adams," she asked, "how are you? How is everything at the cottage? I trust you are finding your new digs satisfactory?"

I nodded, then remembered her blindness. "Yes, thank you. Everything is just fine."

She took her hand away from my thigh and very lightly brushed her fingers across her left breast. I do not know if she did this on purpose, for my sake, or if it was just some simple, unconscious act. Either way, it caught my attention. I think, for several seconds, I actually stopped breathing.

The room grew very quiet. Some time passed. I do not know how much time; perhaps half a minute. I had the distinct feeling Mrs. Richmond expected me to say or do something. Unfortunately, I had no idea what.

And then she stretched her arms high overhead, exposing, for just a moment, her breasts through the armholes of that black kimono; lovely round breasts, small but firm. She sighed then and moved to the real reason for my summons. "I hate to bring this up, Mr. Adams, but there is the matter of the rent."

It took me a moment to catch up. "The rent?"

"Yes. Normally I prefer to receive it on the first of the month. Much simpler that way for everyone. Keeps us all friendly and feeling good about one another."

I had not for a moment anticipated that we would be discussing the rent. Over the past several weeks, really ever since I had met Mrs. Richmond, I had from time to time imagined the two of us sitting on that love seat discussing music, art, philosophy, the important events of the day. She had struck me immediately as an intelligent, interesting, and, of course, quite beautiful woman. And, if I am honest about this, which I intend to be, I suppose I had also spent a bit of time fantasizing about Mrs. Richmond once again running her lovely fingertips through my hair and across my face. Expectations so often slap us right between the eyes.

"Oh," I said, "the rent."

"Yes, Mr. Adams. The rent. The genesis of our relationship."

"But there must be some misunderstanding," I said. "I sent you a check at the end of January. You were not home, so I simply mailed it."

"I have not received it."

"Are you sure? I am certain I sent it."

"Yes," countered Mrs. Richmond, "I am quite certain I have not received it."

I was somewhat shocked by her tone. She sounded

downright hostile, a far cry from her seductive insinuations just moments earlier.

Most of a minute passed. I wanted to suggest that maybe she should look again for my check. After all, she had been away for several weeks. Perhaps my check was buried somewhere in an avalanche of catalogs and department store circulars. But before I could say a word, Miss Julie returned with a pot of tea and two cups on a fancy silver tray.

Mrs. Richmond stood up. "I'll tell you what," she said, her voice puddled with sarcasm, and even, I thought, a touch of venom, "why don't you two kids have tea? I cannot stand the odor in here. It smells like the Great Depression."

Well, I have a pretty good sense of humor, and I don't mind occasionally being the brunt of someone else's jest, but frankly, I wanted to ask Mrs. Evelyn Richmond exactly *how* the Great Depression smelled. Not that she could possibly have known. She was not old enough to have been around during the Great Depression.

But, of course, I did not ask her any such thing. I was brought up always to remain courteous, even in the face of mockery and disdain. My father taught us never to sink to another person's low. Respect and dignity for yourself and others above all else.

Besides, Mrs. Richmond whisked herself out of the music room so quickly I did not have time to open my mouth. She moved not at all like a blind person, but more like a small and very agile fairy. For just a moment I thought I saw her sprout wings. She flew across the room and out the door.

Julie, apparently undaunted by Mrs. Richmond's undeniably rude behavior, placed the silver tray on the Oriental carpet, a few feet from that silent cello.

"Perhaps," I asked her, "you would like to have a cup?"

"I don't drink tea," the English girl announced, and then she too left the music room, her snippy little nose angled toward the heavens.

I stood there all alone for a minute or two. I no longer wanted tea, either. I just wanted to become invisible so I could slip away without being detected.

As quickly as possible I made haste back to the safety of the cottage, back to the enthusiastic good cheer of my tail-wagging pups. I pulled on my cross-country ski gear, and off the three of us went for a lengthy romp through the snow-covered fields.

FEBRUARY 9.

Why, I have been wondering off and on for the past couple of days, did Mrs. Richmond treat me like that? What did I ever do to her? Why are human beings so often rude and cruel to one another?

My parents were never rude or cruel to one another. I cannot remember my father ever saying a harsh word to my mother. Once in a while I would hear them arguing behind the closed door of their bedroom. Not loudly or with any great vehemence, but calmly and rationally. Usually it concerned one of us, one of the kids. Probably we had misbehaved or shown disrespect, and occasionally they disagreed on how to handle the culprit. But their disagreement never surfaced in front of us. In front of us, they were always a united team.

I have decided Mrs. Richmond was simply in the middle of a bad day when she lashed out about the rent. Perhaps she was upset at me for not stopping by

to say hello after she returned from her concert tour. I
should have gone over the next day. It was rude of me
to ignore her.

There is also the issue of her blindness, a disability
that undoubtedly leaves her feeling frustrated and blue
from time to time. Perhaps I said or did something in the
music room to anger her. Her son, Roger, warned me
that she was extremely sensitive about her blindness.

I fully intend to be an excellent neighbor and ten-
ant. I will make every effort to encourage a friendship
between us. As for the rent, well, I can only assume
she must have found my check, for I have not heard
another word about it.

FEBRUARY 10.

I lay awake last night for an hour or more thinking
about Mrs. Richmond and her blindness. It is an extremely difficult disability for a person with 20-20 vision to fathom, but I finally dug up a memory that might
provide me with at least a touch of enlightenment.

It happened when I was nine years old. I very nearly
went blind myself. How different my life would have
been had that happened.

Lime was the culprit. Yes, lime. Simple calcium ox-
ide. I had been hired, let us say indentured, by my father
to help spread the fine white powder on the autumn
grass. "Lime makes the soil sweet," he used to tell us.

My father was, and still is, a gentle soul. He has
taught literature at Dartmouth College since, well,
since the beginning of time. It is from him that I
most definitely get my literary bent.

The Professor, as I often called my father, though

rarely to his face, enjoyed yard work. He wanted his kids, especially his two sons, to enjoy it as well. He would get us out there in the early spring to tidy up the shrubbery beds, loosen the soil, and spread the compost that had ripened during the winter. The classroom has always been my father's preferred domain, but if he cannot stand behind the lectern, he almost equally enjoys being out in his yard on a breezy afternoon with a rake, spade, or trowel in his hand, a hint of perspiration on his brow.

"There is peace and harmony," he often told us, "in even the smallest patch of well-tended earth."

When I was a boy, it was said that my father had the prettiest gardens in all of Hanover, New Hampshire. And the greenest, lushest lawn. Lush, in part, because every fall, after we had raked up the leaves, the Professor would spread a fine white coating of lime over the entire yard. It was a precursor to the heavy snows that we knew would soon follow.

Usually my brother Jack helped my father spread the lime. He was two years older, and he liked doing it. Maybe he didn't like spreading lime specifically, but he thoroughly enjoyed pleasing our father. The Professor never had to ask Jack to help out with chores around the house. Jack always pitched in without protest. I, on the other hand, always had some excuse why I couldn't help out. I always had a Little League game or homework to finish or some piece of pressing business that could not wait. I always had a million excuses. But that fall the Professor cornered me the night before about spreading the lime, so I had no way out short of complete insubordination. Jack, as I remember, was off on a camping trip to the White Mountains with his Boy Scout troop.

Right after breakfast the Professor led me out to the

garage and reviewed my duties. While he cleaned and
oiled the spreader, I started carrying twenty-pound
bags of lime out to the yard. He told me to place the
dozen bags in a grid. I did as ordered, though several
times he had to reel me in, as I had a tendency to drift
off after placing each bag on the ground.

Finally he poured the first bag into the spreader.
The Professor was not happy about the quality of the
lime. "It looks like it must've gotten damp somewhere
along the way," he told me.

I looked at it. I could see the lime kind of clumped
together in chunks the size of baseballs. The Professor
carefully broke up these chunks with his hands. It was
easy to do. The lime turned back to dust practically by
breathing on it. He began pushing the spreader across
the lawn, leaving in his wake a three-foot-wide swath
of white. I stood off to the side and watched him go
back and forth through the thick autumn grass.

After a few passes, he interrupted my idle viewing.
"Why don't you go around, Sam, and open up all the
bags? It'll help expedite the process."

I wandered from bag to bag, slicing open the tops
with a knife. It must have been the eighth or ninth bag
that got me. By that time I was getting pretty bored
just walking up to the bag and slicing it open. I needed
some additional stimulation, something to stir up the
monotony. So what did I do? Well, first I waited for
my father to go into the garage where he had a pitcher
of ice water. Then, when he was out of sight, I reached
into bag number eight or nine and grabbed a chunk of
lime. I tried to throw the chunk against a nearby sugar
maple, but it fell apart before it even left my hand. A
quick look around for the Professor assured me he
was still in the garage. I fished around in the bag for

another chunk. Nothing on top. So that's when I picked up the bag with both hands and lifted it off the ground. Then, with my face directly over the wide opening, I slammed the bag down against the ground.

Not a smart thing to do, Sam.

The fine white lime dust flew out of the bag. A good deal of it went directly into my unprotected eyes. Immediately, the lime began to burn. I knew right away I was in trouble. Big trouble. I dropped the bag, and screaming bloody murder, I took off across the lawn.

My father did not panic. He would have made an excellent battlefield general, except for the fact that he is a staunch pacifist. He put me in the car and drove me to the emergency room. An eye specialist was called in to take a look. Both of my corneas were badly burned. The doctor washed them out with a special saline solution, then he covered both eyes with heavy black patches. I was sent home with orders not to remove the patches, not to expose my eyes to the light of day, for at least a week.

That week turned into a month. A month is a very long time. Especially for a nine year old boy. It was easily the longest month of my life. For an entire month I could not do anything or go anywhere. I was basically a blind person. And the entire time the threat hung over me that I could possibly wind up being a blind person forever. I imagined myself learning Braille, groping in eternal darkness, stumbling around with a stick and a Seeing Eye dog.

But after a month the patches came off and the world came sharply back into focus. Life went on as before. Nothing left but another story to tell. But one that now might serve me well in my efforts to better understand my landlady.

During my month in the dark, I learned one of those very valuable life lessons. I learned that people need to rely on one another. Throughout that month I always had a member of my family nearby. My brother and sister helped me get dressed and clean my room and find my way downstairs. My father read to me and helped me with my studies.

But my mother, she was always at my side. She fed me and bathed me and entertained me. And best of all, she introduced me to music. Classical music. I had heard it playing in the house all my life, coming from the old Victrola she kept in the living room. Never, however, had I stopped to listen. But suddenly blind and ordered to remain as still as possible, I had no choice but to listen. I soon wanted to listen. Mother and I would sit side by side on the sofa listening over and over to the lovely and melodious violin concertos of Wolfgang Amadeus Mozart. Especially Concerto no. 4 in D Major. It was my mother's favorite. And it quickly became my favorite also.

I wonder if Mrs. Richmond can play Concerto no. 4 in D Major? I will have to ask her.

FEBRUARY 12.

My mother was, of course, the first person I called this past Easter Sunday after the tragedy at Sloan's Motel.

My father answered the phone. "Hello?"

"Dad?"

"Sam?"

I was crying, babbling like a baby.

"Sam, what is it? Why are you crying?"

I could not answer. For several minutes my father, in his kind and patient manner, tried to calm me down. But I could not stop crying, could not bring myself under control. Nothing but sobs fell from my mouth.

My mother must have taken the receiver from my father's hand for suddenly her voice came over the line. "Sam, what is it? What's the matter? Is everything all right?"

No, everything was not all right. Everything was all wrong. I felt quite certain nothing would ever be right again.

FEBRUARY 13.

I woke up this morning, looked out the window, and what did I find? Drizzle falling from a low gray sky. That drizzle has now turned to rain. I can hear it beating against the roof. Slowly but surely the rain will wash away all this beautiful snow that Sunshine and Moxie and I have been playing in these past few weeks.

The rain, and surely my memories, have made me blue. Midwinter blues. My mood has always been influenced by the seasons and by sharp changes in the weather.

But today it is the memories. They have been creeping in through the cracks in the walls. And today the memories have made me depressed. I feel the depression gnawing at me, crawling around just below the skin. I do not think I can get out of bed today. I just want to pull the blankets up over my head and pretend like I do not even exist.

FEBRUARY 14.

Valentine's Day. Ellen always loved Valentine's Day, always insisted we make a big show of it. One of us would make the other one breakfast in bed. All day long we would give each other flowers. We always went out for a romantic dinner at one of our favorite restaurants.

Every year I tried to do something extra special for her. One year I filled our apartment with balloons. Another year I got tickets to a Broadway show and a room afterward at the Plaza Hotel. And the first year we had any extra money, I booked us a trip for a long weekend in Jamaica. Every year I made sure Ellen knew I loved her even more than the year before.

FEBRUARY 15.

After our morning stroll on the beach through the rain and fog, after our kisses at the edge of the sea, I wanted only to spend more time with Ms. Ellen Reynolds. I wanted to hold her in my arms, stare into her pretty blue eyes. I fully expected her to appear in the restaurant later that same day, or the next day at the very latest. But she didn't. Her pals came, but Ellen didn't. On the third day I asked them why. They shrugged and said she had other things to do. On their way out, one of them told me Ellen had a cold.

I waited one more day. Then, finally, I fought off my fears and rode my bike out to her family's home on Lighthouse Road. It was an enormous fortress on the bluffs overlooking the beach. The dark, weather-beaten clapboards looked like they had fought off a century's worth of storms. A wide porch wrapped itself around the entire house. Several people lay sprawled across that porch on swings and hammocks and chaise lounges, reading newspapers and magazines. They all looked incredibly cool and relaxed.

Ellen was not among them. I climbed the steps and asked after her. A young man (her brother, I found out later) told me she had gone into town to do some errands. But a young woman said, no, Ellen had gone to the beach. Someone else claimed she had gone up to Boston.

I thanked them all, then turned away, confused and dejected.

FEBRUARY 16.

Two more days passed. I kept asking her friends when they came into the restaurant if they had seen her. They claimed they had not.

That evening I sprained my ankle in a lacrosse game over in Truro. It swelled up like a balloon. I went home, wrapped it in ice, and settled back on the couch to give it a rest.

I was still lying on that couch the next morning when someone knocked on the door. "It's open," I shouted. "Come on in."

"Are you decent?"

"What?"

"Are you decent?"

"Ellen? Is that you?"

She pushed open the door, stuck her head in. "Hi, Sam. How's your ankle?"

She knew all about my ankle injury and my visit to

her house and my endless inquiries of her friends con cerning her whereabouts.

"So why," I asked, "did you disappear? Where did you go?"

"I didn't go anywhere," she told me. Then, "I know it sounds stupid, but I was afraid to see you."

"Afraid? Why?"

"I don't know. I guess because I like you."

"So that's good."

"Except that at the end of the month I'll be leaving for New York and we'll never see each other again."

"Of course we will. If we want to."

She shrugged. "I guess."

I swung my damaged leg carefully onto the floor, sat up on the couch, and drew her near. She came willingly. My ankle hurt pretty bad when I tried to stand, so Ellen sat down beside me. I kissed her on the neck and on the cheek and on the lips. She kissed me back.

FEBRUARY 17.

That same day Ellen asked me if she could read my novel. Flattered she had asked, I told her she could read it as soon as it was finished.

"And when do you think that will be?"

"Hopefully by the end of August."

"Just in time for me to leave for New York."

"Let's not think about that."

But we did think about it. All the time. Every day.

FEBRUARY 18.

One evening, walking on the beach with Reggie, I asked Ellen where she would be working in the city.

"Rockefeller Center."

"That's a good place to work. Which publisher?"

She glanced at me, gave me a slow, curious look. "You mean you don't know?"

"No idea. Just that you're going to work for a book publisher."

"But you don't know which publisher?"

"Should I?"

She gave my hand a squeeze. "I guess I assumed you did."

"Why?"

But she didn't answer. Not right away. Instead, she dropped my hand and started running down the beach. With her long, thin legs she had an easy, graceful stride. I ran after her.

It was a perfect evening: warm and clear with the sun going down and the moon coming up. A gentle breeze blew in off the Atlantic. Ellen kept running until she reached a deserted place on the beach. Then she slowed to a jog and began removing her clothes. First her T-shirt, then her shorts, then her underclothes came off and were left discarded in the sand. So my first view of beautiful Ellen Reynolds perfectly naked was there on Nauset Beach in the fading summer light as she splashed through the wash and dove beneath a breaking wave.

I waited only a few moments before I too disrobed and followed that lovely young woman into the sea.

"Jackson, Jones and Reynolds" was the answer she gave after our frolic out beyond the breakers.

In the warm sea we had held each other close, our naked bodies buoyant and excited in the salty water. We had practically made love right out in the Atlantic Ocean while Reggie, our protector, swam in circles around us.

"Jackson, Jones and Reynolds," I repeated. "Pretty impressive. They're a first-class outfit."

She nodded. "I think so."

We had our clothes back on and were walking slowly across the dunes in the direction of her family's colossal seaside home. And then it dawned on me: the connection came clear.

I stopped. "Wait a second. Are you *that* Reynolds? Is your family the Reynolds of Jackson, Jones and Reynolds?"

She turned and faced me. "You mean you really didn't know?"

I shook my head. "I had no idea.

She gave me a long, serious look. Then, finally, she smiled. "It's my Uncle Stephen, actually. My father's brother. He became a partner in Jackson and Jones back in the late seventies."

I whistled softly. Jackson, Jones & Reynolds was one of the most respected book publishers in the country. They published a small circle of award-winning authors of both fiction and nonfiction. An ambitious young novelist would give up his or her left hand for a contract with Jackson, Jones & Reynolds.

And right then is when another thought suddenly dawned on me.

I looked Ellen straight in the eye. "You thought I knew, didn't you? You thought I knew you were going to work for the family business? You thought I knew and that's why you were afraid to get involved?"

She hesitated. Then, quickly, she nodded. "Okay, I admit it. I was afraid your interest in me had more to do with you being a writer and me being . . . well . . . you see what I'm getting at, Sam."

"Yes," I said softly, "I see."

And then I put my arms around her waist and kissed her passionately on the mouth. We made love for the first time that same night, out on the beach, under the moonlight, wrapped in a swaddle of cotton blankets.

And so what if I had known the details of her family background? It didn't mean that I wasn't falling head over heels in love with her.

FEBRUARY 20.

More rain today. And more memories. And more blues to boot.

I am not equipped to suffer.

FEBRUARY 21.

Miss Julie knocked on my door again early this afternoon. She had, of course, been sent by Mrs. Richmond. The matriarch of Blind Pass sought another audience with me.

What now? I wondered.

I did not rush, but eventually, an hour or so later, I made my way over to the big house. Julie once again led me down the hallway to the music room. She opened one of the double doors and gestured with a sneer for me to enter. As soon as I did, she slammed the door behind me and drifted off to another part of the vast house.

What is wrong with that girl? She does not seem to like me. I have no idea why. Is it possible she sees me as some kind of threat?

Mrs. Richmond sat on a folding metal chair in the middle of that Oriental carpet. Her cello nestled between her legs, its long, slender spike resting on the floor. She held the fingerboard in her left hand, the bow in her right.

"Come in, Mr. Adams. Please, sit down."

I hesitated, fearing her wrath, but eventually I crossed to the love seat. Her perfume, a slightly more subdued fragrance than last time, followed me across the room. This one smelled, I thought, faintly of cinnamon. I did my best not to look at her. I sat down.

"Are you all right, Mr. Adams?"

"Excuse me?"

"Julie tells me you have not left the cottage for two or three days. I thought there might be something wrong."

"I can assure you, Mrs. Richmond, there is nothing wrong." My voice sounded a bit more pugnacious than probably necessary.

Mrs. Richmond must have thought so, too. "No need to get defensive, Mr. Adams. I am simply inquiring, as any good neighbor would, if all is well with you and yours."

"Everything," I assured her, "is just fine."

"I am very happy to hear that, Mr. Adams." She smiled at me from behind her cello; a soft and gentle smile. It made her look like an innocent little girl.

That smile threw me off balance. It made me want to explain the irritated timbre of my voice. "I've had an overload of work lately. Too many manuscripts and not enough time. I can concentrate better at home. Far fewer interruptions."

She seemed only vaguely interested. "I see." The fingers of her left hand ran up and down the fingerboard of her cello. "I believe you told me you were an editor, Mr. Adams?"

"Yes."

"Of books?"

"Yes."

"And you're getting some work done at home?"

"I am, yes."

"So that explains why you've been holed up in the cottage for the past few days."

"I haven't been holed up. I've been working."

She ignored me. "I sometimes have to hole up when I am learning a new piece of music."

"Solitude," I told her, "is good for the soul."

She gave that some thought, then shrugged in response. "May I ask you a personal question, Mr. Adams?"

"It depends how personal."

"Of an intimate nature."

"You can try."

"I just wonder, have you ever made love to an older woman?"

She asked this without changing the inflection of her voice. Still, I knew then she was one of those women who likes to shock. It makes them feel, I don't know, witty and superior, I suppose. But this old dog does not shock easily. I have seen my wife beaten to death right before my eyes.

"Do not think me impertinent, Mrs. Richmond," I answered as I got to my feet, "but I doubt if that is really any of your business." I headed for the door. My shoes made not a sound on that antique carpet. Nevertheless, Mrs. Richmond's vacant eyes followed my movements across the room.

Then, as I reached out for the brass doorknob, she asked another question. "I don't mean a year or two older, Mr. Adams. Or even five or ten years older. I mean an older woman, a woman perhaps old enough to be your mother?"

My arm fell to my side. My brain went to work. I needed a retort, something fast and snappy. But I acted too slow. Before I could say a word, Mrs. Richmond moved her cello into the proper playing position and swept the bow quickly and skillfully across the strings. She played a series of notes, loud and aggressive notes, like something foreshadowing the onslaught of battle. It could have been Mahler, but I was not absolutely sure.

She played for several minutes before the cello finally fell silent.

I put my mouth immediately into motion. "I hate to disappoint, Mrs. Richmond, but you are not old enough to be my mother."

And then, before she had an opportunity to respond, I slipped out of the music room and pulled the door closed behind me.

For the next hour or so I felt pretty good about getting in the last word. But just in the past few minutes, I have realized that Mrs. Richmond actually won our little skirmish. She jabbed here and poked there, and eventually she managed to provoke. That, I believe, was her ultimate aim.

FEBRUARY 22.

Mrs. Richmond is messing with my psyche and I have no idea why. Is she a wild and dangerous woman? Someone to steer clear of? Or is she just into playing games? Maybe she's bored and enjoys toying with me. Or is she mad at me about something? The rent perhaps? Maybe the way I park the minivan too close to the garage? Or maybe she thinks I should put the trash out in the morning rather than the night before. People can become angry and insulting over the most trifling matters.

Of course, maybe Mrs. Richmond's demeanor has nothing to do with me. It could be that Mrs. Richmond is troubled. Or lonely. I should try and find out more about her, about her life, about her blindness.

I am not, after all, the only one in the world who has faced adversity. It is quite likely that Mrs. Richmond has suffered loss also. After all, I have seen no evidence of Mr. Richmond.

But I cannot think about all this right now. I need to concentrate. I have work to do.

FEBRUARY 24.

Yesterday I put out one fire, but today, at work, another blaze began to burn. I am an editor under the gun.

Yesterday I completed editorial work on *The Seduction,* that novel about the man who wants revenge against those who have done him wrong. It was extremely difficult for me to deal with that particular theme, but I burrowed deep and found some common ground. No doubt the author will fail to appreciate my efforts, however. He will rant and rave about my changes, but in the end his ego will back off and his great good sense will recognize the vast improvements over his own substantial work. Writers are an egotistical and stubborn lot, but few of them, I have found, are stupid. I will need to stroke him and soothe him, give him reason to believe that the work is his and his alone, that I am nothing but the cheering section, rooting him on from the sidelines.

Whatever it takes to get the story right.

Today I begin the whole process anew on another manuscript. This one is a science fiction novel about a group of ruthless aliens who come to earth on an evil military mission, their sole aim to annihilate any and all humans. The aliens hope to accomplish this feat by putting some deadly concoction into the water supply. But the scientists back on their home planet did not properly understand human biology, so instead of killing us off, this concoction actually causes us to behave as though we are under the influence of psilocybin mushrooms. The entire human race is suddenly walking around smiling, acting nice, taking time to stop and smell the flowers. Without meaning to, the aliens have brought peace and a touch of harmony to the planet. At least temporarily.

Normally I have little interest in science fiction. I have only edited a handful of science fiction manuscripts before. But the writer is a good friend of one of my finest authors, so I agreed to look at his first draft. Even at that early stage I was both impressed and riveted with his depiction of the powerful collision between the forces of good and evil. And, of course, like most of us, I am a sucker for an ending full of unity and hope.

The rest of the editorial staff at Jackson, Jones &

Reynolds at first scoffed at the idea of bringing out a science fiction title. Until, that is, I managed to get several other editors to read the manuscript. They too were immediately hooked. At JJ&R books are still considered essential to our cultural enrichment. This is not to say that we do not publish our share of tripe, but we still like to think our tripe is superior to their tripe.

FEBRUARY 26.

This morning at our weekly editorial meeting I began to feel dizzy. I excused myself and went back to my office, where I stretched out on the floor. Chills ran up and down my body.

Mitchell brought me some water and a couple of aspirin. "It's the flu," he said, matter-of-factly. "Half the office is home sick."

"It's not the flu," I told him. "I don't get sick."

"You look sick to me."

"I haven't been sick in twenty years. Thirty years. I have the constitution of a brick wall."

"Nevertheless," Mitchell insisted, "you've got it."

I felt sweaty and cold at the same time.

He put his palm over my forehead. "You have a fever. I want you to go home."

I didn't argue with him. I caught the next available train.

I feel like hell.

FEBRUARY 27.

It's the flu. I have the damn flu. It couldn't possibly be anything else. Nothing else feels like this. My whole body hurts.

Fever. Chills. Cold sweats. Nausea.

I feel like I've been run over by an eighteen-wheeler. Like I wouldn't mind just dying, just fading away.

Sunshine and Moxie sit here beside the bed and stare. They look concerned. They have no idea what's the matter with their master. I barely have the strength to fill their bowl or open the door so they can go outside to pee. I have to roll onto the floor and crawl on all fours if I want to get to the bathroom or the kitchen.

It sure would be nice to have someone to help me. When I used to get sick like this, I always had someone to take care of me. My mother or my sister or my sweet Ellen.

Ellen! Where are you when I need you?

MARCH 1.

I've been flying. Flying high through Heaven with God and Jesus and Ellen and Nicholas. Oh what a flight we've had, high above planet Earth with its temples and canyons and wild rivers. But a few minutes ago I crash-landed here on the floor in a raging pool of my own perspiration.

I am alone, all alone. Except for my dogs, who stare at me like I must surely be out of my mind.

MARCH 3.

Man oh man did that bug knock me off my feet.

These past few days I've been delirious, did not even know where I was most of the time. More than once I awoke disoriented, absolutely unable to fathom my whereabouts. That had never happened to me before, not even during my deepest, darkest days following our calamity at Sloan's Motel.

About all I can remember of the past few days is shouting for Ellen, begging for her to come and comfort me. Ellen, however, was nowhere to be found, nowhere in sight.

Instead, Julie came.

MARCH 4.

But I only learned later that Julie came. She entered the cottage under orders from Mrs. Richmond and found me lying practically unconscious on the bed. She immediately retreated to the big house to inform her employer.

They returned together a few minutes later. They found me stark naked and drowning in my own sweat. My fever had soared and soaked the bed sheets straight through to the mattress.

They managed to get me out of bed and make me comfortable on a quilt on the floor. I was too weak to speak, barely able to even open my eyes. They turned the mattress and slipped on some crisp, fresh sheets. And then, with no help from me, they got my body off the floor and back into bed.

I lay there dozing, slipping in and out of the moment.

Once or twice I opened my eyes and saw Evelyn Richmond gently cooling off my feverish and still naked body with a damp washcloth. She, of course, could not tell my eyes had opened, so I watched, with no small amount of interest, as her hand slowly worked that cool cloth around my shoulders, down my arms, across my chest, and over my abdomen.

A clean cotton sheet covered my legs and my private parts. I had just enough mental prowess to wonder if Mrs. Richmond would cool those, too.

She did not. Perhaps she would have, but just then Miss Julie came back into the bedroom. I quickly closed my eyes.

"I think his fever has finally broken," Mrs. Richmond said.

Julie mumbled something I did not quite catch. Probably she would have preferred to leave me there in a puddle of my own perspiration.

"So what did you find in the kitchen?"

"Not much," growled Julie. "Half a loaf of bread, some cheese, some peanut butter, a jar of jelly, a six-pack of Doctor Pepper."

"No wonder he's taken ill," said Mrs. Richmond. "A diet like that would make anyone sick."

I wanted to tell Julie to stay out of my kitchen, but I did not want them to know I was alert. I enjoyed listening when they did not think I could hear, just as I enjoyed watching when I knew Mrs. Richmond could not see. Besides, I wanted them to think I was sick and needed their attention. I did not want them to leave. I wanted them to stay. It was pleasant having someone tend me, care for me, watch over me, take an interest in my life.

MARCH 5.

I feel much better today. Still kind of weak and wobbly, not quite ready to go back to work, but definitely more in my right mind again. That was some potent dose of the flu. I'll bet at times my fever reached 104.

Rarely in my life have I ever been that sick. Knock on wood, but I have been exceptionally healthy my whole life. Most of my health problems have resulted from injuries incurred from athletics: a broken collarbone, a bruised thigh, a sprained ankle, a bloody lip. I need to go back quite a long time to dig up an illness on par with the one I just battled. I think it would have to be the flu I came down with right after my best friend, Russell Petersen, died in the Connecticut River. That time my fever went to 105. They had to put me in the hospital.

MARCH 6.

Russell and I had been best buddies for seven years, ever since our days in preschool. He lived a few houses down on the other side of the street. We weren't allowed to cross the street without an adult until we turned eight, even though it was a very quiet street with a car going by about every half an hour. Sometimes Russell and I would stand on opposites sides and holler to each other. We spent hours yelling back and forth, trading yarns and telling jokes. The first time I ever said a cussword out loud was when I shouted the *f* word to Russell Petersen across the wide open spaces of Rope Ferry Road.

Then, before Russell and I had a chance to do all

the stuff we talked about doing (like going to Africa to see lions and playing hoops for the Boston Celtics and becoming astronauts who would travel to the moon), Russell died. He jumped off the Norwich-Hanover Bridge and drowned in the Connecticut River.

It was my fault. I should have stopped him. But I didn't stop him. I kept urging him on, daring him to jump.

It was a game we played. A stupid, dangerous game. A game kids had been playing on that bridge every winter for as long as anyone could remember. Probably they still play it.

It was December, just before Christmas. But I was not really looking forward to Christmas that year because my mother would not be home to celebrate the holiday with us. She was out in California taking care of a sick aunt.

One day after school Russell and I grabbed our ice skates and took the back trail down to the river. Up until then the ice had not yet firmed up enough to skate, but we thought the previous night's low of fifteen degrees might have done the job. It looked pretty solid along the edge, so we strapped on our blades and ventured out for the season's first glide. The ice creaked and groaned, but held.

We skated around for a while, and then Russell said to me, "I dare you to jump, Sam."

"I jumped first last year," I reminded him. "It's your turn."

Russell did not argue. We both knew I'd been the first to jump the previous winter. But that jump hadn't taken place until the middle of January. Before that we'd been too scared of breaking through the ice. Waiting until the middle of January to jump didn't carry much weight with the kids in town, but it was still better than not jumping at all. We were the only kids in our grade who had ever jumped.

"Jump now," I urged Russell, "before Christmas, and they'll be talking about it for years, till long after we're nothing but dust and old dead bones."

"I don't know, Sam," he said. "It doesn't look very safe."

I ignored him, skated back to the river's edge. Reluctantly, Russell followed. I slipped on my blade covers and started up the embankment to the bridge. Russell, moving slowly, brought up the rear. Together we ventured out onto the span. A few cars sped past in the gathering dusk. The river is not very wide at Hanover, maybe a couple hundred feet. And the steel bridge spanning the river is not a particularly imposing structure. We used to jump off it in the summer. I doubt it's more than fifteen or twenty feet from the top of the bridge to the surface of the river. But in the winter, with the wind blowing cold and the sun already setting by four o'clock in the afternoon, it looks a whole lot higher.

"Go ahead," I said to Russell, "do it. Make the jump. I'll make sure every kid in town knows before we go to sleep tonight. You'll be a legend."

It took some more prodding, but Russell finally sucked in a deep breath and climbed over the safety rail. I could see he was scared but that he wanted to do it. He wanted to make that jump. Kids are so stupid, so unaware of the consequences of their actions.

I climbed over the safety rail and stood beside him. "Ready?"

He nodded, slowly.

But before he could jump, he had to carefully swing

himself down underneath the bridge. You didn't just jump off. That would mean a couple of broken legs when you hit the ice. No, the routine was to work your way under the bridge, grab onto one of the steel supporting rods, and hang from your arms.

Russell did all this. While I watched. And assured him that in no time at all he would be a local hero.

It was the shortest day of the year. Darkness was falling fast.

"Start swinging," I told him. "Get some momentum."

"I'm not sure I can do it, Sam," he said. "I'm not sure I can let go."

I could see him sweating. Way below freezing, but the sweat poured off his face. That's when I changed my tune. "Then don't do it, Russell. If you don't want to do it, don't do it."

But he was swinging now, back and forth. His skates were probably not more than eight or ten feet above the river, but it was still a long way down. He swung some more, so that when he hit the ice he would hopefully stay on his feet and simply skate away. Into history. That was the plan, the way it was supposed to work. But the ice suddenly looked so thin, so fragile.

Right about then is when a streak of fear raced down my spine. "Russell!" I shouted.

"Here I go!"

"Wait! No! Don't!"

But he didn't wait. I saw his hands let go of the steel rod. His body sliced through the air. And in no time at all he disappeared. He went straight through the ice. It was still much too weak out there in the middle of the river.

"Russell!"

I saw him, for a brief instant, my best friend, bob to the surface. He scratched and clawed at the ice in an effort to pull himself out of the water. But the ice kept breaking. The current swept him downstream, away from the bridge.

"Russell!"

I climbed back over the safety rail and stumbled across the bridge in my skates. Right in front of a car. It almost ran me down. I screamed. And kept screaming. Within seconds, several other cars had skidded to a stop. Suddenly I found myself surrounded by adults. They had to shake me to find out what had happened. I must have gone into shock.

I remember peering over the bridge and pointing into the growing darkness at the ice and water below. "There!" I kept shouting. "There!" Men began to appear out of nowhere. I saw them moving along the banks of the river. A few ventured out onto the ice.

But it was no good. It was too dark. And too cold. All that evening and into the night we searched along the riverbank for Russell. I ran back and forth for hours and hours shouting my friend's name into the frozen darkness. Finally I collapsed from sheer exhaustion.

I woke up two days later in an unfamiliar hospital bed. I was sick to the bone and wracked with fever, but still alive. My father held a cold compress to my burning forehead. I asked about Russell. My father told me they had found Russell's body floating in the wash just above Wilder Dam, three and a half miles downstream from the Hanover-Norwich Bridge.

MARCH 7.

This morning I went over to thank Mrs. Richmond for helping me through my bout with the flu. She was not there. Miss Julie told me in her congenial way that Mrs. Richmond had left on a regional concert tour: Boston, Portsmouth, Concord, Albany, Buffalo, and Ithaca.

So I stood there at the back door and instead thanked Julie for helping me through my illness. She said nothing, merely shrugged, then pretty much turned on her heel and strode away. She did not even bother to wish me a good morning.

I nevertheless called one out to her before retreating here to the cottage. I have no idea why Julie has taken a dislike to me. Perhaps it is a gender thing. Or a class thing. Or an immigrant thing.

Who knows? Certainly not I.

Why do we like some people and loathe others? Why this love-hate thing constantly sucking at our souls? It all seems so random, so arbitrary, so pitiful. As though we are more than just particles of advanced protoplasm taking up space for a few ticks of the cosmic clock.

Perhaps, as my science fiction author fictitiously suggests, we should induce some good humor serum into the water supply, some happy fragrance into the air. It might make for better and more harmonious living.

MARCH 8.

I am doing my best to get a handle on the enormous amount of work that piled up during my illness. It will undoubtedly take a week or more to get things back on track. One detail at a time, I keep reminding myself. And in the meantime I am taking long walks with the dogs to get myself back into shape. This morning we walked into town. Two miles each way.

We stopped at Rosie's so I could get a croissant and a cup of coffee. Rosie gave the dogs some day-old cookies. She thinks winter is over, that we can expect an early spring.

"I hope you're right," I told her. Then I told her about my flu.

"I don't mind getting the flu," Rosie said. "It's a good way to lose weight."

When I hear stuff like that, I am reminded there is a positive element to even the most dreadful circumstances.

MARCH 9.

This evening, on the train, coming home from work, my thoughts drifted back to my first days with Ellen. August on Cape Cod. It disappeared in a blur of warm days and tender nights. Ellen and I spent every moment we could spare together. I don't think I slept during that entire month. There simply was not time. I was far too busy falling in love. And going to work. And trying to finish my novel.

I wrote between midnight and dawn, after Ellen had gone home to bed. Often I was exhausted, barely able to keep my eyes open, let alone concentrate. But I wanted to finish before Ellen left for New York. I wanted the manuscript to go with her. I finished the final page at sunrise on the last day of August, the same day she left to begin her job at Jackson, Jones & Reynolds.

That afternoon we sat on the porch of her family's beach house. I handed her the manuscript. "I hope you like it."

"I'm sure I will, Sam."

I was feeling lonely already, thinking about her going and me staying. "I wish you were taking me instead of the book."

She laughed, but not very heartily. "If I could fit you into my suitcase," she told me, "I'd take you, too."

That made me feel better. We shared a long passionate kiss, and then Ellen set off for the big city. I felt pretty forlorn. On the same day, I said farewell to both my girl and my novel.

I have always hated farewells.

MARCH 10.

Ellen returned to the Cape for the weekend a couple weeks later. Neither of us wasted a moment suppressing our feelings. The weekend, we knew, would be over in the snap of a finger.

Ellen recounted for me practically every minute of every day since she'd been gone. In great detail she told me about her new job. Then I told her what I'd been doing: working and playing lacrosse and catching up on my sleep. Then we made love. That took up most of Saturday. Finally, early Sunday morning, out on the beach with Reggie, I had to ask. I had to know.

"So did you get a chance to read the book?"

"Your book?"

"No," I said, "Herman Melville's new one."

She laughed and punched me on the shoulder.

"Wise guy." Then she turned her attention to Reggie. She pulled the Frisbee from his mouth and tossed it into the sea.

I started to worry. "Well?"

She watched Reggie battle the surf. "Sure, Sam," she answered, not looking at me, "I read it."

I took a deep breath. "You didn't like it."

"I didn't say I didn't like it."

"Maybe you didn't say it, but—"

"Sam!"

"What?"

"I liked it fine. It's just that, well, it's not really my kind of story. There was so much violence, so much blood and gore."

I grew instantly defensive. "There's a war going on. When you fight a war, you wind up with plenty of violence and blood and gore."

"I know. I'm sure. It's just not my cup of tea. I like Jane Austen."

"So you didn't like it?"

"Actually, I thought some of the writing was pretty good."

I sighed. I wanted to argue. I wanted to defend my position. I wanted to justify every last word of my novel, insist that *Inside Out* was a serious piece of literature, an effort to show the dissolution of innocence in a strange and troubled and violent world. But instead, I simply sighed a mighty sigh. All of my words, I realized, would be in vain.

Reggie came out of the sea. Ellen turned her attention to the bright orange disk stuck between his jaws. I let my thoughts drift away in the breeze.

MARCH 11.

I do not think Ellen and I ever discussed my novel
again. Some subjects are better left alone even between the best of friends. And Ellen and I were certainly fast becoming that.

I survived this silence by telling myself that Ellen
simply did not understand the depth of my creation.
She was a marketing person, after all; another soldier
of business and commerce. She wanted love and romance and happy endings in her fictional escapes, and
mine was a story of a violent and gruesome struggle
for power.

I made several copies of the manuscript and started
sending them around to various agents and editors.
Despite Ellen's comments, or lack thereof, I felt confident the book would sell quickly and be published to
both critical and popular acclaim.

Tough luck, Adams. Another of life's cruel blows.

The rejections piled up, slowly but undeniably.
Most of them were just form letters saying thanks, but
no, thanks. But occasionally some arrogant underling,
no doubt fresh out of Columbia or Penn, would take
me to task for my melodramatic storytelling or my
adjective-ridden prose.

I did not enjoy being rejected. My skin must have
been thinner than I thought. I grew despondent, and
quite weary of the sea. All that pounding and crashing, that relentless cycle of ebb and flow. And my efforts to begin anew on another novel proved futile. I
found it increasingly difficult to string together even
two coherent sentences. Worst of all, I missed Ellen. A
weekend or two a month was not enough to satisfy
my desires.

MARCH 12.

By late fall I was making frequent trips down to New York City. I usually went by bus since I did not own a car. It was a hellish trip, what with the bus stopping eight or nine hundred times between Hyannis and Manhattan. But I didn't care; Ellen was at the end of the line.

She shared an apartment on the Upper West Side with two other girls. I think those girls got pretty sick of having me around all the time, taking up space, eating whatever I could find in the cupboards. Once one of them even suggested that maybe the time had come for me to get a place of my own.

But I already had a place of my own. Back up on the Cape.

"Maybe," Ellen said to me one night as we strolled along Amsterdam Avenue, "you should think about moving down here to the city."

I had already been thinking about it. Quite a lot, in fact. More and more all the time. But I did not see myself as a city person. I'd always lived in small towns. I liked small towns. They were quieter and safer. And yet I knew if I wanted my relationship with Ellen to grow, New York City would probably have to make room for one more immigrant.

For months I had been secretly hoping that Ellen might suggest I send *Inside Out* to one of the editors at Jackson, Jones & Reynolds. Unfortunately, she never did. I decided not to push it.

She worked long hours in the marketing department, ten- and twelve-hour days. She was ambitious. And I know for a fact she always felt she had more to prove because of her uncle's position in the company.

She never wanted people whispering *nepotism* behind
her back.

MARCH 13.

The months went by. Fall came and went. Winter arrived. And finally I had to admit, after accumulating
more than two dozen rejection slips, that *Inside Out*
was not going to propel me into the literary strato-
sphere. In fact, it was not even going to sell. I probably
could not have even given the manuscript away.

After that realization, I had no choice but to sit
down and figure out what to do with the rest of my
life.

"One of our best editors," Ellen by chance told me
that very same night, "is looking for a new assistant.
Why don't you give it a try, Sam?"

MARCH 14.

Roger Richmond knocked on my door this morning. I
had not seen him since that day last December when I
first stopped to inquire about the cottage.

I do not know why, he certainly had not been particularly friendly at our first meeting, but I felt extremely glad to see him. I reached out to shake hands.
"Hello, Roger," I said. "How have you been?"

He once again refused my offering. Some kind of a
low grunt spilled from his mouth, and then he said,
"Let's not start with the phony pleasantries, okay,
pal?"

I dropped my arm to my side and took a step back.

"Right," I said, "okay. I just wondered how you were and where you'd been."

"Zurich," he mumbled.

"Switzerland?"

He nodded. "That's right. I go to school there." Then, "Mother wants to see you. ASAP."

"Sounds urgent."

Roger did not crack a smile.

I followed him over to the big house. He led me through the kitchen and down the hallway to the music room. His mother sat on her precious love seat, her cello resting on that exquisite Oriental carpet. I had not known she'd returned from her regional concert tour.

Julie, looking pale and hostile, brought tea and biscuits. Mrs. Richmond and Roger and I drank the tea and ate the biscuits and made small talk. Very nice. Very chummy. Very civilized. I learned that Mrs. Richmond had gone to Barbados for a few days after finishing her tour.

"I would have stayed for several more weeks," she informed me, "but I had to get back to see Roger. I absolutely loathe the month of March in these parts. So cold and damp and windy. It never gives you a moment's peace. Like an insecure lover."

I blushed and glanced at Roger. He just stood there munching on a biscuit and staring aimlessly out the window. I had the distinct feeling that he had recently smoked a joint. His eyes were bloodshot and his head sort of lolled around on his shoulders.

He told us a little about Switzerland: skiing in St. Moritz, climbing the lower peaks around Zermatt, sailing on Lake Geneva. His stories sounded tired, spoiled rich-kid stuff. I wondered where he'd gotten his bad attitude.

After we had finished our tea and biscuits, Mrs. Richmond told her son she needed to speak with me alone for a few minutes. That sounded just fine with Roger. No problem at all. He shrugged and retreated without a word.

As soon as Roger had closed the door, Mrs. Richmond said, "I hate to bring up a sore subject yet again, Mr. Adams, but I believe you've fallen behind in your rent."

It was true, I had forgotten all about the rent. "You're right," I said. "I'm sorry. I've been swamped with manuscripts lately." I got to my feet. "Let me go over right now and get my checkbook."

"Maybe I want cash."

"Excuse me?"

"Maybe I'd prefer cash," she repeated. "Maybe I don't want a check. Maybe I don't think your check will be any good."

"My check's fine," I said, insulted. "But if you want cash, I'll go out to the bank and get you cash."

"Easy, Mr. Adams. I sense a certain hostility in your voice."

"Yes, well," I fumbled, "I don't particularly enjoy my honesty and my integrity being put into question."

"You're right, of course. I apologize. It was just a passing thought uttered out loud. So many things better kept to ourselves. Please, come over here and sit down. Relax."

I did not know what to do. I probably should have marched out of the music room, written her a check, and thrown it at her feet, but. . . But instead, I went over and sat beside her on the love seat. I do not know exactly why. Her perfume. Her belligerence. Her beauty. Her blindness. My own loneliness.

The moment I sat down, her hand brushed against mine. The index finger of her other hand brushed against her lips. Or was that just my imagination? I looked at her face and wondered again how old she might be. Forty? Forty-five? Maybe fifty? No, not fifty. Her skin was smooth and clear and not at all ruined by the sun or the passage of time. Maybe she had gone for a face job. A nip and tuck. A pinch here, a pinch there. No, the skin did not look taut or manipulated.

I felt a keen desire to reach out and touch her cheek.

"It's all right, Mr. Adams," she said, "go ahead if you wish."

"Huh? No . . . I—"

"You wanted to ask me how old I was. I could sense you studying my face, wondering how many years had passed since my mother brought me into this strange and deceptive world."

"I'm sorry," I said, absolutely off my guard. "I didn't mean to stare."

"Quite all right, Mr. Adams. I assure you. I rather enjoy being stared at, under the proper circumstances."

I was not sure what to say. I began to mutter something, then stopped.

She let the silence hang there for most of a minute; then, "Relax, Mr. Adams, I possess excellent powers of observation, and I can sense that you are a man with very good manners. Your mother brought you up well. Tell me, are you close with your mother?"

I must have hesitated a tad too long because she asked, "I'm sorry, perhaps the question was too personal?"

"No . . . I mean, yes. . . . We're close," I told her. "Quite close."

"Good. I so enjoy men who are close with their

mothers. They tend to be so much more stable and secure. And far more intimate."

Her unexpected mention of my mother unsettled me. I searched around in my brain for a way out.

"But I'm wondering, Mr. Adams . . ."

"Yes?"

"Were you breast-fed?"

"Breast-fed?" I felt certain I had heard wrong.

"Yes. Did your mother breast-feed you?"

"Well, yes," I answered, "she did. For a while. But then she got an infection. In her nipple. Her milk clogged."

"I see. So she was able to breast-feed you for a few weeks? A few months?"

I suddenly did not mind answering her questions. They seemed somehow perfectly reasonable. I found her interest in me flattering. I jogged my memory for answers. "Actually," I told her, "I believe it was just a few days. Yes. Less than a week."

"Hmm." She seemed disappointed. She ran the middle finger of her left hand up and down her nose. Another minute passed.

Her silence caused me to question the intimacy of our conversation. "Maybe," I said, "I should go over and get my checkbook."

She took several more seconds to respond. She appeared utterly lost in her thoughts. Thoughts of me suckling my mother's breast? This, I told myself, is a very strange lady.

"I was going to say, Mr. Adams," and her hand fell gently upon my leg, "if you are having financial difficulties, I feel sure I could find a way for you to pay your rent without any money passing between us."

What, I immediately wondered, did she mean?

Now what was she talking about? Was she making an advance? A sexual advance? Or was she simply suggesting that I could reduce my monthly rental payment by hauling out the garbage or cutting the grass?

I did not wait around to find out. I stood up, made some absurd excuse, and more or less dashed out of the music room. I raced back to the cottage. I wrote out a check large enough to cover the rent for March and April, then I took the check over to the house, gave it to Miss Julie, and asked her to please give it to Mrs. Richmond.

Julie scowled but said she would.

I thanked her and beat a hasty retreat.

MARCH 15.

Yes, a very strange woman. I wonder, though: Does she want to make love to me?

I have not made love to a woman since Ellen died. Almost a year now. More than eleven months.

Would I like to make love to Evelyn Richmond? I am definitely attracted to her beauty, and also, I suppose, to her strangeness, and to her almost antagonistic attitude.

But would I really want to make love to her?

I do not think it would be a very good idea.

MARCH 17.

For three or four days I contemplated what Ellen had told me. I thought long and hard about applying for that job as an editor's assistant. I weighed the pros and

cons. One side of me kept insisting I should move on,
take my leave, hit the road with my used typewriter until I had spun at least one single phrase of perfect prose.

Of course, had I taken this path, gone for the wander-
lust, Ellen would most certainly be alive today. Had I
squeezed her hand, kissed her on the mouth, and whispered my fond farewells, Ellen never would have passed
that night in room 14 of Sloan's Motel.

MARCH 18.

Alas, I did not say farewell. I had spent enough time
on the road. And besides, I was in love with Ms. Ellen
Reynolds. And she with me. It would have been far
too difficult and painful to part.

So I applied for that job as an editor's assistant,
and with Ellen putting in a good word for me, I got it.
And right from the start I liked it. I liked the structure. And the routine. And the regular paycheck. I
loved my small cubicle with my desk and my typewriter and my shelves filled with books. And, of
course, the close proximity to Ellen. And not worrying for a while about writer's block and becoming the
next great American novelist.

I could just relax.

For six months I camped in the living room of an
old college pal who lived in Brooklyn. Then Ellen and
I decided to take the plunge, to get our own apartment. It was a big decision. Her parents were not
happy about it. Neither were mine. Their generation
did not go in for things like that.

We plowed ahead anyway.

We found a third-floor walk-up on 9th Street, right

around the corner from Washington Square Park. The apartment had two rooms, each about the size of a walk-in closet. We moved in on a torrid August day with both the temperature and the humidity hovering near one hundred. But the heat, the damp, all those narrow stairs, the tiny size of our domicile—none of that bothered us in the least. We were young lovers setting forth on a great adventure. It would have been difficult to imagine anything standing in our way.

MARCH 19.

For months Ellen and I awoke in that apartment and made love before heading off to work. We rode the subway up to Midtown and held hands as we walked across Rockefeller Center. We would always share a kiss before saying good-bye down in the lobby next to the bank of elevators. I worked on the thirty-first floor. Ellen worked on the twenty-sixth.

Nearly every day we would rendezvous for lunch. In nice weather we liked to sit above the ice skating rink and eat hot dogs covered with sauerkraut. We also ate at a small lunch counter around the corner on 53rd Street. You could get a bowl of soup and a sandwich for $3.50, a pretty good bargain even in those days. And on our salaries we were constantly on the lookout for bargains. (Ellen's uncle might have been a rich and powerful publisher, and her father had made a tidy sum as a financial investor, but we lived on our meager salaries and did our best not to beg.)

After work we would ride the subway back downtown to our apartment. Often we would make love again. After dinner we would either go out for a walk or to a movie or to one of the cheap clubs around NYU where we would listen to music and drink bad wine.

It was a pretty nice life. Working and loving and not worrying about anything.

MARCH 20.

Now wait a second. What I wrote last evening is not entirely true. As a matter of fact, I did worry about a few things. I am not a real big worrier, but once in a while I have been known to fret. I do not always go with the flow. I am sometimes forced by my inner self to randomly mess with the controls, fiddle with the dials.

Yes, I was extremely happy in those days, maybe as happy as I have ever been. Ellen was warm and beautiful and sexy. We made each other feel important and vital and safe. And we had endless discussions about virtually everything under the sun: love and lust and families and politics and literature and movies and the fate of the planet.

Still, I sometimes felt troubled. I had this ongoing yearning tumbling around in my head and in my gut. It is difficult to describe, but from time to time I felt like I was going nowhere, like I was doing nothing. At least nothing of any significance. I kept feeling like I should be writing, working on a new novel, developing my craft. As a boy, I had conjured up some pretty lofty ambitions, and now those ambitions were coming back to haunt me.

But there was something else as well, something that caused me to fret, to every so often lose a night's sleep. It was the pretty girl curled up at my side, sleeping peacefully with her chest against my back. Yes, I worried about Ellen. I worried about her leaving me, moving on, finding someone new. She gave me absolutely no reason to think she would ever do this, but the possibility worried me nevertheless.

My fear, of course, had to do with trust. But what I did not understand in my younger and more ignorant days was that I was projecting myself onto Ellen. I did not fully trust myself. Therefore, I could not fully trust her. Somewhere in the back of my mind, the scenario existed wherein I could pack up at any moment and shove off for some faraway post to pursue my boyhood dreams of literary immortality. And since I was capable of considering such an act of betrayal myself, I assumed Ellen had the same kinds of thoughts floating around in her head.

Crazy stuff, I know. The brain can play the most dastardly games.

But this game went one step further. It again concerned Ellen. It had to do with the fact that on two or three occasions during our early days together, I became convinced that I was not good enough for her. I felt certain she would soon grow tired of me, toss me aside, run off with some tall, dark, handsome stranger from a wealthy and prestigious family like her own. After all, went my deluded reasoning, Ellen had initially been attracted to me because I was a writer in the throes of completing his first novel. This was all well and good, except that I soon exposed myself as an utter incompetent in the writing arena. What, I kept asking myself, would the beautiful and intelligent Ellen Reynolds want with an incompetent?

MARCH 21.

The first day of spring. And quite a nice day it has been: plenty of sunshine with a perfumed breeze blowing out of the southeast. Sunshine and Moxie and I went for a long walk. It grew warm enough that I stripped down to my T-shirt. Maybe Rosie was right. Maybe the cold weather made an early exit this year.

The dogs swam in the Delaware. I threw a tennis ball from the bank and they raced to see who could get there first. Moxie usually won. She's almost three years younger than Sunshine, and by nature far more aggressive. But her attention span is also quite a bit shorter. She soon became distracted by some ducks swimming downstream, so Sunshine had the opportunity to make several retrievals on her own.

Sunshine always brings the ball right back to me and hands it over with a very soft mouth. She loves to please. Moxie, on the other hand, never brings the ball back until she taunts you with it for a minute or more. And then you have to pry her jaws open to get it out.

Two golden retrievers, almost identical in appearance, a mother and her daughter, but totally different personalities and temperaments.

It keeps things interesting.

MARCH 22.

All my worrying, all my fretting, all my fears and anxieties, soon passed out of our lives. As the days and weeks and months slipped by, I became more and more secure with my role in our relationship. I slowly but surely began to trust myself. I realized that my love for Ellen was deep and real and committed.

Soon thereafter, my brain sprang forth with the notion that Ellen felt very much the same way. She just wanted me to be kind and loving and supportive. And, of course, she wanted me to make her laugh. She loved me most of all when I made her laugh.

MARCH 23.

Ellen also loved listening to my stories. So I told her stories all the time. I proved an energetic and skilled oral storyteller. Had I lived in ancient Greece, perhaps I would have rivaled Homer with my tales of youth and courage and worldwide travel.

I told Ellen about the places I had gone during and after college. She enjoyed hearing about the people I had met and the things I had seen. I occasionally exaggerated a tale to give it more punch, but that's what novelists do. So what if only bits and pieces of my stories lay grounded in truth? I quickly realized how irrevocably linked were those two supposedly opposed worlds: reality and fiction, fact and fantasy.

MARCH 24.

These realizations, both conscious and subconscious, made me, for the first time in my life, begin to understand and appreciate fully the fictional worlds created by the good and the great novelists. I had always loved reading first-rate fiction, and, of course, I desired more than anything else to write exceptional prose. But suddenly comprehending this intrinsic link between the fictional world and the real world caused me to view myself and my personal responsibilities in a whole new manner.

Perhaps, I reasoned, I was not meant to be a creator, but rather, an interpreter and facilitator.

Soon after this reckoning, my ambitions began to shift. I saw clearly the vital role played by the editor. I immediately started to take my work as an editor's assistant much more seriously.

MARCH 25.

The editor I worked for at Jackson, Jones & Reynolds, a highly respected woman who had been around for three decades, had nurtured a small but very influential group of novelists. Their books rarely reached the best-seller lists, but they garnered lengthy and frequently positive reviews in all of the important literary journals. And they were nominated for, and occasionally even won, the more significant literary prizes.

Madeline Harris was a workaholic. She had her entire life wrapped up in those novels. Overweight and never married, Madeline sucked the juices of life from the very words she edited. Her writers were her children. She made herself available to them twenty-four hours a day, seven days a week, three hundred and sixty-five days a year.

If asked, I would have to describe Madeline as both an earth mother and a monster. Her authors despised and adored her.

My first big break in the publishing business came when Madeline had a heart attack while sitting at her desk eating a pastrami sandwich on rye with extra-hot mustard. Twenty-seven successful years in the business and she still ate at her desk almost daily, poring over manuscripts that demanded her expertise and her always razor-sharp red pencil.

I heard her gasp, then hit the floor. I ran into her office, felt for a pulse, then dialed 911.

"Sammy," she said to me a few days later in the intensive care wing at Lenox Hill Hospital, "you saved my life."

For my efforts, Madeline presented me with one of her new and least favorite authors. "Now listen to me, Sam. Do not tell anyone you're editing this," she told me when she handed over the manuscript. "Not even Ellen. Just do the best job you can, then give it back to me. If you do a good job, more projects will come your way."

I did a good job, an excellent job, a superb job. Madeline told me I had a natural knack for the editorial process. Of course, she took credit for my work, but only because the prima donna author would have blown her fuses had she known some two-bit assistant had actually edited her precious prose.

MARCH 26.

I was summoned again this morning to the big house. When I walked into the kitchen, Miss Julie refused to even acknowledge my presence. I waited for most of a minute while she loaded some dirty plates and glasses into the dishwasher, then I turned and started down the hallway. But just before I left the kitchen, I had to ask, "Julie, have I done something to offend you? It is quite clear from our first meeting that you do not like me."

She glanced at me with narrowed and even angry eyes, then mumbled in her thick English accent, "I don't like any of you."

"I don't understand. Why not?"

"Because you're all so strange," she said, her eyes riveted on the sink. "You have no morals."

I did not know what she was talking about. "Why do you say that? Why do you think I don't have any morals?"

But this time she would not answer. She stood hunched over the sink, a scrub brush in her hand. I sighed and turned away. I took my lack of morals, hiked down that long dark hallway, and knocked softly on the door of the music room.

"*Entrez,*" Evelyn Richmond said in a boisterous voice.

I pushed open the door and stepped inside. Mrs. Richmond sat in her usual spot, but this time she did not sit alone. A young man, not Roger, sat close beside her. A tad too close, I thought.

Mrs. Richmond was not fully dressed. She wore nothing but a silk kimono, not the long black one I had seen her in before, but a short red one that barely covered her thighs.

"That sounds like you, Mr. Adams."

I nearly turned and walked out without a word. Nearly. Not quite. I am far too polite for that. I stood in place and tried not to stare. "Yes."

"Thank you for coming," she said, nice as can be. And then, "Oh, this is Martin, Mr. Adams. A young, and quite brilliant, violinist."

Indeed, a violin lay on the Oriental carpet right

beside the cello, practically right on top of the cello, as though the two stringed instruments had just finished playing some carnal tune.

"Martin and I have been practicing our notes. Isn't that so, Martin?"

Martin nodded but did not speak. I doubt he had celebrated his twentieth birthday. His body was lean, almost feminine. He sat there next to Mrs. Richmond wearing nothing but a pair of tight black jeans and a white rayon shirt unbuttoned most of the way to his navel.

Have these two, I wondered, been sitting in here stroking one another? The notion made me feel slightly sick to my stomach. Or was I actually experiencing a twinge of jealousy?

"I hate to bother you, Mr. Adams," said Mrs. Richmond, "but we've suffered a minor crisis. Our driver has taken ill and I need to get Roger to the airport for his return flight to Zurich. I was wondering if you might be able to help us out?"

"You want me to drive Roger to the airport?"

Mrs. Richmond smiled at me. "I'll compensate you, of course."

MARCH 27.

I took Roger to the airport yesterday afternoon. We drove not in my minivan but in the Richmonds' Mercedes-Benz sedan.

Roger was in a much more gregarious mood than he had been during our previous encounters. He talked and laughed and once or twice even slapped me on the shoulder. Buddy style.

I tried to get him to talk about his mother, but he was far more interested in telling me about his recent golfing expedition down to Myrtle Beach, South Carolina, where he had managed to sleep with, or so he claimed, four different females in three days.

"Don't you worry about AIDS?" I asked him.

"Hell," he said, "you can't go through life worrying about every little stupid detail. But yeah, I think about it. So, if I remember, and I have the time, I slip on a rubber." He shrugged. "I hate the damn things, but hey, you gotta do what you gotta do."

Roger told me he would be eighteen in June.

Then he told me his parents had split up when he was just a kid. "Mother has always been, well, sort of temperamental. An artist, you know. And I guess kind of promiscuous. I think she likes to fuck a lot of different men. Father couldn't handle that, so he moved to Africa. I see him once in a while. When I get out of school, I'm going over there to live with him."

The kid was talking a mile a minute. Probably on amphetamines.

I nodded, my mind whirling with thoughts of his mama's sexual habits, then asked, "Has your mother always been blind?"

"Hell no," said Roger, as though surprised I did not know. "She only went completely blind a couple years ago. It's a degenerative thing."

We drove into the airport. Roger directed me to the appropriate terminal. Just before getting out of the car, he said, "Listen . . . uh—"

"Sam," I reminded him.

"Right. Sam. Listen, Sam, don't let my mother bug you. She's just pissed off about being blind. Never gives anyone a break. Snap your head off at the slightest provocation. Besides, she likes you. I can tell."

I wanted him to stay and talk, fill me in on all the details of his mother's life, but in no time at all he grabbed his bags and flew away.

MARCH 28.

I am still very much in love with my wife. A year after her death and I miss her more than ever. I am painfully aware of how much I miss her every time I sit down to write in this journal. Whereas now I sit alone with my pen and my paper and my thoughts, before I always sat with Ellen. We spent time together every evening talking and just thinking out loud. She heard the words that now I can only write down.

Still, it helps.

But I feel Mrs. Richmond beginning to intrude. I keep seeing her sitting there in her music room, her kimono hanging open, her cello balanced between her legs, melancholy notes drifting toward the ceiling.

I see clearly that Mrs. Richmond has experienced pain, has suffered loss. We have these things in common.

I wonder what else might bind us together?

MARCH 29.

The temperature soared into the seventies this afternoon. The dogs and I took another hike down to the river. Young Kathleen Karr came along. She's a sweet kid, spunky but polite. And oh how she loves Sunshine and Moxie.

We all stopped at Rosie's on the way home. Kathleen
and I had root beers and chocolate chip cookies. Rosie
gave the dogs water and some pieces of stale cinnamon
raisin bagel. They loved it.

I enjoy days like this. But days like this also make
me sad. They make me remember all the good times
Ellen and Nicky and I had together. Give us a warm
sunny spring day, and we could venture outside and in
no time at all become the happiest trio in the land.

But no more of that.

No, no more of that.

I think I'll let the dogs sleep on the bed tonight.

MARCH 31.

Ellen and I got married. Of course we got married.
What else would we do?

I suppose we could have gone our separate ways.
Hindsight tells me we should have gone our separate
ways, that if we had, Ellen would be alive today.

But she said yes when I asked her to be my wife. We
had been living together by that time for more than a
year. Marriage seemed like the right and proper thing
to do. A logical next step.

Her parents, who finally started to like me the day I
slipped an engagement ring on their daughter's finger,
threw us a big, fancy wedding. The ceremony took
place in a lovely white church with a tall steeple out
on Cape Cod on a spectacular June afternoon. Warm
breezes blew big puffy white clouds across the sky.

My brother, Jack, was my best man. My sister, Abigail, was one of Ellen's maids of honor. My mother and
father sat in the front pew.

"Do you, Sam, take thee, Ellen, to be your lawfully wedded wife, to have and to hold, to love and to cherish, for better or for worse, in sickness and in health, till death do you part?"

"I do," I assured my bride, the preacher, and all family and friends present. "I definitely do."

And Ellen did, too.

I kissed the bride. Hard. On the mouth.

We held our reception at the big house out on Nauset Beach. Everyone had a grand time eating and drinking and dancing. We had almost two hundred guests, more than one hundred bottles of fine French champagne. The food kept coming, one course after another. The band played everything from Bob Dylan to Hank Williams to Benny Goodman. And later, as the sun began to set, even though the Atlantic was still a might chilly, the entire wedding party, including Reggie, raced across the cool sand and dove headfirst into the breakers. It made for some very interesting wedding photos.

Ellen and I dried off, then waved farewell and set forth on our honeymoon.

We spent twelve wonderful days on Bermuda. Nothing unusual or out of the ordinary happened during that vacation. We did precisely what honeymooners do on that splendid and tranquil island. We slept late in the morning. We ate breakfast on our balcony overlooking the sea. We tore around on mopeds investigating the island and looking for secluded beaches where we could kiss and swim naked. We went snorkeling. We played tennis. We partook of five-course dinners and fine wines. We made love. A lot. At least twice a day.

But during all of our activities, day in and day out,

something quite out of the ordinary was happening up
in my brain. I felt an incredible sense of calm, of well-
being, as though nothing bad could ever happen to me
or to us again. I did not think it possible, but those
simple wedding vows had brought a whole new feeling
of joy and satisfaction to my relationship with Ellen.
Throughout those twelve days I beamed, so elated was
I to simply stand at my beautiful, loving wife's side.

APRIL 1.

Soon after we returned from our honeymoon, Jackson,
Jones & Reynolds created a new position. I became
the first recipient of that position. It may have had
something to do with marrying into the family, but I
have always liked to believe that I earned the promotion. And I have worked extra hard ever since to justify their initial faith in my potential.

They gave me an official title. Instead of just being a
plain old assistant, I was now an associate editor. Basically that meant I continued to fulfil my duties for
the grand old dame, Madeline Harris, who had fully
recovered from her heart attack and was now eating
yogurt and carrot sticks at her desk, but it also meant I
could begin to look for authors of my own. I was allowed to buy one or two books a year, with, of course,
the unanimous consent of the publisher and the senior
editorial staff.

My first novel, a humorous but fairly esoteric rambling about a young boy who dreams of becoming an
astronaut and visiting the stars out beyond the Milky
Way, exceeded all expectations. It sold over sixty
thousand copies in hardcover.

I was on my way.

To where or for what, I did not know. But nevertheless, I was swept away by the success, by all the attention. Especially when *The New York Times Book
Review* called the novel "a spectacular mix of fact and
fantasy, a perfect blend of innocence and insight. *Icarus
Rises* is easily the best debut novel of the season."

I may not have written it, but I had definitely urged
and prodded the writer into exploring the fantastic
imagination of his young protagonist. By the end of
the narrative, my editorial swirl was present on practically every page. *Icarus Rises* belonged as much to me
as it did to the author.

APRIL 2.

My promotion meant more money, not a whole lot of
money, but enough to keep me interested. Far more
important than the money was the incredible rush of
adrenaline I felt during the editorial process. Red pencil in hand, I felt like God. Well, that might be a slight
exaggeration, but I definitely enjoyed the power I had
over the author's prose.

Ellen was making more money also. In fact, she had
taken the marketing department by storm, first suggesting and then actually implementing several unique
approaches to selling books. She understood what
many editors often ignored: that books were consumer items, nonessential merchandise, luxuries people purchased with excess income. The competition
for this excess income included movies, magazines,
records, and, of course, other books. Ellen realized
that first the consumer needed to know that a specific

book title existed, that it was out there in the stores. Then that same consumer had to be convinced of the necessity of owning that title. That, in turn, led to a sale. And sales meant profit.

The Reynolds clan was into profit. Ellen was most definitely a Reynolds. Ellen Reynolds Adams may have been sweet and silly and even a little bit shy, but as a businesswoman she was extremely savvy.

I think, had she lived, she would have eventually run the company. She would have been CEO of JJ&R.

APRIL 3.

With our extra income, Ellen and I decided to move out of our tiny apartment on 9th Street. After a lengthy search, we headed back to the Upper West Side. We rented a four-room apartment on 77th Street halfway between Amsterdam and Columbus, just a quick jaunt to the Museum of Natural History.

After 9th Street, our new digs seemed positively cavernous. We settled in, happier and more in love than ever.

APRIL 4.

Sometimes I do not know if this is a good idea or not; writing about my life with Ellen, digging up all these old memories. On the one hand it makes me feel good to remember. But on the other hand it makes me feel sad, and it may well be perpetuating my grief.

Still, I want to write. I want to write at least a few sentences each day. I need to write.

And right now, once again, Ellen is in my heart and

on my mind far more than anything or anyone else. So for the time being I will go where she leads me.

APRIL 5.

I did some arithmetic last night. I figured out there are 168 hours in a week. Of those 168 hours I estimated that Ellen and I, on average, spent approximately 120 of those hours in close proximity to one another. I reached this conclusion using the following breakdown: 56 hours per week in bed either sleeping, reading, or making love; 15 hours per week eating meals together; 5 hours per week getting ready for work; another 5 per week traveling to and from work; 20 hours per week on weekends doing chores, running errands, going to movies and museums, etc.; and another 20 hours per week in the evenings relaxing and talking and thinking about the future. A grand total of 121 hours.

Now how, I wonder, does one survive, after spending 121 hours out of 168 hours each week with the same person for years and years, getting along either great or at least pretty darn well, when suddenly, out of nowhere, that person dies, violently, and for no good reason?

Seriously, how does one make it? How does one carry on? Why should I bother to get up in the morning and face another day?

Sometimes it is extraordinarily difficult. I seek simple pleasures. Like walks with my dogs. And, of course, I bury myself in my work.

And I try very hard not to remember that very soon will come the one-year anniversary of our catastrophic stay at Sloan's Motel.

APRIL 6

Rain today. A soft, steady spring rain.

APRIL 7.

Yet another summons late yesterday afternoon to visit
Mrs. Richmond in the music room. I feared at first I
had once again neglected to pay my rent, but then I re-
called paying in advance after our last confrontation.

This time I found Mrs. Richmond alone with her
cello, and quite subdued. In fact, she seemed downright
depressed. She did not even invite me to join her on the
love seat.

"Yes, Mr. Adams," she said, her voice low and hol-
low, "thank you for stopping by. I have a small favor
to ask."

I waited, no longer certain about her small favors.

But it was just that and nothing more. She and Julie
are going away for a few days, and she would like me
to keep an eye on the house. It seems the man who
usually does this, a Mr. Pierson, is in the hospital having some work done on his gallbladder.

I assured her I would watch the house. She thanked
me and handed me a key to the back door. "If you
could come by each day. Just to make sure everything
is all right. I would appreciate it."

"No problem. I'll come over before I go to work in
the morning. And then, again, after I get home."

She thanked me once more.

I decided maybe the time had come to go. She
barely seemed to notice my withdrawal.

At the door I stopped, searched for something to

say. "Well, I guess I'll be going. Have a nice time on your trip." I had no idea where they were going. "I'll see you when you get back."

Mrs. Richmond sighed. "Yes, when we get back."

I hovered in the doorway, uncertain whether to stay or go. "Is everything all right, Mrs. Richmond? You seem distressed. Can I get you anything?"

She did absolutely nothing for several seconds. She did not make a sound or move a muscle. I had the feeling she could have been sound asleep, or in some kind of trance.

Then, suddenly, she sighed again. "Oh, no," she said, "it's nothing. Nothing at all. It's just that, well, you told me before you moved in that you had two friends, two golden retrievers, and now it's been, my God, over three months, and still you have not brought them by for a visit."

I did not waste a second. I went directly over and fetched Sunshine and Moxie. They love to go visiting. They went bounding into the house, and, much to my astonishment, they made a beeline for the music room. Moxie promptly jumped straight onto the love seat and licked Mrs. Richmond right smack on the lips.

"Moxie! No!" I admonished, but Mrs. Richmond hushed me up. In no time at all she was rolling around on that Oriental carpet with those two mutts. Her cello, I noticed, had been safely tucked away in its hard plastic case. She kissed those dogs on the snout and ran her hands lovingly through their thick coats. They have been shedding like crazy ever since the weather started warming up, and so they did yesterday, all over the music room floor. Mrs. Richmond did not seem to mind. She buried her nose in their necks. They gave her a thousand licks and luxuriated in all the extra attention.

I just stood by the door, once again amazed at the subtleties and complexities of my blind landlady.

APRIL 8.

Ellen and I had been married a little over a year when we made the decision to start a family, to have a baby. We had good jobs and plenty of security. The time, we felt, had come.

So Ellen put her diaphragm in that little pink case and placed it in the cabinet under the bathroom sink. If our lovemaking had waned just a bit by this time, the idea of fornicating for a purpose other than our own carnal pleasure renewed our interest in a heartbeat. We made love more often and more passionately than we had since our first few frantic months as lovers. Two, three, even four times a day we took off and put on our clothes. We even found an empty office with a secure lock on the edge of the marketing department where we would rendezvous in the middle of the day if the urge suddenly swept over us.

And in no time at all, within just a few months, Ellen missed her period. A few weeks later she went to the doctor's, and sure enough, just like magic, the seed had been planted.

APRIL 9.

I suppose I would consider the gradual swelling of Ellen's stomach the most emotional and gratifying event of my entire life. Her pregnancy was a purely positive experience. It was something we made happen, something we wanted to happen, something that gave us enormous hope for the future.

When I first heard the news that she was definitely with child, and then, at the first sign of swelling, I felt incredibly proud. For days and weeks I strutted around like a peacock with his tail feathers in full display. I had made love to my wife and created life.

I felt like a lover. I felt like a man. I felt like a husband. I felt ready and able to become a father.

APRIL 10.

Nicholas Michael Adams was born on Thanksgiving Day. And like our Pilgrim forebears, we gave plenty of thanks.

But before he arrived in this world, young Nicky put his parents through the wringer. His mother especially. She was slowly becoming exhausted hauling around those thirty extra pounds. She slept fitfully because the baby kept kicking and rolling in her belly. She waddled when she walked. She spent half the day going to the bathroom. She could not bend down to wash her feet or tie her shoes. I had to do these simple everyday things for her.

Near the end she could not do much of anything but loll around on the sofa, eat, watch the tube, and wait.

The wait proved interminable. That child absolutely refused to come out into the light of day. Labor lasted, it seemed, for months.

Finally, very early on Thanksgiving morning, it must have been about five A.M., Ellen made the announcement: time to go to the hospital. No problem, I was fully prepared. I am not the greatest in times of emergency, possessing an inclination to panic, but I had been making practice runs for weeks. I got Ellen to the hospital lickety-split, in less than thirty minutes, but once we got there, the wait continued. It went on for hours, for what seemed like days. I kept asking the nurses and the doctor if something was wrong, if my wife and baby were okay.

They assured me everything was just fine.

I did not believe them. Months earlier I had once again taken up my call as a worrier. By the second month of Ellen's pregnancy, I began to fret that my child would be marred with some defect: an extra finger, not enough toes, a harelip, a cauliflower ear, maybe brain damage caused by the marijuana I had smoked in college. I read and reread every child-care book I could get my hands on. No doubt about it: I became obsessed. I stayed awake countless nights worrying about all the stuff that could go wrong. It seemed a divine miracle that most of us came out whole and reasonably healthy.

And then, when the kid refused to come out of the womb, refused to separate himself from his mother, my worry turned frantic. I watched Ellen struggling with the waves of labor. Never before had I seen her in so much pain. I wanted her whole and safe. I wanted that baby out of her belly.

I stayed at her side, gripping her hand, sponging her warm, swollen body with a cool cloth. Once or twice I slipped away to catch my breath and stretch my legs, but for most of that fifteen hours I remained within reach.

APRIL 11.

Finally, at 8:35 in the evening on Thursday, November 26, Turkey Day, my son decided to make his grand entrance. Although, in reality, it was not very grand. In the end the doctor literally had to reach up inside my wife, get a grip, and pull him out. Ellen let loose with some pretty horrible screams during this particular phase of the ordeal.

By that time I'd had some fairly negative thoughts about this youngster, but the second I laid eyes on my son, all those thoughts vanished forever.

He came out covered with blood, and for just an instant I thought he might be dead. But the little guy was not dead; he was alive and well, with both eyes, both ears, all his fingers and toes, even a short crop of fine blond hair that later would turn reddish brown, just like his mama's.

The nurses washed him down, the doctor looked him over, and presto—I had my son squirming around in my arms. After a minute or two, he started to cry, really just a whimper, but enough that I handed him over to his mother, who, though practically delirious with exhaustion, instinctively knew how to make the little guy calm and happy and content.

I stood there next to the bed with my eyes all wet with tears of overwhelming joy and happiness while I watched my son suckle my wife's nipple.

APRIL 12.

Tomorrow is the one-year anniversary of that terrible morning in room 14 of Sloan's Motel. Tomorrow is Easter Sunday.

So that I will not find myself alone on that day, I am leaving now for my brother's house in Vermont. I will spend the weekend with my family: my parents, my brother, my sister, and their spouses and children. Sunshine and Moxie will come along with me.

APRIL 14.

We had a good time in Vermont. It was great to get away, to see the family.

Everyone asked how I was getting along. I told them just fine. Jack asked me in private if I'd been out on any dates, if I'd seen any ladies. I told him the truth: that I'd only been out a few times, that nothing very interesting had happened, that I still found it difficult to even think about being with another woman.

But although I did not mention her to my brother, I found myself thinking about my landlady, Mrs. Richmond.

APRIL 15.

Today I found myself thinking about Nicholas. All day long at work I kept wondering what Nicky would be doing today, right now, at this very second, if the creature had not snatched his life away?

He would probably be outside with his pals playing

baseball, running down a pop fly, legging out a squibber down the third base line, swinging for the fences with his twenty-six–ounce Louisville Slugger. Nicky loved baseball. He wanted to be a major leaguer. A New York Yankee.

Maybe he and I would be over at Yankee Stadium with his mother sitting in the Jackson, Jones & Reynolds box, eating hot dogs, drinking Cokes, hollering for the Bronx Bombers to keep the rally going.

God, I am so angry, so totally ticked off.

Of course, the entire scenario was my fault. I have only myself, and no one else, to blame.

I did not need to stop for the night. We easily could have made it to Hanover, driven on to my parents' house. It was not like we were tired. It was not that late in the day. We could have made it. We did not need to pass the night in that crummy fleabag motel.

"You have to stop blaming yourself, Sam," my brother and my sister and my father and my mother and virtually everyone else I know kept telling me. "It was not your fault."

"It was my fault."

"No, Sam, it was not."

"It was."

"Sam, listen to me," my father told me one night on the phone. "You had no way of knowing such an ugly and terrible thing would strike out at your family. It is extremely unfortunate, Sam, but society today is filled with these random and inexplicable acts of violence."

Random. My father had that right. Such a fine word: *random*. It sums the whole mess up.

But why, dammit, why? Why did we wait until the middle of the afternoon to leave home? Why did we have to have that flat tire? Why did the AAA man

make us walt so long? Why couldn't there have been
room at the Holiday Inn? Or the Howard Johnson's?
Why couldn't I have stopped at the next exit? Why did
I have to stop at all? Why couldn't just one small incident that day have happened a little differently?

APRIL 16.

Why did I live?

Why did I survive?

Yes, I know it is easy enough now to sound gallant
and courageous, but I gladly would have died so that
Ellen and Nicky could have lived.

Do I mean this?

Is this a true statement?

Yes, I believe it is. Not only would I like to give my
wife and son life, but living without them is little better than death.

APRIL 18.

I have been working extremely hard, ten and twelve
and even fourteen hours a day, trying to keep my mind
clear and focused on my manuscripts. But I realize
now that I cannot escape my responsibilities. I have to
face the truth about what happened during that terrible weekend last April. I need to be specific and brutally honest.

And I have decided to do much of the work here, on
the train, on the way home from work. It will be easier
this way. At home I need to relax, unwind, spend time
thinking not about my past, but about my future.

APRIL 19.

It was the Saturday between Good Friday and Easter Sunday. We packed up the minivan and set out for my parents' house. An early start had been planned, but we did not get away until the middle of the afternoon. Those inevitable delays: the dogs had to be taken to the kennel, an unexpected telephone call from a distraught author, a lost key, the ritual arguing about what to bring and what to leave behind.

Ellen had enough luggage for a two-week stint to Paris. And Nicky, nine-year-old superathlete, demanded we pack virtually all of his athletic gear into the van: basketball, football, baseball, baseball glove, and, of course, his brand-new twenty-six-ounce, solid maple Louisville Slugger.

I did not really care what time we left. I did not even want to go. I wanted to stay home with my wife and son; spend Easter Sunday reading *The New York Times;* watch a little TV; have a quiet dinner; maybe, after eating too much, take a ride through the neighborhood on our bikes. Nothing too strenuous or stressful. We had enough stress in our lives. We needed a day to just unwind, take it easy.

Sure, I enjoyed seeing my parents, having a few laughs with my brother and sister, but the idea of a seven-hour drive up on Saturday and another seven-hour drive back on Monday did not really strike my fancy.

Nevertheless, by two o'clock in the afternoon we were all set to go, to head north for Hanover.

APRIL 20.

I remember that Saturday as being one of those splendid early spring days. The sun shone brightly under a brilliant blue sky. As we drove off in the minivan, I felt confident the cold, damp sting of winter had finally vanished from the air. The grass had started to turn green, the forsythia bright yellow. Buds appeared magically on the trees. Daffodils swayed in the warm breeze. Everything looked and smelled fresh and hopeful.

We stopped and bought the newspaper and a bag of donuts. Nicky loved donuts. So did his old man. We drove through town, then out along the old east–west highway to the interstate. Lots of traffic. Everybody on the road to celebrate Christ rising from the dead. It was the season of renewal and resurrection.

Ellen drove. Nicky sat in the back playing one of his portable video games. I had tried it once myself. Good knights versus evil knights: an endless bloodbath of violence and destruction complete with sound effects and gaping wounds inflicted by electronic swords and spiked clubs.

I scanned the headlines in the *Times:* a triple homicide on the Upper East Side, a man stoned to death at the Wailing Wall, millions starving in some African country I had never even heard of before, zoo animals dying from sheer boredom, people stealing and swindling and blackmailing.

On and on I read, horrified but still happy to be safe and secure tooling along at sixty-three miles an hour in our dependable American minivan with theft alarm, dual air bags, and automatic door locks.

And the thing is: I did not even see the irony between my son's entertainment and my own.

APRIL 21.

Then, cruising along the interstate, about 150 miles out with another 160 or 170 miles to go, more or less halfway between my manhood home and my boyhood home, Ellen ran over a bottle. A large glass bottle. In no time at all the left front tire went flat.

"Didn't you see it?" I asked her as we limped off the highway. "I saw it half a mile back."

"Old eagle-eye Adams," said Ellen, making light, as usual, of the situation. "A man who never misses a thing. Why, he can see Harry Truman on a dime from a mile away."

I sighed, told myself not to get upset, not to make a bad situation worse. I think I even managed a smile as Ellen maneuvered the wounded minivan onto the wide asphalt shoulder of the interstate.

Safely off the crowded speedway, the engine shut down, the transmission in park, I climbed out to survey the damage. It did not take long. The tire was dead flat, the road and rim separated by only a quarter inch of deflated radial rubber.

I went around to the back, carefully avoiding the endless stream of holiday traffic. I opened the hatch. After moving aside our arsenal of weekend luggage, I reached down into the tire well to pull out the spare. It was one of those dumb little pretend tires. Donut tires, I think the car companies call them. Too bad this one was dead flat also; no more air in it than the one holding up the left front corner of the minivan.

I reminded myself what my father would do: stay calm, remain reasonable, be patient, overcome adversity.

APRIL 22.

While Ellen and I debated what to do, a state trooper pulled up behind us. He tried to be courteous, but we could see the intense volume of holiday traffic was testing his resolve. I asked him if he could give me a lift to the nearest gas station.

"I'll tell you, sir," he answered, his right hand nonchalantly resting on the butt of his revolver, "I've got an accident back at mile marker two thirty-one. The best I can do is try and get you a wrecker. Do you have Triple A?"

Of course we had AAA. Wouldn't be without it. Safe and secure every step of the way.

The trooper called his dispatcher. A couple minutes later the dispatcher radioed back to say AAA would have a man out within forty-five minutes.

It took the AAA guy over two hours to get there. Two hours and seven minutes to be exact. For two hours and seven minutes Ellen and Nicky talked and dozed in the back of the minivan while I read the newspaper and paced around in the weed-choked grass and wished we had just stayed home.

By the time the AAA guy finally arrived, I had pretty much lost my patience. I demanded to know what had taken so long. He just snarled at me, blew up our fake tire, installed it, then drove off without muttering a civil word.

I felt bad after he left. Like the trooper, he was no doubt having a rough day. I should have been more sympathetic. My father always told me to step back when tempers flare and put yourself in the other person's shoes.

Excellent advice.

But it was too late. The AAA guy was gone. All I could do was try harder next time.

We prepared to get under way again. Ellen told me it was my turn to drive. I climbed in behind the wheel, adjusted the seat, and worked my way back into the flow of traffic.

We did not get five miles before that fake tire leaked out all its captive air.

"Damn!" I shouted as I struggled to maneuver the minivan back over to the shoulder. "This is turning into a nightmare."

My son giggled.

So did his mother.

"What are you two laughing about?" I demanded. Then I turned on Ellen. "This whole mess is your fault."

"Oh right," she said. "Like I hit that bottle on purpose."

"You said you did. You said you hit it on purpose."

She just looked at me, rolled her eyes, and shook her head. That's all it took to calm me down. Ellen always knew exactly how to keep me in line.

APRIL 23.

Several hundred yards down the interstate we could see a sign that indicated it was one mile to the next exit.

"Maybe I should just go down there. I'm sure there'll be a gas station."

"Maybe we should all go."

"No," I said, "you two stay here and guard the fort. I'll run down there and see what I can find."

"Okay," agreed Ellen. "But be careful. Don't get run over."

Getting run over was the least of my worries. I was far more worried about getting half a mile from the minivan and having some lunatic descend upon my family. Still, I had to do something. We couldn't just sit there. So I made my move. I opened the door of the van and stepped out. The traffic swept past at a frenzied pace. "Lock up after I go," I told my wife. "Don't let anyone into the car, even if they have a uniform on. These days even the nuts wear uniforms."

She smiled, gave me a thumbs-up. My wife: fearless, cocky, confident.

I had to go up and over a slight rise to reach the exit. As soon as I did, I lost sight of the minivan. That did not give me a feeling of security. I sprinted the rest of the way to the exit ramp. At the top of the ramp I found a gas station. But I had to wait almost an hour before the guy on duty could find someone to man the pumps while he drove me back down the highway in his wrecker.

Most of that hour I stood beside the large red Coke machine. My imagination went into overdrive concerning events back at the minivan. I concocted all kinds of grisly scenarios. I saw droopy-eyed madmen with knives, drug-crazed teenagers with tire irons, convicted sex offenders with ropes and chains. It was not a pretty picture.

By the time I climbed into that wrecker, I had myself pretty well convinced that we would find wrack and ruin back at the minivan.

APRIL 24.

But no, Ellen and Nicky were fine. They were sitting in the back of the van playing Crazy Eights when the gas station guy and I pulled up. No one had stopped to either help or hurt them.

The gas station guy hooked the van up to the wrecker and we all piled into the cab for the short trip back to the gas station. A brand-new tire was installed while we fed quarters into the soda and candy machines in an effort to do our part to stimulate the American economy: Coke and Clark bars and several bags of both plain and peanut M&Ms.

APRIL 25.

"Maybe we should just turn around and go home," I said as we pulled out of the station. "This trip isn't going very well."

"It's going just fine, Sam," Ellen insisted. "We just had a flat tire. People have flat tires all the time."

I sighed, tried another tack. "Then maybe we should stop for the night. Get a room at a motel and do the rest of the drive in the morning."

"That's ridiculous. It's only another two or three hours."

"Three or four would be more like it," I pointed out. "Plus we'll have to stop and eat. It'll be midnight before we get there."

"Yeah," said Nick from the backseat, "let's get a motel room. One with a pool and a Magic Finger."

"It's too early for the pools to be open," said the boy's mother.

Nicholas loved to stay in motels. I liked them too when I was a kid. There was something dark and mysterious about all those locked doors and drawn curtains and cars out front with license plates from faraway states like Montana and New Mexico and California. And, of course, the Magic Finger: the small gray box on the nightstand that took your quarter and magically made the bed vibrate for eight or ten minutes.

We always had the same sleeping arrangements whenever we stayed in a motel: my mother and father in one bed, my brother and me in the other bed, and my sister on one of those foldaway cots. I remember Jack would slip a quarter into the Magic Finger after my father turned out the lights. Then he and I would both roll over onto our stomachs so that we could feel our penises stiffen as that bed did its thing.

I suppose it would be true enough to say the Magic Finger provided me with my first truly erotic experience.

APRIL 26.

Despite Ellen's protests, we decided to stop for the night.

We had to try five or six different motels before we finally found one with a vacancy. The country was on the move that Easter weekend, everyone going somewhere to see someone.

The big, clean, sanitized chain motels were all full: Best Western, Holiday Inn, Howard Johnson's.

We wound up at Sloan's Motel, about half a mile from the interstate, along the old state highway that used to carry the bulk of the north–south traffic before the limited-access four-laner pushed through the area.

Sloan's had obviously been around quite a while,

probably since the late fifties. It was basically a long, squat cinderblock bunker divided up into fifteen or sixteen 20-by-20 cells. It had some character, though, much more than any of the chain motels hugging the exit ramp: a grove of mature shade trees in early bloom protecting the parking lot, a playground with a sandbox and an old steel jungle gym, a small swinging bench outside the door of each room. It looked like a pleasant enough place to pass a night.

I was glad to get off the road.

I carried our gear into the room while Ellen used the bathroom and Nicky ran over to play on the jungle gym. The room looked clean, if somewhat barren, and a quick bounce on the two queen-size beds assured me that I would not wake up in the morning with too bad a backache.

"Bathroom okay?" I asked Ellen as she emerged from the shadows at the rear of the room.

"Oh," she answered, her sarcastic lilt obvious from that single syllable, "it's just swell." She dried her hands on one of those small, coarse motel-room towels. She did not look happy.

"What's the matter?"

"Nothing," she insisted. And then, of course, she told me. "I just think we could've driven on to Hanover tonight without much trouble. Your mother was expecting us."

"We'll get up early," I told her, "and be there in time for church."

"I just think this was an unnecessary stop."

I knew she was right, but I was not about to admit it. I gave the edge of the bed a couple pats. "Come over and sit down."

She ignored me, rummaged through one of her bags.

I decided not to push it. I stood and headed for the door. "You know, El," I said in an effort to lighten the load with a bit of levity, "I only stopped here at the beautiful Sloan's Resort and Casino because we always have such great sex in motel rooms."

She shook her head, balled up that towel, and threw it at me. I slipped out the door before it made contact. I went out into the twilight to find my son. We played together for a while on the jungle gym. Then he wanted me to hit him some ground balls. So we got his baseball, his baseball glove, and his brand-new Louisville slugger out of the minivan. I hit him ground balls in the parking lot until it was so dark we could not even see one another.

APRIL 27.

We carried his baseball gear back to the room where we found Ellen lying on the bed watching some old black-and-white Bible flick on TV. Hollywood's version of the Resurrection. It was almost Easter, after all.

Nick and I washed up, then the three of us walked a quarter of a mile down the road to a diner where we indulged in hamburgers, greasy french fries, and superthick chocolate malts.

Our Last Supper.

When we got back to the room, I called my mother.

"Sam!" she shouted. "Thank goodness! I've been worried sick. Where are you? Is everything all right?"

I explained about the flat tire.

She breathed a sigh of relief, then told me everyone else had arrived in time for dinner. Meaning my sister, my brother, their spouses, and their kids.

I told her we would be there in the morning, hopefully in time for church.

"But what about the Easter egg hunt?" she wanted to know.

"What about it?"

"We have the hunt all set up, Sam. For nine o'clock."

"So have the hunt without us," I said. "Nick doesn't care if he misses the Easter egg hunt."

Wrong. Nicholas might have been nine years old, long over his even feigned interest in the Easter bunny, but he definitely did not want to miss the egg hunt with his cousins. He immediately started whining at his mother.

Ellen glared at me, then grabbed the phone out of my hand. "Hi, Mom, it's me. Sorry we couldn't make it tonight. But don't worry, we'll get up early and be there first thing in the morning."

I sat there and figured the mileage and the time it would take to drive those miles. To make the nine o'clock Easter egg hunt, I would have to get up no later than five A.M. and have the troops on the road by five thirty.

Great. Exactly what I wanted to do on a Sunday morning.

But I would do it. Of course I'd do it. I occasionally used to complain about the demands placed upon me as a husband and father, but more than anything else in life I wanted to please my wife and son. I wanted to love them and make them happy. And I wanted them to love me in return.

After we all said good night to my mother, Nicholas wanted to watch TV. I told him no, we had to get up early to make the Easter egg hunt. He right away began to sulk and protest. Fairly typical behavior for him. He was an only child, after all. We had pretty much spoiled him rotten. He was the product of two working parents who sidestepped their guilt by giving him virtually everything he wanted. We simply could not help ourselves.

But that night, for a change, the boy's mother backed me up, told him he could not watch television. After mumbling under his breath for several seconds, he slipped between the sheets of his own queen-size bed. Within ten minutes he was sound asleep.

Ellen and I read for half an hour or so, just to make sure young Nick was not faking it. The summer before, during a camping trip to the Blue Ridge Mountains, I had caught him watching us from the other side of the tent as we made love inside our double sleeping bag.

Ellen and I always enjoyed making love in motel rooms and tents and old drafty cabins. Something exciting in all those foreign cribs. After a dozen years of lovemaking, we still had a passionate desire to kiss and hold each other close. I am remembering several times a week, and on cold wintry weekends sometimes two or even three times a day.

That night I rolled up on top of her and in no time at all our bodies lay locked together. We moved slowly, our lips barely touching. Because the day had been a strain, because we had disagreed and almost argued, and because our son, the product of our emotional and carnal union, lay so close, we both needed to feel the sexual release.

It did not take us long. We had years earlier developed a keen sense for what the other desired. We came very quickly, almost simultaneously, after just a few moments. And we came so easily, without hardly moving a muscle. We just held on tight as we gently massaged our chests and hips and thighs together.

Our bodies were so well acquainted, so devoted and generous and giving, so highly motivated to please and satisfy.

I sometimes wonder if I will ever be able to make love to another woman.

APRIL 29.

Afterward, we pulled the sheet up over our heads and giggled for a while before going to sleep. Mostly we giggled about me getting so bent out of shape about a stupid flat tire. Ellen loved more than anything else to laugh. She fell in love with me because I could make her laugh. And she stayed in love with me for the same reason.

I suppose I should have made her laugh even more. We did not laugh or giggle nearly enough. Especially as the years rapidly rolled by, as the jobs and the kid and the house and the responsibilities began to mount up and take control of our lives.

But Ellen and I had a good time. We had a grand time. I would not want to take back even a single moment of it.

Not true. I would like to take back that final morning, that terrible morning in room 14 of Sloan's Motel.

I would give up everything to get that one morning back.

APRIL 30.

It happened again last night. Actually, very early this morning. It happened almost exactly the same way it happened back in January. I was sound asleep when suddenly the dogs began to bark. When my eyes snapped open, I saw him, standing there, outside the window, staring in at me, Nicky's Louisville Slugger in his right hand.

Once again I screamed. I screamed when the creature raised that baseball bat over his head and brought it crashing down against my bedroom window. The glass shattered.

And once again that glass shattering shook me from my dream. Yes, just another dream. Another nightmare.

MAY 1

Just before midnight Ellen and I went through our nightly ritual. We kissed, said "I love you," and then Ellen rolled up onto her left side and I pressed my chest up against her back.

I waited until she had fallen asleep, then I quietly got up to make certain of our safety and security. I went outside to make sure I had locked up the mini-van. In the shadows, over by the jungle gym, I saw a man. He was mumbling to himself while drinking from a bottle of liquor. I quickly checked the van, then headed back inside. I threw the dead bolt and secured the chain. The world, I reminded myself, is a very violent place. Criminals and madmen roam the streets day and night. A constant need for caution and vigilance.

Then I returned to bed and set the alarm clock on the nightstand for five A.M. An ungodly hour. I sighed, turned off the light, fluffed up my pillow, and immediately fell fast asleep, my arm draped over my lovely wife's slender waist.

MAY 2.

I have not commented much lately on the weather. I have been concentrating almost exclusively on the events of last Easter. But alas, life goes on: work, a bit of play, even dinner and a movie last weekend with a young lady from publicity. It was pleasant enough. We had a few laughs. But it took some effort. I feel quite sure we will not see each other socially again.

But today, I want to write about today. Today began much the same as any other day, but then it suddenly turned rather bizarre.

It has been a cool and rather damp spring. Fine clear days have been few and far between. But today was a beauty: warm and breezy under a cloudless sky, temperature about seventy-two degrees, flowers in bloom, birds dancing in the trees, and Mrs. Evelyn Richmond sunbathing naked in the walled rose garden out behind her house.

Yes, naked. I came upon her quite by accident. At least I thought it was an accident. At first anyway. Now I am not so sure.

I heard music through my open windows. It sounded like a violin, not a cello, but no matter. Since I moved here to the cottage last Christmas, I have been waiting to hear the sounds of live music through my open windows. This morning my wait came to an end.

I knew immediately the name of the piece being played. It was from Antonio Vivaldi's *The Four Seasons,* the light and airy opening movement of "Spring," a piece much loved by my mother. She used to play it loudly on her Victrola as she swept through the house with her fine feather duster.

At first the violin sounded like part of the natural order, like songbirds singing, like that warm breeze slipping past the leaves of the trees. But suddenly the tone shifted. Spring ended. Vivaldi took his seat. Bach stepped up to take his place. The music turned melancholy, even mournful. I knew it was Bach; I was just not sure which piece.

I pulled on a pair of sneakers and went outside to investigate. The notes had shifted again, brighter now, more pleasant and inviting. I realized then that the music came from the walled rose garden. I went into the side yard to have a look and a listen. The roses had not yet bloomed, but the thorny stems had set their first buds of a new season.

I fully expected to see young Martin the violinist in the garden practicing with Mrs. Richmond. But when I peered over the wall, I saw only Mrs. Richmond perched upon a chaise lounge, violin in hand, not a stitch of clothing covering her slim and quite lovely body. She had that violin cradled in her arm and tucked up under her chin.

Suddenly, the music stopped. "Is that you, Mr. Adams?"

My first impulse was to hide. Then to run. How had she heard me? I had not made a sound.

"Did you come," Mrs. Richmond asked, "to admire my playing?"

I hesitated before responding. "I could hear it through my windows," I said. "It was beautiful, very emotional."

"Yes," she said, "very emotional."

I sensed sarcasm in her voice, maybe even cynicism.

"I didn't know you played the violin."

"A violin," she said, "is just a small cello. Or maybe I have that wrong. Maybe a cello is a large violin. Either way, to make notes one must drag the bow across the strings."

I must have taken some time to consider this comment, for next I heard her say, "So you have admired the music, Mr. Adams. Now would you like to come in and admire an old lady's body? Perhaps you would like to run your hands up my legs and over my buttocks. The sun is growing hot. I could use some sunscreen on my skin."

I swallowed hard, gave my head a shake, wondered if I had misunderstood.

"Come, Mr. Adams, I am only flesh and bone."

I took a silent step or two into the rose garden. Mrs. Richmond had small but still firm breasts, a slim waist, a bit wide only at the hips. Her body could easily have belonged to a reasonably fit woman in her late twenties or early thirties.

"Really," I heard my voice say, "I should go."

"Busy schedule today, Mr. Adams?"

My forehead wet with sweat, my heart firing like a machine gun, I prepared to make my retreat. "Yes. . . . No. . . . It's just that, well, I don't want to interrupt."

She laughed. "You're such a funny man, Mr. Adams. So old-fashioned."

I did my best not to stare. "No, not really."

"What's the matter, Mr. Adams? Don't you like my body?"

"Yes. . . . It's nice. . . . It's just that—"

"Most men find it quite lovely."

This was a bit more than I could handle. I took a step or two backward.

She must have heard my steps, even on that soft carpet of grass, for next she said, "Perhaps next time you can spare a few moments to spread some lotion on my back, Mr. Adams. I will do my best to lull you from your reverie."

"Yes," I heard myself say, "maybe next time." Then I beat it back here to the cottage, where, for an hour or more, I listened to Mrs. Richmond make beautiful music on that violin. Even Sunshine and Moxie seemed mesmerized by the sweet, melodious sounds.

MAY 3.

I wish I could read Evelyn Richmond's mind. I wish I knew her thoughts. Is she attracted to me? Are her rather shocking advances her way of expressing her feelings and affections? Or is she just bored? Using me as a goat? A form of entertainment?

I don't know. And right now I really don't care. I have manuscripts to read and edit, authors to appease and cajole. I have work to do.

MAY 4.

Work was crazy today. So many people making so many demands: authors, agents, reviewers, publicity people, marketing people, sales people. Sometimes I am amazed anything ever gets done. Everyone has an attitude. Everyone has the answers. Everyone knows everything. You think it would be enough to just write, edit, and publish great books.

It feels good to be back on the train. On my way home with a can of beer and a bag of peanuts. And time once again to concentrate on what happened in room 14 of Sloan's Motel last Easter Sunday.

I woke up before the alarm ever sounded. I usually do. An old habit.

A few minutes before five I stirred from a deep slumber. It took me a moment to remember where I was. Room 14. Sloan's Motel. Somewhere off Interstate 91 in northern Connecticut or southern Massachusetts. On our way north to Hanover to spend Easter with my family.

Room 14 was warm, too warm, the air close and stuffy. The heating system must have been working overtime throughout the night.

It was dark and perfectly quiet in that motel room. So dark I could not see my wife or my son. Nor could I hear them breathing. For just one morbid moment I wondered if Ellen and Nicky might be dead, perhaps victims of some strange motel disease. Maybe the innkeeper had been up all night pumping lethal gases through the heating ducts. You read about such things in the newspaper now all the time. Crazy things. Insane things.

Of course, had he been pumping gases, I would

have been dead also. But I was alive. We were all alive and well.

This whole sequence of thoughts made me shudder. I remember lying there trembling, feeling lost and vulnerable. Anxiety on the rise. I reached over and found Ellen's arm. It felt soft and warm. Just that momentary touch made me feel much better. Stronger. Able to face the day.

But still, I knew right then that Ellen had been right: we never should have stopped at Sloan's Motel. We should have driven on to my parents' house. We would have been there now, comfortable upstairs in my old bedroom, surrounded by familiar sounds and smells. Any minute now I would hear my father go down the stairs, out the front door, and along the walk to fetch the Sunday paper. I would hear the clatter of cups and saucers in the kitchen as my mother set the table for breakfast. And I would smell her coffee wafting up the back steps and under my bedroom door.

Safety and security in those sounds and smells.

MAY 5.

But no, I had insisted we stop. I had pulled the minivan off the interstate and started searching for a vacancy. In and out of one motel office after another.

"You know, Sam," Ellen had said calmly from the copilot seat, "we could've made it to Hanover by the time you find us a room."

I had ignored her. Dug in my heels. Occasionally I can be quite stubborn. It comes from my mother's side of the family.

Finally, off the beaten path, I had found Sloan's Motel. Plenty of vacancies at Sloan's. In fact, the parking lot had been so empty, I'd thought at first the place might be closed. Deserted.

MAY 6.

My parents were early risers. My father especially. He usually got up with the sun. Most mornings he went straight to his small office off the kitchen to read over his lecture notes for the day.

My mother would arise not long after. She would make coffee, maybe put a pan of cinnamon rolls in the oven. Then the two of them would sit together at the kitchen table sipping their coffee and chatting excitedly like a couple of brand-new lovers after their first joyous night together.

Many mornings during my youth I crept sleepily down the back stairs only to find my parents giggling or holding hands or just staring into each other's eyes. It always made me feel slightly embarrassed to find them like that, especially as I grew older.

But my parents' lives have always been so intricately intertwined, so much linked by time and place and circumstance, that they are, quite clearly and unmistakably, like one being.

Ellen and I were moving in that direction. More and more every day. We knew each other's thoughts, could finish each other's sentences. People used to tell us we had even started to look alike.

MAY 7.

All right.

I decided to get out of Sloan's Motel as quickly as possible. I wanted to make sure Nicky got to join his cousins for the annual Adams's Easter egg hunt.

Ellen and I had selfishly deprived the boy of any siblings due to our own desires and ambitions. We both had brothers and sisters, and so we both knew well the powerful bonds created by growing up close in a crowded and active household. Friends are vitally important, but blood ties can never be duplicated, just as they can never be fully severed.

Lying there in that bed at Sloan's Motel, the warm, stale air pressing against my lungs, I decided the least I could do was encourage Nicky's relationships with the sons and daughters of my own siblings. Cousins might not be brothers and sisters, I remember thinking, but they still spring from the same blood.

MAY 8.

I let Ellen and Nicky sleep a little longer while I shaved, showered, and dressed. Then, just before I went outside to check the weather and the oil in the minivan, I gave them each a nuzzle.

"Rise and shine, sleepyheads," I said. "Up and at 'em. We have us an Easter egg hunt to attend."

Ellen groaned and rolled over. "It's the middle of the night."

I gave Nicky another shake. "Come on, kid, if your mother wants to spend the weekend here at Sloan's Motel, we'll pick her up on the way home."

Nicholas Michael Adams, a pretty cranky young-ster first thing in the morning, mumbled something under his breath and burrowed into his pillow. I thought about letting him sleep, letting them both sleep, but I was already wide awake, ready to go. Besides, I knew Nick would have a good time once we got to his grandmother's house. So I gave him one more nudge. And finally, he threw back the bedclothes and headed for the bathroom.

I watched him go. My son: thin and wiry with broad shoulders and a long shock of reddish brown hair spreading down his neck. Longer than I liked, but I had decided not to hassle my son about the length of his hair. There would be other battles to fight.

I remember standing there and wondering what he would be when he grew up. He was in his New York Yankees shortstop or fireman mode in those days. One or the other or both.

I just wanted him to be happy.

I turned, slipped the chain off its hook, threw back the dead bolt, and released the lock on the knob so I would not need the key to get back into the room. I turned the knob and opened the door.

MAY 9.

The air had cooled overnight. And grown damp. The sky was still dark, just a faint trace of dawn in the east-ern sky. The only light came from the streetlamps out along the highway and from some low-wattage yellow bulbs just outside the door of each room. Our yellow bulb had burned out.

I took a quick look around. Only two other cars

besides our minivan occupied the parking lot: one outside the motel office and one at the far end of the complex, over near the playground. Not exactly a full house.

At first I did not see him. I did not see anyone. Not a soul. It seemed unlikely that anyone else would be up at such an early hour. But then, suddenly, I did see him. In the shadows. Lurking a few doors down. A tall, bulky, stooped man. The same man I had seen the night before. He looked dirty. His clothes looked shabby and torn.

For just a moment our eyes met. His eyes looked dark and cold. And above his brow he had an angry purple scar. I will never forget that scar.

He shifted his eyes, turned slowly, and shuffled away.

I watched him cross the parking lot. He went out past the Sloan's Motel sign glowing neon red and down the old north–south highway. I kept a close eye on him while I listened to the distant rumble of trucks out on the interstate. I watched until he had disappeared into the gray early-morning darkness.

Then I turned my attention to the minivan. I felt an even stronger desire than earlier to pack up and pull out. Dew covered the windows. I unlocked the door and pulled the lever to open the engine hood. The van was practically brand-new, only a few thousand miles, but like my father before me, I rarely start an engine without first checking the oil.

"A minute or two now," he always told me, "can save you plenty of trouble and anxiety later."

And he was not just talking about checking engine oil, either. My father loathed anger and violence and cruelty. He never understood why children were taught reading, writing, and arithmetic, but rarely how to control their emotions, especially their more aggressive and negative ones. He lectured us frequently, every time he heard us argue or say an angry word, on the importance of checking our behavior, on reining in our more primitive impulses. "The ability to control our most primal instincts," he liked to say, "lies at the heart of civilization."

I went around to the front of the minivan and raised the hood. I located the dipstick, but before pulling it out I decided to go back to the room for a tissue or two so I could wipe it clean.

It was also a good excuse to check on Ellen and Nicholas, see if they had rolled over and gone back to sleep. Experience had taught me they both had a propensity to dawdle.

MAY 10.

Ellen was up. She sat on the edge of the bed brushing her hair. Long, lovely, reddish brown hair. Like her son's. She glanced at me and smiled. "Just waiting for the young prince to relinquish the royal bathroom."

An inside joke. Nicky spent more time in the bathroom than anyone we'd ever known. It amazed us how long he could take to brush his teeth and wash his face.

I rapped on the bathroom door. "Let's move it, Nick. Time to hit the road."

He responded with one of his barely audible mutterings.

When I turned around, I saw Ellen pulling her nightgown over her head. The sight of her naked body, as always, instantly aroused me.

"What are you staring at?" she asked, just the hint of a smile on her face.

"Who? Me? I'm not staring at anything."

She picked up a pillow and threw it at me.

I asked, "Do you let Nicky see you naked?"

She laughed. "I swear, Sam, you're such a Puritan." She reached into her bag for a bra and a fresh pair of panties.

"No, I'm not," I said, defensively. "It's just that he's getting older and—"

"Quiet, Sam. You make a lot more sense when you keep your eyes open and your mouth closed."

She was right, of course, I do.

MAY 11.

I grabbed a few tissues out of the box on the dresser. "Be right back," I told my wife. "I'm going out to check the oil."

MAY 12.

I have thought about it long and hard for over a year now, and I feel quite certain those rather inane remarks were our last bits of conversation.

"Quiet, Sam. You make a lot more sense when you keep your eyes open and your mouth closed."

"Be right back. I'm going out to check the oil."

Going out to check the oil.

Going out to check the oil.

Jesus. Sweet Jesus.

Jesus of Nazareth. He came with only the best and

brightest intentions, with the lofty aspiration of saving us from ourselves.

MAY 13.

It happened so fast. Practically in the blink of an eye. You go along, day in and day out, doing your best, minding your own business, week after week, year after year, nearly four decades on the planet, and then, out of nowhere, when you are least expecting it, not even paying attention: WHAM!

I reached for the knob just as the full weight of his body slammed against the door. And in no time at all he threw himself into our room, huge and lumbering and ominous. He had one leg of a light brown pair of nylon pantyhose pulled down over his face.

Why?

I have no idea. I had already seen his face. I had already seen that angry purple scar stitched across his brow. The pantyhose flattened and distorted his features, made him look oddly menacing and comical at the same time.

Probably only a fraction of a second passed, but I had time to wonder if perhaps I had insulted him somehow out in the parking lot, maybe given him an evil eye or a cold shoulder. But then his lips parted slightly behind that stretchy nylon, and a raspy jumble of words spilled from his mouth. "All your money and valuables on the bed. Now!"

Money. That's all he wanted: our money. A couple hundred dollars. Probably wanted it to buy a bag of crack and a couple bottles of cheap wine. All we had to do was hand over our money. We did it all the time without the slightest ruckus. We gave our hard-earned cash to the electric company, the telephone company, the mortgage company, and most of all to the tax collector without ever even raising our voices in protest.

But Ellen, suddenly Ellen, so feisty and determined, decided the time had come to take a stand, to fight back. "No!" I suddenly heard my wife shout at this filthy drug addict, this petty crook. "You can't just waltz in here and demand we hand over our money!"

I could hardly believe my ears. I turned around to calm her down, to tell her, if necessary, to just shut up. I wanted to give him everything we had, our money and even our minivan if he wanted it, anything and everything if he would just leave us alone, get out of our room, out of our lives.

"My God, Ellen! Let it be! He might have a weapon."

"Shut up!" he demanded. And then, "All your money and valuables! Now!"

I will surely wonder why until the day I die, but at that exact moment, Ellen made another hasty and, I feel, irrational decision. She decided to scream. Very loudly. I suppose she wanted to draw attention to our predicament, perhaps bring the other motel guests scrambling to our assistance. But I knew from the number of cars out in the parking lot that Sloan's had plenty of vacancies, only a handful of guests. It seemed unlikely that anyone would hear her scream.

Our uninvited guest, however, certainly heard her. The piercing sound threw him instantly into a rage. His enormous body sprang across the room. He should not have been able to move all that bulk with such deftness. But he did. He moved like an animal. Like a predator. Just seconds after she screamed, he was upon her. And in his right hand he held something. A weapon!

A baseball bat! Nicky's twenty-six–ounce Louisville Slugger! He had scooped it up off the floor. It looked so tiny and playful in his hand, like some kind of toy. He waved it in the air like a magic wand.

Ellen screamed again. No longer to draw attention, but now out of fear, a deep, primal fear. The sound of that scream sent a shudder of terror straight to the base of my spine.

And then, right then, at that exact moment, is when that bum, that useless human parasite, who just wanted the money in our wallets, turned into a violent and deadly creature. To silence her screams, he raised that magic wand high up over his head and brought it crashing down across my beautiful Ellen's skull.

MAY 14.

Ellen's eyes glanced at me, horribly and pleadingly, before she crumpled to the floor.

I moved instinctively to help her, to attack him, to do something, anything. But my indecision slowed me down.

My son, young Nick, came out of the bathroom. He had his toothbrush in his hand, toothpaste on his face, his hair all slicked back. "What was that?" he wanted to know. "Did I hear Mom scream?"

"Go back in the bathroom and lock the door, Nick! Now!"

Too late. Nicky spotted his mother lying on the floor and the creature hovering over her. He was the next one to scream. A bloodcurdling shriek that once again provoked the creature. He looked crazy, confused, cornered. He leapt over my wife and headed for my son.

I saw the Louisville Slugger held high. I saw Nicky freeze. I saw his eyes. They looked alert and full of fear. Those eyes finally brought me into the action. I made the only move I could: I reached out for that baseball bat so the creature could not bring it crashing down upon my son's fragile skull. The bat struck me across the shoulder and wrist. The pain made me groan and pull away.

The creature, panting now like some caged and frenzied beast, rammed the butt of the baseball bat hard into my abdomen. The air whistled out of my lungs. I doubled over and went down on my knees, not far from my bleeding and unmoving wife.

When I looked up, I saw Nicky trying to strike the creature with his fists. He did his best to inflict some damage. But the creature, his face blazing beneath that nylon, easily threw Nicky aside. And that is when I watched my son fall, in slow motion, back through the door of the bathroom. I watched the side of his small head slam into the sharp corner of the sink. I watched his eyes go blank, and then his whole body slump forward onto the cool white tiles.

Like his mother, my son lay there, unmoving. As still as a corpse.

MAY 15.

A moment later the creature turned his attention back to me. I tried to move, to stand, to rush forward. But my efforts proved futile, utterly useless. I was no match for the creature. He had the strength of ten men. He kicked me so hard in the head I spun completely around and came to rest all the way over on the other side of the room.

MAY 16.

I lay there in the corner of room 14 of Sloan's Motel, dazed and disoriented, while that foul, filthy, violent beast rummaged through our personal belongings, violating everything that was ours. I tried to rise up and strike a blow against this evil, but my eyes would not open. A fierce pounding in my head sapped my energy and my strength. Still, I could hear and feel his presence. I could smell him.

He rifled through our bags and suitcases. Then he took the time to search through the pockets of my wife's and son's clothing. Finally he crossed to me, rolled me over as though I was nothing more than a sack of grain. He ripped my wallet from my hip pocket. He tore loose the currency, maybe $150. And then, perhaps because his take was less than he had hoped, he made ready to kick me once again in the head with his laceless boots.

But this time I was prepared. My survival instincts had kicked into gear. I saw his leg go into motion. In a flash, I grabbed his ankle with both hands and jerked him forward. Startled, he lost his balance. He fell back, slipped off the bed, and hit the floor. His rage instantly returned. But my own rage had gathered momentum. We both struggled to our feet. Like a couple of animals we kicked and clawed at one another. The baseball hat lay on the bed, on top of the pillows. I reached out for it. The creature grabbed me by the hair and pulled me back. I swung around and drove my thumb as hard as I could into his eye.

I knew I was in a fight for my life. I knew he would kill me if I did not subdue him. In all my life I had only ever been in a couple of fights. Three at the most. And two of those nothing more than sibling battles with my brother, Jack. A few fists thrown in anger. A connection or two maybe made. Nothing more.

But this, this was different. This was brutal. This was mayhem. There were no rules. Just kicking, punching, and gouging. As the seconds and then the minutes wore on, I began to worry. I began to feel my strength slipping away. He was too much for me, too powerful. But then I had a stroke of luck. The creature tried to use the top of his head as a battering ram against my chest. Had he connected he would have knocked me to the floor and finished me off. But at the last split second I brought the point of my elbow in front of my chest. His head slammed directly into the rock-hard bone. The blow shook him, made him momentarily dizzy. But long enough for me to reach across the bed, pick up that baseball bat, and swing with all my might in his direction. The first blow caught him across the back. It caused some pain but not much damage. I swung again. The second blow shattered his collarbone. He screamed. But at the same time he lashed out at me, struck me hard across the jaw with his forearm. I recoiled but managed to hold my ground. One more swing. I needed one more swing before I passed out, before every last ounce of my strength melted away. I drew the bat back, both hands on the handle. I swung with all the power I could muster. I swung for the fences. I swung for my wife and son. And I made contact. Sweet contact. I hit that creature right smack in the forehead. Right across his angry purple scar. I heard his skull fracture. I saw his eyes roll back in their sockets. I watched his body crumple to the floor.

Then, a moment later, I dropped that bat and collapsed on the bed. I was done, finished, out of gas, out of order.

MAY 17.

The creature had probably not been in room 14 of Sloan's Motel for more than three or four minutes. Just three or four minutes before I fractured his skull with Nicky's Louisville Slugger.

That's all. Three or four minutes. But in that brief spit of time, a few ticks of the clock, my whole world had changed. The world as I had known it had been swept away, irreversibly shattered.

MAY 20.

I just returned from a long weekend on Cape Cod. The dogs and I spent a few days visiting old friends and walking on the beach.

I think it did me good. I needed a vacation. A break from the rat race.

MAY 21.

This morning, around ten-thirty or eleven, I had an unexpected visit from Mrs. Richmond.

I was out in the yard, lying on a blanket in the grass, doing a first edit on a not particularly interesting manuscript, when Mrs. Richmond suddenly appeared at my side. She had on a long white kimono and dark glasses.

"Hello, Mr. Adams."

I shielded my eyes from the sun. "Good morning."

Her kimono kept lifting in the gentle spring breeze. "I've been thinking about you," she said. "I've been wanting to see you."

"Don't tell me I've forgotten the rent again?"

She laughed. Heartily. Then, "I don't care about the rent. Give the rent money to the peasants. Give it to the communists. Give it to the environmentalists. Give it to someone, just don't give it to me."

The breeze blew her kimono again, and I could see quite clearly that Mrs. Richmond had absolutely nothing on underneath.

Then the dogs, who had been off investigating some sound or smell in the woods out behind the cottage, came bounding back into the yard. They practically mauled Mrs. Richmond with licks and wagging tails. She did not seem to mind. In fact, she went down on all fours and nuzzled her face against their chests. For several minutes, the three of them rolled around in the grass.

I felt aroused. Sexually aroused. I did my best to ignore this phenomenon. But the breeze and that lovely white kimono and Mrs. Richmond's playfulness made my efforts rather difficult.

A squirrel darted across the yard. First Moxie and then Sunshine took off in hot pursuit. They chased that squirrel into the woods and up a tree.

Mrs. Richmond rolled over beside me. "Tell me, Mr. Adams, would you like to kiss me?"

I hesitated, took a deep breath, struggled to find the right reply. "I try and make it a practice not to get involved with my landlady, Mrs. Richmond."

She laughed again. "I see." Then, after a moment, "But would you like to anyway?"

"Well," I said, trying hard to fathom her motives, "you do have pretty lips."

She reached up with her right hand and touched my own. "Thank you, Mr. Adams. You do, too."

It took all my powers of denial not to pucker my lips and kiss the tips of her fingers.

"Why don't we give it a try," she said. "Just to see how it feels."

I managed to get a good, deep breath. "I guess we could do that."

So we did. We kissed. First we licked our lips and then we kissed. A nice gentle one right on the mouth. Only our lips touched, nothing else.

"That was nice," said Mrs. Richmond.

"Yes," I said, "it was."

"Do we dare try another?"

We tried another. A longer one this time. We pressed a little harder. Her hand grabbed my waist. My hand reached up and touched her shoulder, actually the silk covering her shoulder.

We kissed a third time. And a fourth. She pushed the tip of her tongue into my mouth. I welcomed it. Her breath tasted sweet and fresh. But she did not seem to be wearing any perfume today; at least nothing I could detect.

After the fourth kiss she pulled away. Just a few inches. She had a smile on her face. "Tell me, Mr. Adams, have you ever kissed a blind woman before?"

I shook my head. "No, I don't think I have."

"How was it?"

"It was . . . very pleasant."

"Yes." She stood up. "Then I suppose you've never made love to a blind woman, either?"

"You suppose right."

She ran her fingers down the side of my face. "Would you like to make love to a blind woman, Mr. Adams?"

"Do you mean, would I like to make love to you, Mrs. Richmond?"

"That's not what I asked."

"Then," I replied, "the answer is no. I would not want to make love to just any woman simply because she is blind."

Mrs. Richmond gave another hearty laugh. "Excellent answer, Mr. Adams. Very sensitive. Utterly masculine. But, unfortunately, I do not have time to discuss the matter right now. I must be going."

"Where to?" I asked, not thinking.

"Ah, Mr. Adams, an arousal of curiosity. How sweet. I am off to Washington for a few days. I am going to play for the president."

"You're going to play the cello for the president of the United States?"

"So they tell me. I hope he shows up." She laughed at her own joke. Then, "I just came by to ask you to keep an eye on Julie while I'm gone. She has not been feeling very well lately."

"Julie," I mumbled. "I thought you came by to make love, Mrs. Richmond."

"Oh, how naughty of you, Mr. Adams. How could we make love? We're not in love. My God, we're not even on a first name basis."

Then, suddenly, she stepped away from me and danced off across the lawn, more like a pixie than a blind woman.

MAY 22.

All last night and all day today at work, I found myself thinking about Mrs. Richmond. About Evelyn. I actually caught myself wondering about the possibility of entering into a relationship with her.

With Evelyn.

MAY 23.

Enough thoughts of Evelyn Richmond. I have too much work to do. And I need to get back to Sloan's Motel, to the aftermath of the creature's attack.

After I cracked the creature across the skull, I passed out on the bed. Not for long. Just a few seconds. As soon as I could gather myself, I crawled across the bloodied mattress and reached for the phone. I picked up the receiver and held it to my ear. I punched zero.

An eternity passed before a woman's voice finally answered, "Good morning. Front desk."

"Yes," I muttered, my voice barely above a whisper, "this is . . . Mr. Adams . . . in room fourteen. We need help here. Badly. Now."

And then I felt a hand grab my hair and slam my head against the wall. The world went black.

MAY 24.

God knows how long it took for help to finally reach room 14. Time became a blurry mess that morning, and for many days to come. But help finally did arrive. I remember a voice, a man's voice, filled with terror. "Mother of Jesus! What the hell happened here?"

Then I became aware of a heavy weight sprawled across my back. I could not move. My head throbbed. I tried to call out to the voice, but my mouth would not open.

The room filled with voices and activity. Someone with a deep, authoritative voice began barking orders.

Someone else carefully lifted that heavy weight from my back. I managed to turn my head just far enough to see the huge, limp body of the creature being hauled away. I found out later that he had leveled one last attack against me, but then, exhausted and badly injured from the blow I had inflicted upon his forehead, he had collapsed right on top of me.

I put my head back down on the mattress. I closed my eyes. My entire body felt bruised and battered.

When I opened my eyes again, I saw an emergency medical technician hovering over me. He looked spooked, as though he was administering to a dead man.

"Officer," I heard him say, "this one's coming around."

A moment later a policeman, a young one, with a crewcut, just a kid, stood at my side. He looked even more spooked than the emergency medical technician. A horrified expression covered his face.

I tried to sit up, but immediately became dizzy.

"Just lie back, sir," said the emergency medical technician. "You need to take it easy."

"How," I managed to ask, "is my wife? My son?"

"I don't know, sir," he told me. "But I'll find out for you. Everyone is being taken care of as quickly as possible."

They loaded my body onto a gurney and rolled me quickly out of that motel room to an ambulance with its engine running and its roof lights flashing red. Ellen and Nicholas had already been taken out; at least I had not seen them lying on the floor as those first aid workers rushed me from the room.

I remember seeing the sun hanging low in the eastern sky as they loaded me into the ambulance. The door slammed closed. We drove to a hospital in a very big hurry. The siren wailed the entire way, fifteen or twenty minutes. We sped along the interstate, in which direction I could not tell.

I kept asking about my wife and son, but the guy sitting back there with me told me to remain calm and quiet. He assured me we would find out as soon as we reached the hospital.

I kept badgering him, demanding he find out now. Finally he poked a needle in my arm, sent me into some chemically induced Never Never Land.

MAY 25.

I woke up in a hospital bed. There was a nurse at my side. She smiled at me while she took my pulse and my blood pressure.

"My wife?" I asked. "I want to find out about my wife."

"Yes, sir," the nurse said, her voice kind and soothing. "Let me go find the doctor." She left the room.

I felt extremely dizzy, almost delirious, like I might pass out at any moment. It must have been a combination of my fight with the creature and the painkillers. I had trouble drawing a decent breath. Images of Ellen and Nicky lying on that motel room floor kept flashing before my eyes.

A man entered. He wore a suit and tie. "Hello, Mr. Adams. My name is Drew Middleton. I'm a detective with the local police department." He pulled out his wallet and showed me his shield.

Middleton wanted to know what had happened back there in room 14 of Sloan's Motel. I did my best to tell him. But my best that day was not very good. I think I began by babbling about the flat tire we'd had out on the interstate the day before. I didn't get much past that before a doctor came into the room and told the detective to come back later, no sooner than the following morning.

The detective apologized for my trouble, then he left the room.

The doctor, tall, thin, and extremely pale, wearing a sterile white jacket, stood beside my bed. "Hello, Mr. Adams. My name is Dr. Andrews." He looked and sounded extraordinarily grave.

I nodded at his introduction. That simple motion sent a shot of pain straight to my brain. I winced, then asked, "My wife and son? How are they?"

"I'm afraid the news is not very good, Mr. Adams."

MAY 26.

No, the news was not very good at all. The creature had inflicted some very heavy damage.

"Your wife," said Dr. Andrews, "was DOA. We did our best, but there was nothing we could do to revive her."

Ellen was dead. There, I said it. I wrote it down. Ellen was dead. Dead and gone. Forever.

I spaced right out the moment Dr. Andrews passed on the terrible news. My brain, always so alert and healthy and curious, flew off in an instant to someplace far beyond planet Saturn. Nevertheless, I did manage to hear a few key phrases. Lovely, stylish phrases like "massive brain hemorrhage" and "severe trauma to the cerebellum" and "cerebral refraction."

Jesus.

"Blessed are the dead," said the preacher at Ellen's funeral, "who die in the arms of the Lord."

The creature hit my wife on the head with a baseball bat and killed her. Just like that. Just like that my wife and best friend was dead.

MAY 27.

And what about my son? What did the creature do to my son?

He turned him into a vegetable, that's what.

Nicholas had a huge dent in his skull where his head had made contact with the edge of the sink in the bathroom back in room 14 of Sloan's Motel.

For five and a half months my son was a vegetable, a useless sack of skin and bones that could not see or hear or smile or speak or eat except through a tube or go to the bathroom except all over himself.

And then, mercifully, he died. Last September. September 23rd. At 3:57 in the afternoon.

MAY 28.

And what about me? What did the creature do to me?

He did not kill me. I managed to stay alive. But I did not manage to save my wife or my son. Emotionally, I am scarred forever.

Physically, I slowly healed. The creature dealt me several formidable blows. I sustained two broken ribs, a fractured wrist, a concussion, and a wide assortment of bruises.

I spent four days in the hospital. Most of that time they had me sedated.

My parents came to see me. So did my brother and my sister. And Ellen's parents. And Ellen's brothers and sisters. There was not much anyone could do or say. We cried a lot, I remember that.

Undoubtedly we were all in shock.

MAY 29.

Just before I was released from the hospital, Detective Middleton came back to see me. I gave him a detailed account, to the best of my ability, of what had happened in room 14 of Sloan's Motel. I held myself together reasonably well.

After I had finished, after the detective had written it all down, he said, "The man who attacked your family is in a coma, Mr. Adams."

"A coma?"

"Yes."

"From the blow I gave him with my son's baseball bat?"

He nodded. "I should think so. The bones in his forehead are pretty well shattered."

I took a deep breath. "I hit him as hard as I could, Detective. I wanted to kill him."

"I understand."

MAY 30.

And now, more random violence. Is there no end to the atrocities that plague contemporary society?

Last evening Mrs. Richmond returned from Washington. She was mugged. In broad daylight. Just two blocks from the White House.

She'd left her hotel to go out for a walk. Someone was with her, an escort, a woman from the hotel. The woman turned away for a moment to buy them each a soda or an ice cream. They stood right in front of the U.S. Treasury, right under the nose of Alexander Hamilton. The second the woman turned her back, some thug grabbed Evelyn's purse, pulled it off her arm, and knocked her to the ground.

Who would knock a blind woman down on a concrete sidewalk? I swear, I do not get it. I do not understand. What is going on? What has happened to us? We have become a civilization of barbarians.

Evelyn sprained her wrist in the fall, her right wrist, the wrist of her bowing hand. No cello playing for at least two weeks. Maybe a month. Other than that she seems okay: a little shook up, a few cuts and scratches, bumps and bruises.

All this happened the day after she played Mozart for the president. And the vice president. And the secretary of state.

Unbelievable! You would think that troika could have protected her.

I went over to see her this morning. I found her upstairs in bed, recuperating. It was my first visit to her bedroom. There were photographs of her on the walls and on the bureau in the company of various famous persons: presidents, movie stars, musicians.

I was impressed.

Her bed was enormous, king-size, bigger than king-size. She looked tiny lying there in the middle of it. Tiny and vulnerable. Like a little girl home sick from school. She asked me to come over, closer. She squeezed my hand, thanked me for coming. Then she told me all about playing for the president, dining at the White House, chatting with senators, ambassadors, five-star generals.

And then, of course, she told me about the mugging.

I listened to her for over an hour. I must admit that I wanted to touch her, to kiss her once again on the lips.

When she had finished her tale, I asked, "Is there anything I can get you, Mrs. Richmond? Anything at all I can do for you?"

"Oh yes, Sam, there is." It was the first time she had ever used my given name. "You can stop calling me Mrs. Richmond. Evelyn, please."

I laughed. "All right, Evelyn. I think I can handle that. Anything else?"

"Well, if you feel so inclined, you could rub my shoulder. It is quite sore from that maniac ripping my purse off my arm."

So I rubbed her shoulder. I rubbed it with almond-scented massage oil she had over on the bureau. I rubbed her shoulder and her neck and her arm. She kept telling me to rub harder, to really work the muscles with my fingers. I did as she told me and was rewarded with an almost continual moan of sensual delight.

I would have rubbed her entire body, but the doctor arrived to check on her condition. I left, after telling Evelyn not to hesitate calling if I could be of service.

I must say: I hope she calls.

MAY 31.

All day long cars and limousines have been arriving and departing. People alone and in groups of two and three have been going in and out of the big house since early this morning.

I have not heard from Evelyn. She seems to have all the company she can handle.

JUNE 1.

More cars and visitors today. I should have kept count. It must be close to a hundred.

Early this evening, the driveway finally empty, I went over and asked Miss Julie about this endless procession of visitors.

"Friends of Mrs. Richmond" was all she offered.

"So many," I said.

"Yes," she added in her snotty English tone. "They've come to pay their respects and wish her a speedy recovery."

"How is she doing?"

Grudgingly, Julie gave this response: "She's exhausted."

"I thought I'd go up and say hello."

"She is napping," snapped Julie. "She does not wish to be disturbed."

"No?"

"No."

I hesitated, then nodded and headed for the back door. "Please tell Evelyn I stopped by."

JUNE 2.

Today, at our weekly editorial meeting, Jed Barton, the associate publisher, asked me if I would take a look at a new manuscript.

"It's nonfiction," he told me.

"In pretty good shape?"

"I think so. I acquired it off an outline and a couple sample chapters about six months ago. The first draft of the manuscript just came in. After looking it over, I think you're the one to do the line edit."

"I've always appreciated your faith in me, Jed," I told him. "I'll be happy to take a look."

I brought the manuscript home with me tonight. I read the beginning on the train. It is titled:

Social Mayhem:
Violent Crime in America

The first paragraph of the introduction went like this: "Violent crime has become routine and commonplace in modern America. Nearly two out of three Americans will be directly or indirectly involved with some kind of violent crime during their lifetimes."

Try three out of three was my immediate reaction to that.

Reluctantly, I read further. The book is full of statistics, charts and graphs, crime data. But primarily it contains lengthy, vividly depicted accounts of violent crimes, heinous crimes: rapes, tortures, murders. Crimes like the one perpetrated upon us in room 14 of Sloan's Motel.

I had to put the manuscript aside. I could not continue reading.

JUNE 3.

This morning I went to see Jed Barton in his office. I threw the manuscript on his desk. "Is this some kind of sick joke, Jed?"

"Sam," he answered, "absolutely not. I thought you, more than anyone else on the staff, would have the sensitivity and the insight to deal with this material. That's why I gave it to you."

I took a deep breath, allowed my anger a moment to dissipate. "Sorry, Jed. I can't do this. I can't be subjected to this kind of material right now. You'll have to get somebody else."

Before he could sweet-talk me, charm me with his compliments, I turned and left his office.

I won't do it. I won't edit that manuscript.

I do a hell of a good job for Jackson, Jones & Reynolds. For more than a dozen years now I've been a valuable asset to this house. Last year alone I edited our best-selling nonfiction title: *Eden Lost: The Decline of the American Paradise*. And the second–best-selling fiction title, some Euro-spy thriller tripe spewed out by an ex-CIA operative with a chip on his shoulder. We are talking several hundred thousand copies sold. So I think I have the right to draw the line once in a while. I think I have the right to say no.

I am confident that if push came to shove, most of my writers would go with me if I moved to another house. I understand that a book, especially a novel, is primarily the creation of the author. But the editor's role is vital to the process. Few authors, if any, possess the power of absolute objectivity. They need an editor they can trust: one who can smooth the rough edges, strike the hyperbole, eradicate the redundancy.

I think what I do best as an editor is nudge my authors into probing their innermost emotions, into finding the good and evil that lurks within us all. Fiction so often comes closer to depicting reality than reality itself. My greatest success as an editor comes when I subtly manipulate my writers into exposing themselves, into standing emotionally naked right before the reader's eyes.

So I will say it again: I know my worth. I will not budge. Let Barton dump that mess on someone else.

JUNE 4.

I was pretty wound up yesterday. Undoubtedly that manuscript set me off, but that was just the trigger. Work has been extremely hectic lately. And, of course, I've been thinking a lot about what happened at Sloan's Motel. And I've been thinking a lot about Evelyn as well. For some reason I always feel a twinge of guilt whenever I think about her. Strange, I know, but nevertheless true.

JUNE 5.

Today is a special day. Today is Ellen's birthday. She would have been thirty-eight years old today.

We always took this day off from work. A day of celebration. All day long I did whatever Ellen wanted me to do. Every June 5th I was her slave for a day. If she wanted breakfast in bed, I brought her breakfast in bed. If she wanted to shop, we shopped. If she wanted to go roller-skating in Central Park, we went roller-skating in Central Park.

June 5th was her day, Ellen's day. But it was always one of my favorite days as well. I loved making Ellen happy. Seeing her smiling and laughing was the best thing in the world.

JUNE 6.

We buried Ellen beside her maternal grandparents in the small graveyard next to the Episcopal church she had attended as a child. Ellen left behind not only Nicholas and me, but both her parents, her two sisters, her brother, her paternal grandmother, and a whole slew of aunts, uncles, cousins, nephews, and nieces.

"In sure and certain hope," lamented the preacher, "of the resurrection of eternal life through our Lord Jesus Christ, we commend to Almighty God our sister Ellen Reynolds Adams, and we commit her body to the ground, earth to earth, ashes to ashes, dust to dust."

The funeral was a morbid, depressing affair. None of us should have been there. The whole thing was insane. Ellen should not have been trapped inside that box. Ellen had never been sick a day in her life. Ellen had never spent a night in a hospital except the night she gave birth to our son.

JUNE 7.

Actually, Ellen spent two nights in the hospital after Nicky was born. The delivery had thoroughly exhausted her. She needed an extra day to recuperate. I did not sleep at the hospital, but I spent almost every waking second in that room with my wife.

On the Saturday after Thanksgiving, Ellen and I brought Nicky home from the hospital. I carried him into our apartment and placed him gently in his brand-new bassinet. I remember the moment perfectly.

Oh yes, I remember all of it. I remember Nicky waking up in the middle of the night for food and stimulation. I remember the six thousand daily diaper changes, the smell of baby poop permeating the walls of the apartment as well as my suits from Barney's and Brooks Brothers. I remember the various baby-sitters and nannies who came to take care of him after Ellen went back to work. It seems like we had a new one every two or three days. They were either too young or too old or too neurotic or too irresponsible. I remember Nicky crying and crawling and standing and taking that first awkward step. I remember him falling and getting right back up. I remember him mumbling his first words, saying "Dada" before "Mama," saying "Sam" before "Ellen," smiling and laughing and sucking his thumb. I remember him lying in bed with a high fever and me worrying that if I did not get his fragile little body cooled down, he would explode into a million pieces. I remember holding him in my arms and praying to God to please keep my boy safe and healthy and happy forever and ever.

What a schmuck. What a stupid, naive, ignorant schmuck was I. Praying to God. Thinking God would grant me some special favor.

JUNE 8.

Sure, I remember it all, every last detail. Like the summer before Nicky first went off to school. That summer would later be declared the hottest summer on record in New York City. Every day for two months it felt like you were living inside a furnace with six or eight million other hot and irritated human beings.

Crime soared as that heat wave persisted. New York has always been ripe with criminal activity, but that summer violent crime became as commonplace as infidelity. A brand-new expression came into vogue that summer: *drive-by shooting*. We had so many drive-by shootings that you would be walking down Fifth Avenue, minding your own business, when a taxicab would suddenly backfire and ten thousand New Yorkers would scramble for cover.

What a way to live. Murder and mayhem.

Gangs took over the parks, beating and robbing and sexually abusing anyone who dared enter their turf. It got so bad we stopped taking Nicky to Central Park even on Saturday afternoons.

The last straw came one evening when Ellen sent me out to buy a bottle of wine for dinner. I took Nicky with me. I remember he was just a little guy at the time, barely stood as high as my belt buckle. We walked over to Uptown Liquors on Columbus Avenue. We entered the store, wandered over to the wine racks. Ellen wanted a nice crisp Chardonnay to serve with some fish. I held Nicky's arm with my left hand while I picked up and studied the bottles with my right.

I heard some commotion over by the cash register. I turned and looked down the aisle. So did little Nick. The man behind the cash register was arguing with a customer. Suddenly the customer pulled out a gun, a stubby black handgun, and pointed it at the man behind the register. The gun went off. The man behind the register flew backward, a hole in the middle of his chest. I pushed Nicky down on the floor and covered his body with my own. The gunman turned and fled, but not before tripping over us on his way to the door. He took a second to swear and kick me in the head. I fully expected him to shoot me in the back, maybe shoot my son also.

But no, he kept running, down the aisle and out the door. I waited at least a minute before moving. Then, certain the gunman had gone, I picked up my son and went to check on the man behind the cash register. He lay there, in a heap, bleeding, barely breathing.

I used my right hand to cover Nicky's eyes.

I used my left hand to plug up the hole in the dying man's chest.

JUNE 9.

It was hours before we finally got home. I had to make a statement, deal with the police.

Nicky had to make a statement, too. I was impressed with the way the little guy handled himself. He described the gunman better than I did. He stood right there in front of the detective and said, "The man was not as tall as my dad. He had on black gloves and a New York Mets hat that was old and dirty. His skin was white, and kind of pasty like pizza dough. And he had a dark moustache that curled down around his upper lip."

It must have been ten o'clock by the time we got home. Ellen was frantic. She thought we had both been murdered. That's the way people think who live in New York City. She had even called the police, reported us missing.

And that very same night, after we put Nicky to bed, after we did our best to assure him everything would be okay, we made the decision.

Ellen said what I had been thinking. "Maybe it's time we moved out of the city, Sam."

I nodded. "I think you might be right."

"You and Nicky could have been killed tonight."

Again I nodded. "I guess the suburbs beckon."

"I think so."

JUNE 10.

Why not move to the suburbs? Get ourselves a nice little house in a safe and friendly neighborhood?

It suddenly seemed like the right thing to do. We did not want to send Nicky to school in New York City. The idea of sending him out on the streets seemed utterly insane and irresponsible. Maybe he would have been fine, but he was our only child. We were hyper-protective of his safety and security.

So we made our decision. And the very next day we started talking to friends and colleagues who already lived out of town. And then one weekend in late July we rented a car and ventured across the Hudson River to see what we could find.

JUNE 11.

It ate up most of our summer vacation, but by the end of August we had done the suburban shuffle. We had picked out a small town, found a nice house in good repair, made an offer, applied for a mortgage, and hired an attorney to take care of the details.

We could not close on the house until the first of the year, but we felt sure we could safely guide our son

through four more months in the big bad city. And except for an invasion of head lice in Nicky's kindergarten
class, we made it through those four months without
incident. I would not have minded if we had made it
through the rest of our lives without incident. But no, I
had to put off arriving at my mother's house. I had to
pull off the smooth, safe, and secure interstate highway.

I had to check the family into Sloan's Motel.

JUNE 12.

I looked up the word *dead* today at work. Morbid, I
know, but I just wanted to see what it said. I wanted to
see how *Webster's* defined it.

I found over twenty definitions. I could not bring
myself to read them all. The first one pretty much
summed things up: *loss of life, no longer alive.*

Other key words and phrases I spotted as my eyes
scanned the entry: *inert, barren, no longer in existence.*
But I caught one definition that definitely did not ring
true: *no longer having significance or relevance.*

I did not buy that one. Not for one second. Ellen and
Nicholas, for me anyway, have both significance and
relevance. They live on in my mind every moment of
every day. I will do my best to keep them alive forever.

JUNE 13.

This morning it dawned on me that I had not seen
Evelyn for the past two weeks, not since I had rubbed
her sore shoulder after her return from Washington,
D.C. I decided to go over and pay her a visit.

I knocked on the back door. No one answered. I opened the door and stuck my head inside. I called out but no one came. Then I heard the sound of Evelyn's cello. I went through the kitchen and down the dark hallway. I knocked softly on the music room door.

The cello continued to play, something hushed and melancholy. I assumed she had not heard my knock. So I knocked again, a bit louder.

Still she did not hear. So I turned the knob, slowly pushed open the door, and stepped into the music room. And there sat Evelyn Richmond, on the edge of her love seat, stark naked, her legs spread apart to accommodate the presence of that cello. I made some kind of a gasping sound.

Evelyn stopped playing, though she stayed perfectly calm. "Yes? Hello?"

My first thought was to turn and run.

"Is that you, Julie? No, it's you, Mr. Adams. Sam."

"Yes . . . I'm sorry. . . . I didn't know . . . I didn't mean . . . I knocked, but I guess you didn't hear."

She laughed. "I guess not." Then, "Please, Sam, don't go. Just give me a moment to pull on my robe."

I turned away and gave her a moment. Several moments, in fact.

"Okay," she called, "all clear. All private parts stowed away."

I turned around and saw that Evelyn had covered her body with one of her long silk robes. "Again," I muttered, "let me apologize."

"Apology accepted." She patted the cushion of the love seat. "Come over here and sit down. And tell me, where have you been?"

"Where have I been?"

"Yes, I thought you'd lost interest in me."

I stood in the middle of the room, "I thought you were going to call me."

"Oh, Sam."

"You had all those visitors, and well, I just assumed you—"

"Assume nothing, Sam. I have simply been here recuperating from my brush with violence. This is the first day since the mugging that I've even held the cello in my hands." She reached out and stroked the fingerboard of her instrument. "And besides," she added, "I cannot always be the one to make the move. It takes two to tango."

JUNE 14.

Yesterday Evelyn had to leave soon after my arrival to keep an appointment with her doctor. But late this afternoon, we rendezvoused once again in the music room. Evelyn had promised me a massage in return for the one I had given her.

She had me take off my shirt. I stretched out on top of a cotton blanket spread across that Oriental carpet. I had on nothing but a pair of running shorts. Evelyn coated my arms, my back, and my legs with massage oil. And then she went to work with her feet. Standing over me in a long black kimono, she worked my muscles with her toes and her heels. She had perfect balance. And she knew precisely how much pressure to apply.

I could do little else but lie there and moan. She did not want me to talk. "It only gets in the way of the pleasure," she insisted.

Next she went to work with her hands. She massaged

my scalp, my neck, and my shoulders. She rubbed and kneaded all those little fibrous muscles.

"You're all knotted up, Sam," she told me. "It's probably stress. You should learn to meditate and do yoga."

"You're right," I mumbled, "I should." Then, a few moments later, "Will you teach me?"

Evelyn laughed. "Oh, don't worry, Sam, I'll teach you everything I know."

After the massage, we kissed. Right there on the floor. Our bodies pressed together. But we did not kiss for long. Evelyn had somewhere else she needed to go, someone else she needed to see. She slipped away from me and whisked herself out of the music room without making a sound.

JUNE 15.

It is almost midnight. It has been a very long day. I arrived home just a short time ago. After work I had to take an author and her husband out for dinner in the city. She is such a prima donna. I can't stand her. But she writes like a dream. Her sentences are as close to poetry as prose can possibly be. And yet, she is petty and demanding and rude. She is like two entirely different people. I love editing her novels, but I loathe spending even one evening a year with her.

It is, I suppose, the price we pay.

I took the dogs for a walk as soon as I got home. Sixteen hours trapped in the house. They were both ready to explode. Moxie squatted practically on the front stoop. I should have asked Kathleen Karr to come over and walk them.

I hate leaving the dogs alone for all that time. It's not fair. It's downright cruel. Still, they were both so incredibly happy to see me, bursting, as always, with zealous enthusiasm.

As we walked up the driveway, I noticed a few lights burning over at the big house. I wondered if Evelyn might still be up. It would be nice to see her, to spend a few minutes with her before going to bed. But it's late. And I need to get up early. I should really be back in the office by nine.

Maybe tomorrow night we can spend some time together.

JUNE 17.

Last night Evelyn was not at home, but late this afternoon she paid me an unexpected visit.

I sat at the dining room table, editing, the dogs wrapped around my feet. They sprang into action the moment they heard the knock upon the door. I assumed it would be Kathleen, stopping by to see her furry friends. Or possibly Julie, out on an errand. But no, it was neither of them.

I opened the door and there stood Evelyn, dressed in a conservative summer skirt and print blouse. "Hello, Sam," she said. "I've come a-calling."

"This is a surprise."

"A pleasant one, I hope."

"Absolutely. I've been thinking about you."

"How sweet." Evelyn reached out then and took control. "Hold my hand," she said. "Lead me slowly through the living room and into the bedroom. After this, as long as you don't move anything, I'll know the way."

I led Evelyn across the foyer, up the two steps to the living room, and directly across the open space to the short hallway that led to the bedroom. I wondered, of course, what she had in mind. So did the dogs. They followed close behind.

"Take me to the edge of the bed."

I led her to the bed. She sat, then bounced up and down a few times. "Sit beside me, Sam."

I sat beside her. She drew me close, kissed me on the mouth. I kissed her back. After three or four kisses she leaned back into the bed, pulling my weight on top of her. For half an hour or more we kissed and stroked one another. Our hands became very active. We touched each other's arms and hips and backs. I kissed her neck. She kissed my ear. Our bodies felt nice together, close and connected.

We paused to catch our breath. "Do you find me attractive, Sam?"

"I do, Evelyn," I told her. "I find you very attractive."

She laughed. "You want to make love to me, don't you, Sam?"

"I'm beginning to think it might be nice."

"Yes, I think it would." Then, "Will you be sweet and kind and gentle when we make love?"

"Of course, Evelyn. I'll be however you want me to be."

"No, Sam. I just want you to be you."

We spoke all this in a whisper. If there had been another person in the room, I doubt they could have heard us.

Evelyn kissed me once more on the mouth, then she rolled over to the other side of the double bed. She tucked a pillow under her head. And then, in a normal, conversational tone, she asked, "Tell me, Sam,

how many women have you made love to in your
life?"

I did not know. I did not want to know. I did not
even want to think about it. The answer was not
many. Ellen had been my one and only lover, with a
single futile exception, for more than a dozen years.
Before Ellen there had been a few others. Karin, of
course. God rest her soul. And Lauren. Sally Ann.
Maybe eight or ten all together. Ellen was the only one
who ever really mattered.

"I have made love," Evelyn told me without the
slightest hesitation, "to over one hundred men. I love
men, Sam. I love how they make me feel when they are
sweet and kind and gentle."

I was shocked at the size of the number, but I was
also aroused. I rolled up against Evelyn's side, lifted
her blouse, and kissed her belly. But when I tried to lift
that blouse a bit higher, so I could kiss her breasts, she
stopped me. In fact, she pushed me away.

"Easy, Sam. I can't let you touch me that way.
We're not in love yet. There can be no lovemaking un
til there is love."

JUNE 18.

Evelyn likes to play games. She likes to shock and tease.
    So what?
    I enjoy her company. And I am extremely attracted
to her. I think we will make excellent lovers.

JUNE 19.

Evelyn and I spent time together today in the music room. We kissed and stroked and made small talk. Evelyn does not ask many questions. She prefers to talk about herself. She is a great name-dropper. She knows everyone. And she has been everywhere.

JUNE 20.

Evelyn and I are into the slow romance now. I feel like Evelyn's suitor come a-courting. We sit side by side in the parlor holding hands and sneaking wet ones while our chaperone, Miss Julie, stomps up and down the hallway pushing her nuclear-powered Electrolux.

JUNE 21.

After work today I took the dogs for a walk, then we all went over to pay Evelyn a visit. Snotty Miss Julie stopped our advance before we could make it through the kitchen.

She informed me, in no uncertain terms, that Mrs. Richmond was practicing her cello and was absolutely not to be disturbed.

The first full day of summer. And what a beauty: warm and sunny with the grass deep green, the flowers in bloom, the warblers frolicking in the trees. What could possibly make this day better?

Maybe some lovemaking with Evelyn.

Almost. Not quite. She continues to tease.

After lunch I went outside to do some reading and get some sun. Within just a few minutes I fell sound asleep in the grass.

When I opened my eyes, I found Evelyn standing over me, her legs straddling my hips. She wore a long silk robe, tied at the waist.

"Hello, Sam," she purred, pure seduction. "Having a little nap?"

"I guess so," I told her. "I just conked right out."

"I heard you brought the dogs over yesterday to visit."

"I did. But your bouncer threw us out."

Evelyn laughed, then unfastened the drawstring of her silk robe. The robe fell open. I could see her thighs, firm and thin. I could see her soft triangle of dark pubic hair. I could see her flat stomach and her small round breasts.

"Well," she whispered, "I thought I would return the visit."

Evelyn lowered herself slowly down to me. She took quite a long time. I did not move a muscle. I waited patiently. Finally our flesh made contact. An almost inaudible moan fell from her mouth. Or maybe it fell from mine.

I cannot say for sure.

She settled herself on top of me. I could feel the

warmth of her thighs against my thighs. She ran her hands over my stomach and across my chest. Several times. Over and over.

"Relax, Sam," she said. "I can assure you: this will be entirely pleasurable."

She gently stroked my arms and neck and face. For a while I watched her; she seemed perfectly at ease, as though she had perched practically naked on top of me many times before.

I closed my eyes and felt the tension run out of my body, as though my pores were wide-open faucets.

But then, somewhere in the back of my brain, I caught this image of Ellen watching me. Watching us. I felt my entire body grow tense and rigid. My wife's sudden appearance, however, did not strike me as odd. Since her death I have been in the intimate company of other women two or three times. Each time I have experienced this same tension. I do not know what causes it. Fear? Grief? Guilt? I know only that I loved my wife, and that I love her still. Had she not died, there would be no need for another woman. Not Evelyn or anyone else.

Evelyn must have sensed my distraction, my reluctance. Her caresses first slowed, then stopped entirely. She stood up, pulled that silk robe tight around her waist, then took a moment to smooth her tussled hair.

"You're coiled like a snake ready to strike, Sam. You're going to explode with all that pressure running through your body." She turned then and started across the grass. "But don't worry," she said over her shoulder, "we'll work on it. We'll get you nice and relaxed. I promise."

JUNE 23.

We worked on it again today. This time Evelyn had me begging. She knows precisely how to pull my strings. I have never had a woman pull my strings like this before.

Back in the music room. Early evening. But the days so long this time of year. Light poured in through the open windows. Evelyn in her short red kimono. Me in running shorts and a gray T-shirt. Not much time passed before that T-shirt came off. The passion was thick inside that room. We practically mauled one another on the love seat. She opened her kimono and we pressed our chests together. Then down on the Oriental carpet, where I had my hand between Evelyn's legs and she had her hand inside my running shorts.

She ran the tips of her fingers over my testicles. I felt them tighten. She took my penis in the palm of her hand and gently squeezed. I moaned. I wanted to make love to her.

We kissed. Hard and forcefully. I rolled up on top of her, then reached down and started to pull off my shorts. Evelyn stopped me. She held onto the waistband with her right hand. I tried again. She stopped me again.

"Evelyn, what's the matter?"

"Nothing is the matter."

"I want to make love to you."

"No," she said, "you don't. You want to fuck me."

"I want to make love to you."

"You're physically aroused, Sam. You want to fuck me. You're horny."

"Please," I pleaded, "let me enter you."

She rolled out from underneath me. "No."

"Why not?"

"Because you don't love me."

"I do love you," I told her. "I do."

"You just think you love me," she said. "You're confusing love with lust, lover boy." Then, "I have to go away for a few days. If you still love me when I get back, maybe I will let you enter me."

"Where are you going?" I demanded. "When will you be back?"

"I'm going to Chicago," she answered, "to give a concert and attend some lectures. I will be back in a few days."

"Let me make love to you before you go. Right here. Right now."

"Oh, Sam," she said, her hand caressing my cheek, "you tempt me so. But I think not. Better to let our passion simmer. It will give us a chance to make sure we know what we want."

And with that, she was once again on her feet and gone.

JUNE 24.

Back at work today. A million and one things to do. A thick pile of manuscripts demanding my attention.

But my concentration is weak; my attention span brief. Every few seconds my thoughts wander back to Evelyn. To her naked body.

JUNE 25.

I rarely remember my dreams, but last night I had the most vivid dream about Evelyn. About us. It lasted for hours. It took place over many years.

In the beginning we were young and naked. We made love over and over on this rope swing hanging from a tall tree. Then one day the rope broke and we fell into a pool of crystal clear water. Evelyn surfaced barefoot and pregnant. I swam in circles around her until the baby was born right before our eyes. Two babies, actually. Twins. We named them Nicky and Roger. We paddled to shore, and by the time we got there, the twins were young men wearing gray flannels and blue blazers.

Ellen was waiting on the bank. She had wings and a smile on her face. I kissed her and she flew away. Evelyn played the harp. The twins harmonized. I said, "The cycle of life goes round and round."

Evelyn nodded and turned old. She turned so old that her skin hardened and cracked and broke into a million pieces.

I screamed. And woke up.

Sweat covered my forehead. The night air was warm and muggy. I had too many blankets on. I threw them off. I threw them right on top of Moxie who lay asleep beside the bed. She awoke immediately, jumped up beside me, and licked my sweaty face.

JUNE 26.

I wonder if Evelyn will call. I hope she calls.

She has been gone a couple of days now. I think she said she would be gone a few days. No telling exactly what that means. It could mean two days, three days, five days, a week.

It will give me time to get some things done, to do some editing.

JUNE 28.

Mother called last night. She wanted to give me all the details concerning our annual Adams summer reunion. Every summer we all get together for a week at the seashore or up in the mountains. Last summer, so soon after Ellen's death and with Nicky still in the hospital, I decided not to attend. But this summer I will definitely go. We have a house rented for the second week of August up at Kezar Lake in western Maine.

Mother was extremely happy when I told her I would be coming. I did not tell her, however, that I will probably ask Evelyn Richmond to join us. Not that she will mind. Especially if Evelyn brings along her cello.

JUNE 29.

Yes, I have been thinking about Evelyn. And about my dream. I wonder if she can still get pregnant? Still bear babies? I wonder if she would like to have another child? My child? I need another child. A son. Someone to leave behind. Someone to prove I had been here.

Of course, I am getting way ahead of myself. I am really just fantasizing about making love to Evelyn. She calls it lust. Maybe she is right. I don't know. I only know that I want to feel myself inside of her.

The rest of it is just craziness. Evelyn cannot get pregnant. She is too old to get pregnant. My God, she is old enough to be my mother. That's not true. She is probably not more than a few years older than I am. Ten years at the very most. I think closer to five.

But any old way I slice it, Evelyn Richmond has me pretty riled up.

Maybe my attraction to her, this older woman, has something to do with some deep-rooted and suppressed desire to make love to my own mother?

Some Oedipus thing?

Hamlet perhaps? Did not the crazy Dane dream of mounting his mama?

"Seems, madam! nay, it is; I know not 'seems.' "

Ah yes, his mother the queen; nothing but a treacherous whore.

I am just babbling now, running off at the mouth after a stressful day at work and a long ride home on the train.

I cannot remember ever feeling the desire to have sexual relations with my mother. Not that failure to remember proves anything. We remember what we want to remember.

My mother is too old to get pregnant; of that I feel certain.

I wonder, though, if my parents still make love? And if they do, how often? Once a week? Once a month? Do they enjoy it?

I hope they do. I most sincerely hope they do.

They deserve to be happy.

JUNE 30.

Evelyn returned home from Chicago this morning. I went over to see her this evening after work. She was up in bed. Sick. Julie told me she had some kind of stomach virus.

Against Julie's protests, I went upstairs anyway. I

knocked softly on her door and entered. The curtains were drawn closed, but the windows hung open. A gentle breeze blew the curtains about the room.

"Evelyn," I whispered, "hi. It's me. Sam."

She did not answer, did not stir. I crossed to the bed. She was lying on her side, all curled up in a little ball. Her knees were bent. Her head rested upon her hands.

I kissed her softly on the cheek. Her skin was warm, but not hot. I kissed her again, then slipped quietly out of the room.

JULY 1.

Evelyn felt weak and sick to her stomach all day today. When I went to see her this morning, she was happy to see me, but she did not want me to stay.

"I'm terrible company when I'm sick, Sam," she said. "Mean and irritable. I think everyone is much better off if I'm just left alone until I feel better."

So I left her alone. Until after dinner. Then I went back with the dogs. They cheered her up. Moxie went straight onto the bed and gave her a nice big lick on the face.

JULY 2.

Evelyn and I played Scrabble today. Up in her bedroom. Right in the middle of her enormous bed.

She might be the best Scrabble player I have ever seen. I used to think I was the best Scrabble player. Not anymore. We played three games. She won all three. One of them she won by over a hundred points.

She made some incredible words. Playing with nine tiles instead of the usual seven, she fit *parabola* onto a double word score and *quebracho* onto a triple word score. The letters on her custom-made set are raised so she can tell what they are by feeling them. But what truly amazed me was her ability to remember the words that had already been played and the position of those words on the board.

"I have a clear picture of the entire board in my mind," she told me. "I can see it just as well as if I had eyes."

She then made *juxtapose* with the *j* falling squarely on a triple letter score, and that was all the proof I needed.

"Trust me, Sam," she said, resupplying her collection of letters, "I remember everything: sounds, smells, shapes, tastes, the words that spill out of your mouth, everything."

It sounded as much like a warning as a simple declaration of fact. I made the word *fate* on a double word score, took my fourteen points, and kept my mouth shut.

JULY 3.

Today Evelyn felt much better. We played chess out in the rose garden. She beat me the first time in twelve moves, the second time in thirty-four moves. The third game I battled her for over an hour before I had nothing left on the board but my king and a single lonely pawn. But the fourth game, the fourth game I eked out a victory.

"I let you win that one, Sam," she said as we put the pieces away in their silk-lined box.

"No you didn't."

"Yes I did. I could feel how badly you needed to beat me. You're not a bad player, Sam. In fact, you show quite a bit of imagination. If we played fifty games, you might get one legitimate win. If, say, my concentration slipped."

"So why are you telling me that you let me win?"

She glanced at me with those beautiful eyes that could not see a thing. Her mouth curled up in a tempting and delicious smile. "Oh, Sam," she said, "that's the interesting part. That's the part you will have to figure out for yourself."

JULY 4.

Independence Day. The Stars and Stripes. "America the Beautiful." Rockets' red glare. Bombs bursting in air.

When we lived in Manhattan, I used to take Nicky down to the Macy's Fourth of July fireworks display on the East River. My son and I would stand there with our eyes, ears, and mouths wide open as the explosions of noise burst over the New York skyline. Nicky would hoot and holler and point at the brilliant displays of magical color. I would put my hand on Nicky's shoulder just the way my father used to put his hand on my shoulder when he took me to see the fireworks at the fairgrounds on the outskirts of Hanover.

My father, however, did more than just take us to see fireworks on the Fourth of July. We always received a history lesson as well. He wanted us to know what the Fourth of July was all about. One year he told us the story of the Boston Tea Party and, of course, my namesake's role in that party. Another year we heard the stories of Lexington and Concord and Bunker Hill. He made sure we knew about the evils of taxation without representation. And he told us about our ancestors, the great American patriots, John and Sam and Abigail Adams. Oh yes, Professor Adams taught us all about the Declaration of Independence and the United States Constitution and the Bill of Rights, especially Amendment One guaranteeing our freedom of speech.

My father knew all about American history. And he passed his knowledge down to us. But above all, my father had luck. My father had two sons and a daughter. And now, all these many years later, he still does. Not only did my father get to take his kids to the fireworks year in and year out, but he also has had the great good fortune to watch all three of us grow into strong, healthy, and reasonably successful adults.

I, on the other hand, had only one child. One son. And now I have none.

<hr>

JULY 5.

Last night I took Evelyn to the fireworks. Our first time together off the grounds of Blind Pass.

"I am a patriot, Sam," she told me. "A true-blue American. I have been virtually everywhere on the planet, but I would never live anywhere else. The United States is the finest country in the world."

She seemed quite determined on this matter, so I let it go without offering even a mild objection.

Julie accompanied us. I drove the big Mercedes.

Evelyn sat beside me. Julie, silent and frowning, sat in the back.

It was only after we had arrived at the local grammar school, parked, gathered our blanket from the trunk, and found ourselves a spot on the grass wet with dew, that the irony hit me: I, Sam Adams, was about to watch an Independence Day fireworks display with a woman who could not see and a snotty English girl who was apparently still sore about her homeland going down in defeat.

The thought made me miss my wife. And my son.

Still, we had a good time. Evelyn held onto my arm and squeezed every time an explosion rocked the night. And Julie, much to my amazement, actually seemed to enjoy the show. In those fragmentary moments of spectacular light, I more than once saw her smiling. She has a nice smile. She should use it more often.

JULY 6.

More time today with Evelyn. I have even started working at home one or two days a week the way I used to so that we can spend a few hours together in the late afternoon. She seems pleased with this arrangement.

We have not yet made love, but there is an emotional bond slowly developing between us.

Today Evelyn told me that she started playing the piano at the age of three. By age six she had moved on to the violin. By ten she had taken up the cello. By her eleventh birthday the cello had become her best friend. "And," she added, "it has been my best friend ever since.

"You see, Sam," she continued, "unlike most kids who take music lessons, I enjoyed practicing. I loved to practice. No, I lived to practice. Both my parents were extremely accomplished musicians. They filled the house with Bach and Brahms and Beethoven. And being an incredibly competitive person by nature, I wanted to play as well as they did. Soon I wanted to play better than they did. And so I would practice, practice, practice."

I allowed this nuance of Evelyn's character to settle in; then I said, "My mother wanted me to play the piano. She played the violin, although not very well. But she loved music. We always had music playing in our house. Mozart was her favorite."

"Yes," said Evelyn, "mine, too. I remember—"

She started to say more, but I interrupted. I wanted to talk about me, if just for a minute or two.

"I took lessons for a few years. But, like most young boys, I was impatient. I wanted to be outside playing baseball or football. Plus I had this teacher who was a very strict disciplinarian. A little old gray-haired German woman with a thick accent. She used to rap my knuckles with a wooden ruler whenever I hit the wrong key, played the wrong note."

Evelyn laughed. I made Evelyn laugh. Just like that. Just by letting a childhood tale roll off my tongue. She has a wonderful, carefree laugh, not unlike Ellen's.

I could always make Ellen laugh with my stories. Why not Evelyn?

But then her laughter stopped and she returned, as usual, to her own stories, her own enormous role on the planet. Evelyn possesses, quite clearly, a rather expansive ego.

"Try to understand, Sam," she said. "When you

are a mere child and you have one less sense than all the other children, especially one as vital as the sense of sight, you feel extraordinarily vulnerable and inadequate. You go through a wide variety of stages: apathy, anger, denial, dread, fear. I was lucky. My parents were musicians. They gave me instruments and taught me how to play."

Wait. Was I hearing this right? I jostled a few facts around in my head. And then I asked, "But I thought Roger told me you only recently went blind?"

Evelyn's soft features turned hard. She scowled at me. Her tone turned cold and harsh. "Is *that* what Roger told you?"

I shrugged. "Well, yes. He indicated that you had lost your sight in the last year or two."

Another scowl. "Tell me something, Mr. Adams. Do you believe everything Roger tells you? Do you believe everything everyone tells you?"

Before I could answer, before I could mutter a word, she did her disappearing act again: up and out of the music room in a flash, smoke and flames trailing behind as she opened and closed the door with a crash.

JULY 7.

Evelyn's blindness since birth: fact or fantasy?

I lean toward the latter.

But what do I know? Who am I to judge another person's reality?

I went over to see her again this morning. Out in the rose garden filled now with blossoms and the sweet smell of heaven.

I am fast growing used to Evelyn's mood swings. I

suppose these swings could be chalked up to the artist's temperament. Many authors I know act in this same schizophrenic fashion. They assume they can be charming companions one second and belligerent bullies the next simply because they possess a creative flair.

I exact my revenge upon them with my editing pencil. This alteration of their precious prose allows me to put up with their temper tantrums.

This morning Evelyn was quite lovely. She performed a beautiful piece by Schubert. Her playing very nearly made me weep with joy. The sight of Evelyn, the scent of those roses, the sound of the music: incredible. I gave her thunderous rounds of applause.

She smiled and ripped off a few more notes.

"You make love to that instrument when you play it," I told her.

"That's the idea, Sam. Of course, my skills with the cello were a gift. God was kind enough to give me an excellent set of ears and perfect pitch."

Her reference to the Almighty startled me. I am not sure why. "Do you believe in God, Evelyn?"

She ran her fingers silently up and down the neck of her cello. "I am a good Presbyterian, Sam. Of course I believe in God. Don't you?"

"I do, yes." Then I hesitated before changing my tune. "At least I did. But now, sometimes, I am not so sure what I believe."

Evelyn reached out until I offered her my hand. "Poor, Sam. Poor troubled Sam."

She took her hand and placed it gently upon my face. Her fingers caressed my cheek. "I want you to tell me everything, Sam. Maybe not today or tomorrow or even next week, but soon. I want you to feel you can confide in me."

JULY 8.

Confide in Evelyn? Tell Evelyn everything? I do not know if I can do that. I do not know if I can bring myself to tell her about Ellen and Nicky and what transpired in room 14 of Sloan's Motel. To tell Evelyn about that would demand an enormous amount of trust in her and in our relationship.

Of course, it might do me good to tell her. To get it out in the open, off my chest. Not just down on paper, but into the ears and thoughts of a fellow human being.

But I fear Evelyn's response. She can be so . . . I don't know . . . so . . . so complicated. So condescending. So insensitive. I could tell her everything, spill my guts, all about Ellen and Nicky, and she might just laugh in my face.

And yet, she can be so very sweet. So delicate. So gentle. She definitely has two sides to her personality. The tricky part is knowing which side of her will come out each day and play.

I think some more time will have to pass before I tell Evelyn anything very personal about my life.

JULY 9.

This morning I drove Evelyn to the mall half an hour or so from here. We took the Mercedes. I wanted to ask her if she used to drive that big sedan, before she went blind, but I held back. I kept my mouth shut.

"I need a new dress, Sam," she told me on the way. "Something flattering and fancy and flashy."

"For what?" I asked. My voice, I realized immediately after the words jumped out of my mouth, sounded a bit too stern and demanding.

But Evelyn marched on. "For a party, Sam. We're going to a party."

"You and I?"

"Yes."

"What kind of party?"

"Just some stuffy benefit. Do you have a tux?"

I did. Somewhere. Back at the other house. Probably hanging in the closet in the attic. "Yes."

"Good."

I had some more questions, but they would have to wait. We pulled into the mall and Evelyn told me where to park. I did as ordered, then I led her across the hot asphalt and in through the heavy glass doors.

Evelyn shivered at the blast of cold air from the air conditioning. "Brrrr."

I gave her shoulders a squeeze.

She smiled at me and said, "Ladies' fashions, Sam. Second floor."

We took the escalator. I held her hand. Evelyn knew the saleswoman. They greeted one another by name. Friends. Then Evelyn turned to me. "Go buy yourself something, Sam. Maybe a new belt. Come back in an hour. By then I'll have some things for you to look at. You can help me decide."

I stood there for a moment, looking, no doubt, a bit lost. I have never been a big shopper. Once in a while I go out and buy a new suit. Ellen used to buy my shirts and socks and underwear.

But Evelyn had dismissed me, so I had to go and do something. I ventured out into the mall. I bought a couple of overpriced chocolate chip cookies. I watched the crowd. I went into a bookstore and looked at the new hardcover fiction. There were several JJ&R titles, one edited by yours truly. I opened it up, found my name among those the author had deemed it necessary to acknowledge. A perfunctory mention. We did not really care for one another. During a difficult phase of the editorial process, he had called me "a spineless jellyfish more interested in the marketplace than in literary achievement."

An unfair and utterly untrue accusation. I have quite high standards. I took his insult personally. But at the time I said nothing. Not a word. He will get his due when his agent comes looking for a new contract.

An hour slipped away. I headed back to ladies' fashions. Before I got there I stopped and bought a new belt. A brown leather braided one. I needed a new belt. The old one was worn and frayed. I was impressed that Evelyn had noticed. She noticed the new one as well.

JULY 11.

I did it. I started doing it anyway. Over the last couple of days, I have been telling Evelyn some of the more difficult and painful episodes of my life. I have not told her about Ellen and Nicky, but I feel that before long I probably will. The more honest and intimate I am with her about my past and about my feelings, the more sensitive and receptive she becomes.

I began by telling her about Russell Petersen. I told her how he had drowned in the Connecticut River, and how I had blamed myself for his death.

She listened attentively, then, after I had finished,

she held my hands and said, "That's such a sad story, Sam. Of course for your friend to lose his life, but also for you to have to learn about loss at such a tender and innocent age."

I nodded but added nothing. It is amazing that after nearly thirty years I still get incredibly choked up when I think about Russell. If he had lived we would no doubt still be friends. My oldest friend in the world.

JULY 12.

Today, this afternoon, just a few hours ago, much to my astonishment, I found myself telling Evelyn about an episode from my youth that has long been one of my most closely guarded secrets. I, of course, shared this secret with Ellen, but I think she is the only other one I ever told. I may have told my college sweetheart, Karin Dodd. Yes, in fact, I am quite sure I did. But no one else other than those two. Until now.

This secret concerns my parents. I suppose it is not really all that big a deal, but for some reason I have always preferred to keep it to myself. It is not one of the happier episodes of my childhood, so I have probably done my best to bury it, to deny it ever really happened.

But now I have gone and told Evelyn. I must trust her. I know for a fact that I am falling in love with her.

The story begins with me. When I was nine or ten, my parents took me to a psychiatrist to find out why I was so wound up all the time. I had, in their minds anyway, far too much energy. I wasn't a bad kid or even a difficult kid. In fact, I was a pretty happy-go-lucky kid. But I was highly charged and I definitely

marched to the beat of my own drummer. I liked doing things my way. And I always went full speed from
morning till night. I liked going to bed late and getting
up early. Nothing could slow me down. I had then,
and still have now, a rock-solid constitution. All of
this wired determination used to drive my mother
crazy.

So they sent me to see Dr. Blue. Dr. Blue was a
friend of my father's, or so we thought at the time. The
two of them played tennis and squash together over at
the college, and sometimes, afterward, they went out
to drink beer at the Campus Tavern on Wheelock
Street. Dr. Blue had a wife and kids and a house, just
like my father. He also had an office on South Main
Street, where I went to see him. I don't remember a
couch, though there might have been one. We sat
across from one another in a pair of brown leather
armchairs. I squirmed around a lot on that smooth,
cool surface.

For a month or so I went to see Dr. Blue a couple of
times a week. He gave me a whole battery of tests,
asked me all kinds of questions. I answered truthfully,
most of the time. A few times I lied, just to see if he
could tell the difference. I don't think he could.

Once or twice my father took me to Dr. Blue's office,
but most of the time my mother drove me in the family
station wagon. She would sit out in the waiting room
reading *Ladies' Home Journal* or *Good Housekeeping*
while I was in with the good doctor. But afterward, she
always went into his office to powwow with him. I
was always told to wait outside. I figured they were in
there talking about me, but sometimes she would be in
there for twenty or thirty minutes.

After ten or twelve sessions, Dr. Blue called both

my parents into his office for a consultation. "Let me
assure you right off the bat," he said to them in his
silky smooth voice, "that there is absolutely nothing
psychologically amiss with Sam. He possesses above-
average intelligence, a keen sense of curiosity, and excellent cognitive skills. His attention span is, let us say,
adequate, for a boy his age. I'm sure it will improve as
he matures."

"I told you," my father said, turning to his wife,
"that there was nothing wrong with him."

My mother sighed. "So why can't he sit still?" she
asked Dr. Blue. "Why can't he be more cooperative?"

There were no answers. Just some vague sugges-
tions. "Time," Dr. Blue told my parents as he walked
them to the door, "will take care of Sam. Try not to
worry. Try and relax. Sam is a curious and imaginative young fellow. I feel confident he'll be just fine."

JULY 13.

So I stopped seeing Dr. Blue. But my mother did not.

Some months later, my mother called Jack and
Abigail and me into her bedroom late one afternoon.
She told us she had to go away for a while. She had to
go to California to take care of a sick aunt. I had never
heard a word about this aunt before, but nevertheless
our mother was leaving. Right then. That same evening. Before she even put dinner on the table.

She was gone quite a long time. Several weeks. If my
memory serves, she left sometime before Thanksgiving
and she did not return until sometime after the New
Year arrived. It may have been weeks, but to us, her
children, it seemed like years. She called us frequently

on the telephone, almost every night, but whenever I asked her when she would be home, she told me she was not sure.

My father, who was unusually subdued and even irritable during her absence, did not know when she would be home, either. He would shrug his shoulders and turn away when asked. Several times I found him in his small office off the kitchen, staring at a photograph of my mother. A few times I even saw him crying.

It is a terrifying thing for a child not to know when his mother will be coming home. Especially a mother who had never once failed to be in the kitchen with fresh baked goods and ice-cold milk when we arrived home from school. A mother who was always there to tuck us in at night and give us a kiss before turning off the light. I suppose her absence forced upon me, upon all three of us, a rather crude form of independence, but I think we would have survived just fine without this nasty jolt to our sensibilities.

Jack and Abigail and I definitely despaired. We soon started to wonder if our mother would ever be coming home. We eventually decided that we must have done something wrong, something to drive Mother away. And after a few weeks had passed, my sister and brother started blaming me for our predicament. I was suddenly the reason she had left. I was the one, after all, who usually stirred things up, caused the trouble, got our mother all upset.

For the first time in my life, I experienced guilt. In bed at night, when I said my prayers, I always prayed to God for the return of Mother, and I promised to be good from that moment on if she would just come back.

I told all this to Evelyn, and soon she guessed the obvious.

"Your mother had run off with Dr. Blue."

I nodded. Indeed she had.

"You poor kids. It must have been terrible."

I nodded again.

My parents had a good marriage. They loved and supported one another. They still do. They had three children. And they raised us well. They loved and supported us. Financially and emotionally. Both of them did the best they knew how.

My mother just slipped off the deck for a couple of months. That's all. The seas grew choppy, she lost her balance, and in no time at all she found herself in the water, gasping for air.

She had an affair with Dr. Blue. They lost their heads. They ran off for a while. They abandoned their families and their responsibilities. They became, for a time, creatures of the flesh. Their bodily desires far outweighed everything else in their lives that mattered.

"But," I told Evelyn, "they both soon came to their senses. They returned home."

"But the damage," she said, "had been done."

I shrugged. "She held us and loved us and told us what we needed to hear. I think we forgave her before night fell on another day."

"You do? Really?"

Evelyn and I sat out in the rose garden. Side by side on the chaise lounge.

"I do. Yes. Absolutely. We were just overjoyed to have her back."

"The kids perhaps. But what about your father?"

"He no doubt had a more difficult struggle, but he has always deeply loved my mother. In time, he forgave her as well."

"He must be a very special person."

I nodded. "I was extremely lucky. I could not possibly have had a better role model."

JULY 15.

Today it almost happened. Evelyn and I very nearly made love. Almost but not quite. The gods seem to be conspiring against us.

We sat in the music room. Rain tapped the windows. A light summer rain.

We kissed and embraced. Our passion smoldered. I honestly do not know who, but one of us suddenly said, "Let's go upstairs."

"Yes," the other one said, "let's."

A few more kisses, and then we were on our feet and moving toward the door. I opened the door and Evelyn led us out. We crossed the hall and started up the stairs.

I did not reach the second stair before the phone rang. Miss Julie answered in the kitchen.

It was for Evelyn. She took the call in the den across from the music room. I waited out in the hall.

When she returned a few minutes later, she told me Roger had been on the line. It seems Roger is back in the U.S., back from Switzerland. He is up in Boston just now, staying with a friend. I gather there is something wrong. Roger needs his mommy. Evelyn is leaving immediately to take care of his needs. In fact, we're leaving for the airport in a few minutes.

So we almost made love. At least now I know that we both want the same thing, that we both desire each other's intimacy.

But is that what I really want? Do I truly want to become involved with Evelyn Richmond? I wonder what Ellen would say about Evelyn? Would Ellen approve or disapprove?

"Whatever it takes to be happy and satisfied, Sam" is what she would surely say. Ellen was such a fair, honest, and open-minded person.

JULY 17.

This evening, after work, I was out rummaging around in the garage, looking for a screwdriver, when I came across a bicycle. An old ten-speed. The sight of that bike gave me a sudden urge to take a spin.

But first I had to patch a flat tire, oil the rusty chain, tighten the handlebars, and adjust the seat. Then, with the dogs in hot pursuit, I took off down the driveway and along the street.

What a pleasant and invigorating feeling of freedom I had as the wind whipped past my face. I felt like a kid again.

JULY 18.

Today I went for another bike ride, a longer ride, without the dogs. I went out through town and along the river on the old canal path. It felt good to get my heart pumping and to use my muscles again.

I have definitely not been getting enough exercise lately. This is not like me. I have been in good shape most of my life. I have always exercised regularly. It is only since the events at Sloan's Motel that I have lost interest in staying fit. Now the time has come to regain that interest. Bike riding seems like an excellent place to start.

I have decided to ride the bike and do some floor exercises every day. And I'm going to start eating better as well. On the way back from my ride earlier, I stopped at the farm market on the edge of town. I bought broccoli, yams, and a loaf of whole-grain bread for dinner. This is the kind of meal Ellen used to serve, simple and nutritious, very little meat.

JULY 19.

A beautiful summer day. I rose early, swept out the cottage, then hopped on my bike. Well, not my bike. The Richmonds' bike. Probably Roger's bike. But I do not think Evelyn will mind if I use it.

I took a small, lightweight backpack with me and rode over to the farm market, where I bought some fresh fruit, a block of cheese, and a small loaf of dark brown bread. More healthy whole-grain stuff. Then I rode over to the bike shop on Main Street. The rear gear changer was not working properly, but the mechanic turned a couple of screws, gave it a squirt of oil, and in no time at all he had it working smoothly.

"That bike's been around a few years," he said.

"I found it in the garage."

"It's still in pretty good shape."

I asked him about new bikes. He showed me racing bikes and touring bikes and mountain bikes and hybrids. Bikes, I found out, have gotten expensive. He had a bike in there made out of titanium that cost over three thousand dollars.

"I think I'll stick with this old Raleigh for a while."

He nodded and told me to come out Wednesday nights at six for group rides. I told him I would try to make it.

Then I pedaled out of town. I kept a good steady pace over rolling terrain. I rode maybe ten miles before I turned off on a gravel road that ran along a shallow stream. I found a grassy spot in the shade of a tall oak. I sat against the trunk, ate my cheese and bread and fruit, and listened to the stream rush past some large smooth boulders.

After that, I curled back for a nap. I had a dream about Ellen and Nicky. A nice pleasant dream: Disney World with no crowds, no lines, just the three of us in the Magic Kingdom.

JULY 21.

I did not write a word yesterday. And for good reason: I did not have time.

I do not know how much I will get written this morning, either, but I will take a moment to put something down.

She is sound asleep now. I can hear her steady breathing, in and out, in and out. . . .

Last evening, when I arrived home from work, I found a pleasant surprise waiting for me here in the cottage. Right over on the bed, in fact.

The dogs greeted me enthusiastically at the door, then they led me directly to the bedroom. She lay there, between the sheets, perfectly still, her head resting on my pillow, her eyes closed.

"Evelyn?"

She did not answer. I took a few steps into the bedroom. I sat on the edge of the bed and touched her arm with the fingers of my right hand.

She stirred, stretched, and smiled. "Sam, I've been waiting for you."

I gave her arm a squeeze. "Did you just get back from Boston?"

She nodded.

"How's Roger?"

She sighed and turned away. "He's a man now, Sam. No more use for his blind old mother. He has girlfriends now. And plans to run off to Africa and hunt lions with his father."

Loss. The pain and misery of loss. I know the emotion well.

"Sam," she said, "lie down with me."

So I did. I kicked off my shoes and stretched out beside her. We kissed. I could see that Evelyn needed me close and comforting. I stroked her hair and gently rubbed her neck and shoulders. Our passion flared a time or two, then settled down. The room slowly grew dark on that long summer day.

I got up at one point to take the dogs for a walk. When we got back, I found Evelyn lying naked on top of the sheets. "Come here, Sam," she said. "The time has come for you to enter me," It sounded almost like an order.

An order I wanted to obey. I slipped out of my clothes and stood there for just a moment, naked.

And then I crossed to the bed and stretched out at Evelyn's side. I kissed her mouth and we embraced. She rolled up on top of me; such a tiny thing. But potent and powerful. She had me inside of her within seconds. Her rhythm started gently but increased with each push. I tried to get her to slow down, but no, she pushed faster and harder. She had her arms around my waist and her face buried in my chest. I could feel the perspiration gathering in the small of her back. It was damp and warm behind her knees. Then, suddenly, she grew perfectly still. Rigid. And a moment later, she came. As she came, she drove her fingertips so forcefully into my hips that it actually hurt. I suppressed a desire to scream.

Her grip loosened. She relaxed, drew a deep breath, and then rolled onto her side. "Oh, Sam, I needed that. I needed you to fuck me."

I wanted to tell her that I hadn't really done much of anything, but instead, I just ran my fingers gently through her hair.

A bit later I made us some supper. Just salad and French bread. It was all either of us wanted. Then we went back to bed. The night was warm and muggy and still. All the windows were wide open. We lay on top of the sheets.

Evelyn started talking. She told me all about her husband and her son and her divorce. She did not really make it sound like a sad story, but as she finished she began to cry, softly. I comforted her, and soon she fell asleep. I got up, took the dogs for another walk, then stood for several minutes in the shower under a cool stream of water. I eventually made it back to bed, where I fell asleep with my hand on Evelyn's hip, my chest lightly touching her back.

We are lovers now. Evelyn and I.

JULY 22.

Yesterday I waited until almost ten o'clock for Evelyn to wake up. But she kept sleeping and sleeping. So finally I gave up and went to work. Before I left I started writing her note. Then I remembered she was blind.

I thought about her all day long. I thought about her stretched out naked on top of me. I could not get her out of my thoughts. All efforts to concentrate on my work proved futile. I wanted her. I wanted to make love to her. I wanted her sexually, but I also wanted her emotionally.

I went straight over to the big house as soon as I got home. I walked straight into the kitchen without even bothering to knock. Julie stood over by the sink drying a piece of crystal with a hand towel. I gave her only the slightest nod, then kept right on going. Down that long dark hallway and through the music room door.

Evelyn sat on a folding metal chair in the middle of the Oriental carpet, her cello nestled between her legs.

Two or three quick steps and I was upon her. I ripped the cello from her grasp, lifted her into my arms, carried her to the love seat, tore off her clothes, and ravished her. Evelyn loved every minute of it. She came and came. And so, this time, did I.

Dream on, Sammy Boy, dream on.

Actually, I slipped by Julie while she scowled at me, made my way down the hallway, knocked on the music room door, entered quietly, and found Evelyn sitting there with her cello. She was concentrating on tuning the strings. I waited for her to recognize my presence, but after a few moments I received only an annoyed response. "Yes, Sam. What is it?"

I did not take another step. For a good thirty seconds I remained mute. Then, finally, I cleared my throat and asked, "Are you busy?"

"Actually," came her icy reply, "I am. As you can see, I'm practicing."

"Yes."

"I loathe being interrupted when I'm practicing."

This was not at all what I had expected. I had expected passion. I had expected romance. I hemmed and hawed, tried to find some reason for my sudden appearance. "I was just wondering . . ." I wanted to say something about the night we had just passed together, but I could not find the words.

"Yes? You were wondering what?"

"I was wondering . . . I was wondering about that party, that black-tie affair you mentioned a week or so ago. The one you bought the new dress for."

"Party?" Evelyn, her eyes large black holes behind her rose-colored glasses, looked at me with a confused expression. "Oh yes, the party. Forget the party, Sam. I do not feel much like a party girl just now. So . . . if you will excuse me."

I stood there a moment longer, hoping, I suppose, that she might change her mind, maybe ask me to stay. But no, in her mind I was already gone. She had her cello. She did not need me.

JULY 23.

Last evening Evelyn changed her tune. I guess she decided she really did need me. Too bad this time I could not give her what she needed.

She swept into the cottage just a few minutes after I arrived home from work. She was all keyed up, vibrating with energy and good cheer. "I've come for a little snuggle, Sam," she cooed. "And also to apologize for yesterday. I was all jumbled up inside thinking about Roger."

She looked beautiful and vivacious. I took her hands in mine. "That's okay. I understand." But in truth, I did not understand. I do not understand Evelyn's mood swings. They are distracting and damaging.

Still, I wanted her. We went into the bedroom. We lay upon the bed. We kissed and hugged and stroked one another for well over an hour. Slowly, one article at a time, our clothes came off. We proceeded very cautiously, like a couple of young lovers uncertain and insecure. Every once in a while Evelyn giggled. That made it easier.

A warm breeze blew in through the open windows.

And suddenly we were naked, perfectly naked. We wrapped our bodies together, intertwined our arms and legs. Those lovely sounds that new lovers make tumbled from our mouths.

But then, and this is a painful confession for me to make, when our intimacy turned lustful, I could not . . . well, I could not flex my muscle. I could not perform. I wanted to perform. I wanted to make love to Evelyn. I wanted to enter her, make her my own. I wanted to satisfy her so she would love me and want me.

Perhaps I was trying too hard. Perhaps I had Ellen too much on my mind. Perhaps Evelyn's instability was making me insecure. I do not know. I only know that after some amount of time had passed, Evelyn took hold of my flaccid member and said, "Why, Mr. Adams, you're as limp as week-old lettuce."

Undoubtedly she was only trying to diffuse the tension, but still, I became instantly indignant over the remark. I thanked her curtly for her sensitivity and turned away.

She responded with this: "Tell me, Sam, I don't mean to pry, but do you have this problem often?"

I assured her I did not.

She smiled, softened. "Maybe we'll just lie here a little while longer and hold each other close."

"That," I said, "would be nice."

"And who knows? The little guy might just rise to the occasion."

The little guy did not.

Evelyn hung around for another half an hour or so, then she stood, dressed, and departed the cottage. It might have been my imagination, but I am pretty sure she slammed the door on her way out.

JULY 24.

No sign of Evelyn today. I guess she is punishing me for not being able to get an erection.

Nice gal.

Probably she just has other things to do.

And so do I. More than I care to think about.

It used to be things slowed down a bit in the publishing business during the summer months, but no

more. The pressure is relentless: New manuscripts
to read. Old manuscripts to edit. Galleys to proof.
Cover copy to write. Meetings to attend. Presenta-
tions to make. An endless grind. Sometimes I wonder
if it is worth it. The writers are becoming ever more
callous and demanding. The publishers want nothing
but best-sellers. And the public, those who can still
read, seem content with crap.

I would prefer to stay home and play with my mutts.
But not today. Today the meat grinder beckons.

JULY 25.

I had a call at the office this morning from my father.
The Professor. He just wanted to shoot the breeze for
a few minutes, make sure I was still going up to Maine
for the family get-together in a few weeks. I assured
him I was. I even hinted at the possibility that I might
bring along a new friend.

"A female friend?"

"Could be."

"I'll look forward to meeting her."

"I think you'll like her."

"I'm sure I will."

"She's a musician. A cellist."

"Your mother will like that."

"How is Mom?"

"She's good. Busy with the garden."

"You guys are getting along?"

"Of course, Sam," he said after a brief hesitation.
"Never better."

I hoped he was telling the truth. They are both getting too old now not to get along.

My father forgave my mother for her infidelity. I wonder if he regrets forgiving her. I wonder if he wishes he
had handled things differently. I wonder if he has had
a moment's peace since finding out about his wife
sleeping with his good buddy, Dr. Blue.

We sometimes do the most horrible things to those
we love. I cheated once on Ellen, and I have regretted
it ever since. It would be nice to know why we do the
things we do.

I forgave Mother for her infidelity. For abandoning
us. But I did not forgive her quite as quickly as I told
Evelyn. In fact, it took me months to forgive her. A
year. Or more. Much more.

JULY 27.

It was not quite dawn this morning when she entered
my room and crawled into bed beside me. She kissed my
mouth, licked my stomach, aroused me orally, and then
slipped me easily inside of her.

Evelyn was tender and sweet, far more interested in
how I felt than in my ability to develop and maintain
an erection. Yes, she is a very moody, complicated,
and unpredictable woman. But still, I am intrigued
with her. I think I might even be in love with her.

"You're a sensitive one, aren't you, Sam?" She asked
this after our loving had come to an end, after I had
emptied myself inside of her for the first time.

I shrugged. "I don't know. I guess. Maybe I'm just a
little crazy. Like everyone else. You know, tough times
and all that."

"I don't know. All what?"

"I don't want to bore you."

"Oh, Sam, I've never found a man's personal life boring. Especially if he is even remotely honest about it."

I took a long look at her in the early morning light pouring through the window. She really was, really is, quite something, quite beautiful, quite fascinating. She may even be more, I hate to admit this, than I can handle.

She must have felt my eyes upon her face because she leaned in and kissed me softly on the lips. Then, "Sam, I want you to know something. I am not afraid to get close. That's never been a problem for me. The ecstasy of love has no equal. I just think that when two people become sexually and romantically involved, they should be aware of, and they should be able to deal with, the consequences of that involvement."

I was too busy suckling her nipple to respond.

She pulled away. "Did you hear what I said, Sam?"

"Yes, Evelyn," I answered, "I heard you."

"And do you agree?"

I nodded. "Yes. Absolutely." Then I went for her nipple again.

She covered it with the palm of her hand. "Sam, I want to love you. I want to make love to you. And I want you to make love to me. But as I am sure you know, love often goes wrong. People change. Feelings change. Circumstances change. I want to be sure you will be able to cope with the pain and the consequences if anything unpleasant happens."

I did not want to think about it. Not about the pain. Definitely not about the consequences. My God, I thought to myself, we have only just begun. Why worry about things ending already? Her concerns seemed preposterous.

And so I said, "Of course, Evelyn. No problem. I can cope with anything. I just want to love you." Then I pushed her hand away and very tenderly licked her breast with the tip of my tongue.

JULY 28.

Evelyn and I went out for lunch today. I drove the Mercedes. Evelyn picked the place and paid the tab. We ate at a small, quiet, intimate inn across the river. The owner, a woman about my age, greeted Evelyn by name and took our order. It might have been my imagination, but I had the distinct feeling this woman was sizing me up, checking me out, comparing me to other men Evelyn had brought to her establishment.

I found myself working hard to make a good impression. I offered up plenty of coy smiles and witty, offhand remarks.

After lunch and a bottle of white wine, we drove home. We went up to Evelyn's bedroom and made love for the rest of the afternoon. The wine made us loose and drowsy. I could only manage half an erection, but Evelyn did not seem to mind. She stroked me gently, gave me a kiss or two, and eased me inside when the time was right.

Afterward I asked her about the woman at the inn.

"A very pleasant person," she answered. "But frankly, I do not think her sexual preferences are the same as our own." And then, "What about you, Sam? Have you ever been naked with a man?"

I did my best to look insulted. But, of course, Evelyn could not see my miffed expression. "No. Never."

My lover merely shrugged.

I tried not to ask, to remain silent, to mind my own business, but finally I had to know. "Have you ever been with a woman?"

"Of course," she answered, without pause. "But not for years and years. I never found it as interesting, or as challenging, or for that matter, as rewarding as being with a man."

It both excited and repulsed me thinking about Evelyn being naked with another woman. The excited part won out.

"Oh my goodness, Sam! What have we here?"

JULY 29.

Another pleasant summer day with Evelyn. Warm and sunny. Not too humid. A few clouds to occasionally block the sun.

Miss Julie served us lunch out in the rose garden. Every time she came or went she threw me a nasty little glance.

I thought about telling Evelyn but decided to keep it to myself. I did not want to seem petty.

After lunch, Evelyn sent Julie off to do some errands. Before the car had even reached the end of the drive, my lover had her hands on me. We had our clothes off in no time. We rolled onto the grass at the edge of the patio and made love quickly and passionately.

I have not made love like that since my early days with Ellen. It was so easy, so fiery, so spontaneous.

JULY 30.

More time today with Evelyn. My thoughts feel light and free. This was what I needed: someone to love and to love me. We are, I see, nothing without someone to love.

Family and friends assured me my period of mourning would eventually come to an end, that I would find someone to help fill that enormous void left by the deaths of Ellen and Nicky.

I, of course, did not believe them. Not for a second. I thought surely I would grieve alone forever.

Who would have thought a blind woman several years my senior would be the one to drag me out of my depression, rescue me from my war with self-pity and guilt?

JULY 31.

Last night I slept up in Evelyn's bedroom. Evelyn did not want to make love; she wanted to talk. She talked and talked, deep into the night, mostly about her old lost loves.

It was painful to listen, to hear about all the boys and men she had been with over the years. I do not know what she was thinking. Did she really think I wanted to hear about all these ancient relationships? Perhaps a few details would have been nice to help me understand her better, a mention or two of one lover or another, but to go on and on, for hours—it bordered on sadistic.

After a while I stopped listening. I tuned her out. She is a strange woman, this Evelyn Richmond, but I think her apparent cruelties and insensitivities are nothing more than insecurity coupled with a deep-seated inferiority complex. And because I think she is basically a good and decent person, I can see my way clear of her inadequacies. I want to be near her.

Like me, Evelyn has been through her share of suffering. When still just a girl, not yet twenty years old, she lost her fiancé. She cried last night when she told me the story. I could see that more than two and a half decades later she is still strongly affected by his loss.

His death came suddenly and unexpectedly. They had gone to a movie. After the movie they had sat in her parents' kitchen eating ice cream and kissing and planning their wedding. No one wanted them to get married. Everyone said they were too young, that they should wait. But they wanted to go ahead anyway. They were in love, after all.

Around midnight, he left, after a long kiss on the back porch.

"I never saw him again," Evelyn told me. "Not alive." She had tears in her eyes. I wiped them away and waited for her to tell me what had happened.

"Less than a mile from our house. Some drunk ran a stop sign. He didn't even slow down. He smashed into the side of my fiancé's car. And that," she added, the tears now streaming down her face, "was that."

Yes, that was that.

AUGUST 1.

Today I told Evelyn about a lost love of my own. She asked and I answered. I could not bring myself to tell her about Ellen and Nicky, not yet, maybe not

ever, but I did manage to tell her about Karin. Karin
Dodd.

Karin Dodd was the first true love of my life. In
high school and during my first two years at college, I
had weathered a few crushes, brief infatuations that
rarely lasted more than a month or two. But I fell flat-
out in love with Karin Dodd the first time I saw her.
One look at her sitting across the aisle from me in that
Sex and Love in Literature course, and I was hooked.
She was tall and thin with long, dark hair and brown
eyes. She used to sit there in class with her chin resting
in the palm of her hand, her eyes wandering around
the room. An avid reader, she had already read most
of the books on the required reading list.

It was a week or more before I fetched up the nerve
to talk to her. Although actually, she talked to me first,
right in the middle of a lecture on Anaïs Nin. She
wanted to know if I had an extra pen. I immediately
handed her the one in my hand, the one that had been
busy scribbling notes just moments before. She thanked
me, then turned back to the lecturer, a dirty old man
who took great pleasure in reading aloud from the
most explicit sex scenes in all of literature.

I didn't take any more notes during that lecture. I
couldn't. I had no pen. Karin Dodd had my pen. My
only pen. Near the end of the hour she realized the
injustice she had unwittingly perpetrated upon me.
She invited me to come to her room after dinner and
copy her notes. Our first date.

We dated for almost two years. I feel quite sure we
would have married had she lived. It took me a long
time to get over her death. Years. I did not fully re-
cover until after I met Ellen.

Karin, I told Evelyn, was kind and pretty and

easygoing. She loved to smile and have a good time. Especially in bed. We did all kinds of things in bed. We studied, listened to music, giggled, told stories about the past (she cried when I told her about Russell), mused about the future. And, of course, we made love. I should probably protect Karin's memory by not offering too many details about our sexual adventures, but I do not think she would mind if I let it be known that she thoroughly enjoyed making love. Both of us entered our relationship having already lost our virginity, but the potent connection between us broke down any and all inhibitions. Together we discovered the great pleasures of physical contact.

I did not mention this to Evelyn, but once in a while Karin would play her cello for me naked. "You know, Sam," she would say as she placed that cello between her knees, "until recently very few women played the cello. It was considered most unladylike because of this rather promiscuous-looking playing position."

Then she would smile that wicked smile of hers and run the bow gently over the strings, driving me absolutely crazy.

Karin was an excellent cellist. Perhaps not up to Evelyn's standards, but quite talented nevertheless. She played with the college orchestra, as well as with several other ensembles. She used to travel quite often with these ensembles, almost every weekend. They would go to other schools and universities to give concerts and participate in competitions. Occasionally I went with her, but most of the time I stayed behind to fulfill commitments of my own. I had lacrosse and basketball and track.

On the day Karin died, she had only just returned from giving a concert down in Durham at the University of New Hampshire. Four of them had made that trip, a recently formed classical quartet, two males and two females, three violins and a cello.

Karin's death left me devastated. Her death taught me how incredibly tenuous and threadbare the notions of life and happiness can be.

It happened just a few weeks before graduation. She returned from Durham early in the afternoon. I asked her if she wanted to go out for a drive, maybe stop for a picnic. I told her I had some wine and cheese and crackers all packed and ready to go. At first she hesitated, insisting she had too much work to do: final exams to study for, papers to finish. But I urged her to take a brief afternoon respite from her labors. I painted a pleasant and romantic picture of a blanket spread in some green meadow strewn with wildflowers, the sun glistening off the Connecticut River in the distance, the two of us sipping wine and maybe sharing a kiss.

In no time at all, she relented.

Well, my idyllic painting, so carefree and well intentioned, very quickly turned into a terrible nightmare. Trouble that led to tragedy struck just minutes after we found the most tranquil setting in a grassy field not fifty feet from the river's edge. Karin spread the blanket. I opened the bottle and poured the wine. Karin offered a toast to graduation. We both drank.

And then, out of the sky, like a squadron of suicidal kamikaze pilots, a swarm of yellow jackets struck without warning. We must have spread our blanket either on or very near their nest, for their attack proved vicious. Three, four, five times they hit me with their stingers. I did my best to swat them away, to repel their attack. For maybe ten seconds I lost touch with Karin and her defensive tactics; no more than fifteen seconds at the very most. But enough time for her to stand and begin running in a full-fledged panic. Her screams quickly caught my attention.

Those yellow jackets gave chase. They easily swarmed around her as she tried to flee for safety. She screamed louder every time another one struck, leaving its deadly stinger behind.

"Help, Sam! Help me!" she cried. "I'm allergic!"

This last word instantly caught my attention. "What?"

Karin kept running, her arms flailing as she went. "Get my bag! Back in the car! There's a shot of adrenaline! Hurry!"

My God! Yes! She had told me. A year or more earlier. We had been sitting outside on the Dartmouth Green. Just sitting in the grass reading and talking on a beautiful spring day. A couple of honey bees flew by in a peaceful search for nectar. Karin immediately panicked. I could see the terror in her eyes.

"Get them!" she'd screamed. "Kill them!"

"What?"

I found out after I had driven the bees away that a yellow jacket bite as a kid had very nearly taken her life. She was extremely allergic to their venom.

Now a whole swarm of yellow jackets were buzzing around her head. I did not waste time. I sprinted back to the car, maybe a hundred yards away on the other side of that field. I covered the distance in a flash. On the front seat I found her purse. I dumped out the contents. I found nothing that looked like a shot of adrenaline. No syringe or pills whatsoever. Just a set of keys, some lipstick, a pack of gum, odds and ends. I threw the stuff back into the purse, grabbed it by the handle, and raced off to find Karin.

I found her on the ground just a few feet from the river. She must have tried to reach the water in an effort to escape those angry yellow jackets. I could see sting marks, red and swelling, on her face and neck and arms. She looked up at me, her eyes filled with fear.

I held out the purse. "It wasn't there!" I shouted. "I couldn't find it! What should I do?"

She grabbed the purse, turned it upside down, fumbled through the pile of personal items. She was already beginning to have trouble breathing. I could hear her gasping.

"I must confess," I told Evelyn, "it took me a few moments to act. I am not great in times of emergency. I freeze up, my mind goes numb."

But not all that much time passed, maybe a minute or even less, before I picked Karin off the ground, cradled her in my arms, and ran as fast as I could back to the car.

Her face had started to turn blue by the time I settled her as gently as possible across the backseat. She was barely getting any air at all. The poison from those yellow jacket stings had shut down her respiratory system. I did my best to force some of my air into her lungs. But at that time I had absolutely no first-aid training. I had no idea how to administer CPR or mouth-to-mouth resuscitation.

"Still," I added, "I did all that I could."

Evelyn nodded, squeezed my hand. "I'm sure you did, Sam."

"After another few seconds, I decided I had to get Karin to the hospital on the south side of town. I kissed her face and told her to just try and relax. Then I got behind the wheel and drove that car like a crazed maniac south along Route 10 and through the streets of Hanover."

I paused a moment then, took a deep breath. "But," I told Evelyn, "I was too late. By the time I reached the emergency room, Karin had stopped breathing. The doctor did everything he could to resuscitate her, but too much time had passed. Those damn yellow jackets had unmercifully taken Karin's life."

And a little piece of mine as well.

AUGUST 2.

Today was another warm, lovely, midsummer day. Evelyn and I quit all of our commiserating. We concentrated instead on making each other smile. We took the dogs for a walk along the Delaware. Sunshine and Moxie went swimming, and then Evelyn decided she wanted to go for a dip also. So we stripped off all the clothes we could while still remaining publicly decent, and then we waded into the water. I held Evelyn's hand so she would not stumble on the rocks. Once the water got deep enough, Evelyn wanted me to let go. She dove under, utterly fearless, then came up and floated on her back. The sun illuminated her face as she drifted slowly downstream in the gentle current.

I followed her. The dogs followed me. After we had drifted maybe a quarter of a mile, I silently swam over to Evelyn and kissed her on the mouth. Momentarily startled, she quickly recovered. She grabbed my shoulders and pushed my head beneath the surface. When I came up for air, she whispered in my ear, "Fuck me, Sam. I want you to fuck me right out here on the river."

I think I might have blushed. "I don't think I can do that, Evelyn. There's a bridge practically right over our heads. And there's a bunch of kids playing over on the riverbank."

She grabbed my crotch and squeezed. "I don't give a damn about them!" she announced. "Let them look the other way."

Well, we did not make love out there on the Delaware. We came close, but we stopped just short of actually removing our final bits of clothing. No, like good little girls and boys, we waited. We waited until we got home. And when we got home, we made a beeline for the music room, where we ripped off shirts and shorts and made lustful love right smack in the middle of that Oriental carpet. I spent most of the time on the bottom of the pile. I know because those coarse wool fibers rubbed practically raw the skin on the small of my back.

A small price to pay.

Yes, Evelyn and I had a very pleasant day for ourselves. With only one small glitch at the very end. But I do not want to talk about that right now. It's late and Evelyn wants to go to bed. She has to get an early start on the day tomorrow.

AUGUST 3.

The glitch is this: Roger. Young Richmond has changed his tune. He no longer wants to go to deepest, darkest Africa and hunt wild, probably endangered beasts with his dear old dad, Mr. Beauregard Richmond, the former husband of my sweet Evelyn. No, Roger has decided he wants to come home and be with his mommy.

"Roger's adrift," Evelyn told me late last evening

after a lengthy conversation with her son. "He needs direction. He does not know what he wants."

Evelyn never would have admitted it, but Roger's aimlessness gave her a certain maternal pleasure, made her feel necessary and useful.

"He's just young," I said. "We're all adrift at that age."

"Yes," she agreed. "But I think it's important I spend time with him, show him how much I love him."

"Of course," I said. But I was immediately vexed. And probably just a little bit jealous as well.

"I was away quite often when he was young," she continued. "On tour. Playing the cello all over the world. No doubt he often felt abandoned."

"No doubt."

"I need to make it up to him. I have a trip or two planned."

"A trip or two?"

"Yes. It will give us an opportunity to get reacquainted."

A jolt of anxiety ripped through my body. I did not want her to go away. We were just beginning to settle in together. Yes, I admit it, I wanted her to stay, or at least invite me along on this family sojourn.

But that was not her plan. The next thing she uttered was this: "I would rather, Sam, if Roger did not know about us."

I needed a moment to let this settle. "You'd rather if Roger did not know what about us?"

"Sam."

"No, really," I demanded, my voice ever so slightly agitated, "what?"

The blind have an advantage at times like this. They do not have to look at our eyes.

Not that Evelyn Richmond needs any artificial advantages.

"Roger is very vulnerable right now. I do not want him to know," she said, with perfect pitch, "that you and I are lovers."

There it was, laid bare, wide open, no beating the burning bushes to find the hidden meaning in that one.

Perceptive, as well as confident, Evelyn noted the tension that instantly filled the air. "At least not yet, Sam. Not right away. In time we can tell him."

Yes, dear Evelyn, thank you so much for that small crumb, that tiny morsel to help me with my self-esteem. Much appreciated.

AUGUST 4.

So now the prodigal son has returned and I have been relegated to my distant post out here in the cottage. It was not stated in any formal way, but Evelyn made it quite clear that I am not to venture over to the big house unless invited.

I remain here, sulking, I suppose. I watch them come and go, Mama and her boy, smiling and laughing and sharing their own private thoughts.

I remember as Nicky got older—six, seven, eight years old—I used to catch him and Ellen sharing those private thoughts, those intimate moments. It always made me slightly uneasy, just mildly jealous.

One night I mentioned this to Ellen.

She laughed in my face. "Don't be ridiculous, Sam. Every relationship of any value has those private thoughts and intimate moments. Without them you have nothing but a facade, a casual acquaintance."

I feel sure Evelyn would tell me more or less the same thing.

AUGUST 5.

Evelyn came over this evening right after I arrived home from work. It seems Roger has gone off somewhere to see someone. I did my best to act formal and standoffish. To seize control of the situation.

Evelyn saw right through my passive-aggressive behavior. "We only have an hour, Sam. Do you want to stand around being mad and feeling sorry for yourself, or do you want to make love to me?"

I made love to her all right. I hate to say this, it is a phrase I have used only rarely in my life, but I believe it applies to what took place earlier in the bedroom: I fucked Evelyn. I fucked her fast and furiously.

And with maybe a touch of vengeance. But she did not seem to mind. In fact, I think she rather enjoyed it.

While she dressed, she gave me their upcoming itinerary. "We're leaving for Charleston in the morning. Then up to Williamsburg and Washington. We'll be gone ten days to two weeks."

"Ten days to two weeks!" My heart sank. "That's a long time. I was hoping you could go up to Maine with me at the end of next week."

"Maine? I love Maine. What's up in Maine?"

I told her about the annual Adams family reunion.

"That's so sweet of you to invite me, Sam. But the invitation comes rather late in the day. I'm afraid we'll have to do it another time."

I sighed. I should have invited her weeks ago. "So you figure to be gone about two weeks?"

"Maybe less, depending upon who we run into."

"Who you run into?"

"Yes. Friends. Family."

Jealousy clawed at me. I did my best to subdue it. "I wish I was going with you."

"I do, too, Sam," she said, with no great enthusiasm. "Maybe next time we can all go."

"Right," I said, needing the last word, "maybe next time."

AUGUST 6.

Evelyn just left, just a few hours ago, and already I miss her. Ten days seems like an eternity. Two weeks a death sentence. Strange, I know, to be thinking like this, but I have grown very fond of Evelyn. I need her closeness.

But maybe this separation has a positive side. I have piles of manuscripts demanding my attention. All the time Evelyn and I have been spending together has definitely taken its toll on my editorial output.

I wonder if she will call?

She won't call.

Maybe she will.

The reality is this: we need other human beings. Without other human beings to touch us and care for us and love us, we may as well be dead.

I do not want to be dead.

Not anymore.

A year ago, yes. Six months ago, perhaps. But definitely not anymore.

At least she could have left me a telephone number, somewhere to reach her in case of emergency.

AUGUST 7.

I am writing on the train again. On my way home from work. I am writing now because when I get home, I have other things to do. I want to walk the dogs and go bike riding. I might even try to make that Wednesday night ride over at the bike shop this week.

Let me see. What would I like to write about this evening? I don't know. I'm not sure. My mind is a blank. I think I will just sit here and stare out the window.

Maybe tomorrow night something will come to me.

AUGUST 8.

I did not set out in life to become an editor. No, I set out to become a writer, an author, a novelist. From a very early age our father read aloud to us from Twain and Hawthorne and Melville. By the time I became a teenager, I wanted nothing less than to pen the Great American Novel.

On my own I discovered Kipling and Conrad and Hemingway. I decided I was destined to write adventure stories of faraway places. It must have been in the seventh or eighth grade that I resolved to become a wanderer and an adventurer, a combination of Kipling and Conrad and Hemingway all rolled into one. I even ran away a few times during those formative years, never for more than a day or two, and rarely did I get more than ten miles from home, but they were terrifying and exhilarating excursions into the unknown nevertheless.

My father reprimanded me for these unannounced disappearances, but he did so in a lukewarm way. He

secretly enjoyed knowing his boy both needed and
wanted to uncover the wild mysteries of the universe.
My father wholeheartedly endorsed my ambition to
become a writer. He believed literature was the absolute pinnacle of civilization.

Later, my admission to Dartmouth secured, I took a
semester off between high school and college. I worked
over the summer to earn some money, then I set off
across America to see what I might find. I hitchhiked
from New Hampshire to New Orleans to San Francisco and back again. I arrived back in Hanover the
day before Christmas: broke and dirty and scrawny, but
absolutely alive with all I had seen and done.

All through college I packed my bags and headed
off in search of adventure every chance I got: between
semesters, on spring break, during summer vacation.
Give me a few bucks and a few free days and I would
be off to somewhere to see someone or something.

Then, of course, I met and fell in love with Karin.
Our relationship caused me to slow down, to take a
long, leisurely look at my local surroundings.

But after she died and I graduated, I set off again. I
traveled farther and stayed away longer than ever before. I needed to put as much time and distance between myself and Karin's death as possible. I traveled
across Canada. I went south to Mexico and Central
America. Later I tried Brazil and Peru and Argentina. I
made my way to the South Seas: Hawaii. Australia.
New Zealand. I crisscrossed Europe: France. Italy.
Czechoslovakia. Germany. Poland. By train. By bus. By
boat. Even on foot.

I was often sick and hungry and lonely. I rarely had
more than a few dollars in my pocket. But I thrived in

this environment. It was, I believed, the price I had to pay for literary greatness.

It was not, in the end, the difficulties and the discomforts that finally forced me off the road. No, it was something far more profound. The realization did not come all at once but, rather, over many months in many different ports. It slowly but surely dawned on me that millions of others were already out there doing what I was doing. This cheapened and deadened the thrill of adventure. It was true: countless others wanted to be the next Kipling-Conrad-Hemingway also. I was not the only one. Far from it, in fact. No matter where I went, I found them. Americans roamed the globe far and wide in their khaki-colored safari wear. I met them in Auckland, Amsterdam, Berlin, Belize City, Ottawa, and Oslo. Everywhere I went, they had already arrived.

I decided to stay home.

AUGUST 9.

I went back to Hanover for a few months, but that didn't work out. I enjoyed seeing my family, just not every day.

So I headed for Cape Cod. I had a good friend there, and I wanted to live and write near the water.

I got a job at the Orleans Bar & Grill. And then, as I have already recounted in some detail, I began work on my novel, *Inside Out*.

Several months later, I met Ellen Reynolds. We married and had a son, and I figured we would live happily ever after.

Ellen and Nicky and I settled easily into our new life in the suburbs.

I took a keen interest in all those jobs I used to loathe and tried to avoid as a kid: lawn mowing, leaf raking, snow shoveling, gutter cleaning. On weekends I spent almost every waking hour working to maintain order on my half-acre plot of manicured turf. I understood the absurdity and the utter futility of my efforts, but that did not slow me down for a minute. Every Saturday and Sunday I mowed and raked and weeded and pruned and trimmed my little patch of nature. I even spread lime in the late autumn. My neighbors would often stop to chat. They would praise me for the lushness of my lawn, the brilliance of my roses, the tidiness of my flower beds.

Like my father before me, I took pride in my work.

Only after my wife and son tragically died at the hands of the creature in room 14 of Sloan's Motel did I cease my landscaping labors. After they perished, I did not even bother to mow the grass. For weeks I rarely even went outside. I just sat in front of the window and watched my half-acre plot run wild. It did not take long: one season of neglect. Nature imposes its own form of order quickly and without mercy.

From the front window I would sometimes see my neighbors stroll by. They would cast a glance upon my plot, then shake their heads. At first I thought their reactions were a sign of sympathy for what had happened to me and mine, but soon I realized they were simply irked and irritated over the no longer fastidious condition of my yard. I was giving the neighborhood a shabby appearance. I was no doubt causing real estate values to plummet.

<hr>

AUGUST 11.

I called my mother today from the office. I told her I would not be able to make it to the family reunion. She was disappointed and upset, but I told her I simply had too much work and not enough time.

"So bring your work to Maine," she suggested. "I'm sure you can find some time each day to get some things done."

"I really need to be in the office."

It was true: I did. I have more projects going on right now than I have ever had before. But of course, I did not tell my mother the whole story. I could have gotten away, at least for a few days. But Evelyn will no doubt be returning soon, and I do not want to be leaving just as she is arriving. I miss her and would like to spend some time with her. She has been gone now about a week. I suspect she will be back before long.

"Well," lamented my mother, "we'll miss you."

"I'll miss you, too."

<hr>

AUGUST 12.

One of the first things Ellen and I did after leaving the city and moving to the suburbs was purchase an automobile. In New York we had not needed a car; it would have been a nuisance. But a family cannot exist in the suburbs without wheels. Our first car was some kind of Honda, used. It was all we could afford.

The down payment on the house had sucked all our savings right out of our Citibank account.

That Honda was a good, dependable car. In the morning it hauled Ellen and me to the train station, where it sat patiently for the next ten or twelve hours waiting to haul us home.

It took us about an hour to get from our house to the office. First we rode in the Honda, then we rode the train, then we rode the subway up to Rockefeller Center. For more than two years Ellen and I made this daily two-way journey together. We enjoyed it, most of the time. It gave us an hour in the morning and an hour in the evening without Nicky or the telephone or a neighbor or a business associate interrupting. In the morning we would often use that hour to plan our day or the upcoming weekend. Some mornings Ellen would nap against my shoulder while I read a few chapters of a new manuscript. I always had a manuscript close by my side.

And in the evening we would usually moan and groan for a while about all the prima donnas we'd been forced to deal with that day, then we would laugh, maybe share a beer or an ice cream cone. We would use the ride home to just let the tension wash down our bodies and out our toes.

We had good times riding the train together. The train was like our sanctuary against a world turned stressful and chaotic.

And then we bought another car. Our first minivan. A huge mistake.

AUGUST 13.

I was the one who first brought up the idea of a second car. We were in a cab riding from the gas station to the train station. We had already missed our usual train because the Honda had broken down, just a bad alternator or some such thing, but enough to leave us stranded.

"Maybe it's time we got another car."

"We don't need two cars, Sam."

"I don't know. I think we might."

"When? Why?"

I shrugged. "There's plenty of times on weekends when I'm at the lumber yard or the hardware and you need to go shopping or take Nicky somewhere."

"We manage."

"I thought maybe we could get something bigger, like a station wagon."

"A station wagon?"

"Something we could take on vacation. Maybe go camping. We have a lot of gear now with Nicky and Sunshine and—"

"I can see you've been thinking about this."

She was right. I had.

So we went ahead and did it. Not a station wagon but a brand-new minivan, fully equipped with air-conditioning, cruise control, AM-FM stereo cassette, power seats, power door locks, power mirrors, the whole shebang.

The new minivan changed everything.

AUGUST 14

What I said yesterday is probably an exaggeration. Minivans do not change everything; people do.

It was not long after we became a two-car family that Ellen and I began driving separately to the train station in the morning: her in the minivan and me in the Honda. (She only agreed to the purchase of the minivan after I agreed that it would be her car.)

At first we only went in separate cars if, say, I needed to catch an earlier train because of an early meeting. But little by little, day by day, month by month, we started taking both cars even when we caught the same train.

"I need to go to the grocery after work."

"I need to stop at the dry cleaners."

"I need to take Nicky to baseball practice."

"Then maybe we should take both cars."

"Right. I think we should."

That kind of thing. Little things. The kinds of things that can slowly but surely set a marriage adrift, erode the bonds that bind us.

AUGUST 15.

Then the head of the marketing department quit to take a more lucrative offer at another publishing house, and Ellen got promoted to the top spot. And not just because she was the niece of Mr. Stephen Reynolds, either; no, Ellen got the top spot because she was creative, innovative, and extremely hardworking. She deserved the top spot.

The promotion meant more money. It also meant more hours. She had to go into the office earlier and she usually got home later. Out of the ten train trips per week, we suddenly did not make more than two or three of them together. And we rarely, if ever, saw one another during the workday. Maybe once a month we found the time to share a quick lunch, usually at her desk between phone calls.

No doubt feeling nostalgic for our younger and more carefree days, I would occasionally complain about the subtle changes taking place in our lives.

"Most couples, Sam," Ellen would respond, "say good-bye in the morning, and then don't see each other again until that night."

She had a point, but somehow I still felt off-kilter. It is difficult to describe, but I felt something slipping anyway. Something vital and emotional.

And I also felt that our son, who spent more time with his baby-sitter than he did with his parents, was being neglected more than ever by his mother.

When I finally found the nerve to mention this particular concern to Ellen, she replied by asking, "Then why don't you stay home?"

"What? How would I manage that?"

"You could stay home one or two days a week, Sam. More and more editors are working at home. If you planned your time wisely, you could probably get by with three days a week in the city."

She was right, of course, I probably could.

I thought it over for a week or two. I weighed the pros and cons: I might miss out on some of the action at the office, but at home I would probably get more work done. It is virtually impossible to edit in my office. People stop by to chat, the phone rings, one interruption after another. So I decided to give it a try. I would do it for Nicky. He was, after all, my only son, my flesh and blood. And he would not be a boy for long. Before I knew it, he would be a man.

I presented the idea to Jed Barton. He thought it over for a day or two, then gave me the okay.

So I set up a small office upstairs in the spare bedroom. I bought a fax machine and a copier and a computer. And on Mondays and Fridays I started working at home.

It worked out great.

For a while.

I soon realized Ellen was working even longer hours than ever, and that I was suddenly being inundated with most of the domestic duties: cleaning, shopping, cooking, hauling the kid all over creation.

It got to the point where Ellen would actually become annoyed if I did not have dinner ready when she got home from the office. She did not have the nerve to say anything, but I could see the annoyance on her face, read the agitation in her eyes and on her lips. Same thing if she went for the milk in the morning and found the carton empty. Or if she discovered her precious undergarments lying wrinkled and unfolded in the clothes dryer.

I suppose, if you give women half a chance, they can act a heck of a lot like men.

AUGUST 16.

And then there was the travel.

Yes, just like Evelyn, Ellen did her share of traveling. More and more, as time went on.

Which reminds me: what has become of Evelyn? It has been well over a week since she left, but I have not heard a single word from her. She does not call, she does not write, she does not return.

I would merely suggest that this is a pretty crummy way to treat your lover. A simple telephone call does not seem too much to ask.

AUGUST 17.

Lo and behold, as if she had read my mind, the Great Cellist finally returned home late last night. I did not see her, except from a distance.

I have not seen her today, either. But I did run into son Roger an hour or so ago out in the driveway.

"Hello, Roger."

"Hi . . ." He hesitated, unable to remember my name.

"Sam."

"Right. Sam."

"So," I asked him, "how was your trip?"

He needed a few seconds to decide. "You know, okay. Played some golf, did some sailing, cruised for babes."

I felt a very faint impulse to knee him in the groin and leave him writhing there on the asphalt. Of course, I did no such thing. "Sounds like a good time."

"Yeah." He seemed anxious, as though he might be late for an appointment with his stockbroker or his marijuana salesman.

"So, how's your mother?"

His eyes wandering, he answered, "She's good. You know."

He wanted to get away, but I had another question or two. "Did she have a good time? On your trip?"

This made Roger laugh. Well, maybe not quite a laugh, more like his own private little snicker. "Mother? A good time? Hell, I guess she had a good time. It's always tough to tell with her. If she does have a good time, it's usually at someone else's expense."

I wondered what he meant, but I laughed politely, as if I too was in on his little joke.

I said so long to Roger then, let him go about his business. I could feel him chafing at the bit.

AUGUST 18.

I spent the afternoon and part of the evening with Evelyn. Roger was off in the city visiting with some old school chums, probably partaking of illegal substances and women who reduce the size of your billfold.

We rendezvoused in Evelyn's bedroom. I could not resist playing the martyr's role: cool and detached. After a brief kiss, I said, "I saw Roger yesterday. He told me you had a good time."

"We did, yes," replied Evelyn. "A very pleasant time." Then, "I think the trip did him a lot of good."

I took a step back. "That's nice."

She ignored my pettiness. "What I enjoyed most was the movement, the coming and going, the arriving and departing. I love to travel. I could stay on the road ten months a year."

I heard the words coming out of her mouth, but I had my own agenda. "You could have called."

She hesitated a moment, then, "Oh, Sam, I wanted to, but . . . well, it would have been so . . . so unsatisfying. More like a tease than a release."

"Still, I would have appreciated it." Then, in self-defense, I added, "Knowing you were all right."

Evelyn sighed. "Oh, Sam, believe me, I'm always all right. I am not someone you need to worry about. Worry about the starving masses, but not me." Then she reached out, found my arm, and drew me close.

I wanted to reject her, push her away for her insensitivity, but physical desire took control after the long absence.

We had most of our clothes off when a rush of apprehension washed over me. No doubt that apprehension had some venom mixed in with it also.

I suddenly ceased my kisses. I sat bolt upright.

"Sam! What is it?"

"I don't know. . . . I just . . . I hate to . . . but . . . but . . ."

"What, Sam? What's the matter?"

"It's just that, well, there's so much . . . so much disease around today."

"Disease?"

"Well, AIDS."

"AIDS!?"

"Yes, you know, autoimmune—"

"Good God, Sam, I know what it is! What are you telling me? That you have AIDS?"

What was that? In her voice? In her expression? Fear? Maybe even a touch of terror?

Yes, fear. Real fear. Fear and terror. Finally I had scared Evelyn half to death. I thought about pushing the emotion, making her fret a while longer for remaining incommunicado over an entire fortnight.

But once empowered, I backed off. "No, of course I don't have AIDS. It was more, well . . . I was wondering—"

Evelyn caught my drift, recovered quickly. She laughed in my face. The same way Ellen used to.

"Oh," she said, "I see where this is going. You thought maybe I had stumbled upon a friendly little case of AIDS while off touring with my son. Nice, Sam. Very refreshing to know you trust me so."

"No, I didn't mean . . . it's just that—"

"Give me a break, Sam. You've been stewing ever since I left, worrying about me out there screwing anything and everything that moves."

I felt my power slipping away. "No, I—"

"I swear to God," she added, "men are such belligerent hypocrites. You are willing to stick your wands in any old hole, but when a woman spreads her legs, it's suddenly a felony. Well I've got news for you, Sammy Boy, this old girl's had her share of lovers, true enough, but one at a time, son, one lover at a time. That's the only way it works for me. Now do you want to fight with me or do you want to fuck me? Your choice. I can be stimulated either way."

AUGUST 19.

Evelyn is leaving again. She told me last night. She is leaving tomorrow morning. She and Roger are headed for the West Coast: San Francisco. Roger starts school at Stanford in the fall, and I guess she wants to get him settled. She will not be back till Labor Day.

We spent a few hours together this afternoon. Young Roger went off to get himself a haircut.

After we made love, I asked, "Why don't we just tell him?"

"I don't think so" was her response.

"Why not?"

She sighed and said, "He's still feeling rather insecure about things. I don't want to upset him. But soon, Sam. We'll tell him soon."

I had my doubts about that. Serious doubts. But I chose to ignore the alarms going off in my head. I needed to feel Evelyn's warm and naked body close against my own.

The sexual urge rules the world.

AUGUST 20.

They left this morning just after dawn.

Evelyn told me yesterday that she can sense the dawn. She cannot actually see it, but the brightness somehow reaches her brain and gives her a sensation of light.

I suppose it is something only a blind person can fully comprehend.

I think a lot lately about being blind, immersed in darkness, unable to see my own fingers, my own toes, my own face, my lover's face, my lover's eyes, the sun, the moon, the stars.

Something else Evelyn said to me yesterday after we had made love: "You know, Sam, I think, in some strange emotional way, you're glad I cannot see."

"What? That's not true."

"Oh, I think it is. I mean, I know you don't wish blindness on me, but it is just fine with you that I am blind."

"That's absurd, Evelyn. I don't wish that at all. Why would I want you to be blind?"

If you don't want to know, don't ask.

Evelyn shrugged. "I'm not exactly sure, Sam. I can tell by running my fingertips across your face and over your body that you are an attractive man. Friends of mine who have seen you tell me you are quite handsome. 'A knockout,' the woman from the inn across the river called you."

"Who? The lesbian?"

"Oh, Sam. Don't be ugly."

"Okay, then what's the reason? Why would I want you to be blind?"

She thought about it long enough that I thought she would not answer. But then, finally, "I can only guess that you must be hiding from something."

I wanted to again call her insinuations absurd, ridiculous, ludicrous even. But instead, I kissed her on the mouth. I kissed her neck and licked her ears. I did my best to arouse her for a second go-around. It didn't take long. Evelyn quickly succumbed to my advances. She enjoys sex more than any woman I have ever known.

AUGUST 23.

I have not written a word in three days. I needed a break from the pen and paper routine. Also, I have been spending large amounts of time at the office trying to catch up with my work. I have decided I will probably never catch up. It will simply stay a step or two ahead of me for the rest of my working days. On the day I retire I will still have a mountain of unread manuscripts sitting on my desk.

Also I have not written because we are in the middle of a pretty rough heat wave; it hit one hundred degrees yesterday and never went below ninety degrees all night long.

I finally had to go out and buy an air conditioner. Not so much for me, but for Sunshine and Moxie. Those poor mutts with their long golden coats suffer in this kind of heat. Now that the cottage is air-conditioned, I have to practically shove them out the door. I'll be glad when it cools off again. I like warm weather but this is too much even for me.

Several days ago I made an important decision. I have been thinking about it for months, and now I have decided to do it. I am going to put the house on the market. I do not know exactly when. Maybe in the fall.

Not only is it a waste of money to keep paying the mortgage, but I know now I can never live in that house again. Not without them. Not without Ellen and Nicholas.

I rarely go over there anyway. I used to stop by once a week or so. Now I go maybe once a month. Usually I go to pick up something; a suit or a pair of shoes or a book or some piece of kitchen equipment. Little by little I have brought over here everything I need.

So the time has come to sell. I do not know what I will do after I sell. For a while I am sure I will continue to live here. Who knows? Perhaps I will move in with Evelyn. We will have to see how things go. I could always move back into the city, though I doubt I could handle living in there again. It grows more desperate and violent with each passing day.

No, if I am honest about it, I would prefer to stay here at Blind Pass. I like it here. It is safe and secure. The dogs have room to roam. There is no need to lock the door or even take the key out of the car. Yes, it would be nice to stay here with Evelyn. Making love and listening to her play the cello. I only wish she would not go away so often.

AUGUST 24.

More heat. Killer heat. The newsman on TV this evening said the heat wave had claimed the lives of six people in New York City. And that does not include the increased number of homicides indirectly attributable to the weather.

I have lived in Manhattan. The Big Apple. The Rotten Apple. I know what this kind of heat does to people. It makes them mean and wild and crazy. They will shoot you, break your legs, kick your head in if you so much as look at them the wrong way.

AUGUST 25.

Ten days till Labor Day. Maybe eleven.

School days are nearly upon us.

I wish I was going back to school.

When I was in school, I hated going back, dreaded the end of summer vacation, but now I wish I was twelve years old again and getting ready for the sixth grade.

I had Mrs. Hirsch in the sixth grade. She was tall and slender with long blond hair. I used to sit at my desk in the back of the room and stare at her for hours without hearing a word she said about square roots or Jack London or the War of 1812. I used to get an erection staring at Mrs. Hirsch. Once, right in the middle of social studies, I came right in my Fruit of the Looms.

It scared the heck out of me. But I also enjoyed it.
I soon began to masturbate.
A boy and his hormones.

AUGUST 26.

I had a productive day today at work. I got quite a lot
done. I even slipped out of the office a little early so I
could get back here and go for a bike ride. I took the
dogs with me. They needed a good run. We went out
along the old canal path. I rode and they ran. Moxie,
the younger one, kept up, but Sunshine kept falling behind. She's getting older now, starting to show a little
gray around her muzzle. I do not like to think about
Sunshine growing old. It seems such a short time ago
that Ellen and I brought home that tiny furry puppy.

Now we have all eaten and settled down for the
night. It would be nice if the phone rang. If Evelyn
would humble herself to give me a call. But she won't.
I know she won't. She won't call. She won't write.
She'll just come floating in here in a week or so, all
smiles and seduction, and right away she'll want me
to make love to her.

And, of course, I will. I will do exactly what she
wants.

AUGUST 27.

I have a confession to make. Two confessions actually.

The first is this: I have been watching television.
Mostly late at night when I cannot sleep, but other
times as well. I will watch practically anything: News.

Sports. Documentaries. Weather. Sitcoms. Old movies. New movies. Bad movies. Talk shows. Nature shows. Any shows at all.

But I have recently become obsessed with one particular genre: the afternoon soap opera. I cannot watch my favorite soap during its regular broadcast time, so I tape the show on my VCR and watch it at night. I first heard about *Moonlight Love* from my assistant, Mitchell. He is a big fan. So is Elaine, the assistant who works next to Mitchell. Every day I used to hear them discussing the latest intrigue on this show called *Moonlight Love*. They were obsessed by it. I would make fun of them. But soon enough I found out that half the people in the office were taping the show and watching it at night. The other half may have been watching it also but were simply not willing to admit it. I tuned in one rainy afternoon a few weeks ago, and I quickly became a clandestine viewer. One or two episodes and I was hooked. In no time at all I became like a junkie who needs his daily dose of melodrama.

Which brings me to my second confession. This evening, a couple of hours ago, around nine or nine-thirty, after I had set aside a manuscript, I rewound the tape and turned on the tube. But tonight, I must admit, I reached the end of my soap opera rope. No, it was not just the insidious story lines, the convoluted plots, the absurd characters playing out their ridiculous make-believe lives; it was more than that.

It was the way they killed off Monique, the sweet and beautiful young social worker who helped the homeless and the downtrodden and never had a bad thing to say about anyone, not even Daphne, the wicked wench who plotted incessantly against her rival.

The writers killed off Monique suddenly and

violently. She was attacked and raped, then murdered by gang members while delivering food to an inner city homeless center.

I was appalled. So appalled I jumped out of my chair and headed for the set. I marched right up to it and put my right leg into motion. Thank God I had my shoes on because I slammed my foot into the television screen with all the power I could muster. The glass did not give but the set fell back off the table and landed in a heap on the floor. The picture continued to flicker. A commercial this time. First, one for female douche. Then one for some disposable baby diaper.

Antacid.

Constipation.

Aches and pains.

I turned away and located the broom. I picked it up and marched back to the fallen television. Without a second's hesitation I began to smash the handle of the broom against the TV screen. It took some time but I finally caused a crack. Then another crack. And another. I kept raising the broom high up over my head and bringing it down hard against the screen. Before long the glass shattered, gave way completely. Sparks and electrical energy flew around the room. First the image died. Then the sound.

The TV was dead, stone dead.

I thought about taking it out in the yard and burying it, but instead, I shoved it back into the closet where it belongs.

AUGUST 28.

Do I see the irony in my actions?

　The terrible irony.

　I suppose.

　Let me put it this way: I did not get much shut-eye last night.

　I wish I could say that when I peered into the closet this evening I found my television set whole and healthy and ready for some prime-time viewing, but, alas, I cannot.

　Brought to my knees by a soap opera.

　My God, what next?

　Actually, I am glad I busted the television. Watching the damn thing is such a miserable waste of time. Now I will not even be tempted.

AUGUST 30.

The end of August. The days are growing shorter. That high summer light has begun to wane.

　I am not at all sure I can stand the slow, methodical onslaught of another winter.

　What is the alternative?

　I could hit the road.

　For where?

　I don't know. Maybe the South Seas.

　You've already been there.

　So I have, so I have.

　But maybe Evelyn has not. Maybe she would like to go. She said she loves to travel. We could go together.

　I really do need to get away. Do some traveling.

Editing these manuscripts has recently become an incredible strain. And all the rest of it.

Maybe I should think about taking some time off and writing another novel. I know so much more than I did as a younger man. My experiences are far more varied and intense. I could hit the road, find some wide open spaces, open my eyes, do some scribbling.

It would do me good.

But first I need to sell the house. In fact, I have several things I would need to take care of before I could just pack up and take off. Evelyn, for instance. Would she stay here or go with me? We will have to talk about all this. Soon. As soon as she gets home.

AUGUST 31.

I did it. I made the first move. I drove over to the old homestead this morning, parked out on the street, and stared at the house that used to be our home. The home of Sam and Ellen and Nicholas Adams.

After sitting there for half an hour or so, memories exploding left and right out of my brain, I decided to go ahead and sell.

I drove into town and stopped at the first real estate office I could find. I went inside and did the contract thing with the realtor, some slightly overweight middle-aged divorcée who had not worked in twenty years and now was trying to make a living pedaling other people's property while raising her two teenage sons. She told me all this in one long breath. Finally she slowed long enough to take down some information.

Along the way she asked, "So, Mr. Adams, are you moving on or moving up?"

"I'm just moving," I told her.

"I see." She gave me a big smile. With lips painted blood red. "Just looking for a change?"

"No," I said. "My wife had her brains beaten in by some lunatic and I don't want to live alone in our house anymore."

I didn't really say this. I was far more polite about it. I said, "My wife died last year. The house holds too many memories."

She looked at me with a sad set of eyes. "Oh, yes, I imagine it would. I'm so very sorry for your loss." She showed her deep and sincere respect for my pain and suffering by remaining silent for a full thirty seconds while jotting down the rest of the information on my real estate contract. And then, "I gather you would like to price your home to sell."

How perceptive. "I would, yes."

"Excellent choice. So many people today want so much more for their homes than the market will bear. Price your property competitively and it'll sell in a flash. That's what I tell all my clients."

I nodded and signed my name wherever her blood-red fingernail pointed. Then I thanked her and got out of there lickety-split.

SEPTEMBER 1.

September. I can hardly believe it. The first of June was just a week or two ago. Incredible as we get older how the days and weeks and months so rapidly slip away.

Just a few more days until Evelyn's return. I am very much looking forward to seeing her, putting my arms around her waist, my lips upon her lips. I will be glad when she returns from her travels.

SEPTEMBER 2.

Evelyn and her traveling. Ellen and her traveling. Her business trips. They soon became a problem.

Jackson, Jones & Reynolds had a West Coast office. In Los Angeles. I use the past tense, but that office still exists. Ellen may be gone, countless others may have quit and died and retired, but the company, powerful and omnipotent, persists, casting books and films and periodicals to a weary and entertainment-saturated public.

But that West Coast office had a very personal and profound impact on me, on my marriage. To put it bluntly: that office, along with Ellen's frequent-flyer miles, really started to get on my nerves. After a while I found it very difficult to suppress my feelings.

"You're practically a bicoastalite," I told her one night while she hovered between the bed and the bureau filling her suitcase with silk undies and various colored pantyhose.

"Easy, Sam."

"Oh, I'm easy, Ellen. Plenty easy."

"Let's not fight, Sam."

I ignored her, cast another fly. "I've been thinking. Maybe we should buy a little condo out in Malibu. Right on the beach. We might as well. You spend half your life out there."

She took the bait. "I don't spend half my life out there. I spend three days and two nights in L.A. every other week. And once we get this new marketing strategy into full swing, I'll probably cut the trips down to once a month."

Her account was accurate, but did not include the occasional trips to our other important markets: Dallas, Chicago, Miami, London.

Besides, I was in a mood to rumble.

"Once a week, once a month, what's the difference? You're away far too much. Your son is only going to be a boy once, Ellen. One time and then his childhood will be gone. He'll be gone. He'll vanish into thin air. You'll wake up in some hotel room somewhere and he'll be a man and you won't know what happened to him."

She dropped some accessory items into her bag: scarves and belts and those turquoise earrings I'd given her for Christmas. "Your concern for Nicholas is admirable and touching, Sam, but don't you think you might be exaggerating a tiny little bit?"

"Exaggerating? No, I don't think I'm exaggerating."

"I do."

"I don't."

"I do."

"Well I don't, dammit."

She looked at me, shook her head, and sighed. "This isn't about Nicky, is it, Sam? This is about you. You're feeling neglected and abandoned. It's perfectly natural."

"Don't hand me the pop psychology crap, honey."

"And why not, Sam?"

"Because I don't want to hear it."

"Of course you don't. It's too close to the truth."

"Bullshit."

"It's not bullshit, Sam. You only think it's bullshit

because, unfortunately, you often interpret your feelings as a sign of weakness. And you can't stand weakness. In yourself or in others."

"You're such a know-it-all, Ellen. Never in my life have I known anyone who knows everything the way you do. It's such a comfort to be your husband."

Then, before she could muster a reply, I threw her an evil eye, marched across the bedroom, and slammed the door on my way out.

I slept on the sofa that night. At least I tried to sleep. Mostly I lay there waiting for Ellen to come and make things right.

But she didn't come. In the back of my mind I knew she wouldn't come. Ellen did not tolerate fools. And I, of course, had acted like an utter fool.

She was absolutely right. I did feel neglected and abandoned. My mother had abandoned me when I was a boy, and I could not stand seeing my wife, my anchor, the mother of my son, packing her bags every week and deserting her family. It made me pretty upset.

SEPTEMBER 3.

I lay awake on the sofa all that night thinking about Ellen and how much I loved her. But because I can occasionally be quite stupid and incredibly stubborn, I did not go upstairs, cuddle up beside her, and tell her how I felt. No, instead, I held my ground, guarded my turf.

Finally, in the morning, just before dawn, I heard her get up, shower, and dress. I heard her go into Nicky's room and kiss him good-bye. I heard her come downstairs, set her bag by the front door, and enter the living room. I could feel her eyes on me, but I pretended to be fast asleep. I wanted . . . no, I needed her to make the opening move.

She stood there for at least a minute. Watching. Waiting. Giving me every opportunity to stand up and act like a man. But I did not move a muscle. I was too damn bullheaded. Maybe too afraid. Too ashamed.

Then I heard her sigh as she swept past the sofa on her way to the kitchen. She opened the refrigerator and poured herself a glass of juice. I heard her go back upstairs and into the bathroom. I heard the taxi pull up outside and blow its horn. I heard her make her way down the stairs. I heard her pick up her suitcase. I heard her open the front door. I heard her slam it closed.

A minute or two later, after I felt certain the taxi had pulled away, I climbed the stairs to shower and shave. I found a note written across the bathroom mirror in red lipstick. It said: "YELL AND SCREAM. ACT LIKE A CHILD. STOMP OUT OF THE ROOM. SLEEP ON THE SOFA. PRETEND TO BE ASLEEP. REFUSE TO SAY GOOD-BYE. AND YOU HAVE THE GALL TO CALL YOURSELF A HUSBAND AND A FATHER AND A FRIEND?"

It took me quite a while to clean the lipstick off the mirror. I had to rub and rub and rub.

SEPTEMBER 4.

I think it was that very same day I made the moves on Fiona. And if not that day, it was soon thereafter.

The male ego. Unbelievable how it responds to

threats and adversity. In fact, the twisted rejoinders of the male ego can go a long way in explaining the whole history of the world.

SEPTEMBER 5.

Evelyn got home late last night, a day early. I was asleep when the limousine pulled into the driveway. But the headlights shining in my window and the sound of the engine idling woke me up.

I thought about pulling on some pants and going out to see if she could use some help. But before I got even one foot on the floor, I changed my mind. I decided to wait for Evelyn to come to me.

SEPTEMBER 6.

Last evening, when I arrived home from work, I found Evelyn sitting on the living room floor kissing and petting the dogs. We greeted each other with warm hugs and kisses.

She was extremely happy to see me. And I her. She told me she had missed me. I chose not to ask why she had not written or called. We had been all through that the last time.

Then something happened that I am reluctant to describe. I will not give many details. Let it be enough to say that we made love with a tenaciousness and an intensity bordering on desperation. We had each other right there, on the floor, then again, not long after, in the bedroom.

Ellen and I sometimes made love like that after she

returned from one of her business trips. Maybe absence does make the heart grow fonder.

Unfortunately, I think it also causes the brain to nurture thoughts of uncertainty, jealousy, and infidelity. Even while fully connected to Evelyn, both physically and emotionally, I wondered if she had been faithful to me during her two-week West Coast frolic.

SEPTEMBER 7.

It is nice to have Roger out of the picture. Evelyn is so much more relaxed, so much more attentive, so much more interested in our little sexual games with the boy off at college furthering his education. His mother tells me he will not be home again until Thanksgiving. Maybe Christmas.

SEPTEMBER 8.

Another lovely day on the sexual playground. Evelyn asked me if I loved her. I assured her I did.

She laughed and laughed and laughed.

SEPTEMBER 9.

I wonder how far we can go?
  Sexually?
  Emotionally?
  Domestically?
  I wonder if Evelyn and I could make a life together?

SEPTEMBER 10.

This morning, for the first time in my life, I took a limousine to work. The driver pulled right up in front of my Midtown office building. I kissed Evelyn good-bye, told her I would see her later, and then I stepped boldly out into the morning light like some big shot off to cut a major deal.

Evelyn had a meeting just a few blocks away, so last night we decided to drive into the city together. Her meeting was with some record company executive who wants her to play the cello on a new Mozart recording.

I asked her on the way in if she wanted to have lunch after her meeting, but she told me she already had plans for lunch. I waited for her to elaborate, maybe tell me where and with whom, but no other information was forthcoming. I decided not to push it.

As we exited the Lincoln Tunnel and started uptown, she more or less told me she would see me back at Blind Pass.

Well, I'm home now, have been for a few hours, but I have seen neither hide nor hair of Evelyn. I had to take a cab home from the train station.

It has been raining ever since I got home. A light, steady rain. But it's warm outside; no, not warm, hot. Hot and muggy. The air feels heavy. Sluggish. This is the kind of weather they probably get in Purgatory. Not that I am a big believer in Heaven or Hell or any of the stops in between.

I just wish Evelyn would get home so I could go over and make love to her before it's time to go to bed.

Almost noon now, but still no sign of Evelyn. I stayed home from work today to finish editing a novel. Not a particularly good novel, but I suppose they cannot all be *Crime and Punishment*.

Also I stayed home to be here when Evelyn arrives. If she ever does.

I cannot believe she has not called.

An hour or so ago I got tired of waiting for her. I needed a work break anyway, so I decided to go out for a bike ride. When I left, the skies were still dark, but the rain had finally ended. It looked like it would soon clear.

Well, it didn't clear. I got maybe five miles from the house when a fresh batch of black clouds rolled in and the skies opened up right on top of me. I mean the rain fell in buckets. Torrential. I slowed to a crawl and headed home. Probably I should have gotten off the bike and walked. But I thought I could make it as long as I took my time.

Wrong.

Less than a mile from here there is a short but rather steep hill. Very steep. I got up a little too much speed coming down that hill. A pickup truck flew by me. I got spooked and hit the brakes a bit too hard. The front tire locked up. I lost control. In the snap of a finger the bike went down. I went down. Slammed right into the slick asphalt.

I made off with just a few cuts and scratches, a pretty good piece of road burn on my right thigh, but other than that I'm okay. The bike took the brunt of the abuse. Both tires went flat. The front rim is all bent. The handlebars are twisted. The rear derailleur snapped right off.

Obviously I could not ride the bike home. I could not even roll it home. I literally had to carry it home.

And when I got home, not all that long ago, Evelyn was still not here. She left yesterday morning for a ten o'clock meeting. And still she is not home. And she has not called. I have not heard a word from her.

I mean, that's just plain inconsiderate. Common courtesy demands a phone call, if nothing else.

If Evelyn was my wife and she pulled something like this . . . I don't know . . . I think I'd be pretty upset, pretty ticked off.

SEPTEMBER 12.

Evelyn finally arrived home last night. Late. After dinner. Well after dinner.

By that time my anger and annoyance had waned. By that time I was just flat-out worried about her. By that time I had convinced myself that something bad had happened to her.

Miss Julie had not heard from her, either. But she did not seem to share my concern. She more or less slammed the back door in my face when I went over to inquire if she had received word from her employer.

I have no idea what is wrong with that girl.

Later, when headlights appeared in the driveway, I dashed out into the night in a rather harried state and swung open the back door of the limousine.

Twenty-four hours of worry and concern came pouring out of me. "Thank God you're home, Evelyn. I've been worried sick."

She sighed right in my face, then nonchalantly

gathered her belongings from the seat beside her. "Hello, Sam."

That's when I snapped. It might have been all the time that had passed, or it could have been her passive, blasé greeting. I do not know. "Where the hell," I demanded, "have you been?"

She glanced up at me, as though she could actually see. "Excuse me?" She did not care for my tone, not one bit.

But I had worked myself into quite a dither by that time. "I said, where have you been?"

"I have not been shacking up with another man, Mr. Adams, if that is what you are insinuating."

"That is not what I am insinuating."

"Of course it is."

"It isn't."

"Then what?"

God, she can be so damn difficult to deal with.

"I've been worried about you. I—"

"Worried that I've been fucking some other—"

"No!" I shouted. "That's not it at all. For chrissakes, Evelyn, when we said good-bye yesterday morning, right outside my office, I assumed you would be back here long before I got home from work. Certainly I assumed you would be home last night."

Her expression gave off nothing but impatience. She took her time offering a response. Then, after another sigh, she said, "As I've said before, Sam, assume nothing. Perhaps I said I would be home yesterday. Perhaps not. I cannot really recall exactly what was said. But whatever was said, the day's events took control, and I had no choice but to take a particular course of action. One meeting led to another. Nothing was resolved. It got late. I checked into the Regency. It seemed like a better idea than coming all the way out here last night, then traipsing all the way back to the city this morning."

I listened, and while I listened, I tried to stomp out my burning fuse. "Okay, fine, I understand. But why can't you take a minute to call? It wouldn't kill you to let me know you're all right."

Her voice softened. "Oh, Sammy, I can tell you're upset." She offered me a condescending smile, grabbed my cheek, gave it a squeeze. "What's the matter? Did you miss your mommy?"

I frowned, pushed her hand away. "What?"

"Did you miss me?"

"Give me a break, dammit. I was worried about you. Why can't you just accept that?"

She shrugged and stepped out of the limo. She sighed, for a third time, right in my face. Then she turned and headed for the back door. Blind or not, Evelyn Richmond walked those steps with total confidence.

"Don't worry about this old girl, Mr. Adams. Let me assure you: I can take care of myself."

SEPTEMBER 13.

The skies have cleared. Another warm and pleasant late-summer day. Evelyn and I are bosom buddies again. We made up this morning. We made up and made love.

Amazing how a little romp around the bedroom can make everything fine and dandy. Twenty minutes between the sheets and the world suddenly seems once again like a very rosy place.

Ellen and I used to occasionally employ the same remedy when tempers flared, when times got tough.

SEPTEMBER 14.

This afternoon Evelyn and I took a ride in the mini-van. I described the scenery to her: the colors and shapes, the hills and valleys.

"Yes," she said, "I can see it. If I concentrate, I can conjure up the images in my mind."

She managed to smile, but I could hear strains of melancholy and even bitterness in her voice.

I had the most intense desire to lend Evelyn my eyes so she could glimpse the world around her once again. But, regrettably, there is only so much we can do for one another. In so many ways we are solitary sailors.

We ate lunch at the edge of a pretty field I had found while out bike riding. After our cheese and bread and fruit we laughed about something, I cannot remember what, something trivial and silly, but it was a good, genuine belly laugh, and after the laugh we rolled into the tall grass and kissed, our bodies tense and active with the thrill of sexual expectation.

I cannot begin to describe how happy and fulfilled it made me to see Evelyn laughing and then taking pleasure in my physical presence. We are, at least at times, very good together. Friends. Lovers.

SEPTEMBER 15.

Today the rains returned. And the air feels cooler. The breeze holds an early hint of autumn.

Evelyn and I made love in the music room to the sound of raindrops pattering against the windows. It was a calm, almost pensive affair, undoubtedly the result of so many encounters these past several days.

Afterward we sat on the love seat, quiet and touching. Evelyn ran her fingers up and down my arm, over my hand and fingers.

And then, out of nowhere, in the midst of all that tranquillity, she said, "You've never told me about your wife, Sam."

The air caught in my lungs. I could not exhale. Finally, I mumbled, "My wife?"

"Yes, Sam. Your wife. The woman to whom you must have at one time been married. Or perhaps, for all I know, you still are."

I looked down. Her hand was on my hand. My wedding band shone there on my finger like some giant gold goblet. No doubt she had noticed it long before this, but for reasons only she knew, it was a topic she had chosen to avoid.

Just as, for reasons only I knew, I had chosen to avoid it as well.

"She . . . my wife . . . she . . ."

"It's all right, Sam," said Evelyn, her fingertips gently stroking my hand. "You don't have to if you don't want to. Believe me, I know very well how unpleasant the past can be, how very painful."

"You do?"

She put her arms around me and squeezed, the same way my mother always did whenever I felt sick or threatened or forlorn. My mother hugged and squeezed me that way the day she returned from her sexual odyssey with Dr. Blue.

"Yes, Sam," said Evelyn, "I do."

We sat there, my head buried against her breast. I felt myself trembling. I actually began to cry, just a few brief sobs. Evelyn comforted me. She did not ask me again to tell her about Ellen.

But I wanted to tell her. I wanted to let it out. Perhaps, soon, I will.

SEPTEMBER 17.

I have told Evelyn everything. Every last detail. The whole violent mess.

Over much of the last couple of days, Evelyn has listened to my terrible tale without hardly saying a word. If I began to cry, she drew my face against her breast. If I grew silent, she gently insisted I continue.

"You have to let it out, Sam," she whispered more than once. "All that pain and pressure has to be released. You can't hold it inside forever. You'll explode. It'll blow you apart. I see now that it very nearly has already."

She held me close as my tale closed in on that horrible day. I took her straight through that Saturday before Easter Sunday: packing up the minivan, driving up the interstate, the flat tire, the delays, the day quickly slipping away, the decision to stop for the night, the search for a room, our arrival at Sloan's Motel.

I went into quite a lot of detail about events at Sloan's Motel: playing baseball with Nicky out in the parking lot, eating dinner at that greasy spoon down the street, settling into our beds for the night.

And then the time arrived; nothing more to discuss; I had to tell Evelyn about the creature with the angry purple scar. I told her how he came crashing into our room, how he lifted Nicky's Louisville Slugger high up over his head, how he used that baseball bat to bludgeon my wife and son to death.

I told Evelyn about the blood. And the screams. And the terror.

She held me tight, her hand caressing the back of my neck. "My God, Sam, I had no idea you had been through such a terrible ordeal. I just assumed you were another victim of divorce."

I pressed my face against her chest.

She encouraged me to do so. "Poor Sam. Poor, poor Sam."

We sat there then, very quietly, for a long time. I was emotionally spent. And very thankful Evelyn did not ask any questions. Had she asked, I doubt I could have answered.

SEPTEMBER 18.

I awoke early this morning to the sound of a car idling out in the drive. When I looked out the window, I spotted Evelyn climbing into the back of a limousine, and then that limousine pulling swiftly away. Where was she off to now? She had not mentioned anything to me last night about going anywhere.

I spent the morning and part of the afternoon editing a manuscript here at the cottage. After lunch I took the dogs for a walk. We arrived back just as Evelyn was pulling up the drive. I was right there to open the door for her and help her out of the limo. She thanked me and kissed my cheek. I inquired about her day. She would say only that she had been out running a few errands, taking care of some unfinished business. Then she steered herself toward the back door, insisting she had some practicing to do and some telephone calls to make. But before she disappeared into the house, she asked me to please come for dinner at seven o'clock.

I showed up at seven o'clock sharp. We ate in the dining room. Just the two of us. We used the fine china and the crystal and the sterling silver. Julie served the meal. Evelyn sat at the head of the table. I sat just to her right. We shared a bottle of wine.

At first we just spoke about this and that, books and music, the latest political crisis. Evelyn told a dirty joke. I laughed and squeezed her thigh under the table. I felt better, more at ease, after having shared my painful memories with this woman I now loved.

But then, about halfway through the meal, Evelyn once again broached the subject. She suddenly wanted to know more about what had happened at Sloan's Motel. I think I had secretly hoped to never discuss the matter again.

She began with a comment that sounded very much like a question. "You never actually told me what happened to the man responsible for committing such an atrocious crime against your family."

I felt my appetite vanish. "He's in jail."

"So he was convicted?"

"Yes, he was convicted."

"Tell me what happened."

"There is not much to tell. He was obviously guilty. The police found him in our room."

"But you said he was unconscious."

"Yes, he was unconscious. From the blow I had leveled against him with Nicky's bat."

"But he must have mounted a defense?"

I hesitated, remembering the oft-repeated details. And then I told Evelyn the tale of the creature's trial. "It was several weeks before he recovered from the injury to his head. When the police finally questioned him, he claimed to have no knowledge of the incident whatsoever. He claimed he could not remember breaking into our room or threatening us or striking my wife or my son. So they put him in jail, got him a lawyer, and set a trial date."

Evelyn shook her head. "Memory loss, huh? Pretty imaginative alibi."

"I guess that was about his only option."

"Did this maniac have a criminal record?"

"A mile long," I answered. "Misdemeanors mostly. Vagrancy. Vandalism. Petty theft. Things like that. But he also had a felony for armed robbery. Plus some psychiatric problems. The guy was a mess."

"So what happened at trial?"

"Months passed before the trial began. They postponed it several times, the last time because my son passed away early last fall. Nicky's death changed the charge. Now, instead of being tried for one count of murder and one count of aggravated assault, the creature faced two counts of murder in the second degree."

"My God, Sam," said Evelyn, her hand on my forearm, "this must have been incredibly difficult for you."

I nodded and took a deep breath, then continued. "By the time the trial finally started, the creature's lawyer had concocted a whole new story. Suddenly he remembered being in our room. But now he claimed he had been attacked outside the motel in the middle of the night, beaten unconscious, and then dragged into the room where it was made to look as though he had committed the murders."

"You're kidding? That was his defense?"

"That was it. I sat there in court for over a week

listening to this cock-and-bull story. It took all my powers of restraint not to jump out of my chair and attack that murderous bastard."

"So what was the defense theory?" asked Evelyn. "If the defendant didn't do it, who did?"

I shrugged.

"You?"

"They never actually had the gall to say such a thing, but they definitely insinuated it."

She shook her head again. "Unbelievable. So what was the outcome?"

"Well, I think the jury was annoyed and even insulted with this defense. They brought back a verdict of guilty on both charges in less than four hours."

"It took them that long?"

I glanced at her. "Something like that, yes."

"And his sentence?"

"Two consecutive life terms."

Evelyn slowly nodded her head. She whistled very softly.

A minute or more passed. Finally I said, "Why don't we quit all this gruesome talk and finish this fine meal now?"

Evelyn smiled. "Of course, Sam. I'm sorry for being so curious."

We went on eating. In silence. For maybe three or four minutes.

Then, a forkful of food at her mouth, Evelyn asked, "So then you were never a suspect?"

"Excuse me?"

"The killer's accusation about being dragged into the room. This never led to the police considering you a suspect?"

"My God, Evelyn, what kind of question is that?"

She chewed and swallowed. "I don't know. Just a question."

"A pretty offensive question, if you ask me."

"I didn't mean it to be."

"Maybe not," I said, a touch of anger rising in my voice, "but if you had any compassion at all for what I have been through all these months, you never would have asked it. I was battered and beaten that morning. I was definitely not a suspect. I was a victim."

"Of course, Sam. I apologize. It was a stupid question better kept to myself. I think we should just drop the whole subject."

"Excellent idea. Let's just sit here and enjoy this food and one another."

But thereafter we had very little left to say. In fact, our conversation pretty much ground to a halt. And almost as soon as we finished eating, Evelyn complained of a throbbing headache and went straight up to bed.

I was glad. I did not really want to be with her. So I came home. But I wasn't tired, so Sunshine and Moxie and I went out for a long walk under an almost full moon.

SEPTEMBER 19.

Late this morning I went to see Evelyn. I wanted to fix what last night we had broken. I went upstairs to her bedroom and tried to arouse her for lovemaking. She did not seem particularly interested.

"What's the matter?" I asked.

"Nothing."

"Something?"

"I suppose, Sam, my head still hurts."

"You suppose?"

"Yes, I suppose." And with that she climbed out of bed, pulled on her silk robe, and went into the bathroom.

I was still sitting there several minutes later when she came out. Right away she had a question, "Tell me something, Sam. Were you angry at her?"

"Angry at who?"

"At your wife?"

"When?"

"When she died."

I needed a moment to answer. "Angry at her? Of course not. Why would I be angry at her?"

"Easy, Sam," she said, as she dried her face with a plush towel. "I don't mean before she died. I mean *after* she died. Were you angry at her after she died?"

"For what? For dying? That's absurd."

"Probably it is. But I remember being furious with my husband, Roger's father, after we got divorced. I did not want to be married to him anymore, I hated him, but still, once it was over, I was incredibly angry at him. Angry because we had failed, angry because of all the ugliness we had inflicted upon one another, angry because I was suddenly all alone."

I listened, then asked, "So what does this have to do with me? Divorce is a very different matter."

"You're right, Sam, it is. It's just that you told me the other day that the two of you had been together for so many years, and that you were still very much in love. Then, suddenly, out of the blue, she dies. She dies and leaves you utterly alone. It would be very normal for you to feel a certain amount of anger and even animosity toward her for abandoning you like that."

I could do nothing but shake my head at her logic. "I can assure you, Evelyn, I was not angry at Ellen for being brutally murdered. I was angry at that creature who took her life. And I was angry at myself for not doing more to save her."

Evelyn did not respond for most of a minute. I wanted her to respond. I wanted her to apologize for asking me if I had been angry at Ellen for dying. But she said only, "I see." And then, "Of course. You're right. I understand perfectly."

I sat there wishing I had never said a word to Evelyn about Ellen or Nicky or Sloan's Motel. And then I decided the time had come to move on, to change the subject. "What would you like to do today?"

"Actually, Sam," she replied, "I've been neglecting my cello lately. I really need to practice. I have the fall tour coming up soon and several new pieces to learn."

"Fall tour?" This was news to me.

"Yes. In October. I must have mentioned it to you?"

"I don't think so."

"Well, it's not really a tour. Just an invitation from the London Philharmonic to play a few dates in England. And I think one in Scotland. Or maybe Wales. Nothing very demanding, but an honor nevertheless."

"And when do you go off on this fall tour?"

She ignored my tone. "What's today? The nineteenth? In a week or so. I may go a little early and do some visiting."

My mouth went to work before my brain could catch up. "Why did you wait so long to tell me about this?"

She busied herself in front of her bureau. "I don't know, Sam. I thought I had told you. Anyway, I'm telling you now."

I took a chance. "Maybe . . . maybe I could go along. I could use a vacation."

"Oh, Sam, you'd find it excruciatingly boring."

I sensed a crack. "No I wouldn't. I'd find it fascinating. And besides, you could certainly use the help."

The crack quickly closed. "What does that mean? That a blind woman can't take care of herself? That she can't travel alone? Can't fill her own cup with tea?"

"No, I didn't mean it that way. You know I didn't mean it that way. You're the most independent woman I've ever known. I just mean—"

She laughed. Right in my face. "You haven't known many women, have you, Sam?"

I felt the moment slipping away. Was it not just yesterday, or perhaps the day before, that she had been so sweet, so gentle, so sensitive, listening to my woeful tale, comforting me, allowing me to suckle her nipple?

"I don't want to argue," I assured her. "I just thought it would be nice for us to maybe go on a trip together."

This brought a brief smile to her face. "You're a sweetheart, Sam. Really. But try to understand. I prefer to travel alone."

"I won't get in your way."

She did not even hear me. "You meet the most fascinating people when you travel alone. Especially when you're blind. Strangers come out of the woodwork to help the blind."

I could not think of much to say. Actually, I could think of all kinds of things to say, but I feared the sound of my own voice, or at least the fool I would make of myself if I opened my mouth.

Evelyn did not fear anything. "Believe me, Sam, I

get plenty of help when I'm on the road. The people who invite me to these affairs make sure I am properly pampered. I get treated like royalty."

I thought I might say something then, but she got there first. "My advice to you, dear Sammy, is take a trip of your own. You need to get away for a while. Trust me, it will do you a world of good. You have been through hell. I understand that now. I have a clear picture. But you are young and handsome and sensitive. Experience will seek you out and stick to you like road tar. Go for it, Sam. Go out and have yourself an adventure."

And then, all talked out, Evelyn told me she had things to do. She told me she would see me later. And, with a wave of her hand, I was dismissed.

SEPTEMBER 20.

An adventure.
 Right.
 I've done the adventure thing. Back in the old days. Remember?
 My big adventure right now is to get my butt into the office and get some work done. I've got writers closing in on me from every direction.

SEPTEMBER 21.

I tried once again to get Evelyn interested in making love. I went over to see her right after I got home from work. I even took the dogs. But my efforts proved futile.

She seemed distracted, distant.

"What is it?" I asked.

"Nothing," she answered, "I have my period."

I did not even know Evelyn still got a period.

Maybe she doesn't. Maybe it was just a ruse, a little white lie to throw me off the scent.

SEPTEMBER 22.

And today, the first full day of autumn, she has taken refuge in the music room. She refuses to come out. She insists she has to practice. And practice she does, for hours and hours. And when she is not practicing, she is yacking on the telephone, yacking and laughing so loud that earlier I could hear her out in the driveway where I sat on the asphalt trying to fix my bicycle. Roger's bicycle. The Richmonds' bicycle. But I could not fix it. The tires are flat, the rims are bent, the handlebars are all twisted. It looks like a trip to the bike shop if I want to keep riding.

An hour or so ago I came inside to answer the telephone. I thought it might be Evelyn calling.

But no, it was my realtor. "Mr. Adams! You won't believe it. Someone has made an offer."

"An offer! Already?"

"Yes."

"How much?"

"They're lowballing, but I can tell they're interested."

We discussed numbers. I told her what I wanted. She assured me she would do her best.

SEPTEMBER 23.

I thought about telling Evelyn that I am selling the house, but for reasons I do not fully comprehend, I have decided against it. I do not want her to know. I have been regretting telling her about Ellen and Nicky, about the terrible trouble we had at Sloan's Motel. I should not have told her.

I should have kept my mouth shut.

I should have kept my misery to myself.

I talked to the realtor again this afternoon. The potential buyers have come up another ten thousand from their original offer.

I told her if they will come up another ten thousand, they can have the house, the house where I used to live with my wife and son, the bedroom where I used to sleep with Ellen, the backyard where I used to play ball with Nicky, the garage where I used to keep my car, the office where I used to edit manuscripts, the den where we used to watch TV, the dining room where we used to eat our meals, the kitchen where we used to mill around and talk about our lives.

Another measly ten grand and they can have the whole damn package.

"Very sensible, Mr. Adams. I think you're making an excellent decision."

I hung up without saying good-bye.

SEPTEMBER 24.

I asked Evelyn to accompany me to the bike shop this morning. She agreed to go. She wanted to go. I wanted to take the bike in and have it fixed. But I did not get it fixed. No, I bought a new bike, instead.

"Yes," said Evelyn. "Get a new bike. A red one. A bright red one." She sounded happy and enthusiastic.

The shop was having an end-of-the-season sale. I splurged. I bought a fancy new touring bike, fire engine red, with all the bells and whistles.

"Do you think," I asked the salesman, with Evelyn standing at my side, "that this bike could carry me all the way to California?"

"If you can ride it that far," he told me, "it can definitely get you there."

"All the way to California on a bicycle," said Evelyn, once we were back in the minivan. "Now that sounds like an incredible adventure."

"We'll see," I told her. "Maybe we'll have to start with something a little more reasonable first."

"Why, Sam?" she wanted to know. "Why not just go for all the marbles on the first throw?"

But when we got back to the house, she did not want to play marbles with me. She wanted to play by herself. She wanted to play with her cello.

SEPTEMBER 25.

I drove over and picked up my new bike today. I brought it home and went straight out for a spin. It's a beauty, a very smooth ride.

Evelyn was standing outside the garage when I rode

up the driveway. "How's the new bike?" she wanted to know.

"Pretty sweet," I told her.

She sighed and reached out to touch the bike.

I led her hand to the handlebars. She ran her fingers over the smooth steel. "I haven't experienced the thrill of operating a bicycle, of pedaling full speed downhill with the wind in my hair, since, I don't know, probably since I was a little girl."

I studied her face. I saw immediately the melancholy in her vacant eyes. God, how she can swing my emotions in a thousand different directions.

A tear rolled out of her eye. I could not help myself. I wiped that tear away, and then kissed Evelyn softly on the mouth.

She gave me a brief smile. "I don't know, Sam. It's all so crazy. Nothing makes sense. Right is wrong and wrong is right. Your wife dies and we live. Life is lovely and life is cruel. You hate me. You love me. You go out and buy a new bicycle and you don't even ask me to go for a ride."

I wanted to say something about going all the way to England without asking me to go, but instead, I asked, "Do you want to go for a spin?"

She took a moment to think about it. "I do," she answered. "Absolutely."

"Then let's go."

We started down the driveway. Halfway down, Evelyn stopped. "Can I trust you to keep me safe, Sam?"

I assured her she could.

She sat on the seat while I stood on the pedals. It did not work very well. We did not go very far. Just out the driveway, along Valley Drive, and down the fairly steep hill on Church Street.

It took all my concentration and physical strength to keep the bike from tipping over as we made our descent. Evelyn, with no clear perception of the mechanics involved, balanced on the seat like a sack of potatoes, her arms tight around my waist. She felt like dead weight. Still, she screamed with delight as we picked up speed and the wind rushed past our faces.

When we reached the bottom of the hill, Evelyn squeezed my arm and pleaded, "Let's do it again, Sam! Please, one more time."

We did it three more times, four times altogether. I had to walk the bike up the hill, one hand on the handlebars and the other hand leading my blind companion along the street littered with the first fallen leaves of the approaching fall.

It was one of the most satisfying days of my life in a long time. It feels so good to make another person happy. And yet, somehow I knew the satisfaction would not last.

SEPTEMBER 27.

"I'll be leaving soon, Sam."

I did not want to hear it. I did not want to talk about it. But I had to ask, I had to know. "When?"

"The day after tomorrow. No, I'm sorry, the day after that. The thirtieth."

I stood in the middle of the music room. Evelyn sat curled up on the love seat.

"And you're flying to London?"

"Yes."

That seemed like enough questions, but I could not

stand the silence floating between us. "So . . . how long will you be gone?"

"Not long," she said quickly. "Two or three weeks."

I felt a whole host of emotions: anxiety, jealousy, and finally, sadness. I could not help myself. "I'll miss you."

"Oh, Sam."

"I will."

She moved immediately to change the subject. "So, have you decided what you're going to do? Where you might go on your adventure? Is California still in your plans?"

"What adventure?" I wanted to ask but didn't. I needed something better than that. I needed something as good as jolly old England. "I don't know if I'll make it all the way to California, but I'm definitely going to take a hike trip."

"And where do you think you will go?"

"I'm still poring over my maps," I lied. "But I figure with the weather turning colder, it would be wise to head south."

"South! Yes!" She sounded all worked up. "South would be best."

"Maybe Virginia," I said. "The Carolinas. Tennessee and Kentucky. I've always wanted to see the Great Smoky Mountains."

Evelyn had a wide smile on her face. "The Great Smokies! Yes! It sounds wonderful. You'll have a grand time, Sam. How long do you think you'll be gone?"

I had the feeling she hoped I would say forever.

SEPTEMBER 28.

I just spoke with my realtor. Things look good. It looks like we have a deal.

I have to go over there tomorrow and meet the buyers, sign some papers, move the sales ball along.

I hope it does not take too long. Tomorrow is the last day I will get to spend with Evelyn before she heads across the Atlantic. Not that our time together lately has been particularly exhilarating.

Nevertheless, I want to see her, even if just to hold her hand. I feel sure, with time, that things will improve between us.

Or am I just kidding myself?

SEPTEMBER 29.

I did not get to see Evelyn at all yesterday. She went out and did not return until after I had gone to bed. And then I had to slip away early this morning to make my meeting at the real estate office.

I almost turned around and walked out after meeting the people who want to buy the house: a young couple with a five-year-old son. The same age as Nicky when we bought the house. The husband works in New York. The wife used to work in New York, but quit her job to take care of the kid. They used to live in the city, but then it became too dirty, too violent, too dangerous.

"A horrible place now," the wife told me. "Absolutely hellish."

They babbled on and on about the house, about what a wonderful place it will be to raise their son. I gathered they did not know what had happened to my wife and son, or if they did know, they simply did not care.

On a more positive note: they are in a hurry to leave the city. They would like to close on the house by the first of November.

"Great," I told them, a great big phony smile on my face. "Fine with me. The sooner the better."

Evelyn was out when I arrived home a few hours ago. Miss Julie claimed she did not know where Evelyn had gone or when she would be back.

It is now almost eight o'clock. I am still waiting.

SEPTEMBER 30.

Once again Evelyn did not get home until late. But this time I was still awake. I was up. Waiting for her. In the shadows.

The moment she stepped from the limousine, I sprang out and hit her with our favorite question. "Where have you been?"

Startled, she jumped. "Sam," she said, recovering quickly, "hello. I was just out taking care of some last-minute details."

Last-minute details. Right.

And then she invited me into the kitchen. For a cup of sleepy time tea. For a few minutes of neighborly chitchat before bed. Not to spend the night or spread her legs. Her long, thin, lovely legs.

Before I had drained my cup of tea, she pleaded exhaustion, told me she had a long and difficult journey ahead of her in the morning.

I did not care about her long and difficult journey. I

had so many things I wanted to tell her. So many things I wanted to do to her. I wanted to throw her down on the kitchen floor and ravish her. But, of course, I did no such thing. Not me. Not Gentle Sam. I let her kiss me lightly on the mouth, then I let her send me home with fare-thee-wells lingering on our lips.

OCTOBER 1.

And now, once again she is gone. The limousine pulled out of the driveway just a few minutes ago. I wanted to accompany her to the airport, but she said no. "I hate good-byes, Sam," she insisted. "Especially airport good-byes. They are so melodramatic."

So we kissed out in the driveway, a few drops of cold rain spitting out of a dull, gray sky. "Have a nice trip," I heard myself say. "Call if you have the time. See you soon. I'll miss you."

She nodded to each of my clichés, then she climbed into the backseat of the limo, closed the door, and lowered the window. "Time now to be strong, Sam," she whispered when I bent down to her. "Time to be a man. Time to find your way through the madness."

For some reason, I nodded. And a moment later, the limo was on the move.

I stood there, the rain falling faster, her words echoing in my ears.

She turned and waved.

Just the way Ellen used to do.

"Time to be strong, Sam. Time to be a man. Time to find your way through the madness."

What, I wonder now, was all that about?

OCTOBER 2.

I am feeling pretty good tonight. Tired but good. I took the longest bike ride of my life this morning. I rode 42.6 miles, averaged 15.4 miles per hour, and had a top speed of 38 miles an hour. I know all this because of the little computer gadget attached to my handlebars.

If I rode fifty miles a day and it is, say, three thousand miles to San Francisco, I could ride clear across the country in two months. Why not do it? Why not give it a try? What else do I have to do? What do I have to lose?

I guess I could wait around for Evelyn to get home. See if maybe she will give me the time of day.

All right, I'll do it. I'll go for it. I'll spend a month getting in shape, obtaining all the right equipment, plotting my route. And then, right after I close on the house, I will make my escape.

I'll fly the coop. Gone with the wind.

OCTOBER 3.

Weather today: clear and cool, just a slight breeze. Perfect riding weather. I did 44.5 miles at 15.2 mph.

Not bad. Tomorrow I will do fifty. Already have my route planned out.

OCTOBER 4.

Today I will not do much of anything.

Today it is raining and about 45 degrees.

I thought about going out anyway and at least

doing a few miles. If I plan on riding across the country this time of year, I better be prepared for some lousy weather. Maybe I should go over to the bike shop and see what kind of gear they have for rotten weather riding.

Wait a second. Why ride all the way to sunny California? Why not drive the minivan? Leave tomorrow. Leave today. Leave right now. I can bring the bike with me, take a ride every morning before getting back on the highway.

That makes a lot more sense than pedaling all those miles. Besides, I have the dogs to think about. What will I do with the dogs if I ride across? I can't put them in a kennel for all that time. I don't like putting them in a kennel for even one night. If I drive across, I can bring them with me. I can also bring my laptop and my books. Do some writing along the way.

But I don't know if driving will do the trick. I need more of an adventure than that, more of a challenge. I need to ride to California.

Just to prove I can do it.

What did Evelyn say just before she left? Be a man, Sam. Find your way through the madness.

<hr>

OCTOBER 5.

More rain today. And more rain, the weathermen say, tomorrow.

But today, after work, I bought this special Gore-Tex rain suit at the bike shop and went out riding anyway. I did about ten miles. It was miserable. Cold and wet and dangerous. Cars and trucks splashed water all over me. The road was slick and slippery. I went down going around a corner, scratched my new bike, tore a hole in my new rain suit.

This whole bike thing is beginning to seem like a pretty stupid idea.

OCTOBER 6.

I woke up this morning thinking about Fiona. No idea why. She just slipped into my thoughts. I mentioned Fiona several weeks back, but I never got around to bringing her into focus.

Now I'm on the train, heading home after a long and stressful day at work, one of those days that makes you want to quit and never go back. I don't feel this desire very often, maybe three or four times a year. Although, I'm beginning to feel burned out, like a leave of absence might do me a world of good.

Anyway, Fiona has popped into my thoughts again. Yes, young Fiona, my one and only fling during a decade and a half of married life. And I doubt very much I would have had that one if my wife had not been flying all over the country on business.

And, I found out later, a little pleasure as well.

OCTOBER 7.

I met Fiona on the train coming home from New York one night after work. The evening express.

She got on just seconds before the train pulled out of the station. Breathless, she threw herself down beside me. Her long dark hair and thin, compact body caught my eye immediately. And the eye of just about every other male commuter on that train as well.

Fiona had great hair and a great body but not much of a face. Her nose was too long, and her eyes, I don't know, they just looked a little funny, especially the right one, which tended to wander. She had a great set of lips, luscious and lustful, but when she parted those lips to form words, ouch! Jesus Himself would have plugged up His ears.

Fiona had grown up in Brooklyn. And she had the accent to prove it. She did her best to cover it up, but it was there with every word she uttered. She told me that night on the evening express she wanted to be an actress. "Actually," she said, that voice making me flinch, "I already am an actress. Been one for years. Just haven't made it to the big time yet."

I wanted to suggest some elocution lessons but decided she might take it as an insult. And I did not want that. Not at that stage of our relationship.

OCTOBER 8.

Fiona's face might not have been a dream come true, and her voice might have sounded like fingernails on a chalkboard, but her body, my goodness, now that was something worth groveling for. All those silky smooth curves and fine lines: enough to drive a married man to distraction.

I sat on the train with Fiona maybe half a dozen times over a month or more before I finally got up the nerve to ask her out. By that time I was editing at home two and even three days a week. With Nicky in school and Ellen piling up the frequent flyer miles, I had plenty of time to kill. So one day I just casually asked Fiona if she wanted to maybe go to a movie or something.

She glanced at me suspiciously with her wandering eye, but then she smiled and said in her thick Brooklynese, "Sure. Okay. I love the movies."

"I do, too," I told her, even though I probably had not been to one since Nicky'd been born.

So we did the movies. Once or twice a week for two or three weeks. We held hands. Then we started to kiss.

And then, excuse the metaphor, we did each other.

"You know, Sammy," said Fiona, after I gave her a not particularly long ride on my marital bed, "I've always wondered what it would feel like to make love to a married man."

"And how did it feel?"

She put those lovely lips against mine, then she whispered the following question in my ear: "When do we get to do it again?"

"Soon," I assured her. Very soon.

OCTOBER 9.

So what did I see in Fiona? Fiona Sabrio?

I saw a girl in her midtwenties willing and wanting to have sex with me, a married guy more than ten years her senior, a guy sliding fast toward middle age. I saw that naked body willing to accept my weight. I saw, no doubt, a means of holding on, a little longer, to my youth. And I saw, perhaps, a way to get back at Ellen for abandoning her family.

Fiona and I had sex. We just had sex.

And oh yes, we went to the movies. We always went

to a matinée. Usually out at the highway twelve-plex where I felt confident no one would recognize me.

Fiona was extremely cooperative in bed. She even allowed me to tie her up a time or two. Yes, we did the bondage thing with my neck ties. Something Ellen would never do.

I tied Fiona to the four corners of our poster bed, but it was the bed I shared with Ellen, so guilt quickly came into play. I could not get an erection. I had my prey bound and gagged and perfectly naked, but I did not have the tools to move in for the kill.

Unlike Evelyn, Fiona did not mind when my maleness lay limp against my thigh. In fact, I think she rather enjoyed it in that benign state.

Fiona was an extremely playful and giddy partner. She giggled when she came. No, Fiona did not take her sex very seriously. Certainly she took it far less seriously than I. Of course, we were not doing the deed in the bed she shared at night with her husband. Fiona did not have a husband. She did not even have a boyfriend. Fiona had me.

OCTOBER 10.

So I became an adulterer. I made love to Fiona two or sometimes three times a week. We always rendezvoused at my house, at Ellen's house, in our queen-size bed, primarily because Fiona lived with her gray-haired aunt who rarely ventured out of doors.

Every day, or practically every day, I suffered through a bout of intense guilt, and always I swore to myself that I would not see her again. Then the morning would pass, I would do my editing, get my work done, make my telephone calls, and suddenly there would be a whole afternoon spreading out before me, three or four hours to kill until Nicky got home from school. So I would ring up Fiona. And the cycle would begin anew.

I have no idea what Fiona got from our relationship. If she expected some long-term commitment from me, I never heard about it. Not a word. She lived from second to second, from movie to movie. The sex and the cinema seemed more than sufficient to keep her content.

And not necessarily in that order. Sometimes we would be in bed and I would catch her staring off into space, her thoughts obviously preoccupied with things cinematic, things other than the rhythm of my pelvic thrusts.

I never wanted to admit this before, but I think she faked most of her orgasms.

I wonder if Ellen faked orgasm?

I wonder if Evelyn fakes it?

OCTOBER 11.

Maybe Fiona was just lonely.

Maybe she figured someone was better than no one.

OCTOBER 12.

We have had a pretty nice stretch of autumn weather these past few days. I have been getting my rides in, piling up the miles, building up my leg muscles for the long trek ahead.

The question is: Will I really do it? Will I really make

this trip? Will I really ride my bike across the Golden Gate?

And what about Evelyn? Somehow she does not seem like the kind of woman who will sit calmly by and wait for her lover while he is off on some cross-country bike ride for two or three months.

So what am I to do? How am I to decide? I cannot even get in touch with her. I do not even know where she is.

Let me think rationally about this for just a moment. Can I reasonably assume that Evelyn and I have a future together? Does she want me? Do I want her? Is there anything more between us than a wild sexual connection?

There may be. I am not sure. But I would like to find out.

So, I suppose I should stick around at least until she returns.

OCTOBER 13.

I called the realtor this morning to see how things were progressing on the sale of the house.

"Beautiful, Mr. Adams," she told me. "Never have I seen a deal come together so well. It seems the wife's father is a lawyer and the husband's father is a banker, so all the legal and financial details are getting done lickety-split."

"Isn't that nice?"

She either missed or chose to ignore my sarcasm. "So," she continued, "unless a problem arises with the title search, it looks like we'll close on the second of November."

"There won't be a problem with the title search," I assured her.

"Beautiful, Mr. Adams. Excellent."

I hesitated, then said, "I'd like to find out if they might want to buy some of my furniture."

"Certainly. I'll give you their number."

"No, I don't want to talk to them."

"Excuse me?"

"I want you to do it. You find out if they're inter- ested. If they are, I'll give you a percentage of the prof- its."

She liked the sound of that. I could hear the bells ringing in her head. This middle-aged divorcée would do just about anything for a little cash, even hawk some dead woman's flatware.

It is a bitch of a world out there.

OCTOBER 14.

I guess my romantic entanglement with Fiona had been going on for five or six months when it all suddenly came to an abrupt end.

It was bound to happen. It had to happen. I think secretly, subconsciously, I had been hoping it would happen. I needed something to break the cycle of guilt and desire, of repulsion and lust.

Too bad that something turned out to be someone.

At least Ellen did not actually catch us in bed, her bed. At least she did not walk into her bedroom and find Fiona's firm and voluptuous young butt bouncing up and down on her silk sheets.

At least the fucking had ended for the day.

But just barely.

If Ellen had arrived five minutes earlier, she would have caught us doing the dirty deed. But that day we had finished up quickly and pulled on our clothes. We were late for the movies.

We buttoned our shirts, dashed down the stairs, and grabbed our jackets. It was spring, I remember. Oh yes, I remember well. Spring had sprung, but it was still rather cool outside.

And damp. It had been drizzling off and on all day.

"Ready?" I asked.

"Ready," she replied.

I pulled open the door. Fiona slipped past me. I followed her out and closed the door.

And right there, almost close enough to touch, stood my wife.

OCTOBER 15.

She stood right in the middle of our brick sidewalk. Our walk that I had recently weeded and swept. It looked perfectly neat and tidy.

Out of the corner of my eye I saw a taxi, her taxi, winding down the street.

Ellen stared at us. Her suitcase sat on the walk to her right, her briefcase to her left. She held her purse in her left hand. She must have stopped to search for the front door key.

Now the key no longer mattered.

I could see her sizing up Fiona, passing judgments left and right on her husband's lover, my "whore," as she would relentlessly refer to her in the days and weeks and months ahead.

A good minute passed.

I made no effort to explain.

No one moved. No one said a word.

Then Ellen picked up her bags, adjusted herself, and marched directly toward us. We made way. The lovers parted.

As she passed, she had only this to say: "Get rid of her."

OCTOBER 16.

I got rid of her all right. Pronto. In the snap of a finger. Just like that.

"I'll call you," I said.

"Maybe you shouldn't," she said.

"You're right," I said, "maybe I shouldn't."

I finally did, a week or so later, but only to apologize and say good-bye.

Fiona, I realize now, was lucky. She escaped.

OCTOBER 17.

Inside I found Ellen standing with her arms crossed in the entrance hall at the bottom of the stairs. "Have you been fucking that whore in our bed?"

I could not get my mouth open.

"I want you to get rid of it. All of it. Right now. Do you hear me?"

I heard her all right. Loud and clear.

"The sheets, the pillows, the mattress, the box spring. Get all of it out of my house. Now." Ellen spoke in a very calm and collected voice. It scared me. She continued, "I want a new mattress with fresh sheets in place by the time I am ready to go to bed."

I did not argue. I did not say a word. I did exactly as she ordered. I hauled the evidence out of the bedroom, down the stairs, and out the front door. I piled it into and on top of the minivan and headed for the town dump. I dumped it, then drove straight to the bedding store. I bought the best bed the guy had, cost me almost a thousand dollars. I hauled it home, carried it upstairs, and set it up. Then I drove to the mall and bought all new sheets and pillows.

I made the bed up neat as a pin and waited silently to see what would happen next.

OCTOBER 18.

I guess what happened next was a classic case of Show and Tell. Truth or Consequences.

I soon found out that Ellen, my once faithful wife, had been doing more than business on her frequent journeys to the West Coast. She had been doing the dirty deed as well. Only it sounded as though she had been doing it longer and with far more gusto than yours truly.

Her lover, it turned out, was someone from the L.A. office. Some lowly publicity dweeb. Try though I did, I never really got the whole story.

"Why do you want to know?" she asked when I probed for more information about her suitor.

I was working overtime to suppress my anger. "I just do."

"Why, Sam? What does it matter?"

"Believe me," I told her, "it matters. How old is he?

Is he married? Does he have kids? Do you love him, Ellen? What about sexual diseases? Do you think he has any of those?"

No answers were forthcoming from my bride, but this last question became a major concern for both of us. I doubt we would have engaged in sexual intercourse for quite some time anyway, but with the threat of sexually transmitted diseases hanging over our bed, we made a quiet pact to remain celibate for three months and then go for tests.

All tests proved negative, but still our celibacy, at least between the two of us, stretched on month after month after month. All through that spring and into the summer and fall.

Although, I must admit, rarely did a day slide by when I did not wonder what Ellen was doing out of my sight. Every night I spent alone in bed, when she was away on another business trip, I would lie there and wonder if she was sharing her bed with someone else.

The bond between us had been broken. Our trust and faith in one another had been snatched away. Just like that. In the blink of an eye. Terrifying how fast it can happen.

OCTOBER 19.

Yes, our sexual sojourns very nearly ruined our marriage.

No, that is not quite true. Our sexual sojourns did ruin our marriage. Our lies and our infidelities tore our marriage to pieces. There can be no question about that.

I had a difficult time being around my wife knowing that she had slept with another man. Sometimes it would make me crazy. We would be sitting, having dinner, everyone quiet and calm, and all of a sudden I would get this overwhelming desire to reach across the table and grab her, shake her with all my might. Of course, I never did. I would merely stand, go in the other room, and wait for my indecent desires to abate. They always did. They did because I loved my wife. I loved her more than anything in the world.

I would also remind myself that I too had been unfaithful. Although, in truth, I found my own adulterous behavior inconsequential. The fact that I had fornicated with another woman did not mean for one second that I did not love Ellen. My affair with Fiona had been nothing but a harmless flirtation. Fiona meant nothing to me. She was just someone to help pass the time.

Ellen felt quite differently. Her anger, and the point of reference she kept going back to again and again, every time the subject came up, was the bed. She could not believe I had violated the sanctity of our bedroom, that I had invited that "whore" between our sheets.

"If you had to fuck her," she would demand, "why couldn't you at least have had the decency to do it in a motel? Or in the back of the van? Or out on the front lawn? In our bed, Sam? In our bed!"

The reality is this: we still had not recovered from our indiscretions by the time Easter rolled around nearly a year later. Not once in all that time had we made love or been even remotely intimate. No, not even that night in our room at Sloan's Motel. I like to think we made love that night, I like to fantasize that we did, paint a nice rosy picture of the two of us bound lovingly together. But we did that night exactly what we had been doing for the past many months: we turned off the lights and turned our backs on one another.

OCTOBER 20.

I went over to see Julie this morning. I wanted to find out if she had heard from Evelyn. I guess I have no intention of leaving before she gets back. I know I should leave, be on my way, but I also know I will not leave. I want to feel my lips against her lips, my chest against her breasts. I want to feel the sweat behind her knees just before she comes.

"Have you spoken to her?" I asked Julie.

"She called a few days ago."

"A few days! Why didn't you tell me? Come over and get me?"

"I did," she answered with a sneer. "But when I knocked on the door, you didn't answer. You weren't home."

"But she wanted to talk to me?"

"I gather that's why she sent me over to fetch you." Young Miss Julie could not contain her sarcasm. It oozed out of her mouth. Her tongue moved like a dagger on my heart.

I wandered out of the big house content with the knowledge that Evelyn had tried to communicate with me. I climbed onto my bike and went for a ride. I pedaled like a man possessed. I charged up and down the steepest hills. My legs felt like bands of steel.

OCTOBER 21.

I talked to my realtor again today. She said the couple buying the house was not interested in purchasing any used furniture. That's what she called our belongings, "used furniture."

Which means I have to get rid of the stuff myself. There is so much. Five and a half years we lived there. Five and a half years of my life occupy that house.

And yet, I do not want to go near the place. I do not even want to drive down our street. I do not want to see or touch anything. I fear the memories. I fear the pain and the sadness.

Still, I will have to make a plan. I will need to figure something out. The closing is less than two weeks away.

OCTOBER 22.

I went over to the big house an hour or so ago to ask Julie a question I had meant to ask her during our last amiable encounter. "Did Mrs. Richmond say when she'd be back?"

"She did, yes."

"And do you think you could tell me when that might be?"

She no doubt would have preferred not to tell me, but she had an extra dagger to cast in my direction. "Early November," she finally mumbled. "The second or the third."

I thanked her and turned to go. But before I could reach the door, Julie shoved another blade through my rib cage. "Her concert tour is over," she said, and I could have sworn I saw her smirk. "But someone invited her for a holiday in Switzerland. I would think she is probably there now."

I stopped dead in the doorway to receive this information, but I left without giving a response.

Switzerland? Why Switzerland? Evelyn said nothing to me about a holiday in Switzerland. Who would have invited her to Switzerland? An old friend? A new friend? A devoted fan? Albert Schweitzer? St. Thomas Aquinas?

Come on, Sam. What you really want to know is whether or not the invitation came from a man or a woman. And if it came from a man, is that man, at this very moment, making love to her?

OCTOBER 23.

I made a few trips to Switzerland in my younger and more carefree days. And I made another trip over there not too long ago, I went there during the disintegration of my marriage.

One of my authors, a novelist, a very macho fellow, a true throwback to the days when men were men and all that nonsense, liked to slip away several times a year on various types of adventures. He had been trying to get me to accompany him on one of his adventures ever since I had edited his first novel. But I always had some excuse, some reason why I could not go.

Then one day at lunch he asked me, "So tell me, Sam, how's things on the domestic front?"

It had been six months or so since I had bought the new bed. Ellen and I had not made love, had not even held hands or shared a kiss in all that time. "Okay," I told him.

"Come on, Sam, I hear different."

I looked up from my plate of smoked salmon. He sat there smiling at me. His name was, still is, Mark McWilliams. His friends call him Will.

Simply stated, Will is who I wanted to be. He writes clever literary novels that sell pretty well and get good reviews. He effortlessly travels the world, speaking in any of several tongues. Nothing bothers him. He allows the trials and tribulations of life to roll easily off his chest. Yes, I once yearned to do the Conrad-Kipling-Hemingway thing. Mark McWilliams did it. Does it. He is out there doing it even as I write these words.

"What do you hear?" I asked him.

He gave me that sly smile of his to indicate that this was nothing more than fodder for his fiction. "I hear you and Ellen are, well, at odds. I hear she caught you . . ." and he stuck the middle finger of his right hand through a small hole he formed with the thumb and index finger of his left hand. He slipped that middle finger in and out of the hole.

"Jesus," I said. "Isn't anything private anymore?"

"Look, Sam," he said, "when things go wrong with the wife, you have to get the hell out of the house for a while. It's no big deal. Sometimes all you need to do is go down to the local gin mill for a couple cold ones and a rack or two of pool. Other times a day trip out to the track will take care of the wolf at the door. But every so often you need to clear out, blow town, slip away trailing nothing but a cloud of dust."

I looked at him and shook my head. "How would you know what a man needs to do when things go wrong with his wife? You've never even been married."

He just smiled again and said the time had come to head for the mountains.

"What mountains?"

"The Alps," he answered. "The Swiss Alps."

I told him I would think about it. But Will kept after me. By the time we finished lunch, and our second bottle of California red, I had agreed to go.

OCTOBER 24.

When I mentioned the trip to Ellen, she just glared at me and pretended as though I did not exist.

But finally, a few days later, she said, "Take your stupid trip, Sam. I don't give a damn." And then, for good measure, "And take your slutty whore with you. You can share her with Willy McWilliams."

Ellen did not like Will, never had, not the man or his prose. "He's a selfish and sexist pig," she would occasionally crow. "And his female characters have about as much depth as a kiddie pool."

A fairly accurate description.

Men, nevertheless, loved him.

OCTOBER 25.

The trip was a disaster right from the beginning. We flew to Germany in late February. We met up with a couple of Will's pals, hard-drinking Scotsmen who seemed to thrive on whiskey, bad jokes, and not more than two or three hours' sleep a night. We piled into a huge BMW sedan and drove south on the autobahn at around 150 miles an hour.

By the end of the first week, somewhere along the border between Germany and Austria, I was exhausted, hung over, and homesick. I had not been away from home without my wife since . . . well, since back before we were married. I suppose I had been away on short business trips. A day or two at the most. But never in all those years had I been away on vacation without Ellen. We always took our vacations together.

All I wanted to do, practically every second of every day, was call Ellen, tell her I was sorry, tell her I loved her, tell her I would do anything to make things right again between us.

But my good buddy Will had a better idea. "Give it a break, Sam. Just let her simmer. She'll appreciate you all the more for it. A couple weeks of wondering will do her good."

That day I had enough booze in me to believe him. But several days later, in the middle of a frigid alpine night, unable to sleep, the cold wind whipping against my bedroom window, the need to call her finally overwhelmed me.

I looked over at Will in the other bed. He had finally passed out. I slipped out of the room and crept down to the lobby to use the telephone. It must have been around nine o'clock at night back home. Nicky's bedtime. I dialed our number. The phone rang and rang and rang. The answering machine eventually picked up. I heard my own voice, calm and friendly. "Hi. Sam and Ellen and Nicky aren't here right now to take your call. But please leave a message after the beep, and we will get back to you as soon as possible."

I waited for the beep, but once it came I did not say a word. I just sat there with the receiver against my ear and wondered where she was, what she was doing, who she was with. I know of no lonelier feeling than calling home in the middle of the night from a foreign country and having no one answer.

I hung up the phone and went back up to bed. "To hell with her," I kept telling myself. "She's not worth worrying about." Maybe not. But I crawled back into bed, and all night long I had visions of her naked in the arms of that dweeb from the L.A. office.

I did not sleep a wink.

OCTOBER 26.

I made arrangements this morning to put our furniture and other household belongings in storage, into one of those cinderblock complexes that now dot the suburban landscape. I used to wonder who needed those storage facilities. Now I know it is people like me, people who have lost their way.

I also found some rinky-dink moving company to help me move the load. But they cannot do it until the first of the month. Maybe not till the second. That cuts things pretty close with the closing.

What choice do I have? I cannot do it all myself. It is too much work, too much effort. I do not have the time. Or the strength.

OCTOBER 27.

In the past few days the weather has turned cold and raw. All of a sudden it feels like winter lurks right around the corner. And I noticed going in on the train this morning that all of the leaves have fallen from the trees. Nothing but brown now everywhere you turn.

I do not know if I can ride a bike in weather like this. I bundled up in all the cold weather gear I own and went out after work for a ride, but I still froze my tail off, turned back after just a few miles.

Maybe I need to drive down to Florida and leave from there on my cross-country bike trip. I will take the southern route.

Come on, Sam, you are so full of it. You will never ride that bike across the country. Two and a half weeks in Europe were more than you could handle. And you were there with friends, laughing and joking, drinking and skiing. How are you going to cope with three months on the road? Solo? On your own? You are kidding yourself. Fantasizing to help you through another rotten and painful day without Ellen.

Or Evelyn.

OCTOBER 28.

I drove over to the house today thinking I might pack up some things, throw some things away. But I could not even get myself out of the minivan. I just sat out in the driveway staring at the house and at the For Sale sign at the end of the brick walk. Plastered across the sign was a sticker that said: SORRY, TOO LATE! SOLD!

After a while I put my head down on the steering wheel. Within a few seconds I started to cry.

All this time has passed, so much time, over a year, a year and a half, and still I am an emotional mess, nothing but a shell of my former self.

OCTOBER 29.

Maybe I should call Will McWilliams. See how he is. See what he is up to. Ask him if he is working on a new novel. He might need some editorial advice. He might even want me to edit his next novel.

OCTOBER 30.

I swear, Sam, sometimes you can be so out of touch with reality. You sat there in that pub in Zermatt, Switzerland, and verbally castrated Mark McWilliams in front of his friends and several strangers for a good twenty or thirty minutes. You called him every foul and filthy name in the book. You told him he knew nothing about women. And then you told him if he said one more goddamn word about Ellen you would knock his teeth out. You called him a windbag and a pompous horse's ass. You told him he had the sensitivity of a stone. And finally you told him—and this really cinched the deal, pal—you told him, in no uncertain terms, that his prose sucked and that his sentences sounded as though they had been created and constructed by a hyperactive fifth grader.

Nice work, Sam. First-class. Attaway to hang on to those National Book Award nominees.

And now you want to call him up out of the blue and ask him if he has been having a nice life.

OCTOBER 31.

I had no choice. I had to go over to the house today, roll up my sleeves, and begin to take care of some nasty business. At first I moved at a snail's pace through the silent, familiar rooms. Every pot and pan, every picture hanging on the wall, every piece of furniture stirred an emotion deep within me. Over and over I found myself smiling at some distant memory, at some faded moment from our domestic lives. But the smiles did not last for long. Sadness quickly became the prevalent emotion of the day. Sadness and melancholy.

Nevertheless, I battled on. I fought the memories with speed and agility. I literally ran through the house, stuffing toys and books and clothes and household gear into heavy-duty plastic bags. I found Nicky's underwear still folded in the top right-hand drawer of his dresser. I scooped up the neat piles of cotton briefs and flung them into a bag. I had tears, big wet tears, streaming down my face, clouding my vision.

Ellen's closet really messed with my psyche. Her skirts and dresses hung there crisply, some of them still protected by the dry cleaner's plastic wrap. I could see her in those skirts and dresses. And I could see me, late at night, after a party, back in the good old days, helping her out of those skirts and dresses, tossing them onto a chair, then leading her over to the bed.

That was all before.

Before Fiona.

Before the dweeb from the L.A. office.

Before Switzerland.

Before Sloan's Motel.

Tears pouring down my face, and every so often

wailing at the top of my lungs, I pulled the clothes off the hangers and shoved them into the black plastic bags.

As quickly as I filled the bags, I carried them down to the end of the driveway so the trash man could haul them away.

Out of sight, out of mind.

My God, what a day!

What did I do to deserve a day like this?

NOVEMBER 1.

If yesterday was the worst day of my life, then I wonder what would you call today?

No, the worst day of my life, by far, without a doubt, was that day, that terrible morning, at Sloan's Motel.

And I have had plenty of bad days since. But these last couple days definitely rank right up near the top.

Today's pain started early, before nine. I drove back to the house and found the moving van already in the driveway. And my movers, Tony and Vinnie, peering in the living room windows. Tony and Vinnie: big, rough, surly guys.

I tried to act nice, strike up a rapport. "Good morning. Sorry I'm late. I wasn't sure when you were coming."

They grunted, then one of them asked, "What goes? Everything go?"

"Everything," I told them.

"Basement? Attic? Garage?"

"Everything," I repeated. "Except for the stuff I throw away."

We went to work. Tony and Vinnie could really work. Like animals. Beasts of burden. They picked up Ellen's solid cherry dresser without bothering to remove the drawers. I had not emptied the drawers yet, either, so it was still filled with her sweaters and nightgowns and underwear. They hauled that dresser down the stairs, out the front door, and into the truck without the slightest sign of strain.

They trudged in and out of the house like worker ants. I guess they rested during the inbound trip. But they never actually sat down, not for hours. Slowly, very slowly, the house began to empty.

I stayed busy with my plastic bags. I felt sad and miserable. My head hurt and my stomach kept churning. At one point I even slipped into the bathroom and threw up. But like Vinnie and Tony, I kept at it, kept moving, one chore at a time.

Early in the afternoon I hauled a load of garbage bags over to the dump. On the way back I stopped and bought coffee and donuts. Tony and Vinnie ceased their labors just long enough to guzzle the coffee and stuff a few donuts into their mouths. They did not even sit down, just stood near the back of the truck.

I hung around, trying to make eye contact, hoping maybe to strike up a little conversation.

They ignored me as long as they could, but finally Vinnie gave in, grudgingly. "Moving, huh?"

"Yes," I said, "I'm moving."

"Where to?"

I shrugged. "I'm not sure."

Vinnie shot Tony a glance. It said, "Who's this bozo? Doesn't even know where he's moving." But he said to me, "What about the stuff? Where's it go?"

"Storage."

Vinnie thought this over as he shoved another donut covered with sugar and cinnamon into his mouth. "Divorced?"

At first I did not know what he meant. "Huh?"

"You get divorced? That why you're moving?"

"Oh," I said, "no, I didn't get divorced." And then, I am not sure why, I told them the truth. "My wife died."

Tony and Vinnie did not even stop chewing. They did, however, fix their gaze on the ground for three or four seconds, kick at some invisible dust. That was their show of sympathy, their moment of respect for the dead. Everything they had to offer.

And then, believe it or not, Tony said, "No shit? Like, that sucks."

And Vinnie: "We figured you was divorced. Lots of people we move now 'days is."

And then, the coffee cups sucked dry, the donut box empty except for crumbs, the boys went back to work.

I slipped away to a private corner and had myself a good cry. And while I cried, I tried to figure out why God had bothered to create human beings. With our huge brains and tiny hearts we make such giant buffoons. Not a single graceful bone in our bodies.

But the day was not over. Oh no. Not even close. Not by a long shot. I had a long way to go.

We worked until dark. And still all the possessions Ellen and Nicky and I had accumulated over the years were not out of the house. So Vinnie and Tony and I agreed to rendezvous tomorrow morning at eight. The realtor would be coming by at noon to check the house, and then I had the closing at the lawyer's office at two in the afternoon.

A lot of things to do. Lots of details. Stress and strain.

On the way home I stopped at a diner for something to eat. I ate one of those turkey dinner specials with white meat, dark meat, stuffing, mashed potatoes, peas, and plenty of gravy. It tasted pretty good. I even ordered a second platter. All that work had brought on an appetite.

I wondered if it might do me good to go to work as a manual laborer for a year or two. It might give me a whole new perspective on life. I could be like Vinnie and Tony: lifting and carrying, lifting and carrying. Hour after hour after hour. Maybe I could work for them: Vinnie and Tony and Sam's Moving & Storage.

Then the second plateful of turkey and gravy came, and I realized in a few weeks it would be Thanksgiving. I decided, definitely, to have dinner with the family, to go up to Hanover and do the whole Thanksgiving weekend thing with Mom and Dad and my bother and sister: the big meal, the long walk, the endless football games on the tube, my hand wrapped around a tumbler of bourbon, the ice cubes chinking against the glass.

I decided to invite Evelyn. Introduce her to the family.

Then I had an insight, an inspiration. Maybe call it intuition. Whatever you want to call it, I suddenly knew that Evelyn had returned home, a day or two early, so I wolfed down my food, paid the bill, and hurried home.

I pulled in the driveway a few hours ago, a little before nine. Evelyn's bedroom light was on. So was her bathroom light. She may be blind but she still likes to turn on the lights when she enters a room. She says she can sense the brightness.

I stood out in the driveway. It was cold. I could see my breath. And then I saw Evelyn pass in front of her bedroom window.

Finally, she was back.

I thought about going directly over, even if just to say hello. But I needed a shave and a shower, just in case our hello turned a bit more ambitious, perhaps more passionate. So I walked and fed the dogs, then I shaved and took a long hot shower.

I cannot tell a lie; vivid images of lying warm and naked with Evelyn danced through my brain.

Too bad things did not turn out that way. No, they surely did not. Not by any stretch of the imagination. If I had a rope and a strong branch handy, I would hang myself, suck the life right out of my lungs.

I left the cottage and started across the drive. It was even colder now, down around freezing. But perfectly clear. And absolutely still. The moon, enormous and white, lit up the sky.

I stopped, glanced up again at Evelyn's bedroom window. And there stood my lover in one of her long silk kimonos. She had her hand on her hip, a smile on her face.

I saw her laugh then, a big happy laugh. Full of merriment and joy. But what was she laughing at? Whom was she laughing with?

Julie? Was Julie up there with her? Julie has no sense of humor.

Maybe Roger? Perhaps Roger had come home unexpectedly for a visit with his mommy.

No, it was not Julie. And it was not Roger, either.

But it was a man.

There was a man up in Evelyn's bedroom. A fucking man.

As I watched her smiling and laughing, he walked right into the picture. He filled the window frame. He filled it with his size and his presence. And then, right in front of me, he reached out and embraced her. He held Evelyn close against his chest. And a moment later he kissed her, hard, on the lips.

Something in my stomach heaved. I bent over at the waist and puked. Right there on the driveway, for the second time today, I threw up. Turkey and stuffing and peas and potatoes and gravy rose up out of my gut and spewed out of my mouth onto the cold asphalt.

And when finally I stood erect again, and I glanced up at her window, they were gone.

Long gone.

To where and for what, I could only imagine.

NOVEMBER 2.

Another rough day.

Let me see if I can gather myself and get what happened down on paper. It is late, close to midnight, but I know I will not be able to sleep. I did not sleep last night, I will not sleep tonight, I may never sleep again. I feel like I am moving a million miles an hour. I cannot sit still. I am vibrating here in this chair at the dining room table.

Last night, after I threw up on the driveway, I started for the back door of the big house. I fully intended to barge in on Evelyn and this new Romeo character she has toted home from Europe. But no go: the door was locked. And I did not have the guts to break the glass or knock down the door. So I turned and slunk back here to the cottage. I lay in bed wide awake. I could not even keep my eyes closed. My body tossed and turned while my brain hissed and hummed.

Finally, around dawn, I dozed off. And when I opened my eyes, the clock on the stand beside the bed read 7:49 A.M.

I scrambled out of bed, back into my clothes, and headed for the door. As I crossed the driveway to the minivan, I glanced over at the big house. I looked up at Evelyn's bedroom window. I saw nothing. Not a thing. Not a soul.

"Fuck it," I heard myself say right out loud, right into the cold morning air. "I'll deal with her later."

I drove like a maniac over to my old half-empty house. It was almost nine o'clock by the time I pulled in the driveway. Tony and Vinnie had already arrived. They barely acknowledged my presence when I said hello.

I went to work on the basement. Up and down. Up and down. So much stuff: toys and tools, ladders and lumber, old clothes, old magazines, old books. I filled one plastic trash bag after another.

By noon we had the house pretty close to empty. The realtor showed up in her spiffy white Mercedes. "Still at it, hey, Mr. Adams?"

I wanted in the worst way to stuff her into one of those plastic garbage bags, tote her off to the dump. But, of course, I did no such thing. I am a good boy. I even showed her a few teeth. "We've just about got it licked."

She gave me a phony smile, then made her room-by-room inspection. I had been busy sweeping and vacuuming, so the house looked reasonably clean.

She made voluminous notes, which I heard about later at the closing: cracked panes of glass, holes in the doors, holes in the cupboards, holes in the sheetrock, blah blah blah blah blah.

As she drove away, I flashed her the bird. Behind her back.

Then back to work.

By one-thirty we had everything out of the house and garage. Tony and Vinnie finished packing the truck while I made one last trip through the empty rooms. The desire to back out of the deal, to hang on to the house, kept kicking me in the side of the head. Every empty room I entered brought back fond memories: Nicky and I wrestling in the living room, Ellen and I making love in the bedroom, the three of us sitting around the Christmas tree in the family room. Out, memories, out! I started to cry.

I might have just collapsed right there on the floor of Nicky's bedroom, given up entirely, had I not heard a noise emanating from the attic. There was someone up there. I could hear footsteps. I could hear the rafters squeaking. I glanced out the window. Tony and Vinnie stood out by their truck. So who was in the attic? It had to be the creature. He must have escaped from jail. Who else would be lurking in the dark, creepy places?

I did not wait around to find out. I sprinted down the stairs and out the front door. I did not look back.

I drove to the lawyer's office downtown. The attorneys talked and talked. They carried on for hours about the most mundane details. For a few minutes I actually fell asleep.

I must have signed my name a hundred times, a thousand times. I felt like a trained chimp. They did everything for me but hold the pen.

By five o'clock the deal was done. I no longer owned a house, but I suddenly had a sizable chunk of cash at my disposal. After paying off the mortgage and the property taxes and the attorney, I made myself $156,000. A tidy sum of money. Which modern technology transferred directly into my bank account faster than I could reach into my wallet and pull out a one-dollar bill.

Incredible.

It happened even faster than Ellen's death.

I shook a few hands and blew out of that lawyer's office as fast as my feet could carry me. The time had come to head for home and the confrontation with Evelyn that had been brewing in my head ever since I had caught her and Romeo through yonder bedroom window.

But not so fast. I still had one more stop to make.

Tony and Vinnie were already at the storage facility waiting for me. I got my key from the guy in the office, and we drove into the huge cinderblock complex. It took a while but we finally found number 338. I rolled up the garage door. One look inside and we all three knew that all the stuff in the truck would never fit into that 15-by-15 cell.

We started shoving it in anyway. No choice but to keep going, keep pushing forward.

It grew dark long before we had the truck even half-empty. We once again agreed to meet in the morning. They left the truck and drove away in Tony's Chevy Blazer. I hung around for a while and stared at my possessions. I wondered how long I would have them in storage, if I would ever use the lamps and the desks and the beds again. Maybe I should have just sold everything, or donated it all to a worthy charity.

I closed and locked the door and drove away. The time had finally come to deal with Evelyn.

But Evelyn was not dumb. Evelyn was as sharp as a tack. Evelyn was not home. Evelyn had flown the coop.

"Where is she?" I demanded of Julie, who had reluctantly answered my knock on the back door.

"She had to go out" came the snippy reply.

"Out where?"

"Just out."

"When will she be back?"

"I don't know." She slammed the door in my face.

I retreated here to the cottage. I paced for an hour or more. Back and forth. Like a caged panther. I could not decide what to do next.

So I did the smart thing. I took Sunshine and Moxie out for a long walk in the moonlight. It did us all a lot of good.

NOVEMBER 3

I met Tony and Vinnie over at the storage facility early this morning. We finally finished unloading the truck. We crammed everything into that cell as best we could. By the end we were more or less throwing the lighter stuff up on top of the heavier stuff. A real mess.

The few things that would not fit, I gave away to Tony and Vinnie, my good buddies. Then I wrote them a check for their labors, shook hands, and we parted company.

Never, I feel sure, to meet again.

Now I am back here at the cottage with nothing to

do, nowhere to go. I should probably go to work, but I think that will have to wait until tomorrow. I could do some editing here at home, but I fear the damage I might do with my red pencil. I could go out for a bike ride, but there is a nasty chill in the air.

I've already been over to the big house looking for Evelyn. Too bad no one answered my knock. Not even Julie.

I don't care. It's just as well she's not home. I'd only get mad. My jealousy would only make me angry. Besides, I'm whipped. Beat to the bone. These last few stressful days have left me exhausted. I need sleep.

NOVEMBER 4.

Still no one home over at the big house. All last night the place was as dark as a tomb, not a light on anywhere, not a soul in sight.

Where is she?

Probably off screwing that dweeb from the L.A. office.

No, wait, that was Ellen. This is Evelyn. She's probably off screwing that Romeo scoundrel who swept her off to Switzerland. The one I saw through her bedroom window.

NOVEMBER 5.

I feel much better today. I feel rested and calm. I put in several good hours at work. I began editing an excellent new manuscript, one so tight with suspense that it might actually hold my attention throughout.

When I arrived home from work, there was still no one over at the big house. This is quite upsetting. I certainly would like to know where Evelyn is, and why she seems to be avoiding me.

Maybe I should just pack up my gear and blow town. I have money: money in the bank, money in my wallet.

I could go anywhere, do anything.

But go where?

Do what?

NOVEMBER 6.

Still no sign of Evelyn. No sign of Julie. No sign of anyone. I am beginning to worry that something bad has happened.

I wonder if maybe I should call the police. Report Evelyn missing.

NOVEMBER 7.

I called my mother this morning before I went to work. She wasn't home. Nor was my father. No one answered.

I called them again from the office. Still no answer.

And I have just called them again. Just a few minutes ago. From right here in the cottage. But still they are not home. Neither is my brother. Or my sister. The whole family seems to have suddenly disappeared.

Their phones just ring and ring and ring.

I wish someone would answer.

I wish someone would talk to me.

NOVEMBER 14.

I have not written a word in days. And for good reason: there has simply not been time.

Tragedy has intervened in our lives.

It happened a week ago, exactly one week ago today. I believe it was the same day I tried to call my mother. No, it was the next day, early the following morning.

But I cannot talk about it, not right now.

I have to get to the hospital.

NOVEMBER 15.

Last week . . . early morning . . . not too long after dawn . . . I got up, pulled on some sweatpants and a jacket. . . . Took the dogs out for a walk. . . . I always take the dogs for a nice long walk before going off to work. . . .

That's what I expected, what I fully anticipated: just another day on the job. But no, something highly unusual was on the agenda . . . something way beyond my control.

As we came across the driveway, Sunshine and Moxie and I, I saw the lights on over at the big house. . . . I saw lights in the kitchen. . . . In the hallway. . . . In the music room. . . . In the bedroom . . . Evelyn's bedroom.

Finally, I thought, she's home!

I gave the dogs time to do their business, then I chased them back into the cottage. At least I thought I did.

And then, without another thought, I headed back to the big house to see Evelyn, to find out where she had been all this time.

So little do we know what the future holds in store.
It is all such a mystery until the moment it happens.

I should have walked the dogs, taken a hot shower,
gone off to work, and buried myself in my unedited
manuscripts.

Ah yes, hindsight is a wonderful catharsis.

NOVEMBER 16.

The back door of the big house was locked. I knocked.
I rang the bell. No one came. No one answered. I
knocked a little harder. I knocked as hard as I dared.
I did not want to break the glass.

A minute passed. Two minutes. Three minutes. I
continued to slam my fist against the door frame.

Finally, Evelyn's bedroom window opened directly
over my head. "Yes? Who is it? Who's there?"

I stepped back and looked up. "It's me."

"Sam?"

"That's right, Sam."

Evelyn took a moment, surely to think things over.
Then, "I'll be right down."

I waited. My body hummed along at an exaggerated speed. "Stay cool, Sam," I told myself. "Stay
calm."

Yes. Excellent advice.

NOVEMBER 17.

I watched her through the glass as she stepped out of
the shadows. She walked across the kitchen and approached the back door. Her feet barely touched the

floor. Light as a feather. She had such a smooth, easy gait, confident and, yes, even graceful. One of God's few.

She knew exactly how many steps to take. She reached for the doorknob and found it immediately. The lock released. I had to hold myself back, keep myself in check. I felt like a wild beast who had been tied to a stake and deprived of food and water for many weeks.

I should have just turned on my heel and headed home. Come again another day. But the door swung open.

"Sam," said Evelyn, smiling, "I'm so glad you've come over."

I glared at her. Stepped inside. Walked right past her. Sweat covered my forehead even though it was freezing outside. My hands shook. My eyes darted around the room, no doubt searching for Romeo.

Evelyn wore her long red silk kimono. "I was asleep," she said. "Is it still early? It feels early."

I mumbled something about the time.

She must have sensed my irritation. She retreated into the kitchen.

I pursued.

"I arrived home quite late last night," she said, her voice steady. "The flight was delayed for several hours. It must have been after two o'clock by the time I got to bed."

I said nothing. I simply watched with narrowed eyes as Evelyn crossed to the sink and filled a glass with water. As it filled, she said, "I can't tell you what a relief it is to finally be home."

I made no response but continued to watch as she drank the water in one long swallow. Then, "Would you like something, Sam? A cup of tea? Coffee? I really don't know what's here."

I wanted her to shut up. "No, I don't want anything."

She shrugged, refilled her glass. "So, how are you?"

"Me? I'm swell."

Evelyn, her working senses remarkably acute, knew without question that I was annoyed and probably furious. She could hear it in my voice, feel it in my body language, smell it gushing from my pores. But she had no intention of recognizing my rancor. My petty anger was beneath her. In her mind, my emotional bile had absolutely no validity.

She polished off a second glass of water, placed the glass in the sink, brushed by me, and headed down the long dark hallway toward the front of the house.

I followed close behind.

"So, Sam," she asked, cool as can be, "tell me, how has the weather been? I normally loathe the weather around here this time of year. So damp and gray and dreary."

NOVEMBER 18.

I could not believe she asked about the weather. The gall. The unmitigated gall. For just a moment I felt the desire to sprint down that hallway and crush her throat with my bare hands.

But, of course, I did no such thing.

I held myself together.

I kept myself calm.

My God, look at the time. I should have left an hour ago. I have to get out of here. I have to get to the hospital.

NOVEMBER 19.

Okay.

I told Evelyn the weather had been swell, just like me. And then, because I had to, I asked my favorite question, "Where have you been? You told me back at the end of September that you would be gone for two or three weeks. It's now the second week of November. You appeared one night a week or so ago, and then, just as suddenly, you disappeared the following morning."

Evelyn had by this time passed the doors leading to the music room. She stood at the bottom of the long, steep flight of stairs, her right hand grasping the beautiful mahogany banister. She turned and faced me. "You mean Julie didn't tell you?"

"Tell me what? Julie doesn't tell me anything. Julie hates me. I haven't even seen Julie for three or four days. I haven't seen anyone. What the hell is going on, Evelyn? Where have you been?"

Her voice softened. Her face grew tense. "Roger was in an accident."

"An accident? What kind of accident?"

She sighed, then took a shuddery breath. "Come up stairs, Sam. I need to use the bathroom and get dressed."

NOVEMBER 20.

"The accident occurred," she told me after we had reached her bedroom, after she had used the bathroom, "the same night I returned from Switzerland. Julie did tell you I went to Switzerland after the concerts in England, didn't she?"

"Yes," I said, struggling to control my anger, impatiently waiting to learn the details about Roger and his alleged accident, "she told me."

I sat in the leather armchair in the corner of the room. Evelyn, still wearing her red kimono, moved easily about the room, unpacking her suitcases, putting things away.

Her cello rested on the floor beside its hard plastic case.

She stopped moving. For several seconds she stood perfectly still. Then she sighed once again and sat on the edge of the mattress. "The telephone," she said softly. "The telephone rang in the middle of the night. I hate when the telephone rings in the middle of the night. It is such an ominous sound. Inevitably it means trouble."

"It was Roger?"

"No, it wasn't Roger. It was the hospital in Palo Alto. Roger and some of his friends had been up in San Francisco. They'd been drinking. On the way back to Stanford, just a mile or two from campus, they slammed into the back of a bus and the car flipped over."

"They ran into the back of a bus?"

"Yes."

For a second or two I was not sure if I believed her. Then she said, "The boy who was driving hit his head on the windshield. He died."

I took a deep breath. "And Roger?"

"Luckily, Roger was riding in back. But he came over the seat on impact. He broke two or three of his ribs, sprained his neck and his wrist, hit his head on the dashboard. He has a concussion."

I was not sure how I felt about all this. But I nevertheless knew the right things to say. "That's horrible, Evelyn. Is he going to be okay?"

"I think so. He's having some pretty bad headaches, but the doctor insists it's nothing to worry about."

I allowed some of my anger to dissipate. "So you flew out to California that same night?"

"Early the next morning. As soon as I could get a flight. Julie came a day or two later to help out. She'll be back day after tomorrow."

Evelyn began to sob. She did her best to hold back the tears, but I could see the strain on her face. I stood and crossed the plush carpet covering the bedroom floor. I sat down beside her.

"It's okay," I whispered. I put my arm around her and drew her close. "He's going to be fine. I'm sure of it. You said so yourself."

"I hope so," she said between sobs. "I don't know what I'd do if something happened to Roger. He's the only good thing I've ever done in my whole life."

"That's not true," I told her over and over again as I gently rocked her back and forth in my arms. "That's not true at all. You know that's not true."

NOVEMBER 21.

Evelyn calmed down after a few minutes. She dried her eyes and smiled at me. Then she stood, crossed the carpet, and went back into the bathroom to wash her face.

I wondered what I should do. I had come here to confront her, to have it out about what I had seen that night through her bedroom window, to demand the sordid facts about Romeo.

But now, this thing with Roger. It was all so complicated, so confusing.

Why didn't I just comfort her? Why didn't I just hold her close, let her know I was there if she needed me? That would have been the loving and humane thing to do.

NOVEMBER 22.

"Evelyn," I said, as she emerged from the bathroom, her face moist and cool from the water she had splashed on her eyes and cheeks, "I really need to talk to you about something."

What? The rent? The dripping faucet in the kitchen sink? The broken gutter on the back of the cottage? The potholes in the driveway?

I could have talked to her about anything, anything at all, any trite or trivial thing in the world. But no, I had to talk about that night, about what I had seen through her bedroom window. I had to. There was nothing else on my mind.

Not my past.
Not my future.
Not Ellen.
Not Nicholas.
Not Roger.
Nothing.

"What, Sam?" she asked. "What is it?"

NOVEMBER 24.

Yesterday was Thanksgiving. I spent the entire day at the hospital. I did not spend the day in the bosom of my family as I had planned, as I had hoped.

I did, however, spend quite a lot of time over at the hospital thinking about my family. Especially Nicky. Yesterday would have been his birthday.

"The Lord is my shepherd," said the preacher at Nicky's memorial service, "I shall not want."

I sat there in the front pew, tears pouring down my cheeks. I caught only bits and pieces of the psalm. "Yea, though I walk through the valley of the shadow of death, I will fear no evil. . . . Thou anointest my head with oil; my cup runneth over. . . . Surely goodness and mercy shall follow me all the days of my life. . . ."

Amen.

I suppose, in the end, we always have hope.

NOVEMBER 25.

"Who was he?" I asked as she drifted across the bedroom carpet, her feet not making a sound.

Evelyn gave me a glance even though she could not see. "Who, Sam? Who are you talking about?"

"That guy."

"What guy?"

I had been fairly calm up until then, and quite certain I could discuss this in a quiet and reasonable fashion. But her denial sent a powerful rush of blood through my system.

"You know exactly what guy."

"You're wrong, Sam. I don't know."

"Bullshit, Evelyn."

"You'll have to calm down, Sam," she said. "Give me some idea what you're talking about."

My anger instantly escalated into rage. "You know exactly who and what I'm talking about!"

"I don't, Sam. I don't have any idea. Why don't you tell me?"

NOVEMBER 26.

I could not write anymore yesterday. Nor today.

I do not want to think about this.

I do not want to think about anything. I just want to be Sunshine or Moxie, with a kind and loving master like me who feeds me twice a day, takes me for long walks in the woods, and lets me sleep on the bed.

Or at least under it.

NOVEMBER 27.

I just got home from the hospital.

Things do not look good.

NOVEMBER 28.

I lay in bed all last night and most of today thinking about Ellen. My wife. My beautiful dead wife. I started back with that first time we met out on Nauset Beach all those years ago. From there I moved forward through our courtship, our days at the apartment on 9th Street, our marriage, the birth of our son, the life we built and shared together. For a long time, for many hours, I managed to focus on the good times, on the many positive things that had happened between us.

But just before dawn, the bad times started to inflict themselves upon my thoughts. I did my best to suppress them, to drive them away, but they contained too much momentum, too much power, too much fury. As the first light of a new day filtered into the bedroom, I had no choice but to deal with the events that had transpired during and immediately after my journey to the Swiss Alps with Mark McWilliams and his Scottish cronies.

For three or four days, out there in the snow-covered mountains, I tried to reach Ellen on the telephone. I dialed our number morning, noon, and night. In vain. No one answered my calls. Not Ellen. Not Nicholas. No one but my voice on that damn answering machine. It started to drive me nuts. Sure, I was worried that maybe something had happened to one of them, but more than that, if I am entirely honest about it, I had this vivid and ugly image in the back of my mind of Ellen being mounted by the publicity dweeb from the L.A. office.

Then, finally, exhausted, irritated, ripe with anxiety, and just plain stressed out, I had my confrontation with Will McWilliams. The one in that Zermatt pub wherein I told my leading author his prose sucked and his sentences sounded as though they had been constructed by a fifth grader.

Our desire to travel together waned after my verbal assault.

The next morning I packed my bags and bid Will and his Scottish cohorts a fond farewell. I had seen enough of Europe. I wanted to go home and have it out with my two-timing wife.

I called her from the airport in Geneva. No answer. I called her from the airport in London. No answer. I called her when I landed in New York. No answer.

I caught the train to our local station. Then a cab out to the house. I spotted the minivan in the driveway

as I stepped out of the cab and marched up the front
walk. The brand-new minivan. Our second minivan.
The one that would have a flat tire out on the interstate
in the not-too-distant future. The one sitting outside
right now waiting to haul me over to the hospital.

I went up the front steps. I put down my bags. I
fished my key out of my pocket and inserted it into the
lock. I turned the lock and pushed open the front door.
And right away, immediately, I heard it: Ellen's laughter. Coming from upstairs. No, not from upstairs.
From the kitchen. Yes, the kitchen.

Very quietly I closed the door and crept along the
hallway. More laughter, then voices. A man's voice!
He must have been telling a joke. Something about the
pope running for president. I did not get it all. But
Ellen got it. Ellen responded like it was the funniest
damn joke she had ever heard in her whole life. She
cackled at the punch line of that joke.

I eased my way through the doorway of the kitchen.
They sat there at the table, side by side, drinking coffee,
yucking it up: Ellen and, I felt sure, the publicity dweeb
from the L.A. office.

He was tall and broad and good-looking. And several years my junior. He glanced up and saw me. Guilt
all over his face.

Ellen turned quickly. "Sam!"

"That's right," I said. "Sam. Your husband."

NOVEMBER 29.

The publicity dweeb, all smiles and muscles, was dismissed after a cursory introduction.

Before he left I was told his name was Ken Something

or Other. That he worked for Jackson, Jones & Reynolds in the marketing department. That he had just been transferred from L.A. to New York. That his wife had recently given birth to twin daughters. That he was looking for a house in the suburbs. That Ellen had brought him out to have a look around our neck of the woods.

I did not buy a word of it. Not one stinking word. I knew he was the publicity dweeb from the L.A. office. I knew it. And I knew, without question, that he had been upstairs in our bed screwing my wife.

"Where the hell have you been?" I demanded the second we closed the door on the back of Ken Something or Other.

"Excuse me?" Ellen, like Evelyn, did not respond well to oral commands.

I did not give a damn. Not that day. "I want to know where the hell you've been! I've been calling you for a week!"

"I've been in Los Angeles, Sam. You knew I had to go to Los Angeles."

"Bullshit, you've been fucking that twit Ken up in my bed!"

"What!"

"You heard me!"

"I hope I didn't."

"You bitch! You lying bitch!"

"Shut up, Sam. You're making a fool of yourself. We have enough troubles with our marriage without you behaving like this."

"You told me you were finished with him! But the second I turn my back, you have the bastard here in my house, in my bed!"

"You're delusional, Sam. And obviously suffering

from repressed guilt." She turned her back on me then, headed down the hallway.

"Wait one goddamn second, Ellen!"

"Wait for what? For you to explode? I suggest you go upstairs and lie down for a while. Take a Valium. Try and calm yourself. Then we'll talk." She kept moving, farther and farther away from me.

I started after her. "Where's my son?" I shouted. "Where is Nicky?"

"He's at my mother's."

"At your mother's? Why the hell is he at your mother's?"

She turned and glared at me. "Spring vacation this week, Sam. You knew he was going to my mother's. We discussed it before you went to—"

"Bullshit! You shipped him off to your mother's so you could fuck your lover on the kitchen table without Nicky seeing you!"

"You're totally irrational, Sam. You don't know what you're saying." She turned her back on me again and started to walk away.

I caught up to her in the doorway between the kitchen and the dining room. I grabbed her shoulder. "You whore!" I spun her around. "You lying whore!"

Her eyes met mine. They looked both frightened and furious. "I'm warning you, Sam—"

But I did not wait to hear her warning. I should have, of course, but I did not possess the power to hold myself in check. Before another second of our lives could pass, I struck Ellen across the face with the back of my hand.

Yes, I know I claimed some time ago that I had never laid a hand on my wife in anger. But that was a lie, a cover-up. I did strike my wife in anger.

But only once.

Just once.

Just that one time.

I hit her hard enough to knock her down.

NOVEMBER 30.

She was not hurt. Not physically.

Just stunned.

And humiliated.

She stood up, collected herself, and calmly made an announcement: "If you ever hit me again, Sam Adams, I swear to God, I will leave you. That is a promise. I will leave you and I will take Nicky with me. And I will not come back. Ever."

She then turned away once more. She went quickly down the hallway and up the stairs. At the top of the landing she paused just long enough to add this to the mix: "And by the way, you bastard, there never was any West Coast lover. Do you hear me? There was no lover. I made him up. To hurt you. To get back at you for what you did to me."

DECEMBER 1.

There was no West Coast lover.

There was no publicity dweeb from the L.A. office.

The dweeb was just a fictional character. A fantasy. The polar opposite to my factual Fiona. Or so she claimed.

But striking my wife: that was no fantasy. That was as close to reality as I had ever stumbled.

Too bad I did not believe her. Not for one second. I felt fully confident that Ken Something or Other was, in fact, the publicity dweeb from the L.A. office. And I also felt certain that he had been in my house, upstairs in my bed, having sex with my wife.

Ellen could not convince me otherwise.

Ken, the son of a bitch, even had the nerve to call her on the telephone. He called her several times. Even at night and on weekends. Supposedly it all had to do with business.

"Hello, Sam," he would say, nice as can be, as though we were old school chums. "It's Ken. Is Ellen there?"

DECEMBER 2.

Her threats aside, Ellen was not going to leave me. Not a chance. And no way was she ever taking Nicky from our home.

My mother left me when I was just a boy, a boy about Nicky's age.

No one was ever going to leave me again.

DECEMBER 3.

Not Ellen.
Not Nicky.
Not Evelyn.
No one.
"Who was he?" I demanded of Evelyn as she came out of the bathroom.
"Who, Sam?"
"That guy."

"What guy?"

Blood pounded against my temples. "You know exactly what guy."

"You're wrong, Sam. I don't know."

"Bullshit. You do, too." I could feel my rage clawing at me.

"I don't," she said. "Why don't you tell me what you're talking about?"

"Tell me who he was, dammit!"

"Don't get angry, Sam," she pleaded. "It doesn't do anyone any good to get angry."

But I was angry. Angry and agitated. And jealous. Extremely jealous. It had been building for days. "I'll get angry if I feel like getting angry!"

She started for the bedroom door. "Maybe you should go."

I was off the bed, on my feet. "I'll go when I'm damn good and ready to go."

"You're not going to get ugly, are you, Sam?"

Ugly? I had every intention of getting ugly. "I'll go after you tell me about Romeo."

"Romeo?"

"Yes, Romeo! The son of a bitch who was up here in your bedroom licking your nipples."

"You're sick, Sam," she said. "Sick, and obviously delusional."

"Screw you, delusional!" I had heard that one before. From Ellen. I did not need to hear it again.

"Listen to me, Sam," I heard Evelyn say. "Try to remember. You and I had an agreement. Yes? An agreement between two mature and consenting adults. An agreement that said we would both be able to cope with the consequences if we chose to become romantically and sexually involved."

Evelyn spoke quickly, almost frantically, as though she knew time might be running out.

"Yeah!" I shouted. "And where in that agreement did it give you the right to go off and cheat on me?"

"I didn't cheat on you, Sam."

"Bullshit!" The beast was taking full control now. "You're no better than my mother. Or my wife. Or Karin Dodd!"

Evelyn stood by the bedroom door, almost in the hallway. She had her arms wrapped around her chest. "Please, Sam, go. I really think you should go home. We'll talk about this later. Once you've had a chance to calm down."

Calm down. Right. Something else I had heard before. I moved forward. "Who was he, dammit!?"

"Sam. Please!" She sounded desperate.

I wanted her to sound desperate. "Tell me who he was!"

"I can only assume," she said, "that you mean the man who was in the house the night I returned from Switzerland, the night the hospital called about Roger."

The beast prowled around the bedroom, sniffing and snorting, ready to attack, ready to pounce.

"Is that who you mean, Sam? Is that who you saw?"

I managed to nod. "Damn right that's who I saw."

"For chrissakes, Sam, that was my brother! That was—"

"Bullshit!"

"Bullshit yourself. That was my brother! James!"

"I saw him kissing you, Evelyn! I saw him kissing your mouth and licking your breasts. Brothers don't kiss and lick, honey."

"You're crazy, Sam. Absolutely out of your mind.

You didn't see any such thing. You may have seen him hug me. Nothing more."

"I don't believe you! You're a lying stinking rotten whore."

A moment of silence passed between us. My words had brought it on.

Evelyn took the time to retreat inside of herself. And then, "You get the hell out of my house! Do you hear me? Get out! Now!"

But I was not ready to get out. Not quite yet.

I crossed the floor and picked up her precious cello. Plucked the taut strings.

"Damn you!" she cried out. "Put that down!"

"I'll put it down if you let me suck your nipples."

"Go to hell!"

I already had.

The beast, cello in hand, lumbered across the bedroom floor.

The prey backed away, through the doorway and out into the hall, near the top of the stairs.

The beast pursued.

"Sam! Please! Think about what you're doing."

But the beast could not think. The beast was pure instinct. His breath came in short, frantic bursts. I could feel the blood pumping through his body, exploding against the walls of his chest.

"Please, Sam! Please!"

The beast raised the cello high up over his head . .

"Sam!"

. . . And brought it crashing down against the wall just over her shoulder.

The fragile instrument shattered. The tension on the strings snapped. As they snapped, they made a high-pitched twanging sound.

The last sound they would ever make.

"My God!" I heard her cry out after the silence had descended upon us. "Oh my God!"

DECEMBER 5.

I have no idea what has happened to the past two days. Yesterday simply does not exist in my memory. I do not think yesterday happened. Of course, it did happen, but what happened?

The day before yesterday I was writing, trying my best to record the events that transpired up in Evelyn's bedroom, when suddenly, I blacked out. My mind went completely blank. My body went dead. I have no memory or recollection whatsoever of the past forty-eight hours.

I better get to the hospital.

For her.

For me.

DECEMBER 6.

Things at the hospital are not good.

No, things do not look good at all.

Or am I wrong about that?

Do they actually look very good? Very good indeed.

Two sides to every story. All depends on the editor's little red pencil.

DECEMBER 7.

I need to continue. I need to get down the rest of what happened.

"You've destroyed it!" she screamed. "You've destroyed my cello!"

I could not deny it. How could I deny it? I held the fractured fingerboard in my right hand. The belly, the bridge, the tailpiece, the tuning pegs—the whole delicate instrument lay scattered across the upstairs hallway. A few pieces had even flown down the steps.

"Thirty years," she cried. "Thirty years I've stroked and coddled that cello. Thirty years we've been together. Through good times and bad. Thirty years," she kept repeating, "thirty years!" Tears welled up in Evelyn's eyes. She began to sob, and then to actually weep.

I did not know what to do, did not know what to say. My rage vanished. It had started to dissipate the moment that instrument shattered. And it had disappeared entirely as soon as Evelyn began to cry. I felt bad. Very bad. I wanted to put her cello back together again. I wanted to rewind my life. Rewind it, if not back before the tragedy of Sloan's Motel, at least back before I slammed the cello against the wall, before I called her a liar and a whore.

But for all of our advanced technology, reality rewind is still not an option.

Evelyn's sobs suddenly faded, replaced by fury. Her whole body seemed to tense and swell. "Do you hear me? You cowardly bastard! Thirty years!" Her voice was strong again, fully in command. "Thirty years! And in less than thirty seconds you destroy it. A thirty-year relationship, long and fruitful, reduced to rubble because of your rotten, disgusting jealousy and your petty possessiveness. You're a sick man, Sam Adams. Most men are sick, but you, you are both sick and dangerous."

I stood there staring at her, wishing she could see me, relieved she could not, hoping that something would happen to make everything better again.

My right hand relaxed. The fractured neck of the cello fell silently onto the thick carpet.

But not so silently that Evelyn, with her superacute sense of hearing, did not pick up the sound and identify it immediately. "You bastard!" she screeched. "You miserable, no-good bastard! How could I have been so stupid to allow you into my life for even an instant?"

"No, Evelyn," I pleaded. "Don't say that. Don't even think it. You don't mean it."

"Damn you, I do mean it! I absolutely mean it. How could I not? I've made some bad choices when it comes to men, but you are easily the worst, the most destructive, the most—"

"No!"

"I tried to tell you before I went off to England that it was over between us. I made it as clear as I could without being ugly about it. You just wouldn't listen. You only hear what you want to hear, Sam. We had a nice run. Short and sweet. But any idiot could see the time had come to move on."

"No. Evelyn. You can't leave me."

"Of course I can, Sam. And I will. I already have. You're far too sick and needy for me. The whole time I was gone you must have been wallowing in your petty, jealous thoughts. And now you stand here and threaten me and abuse me. I can't stomach you. Not for one more second. You make me sick."

I waited for her to stop, to wind down. I took the time to gather my thoughts, to pull myself together. Then I said, very softly, "It's about to get worse, Evelyn."

She froze. She tried with all her might to see me through blind eyes. But, of course, she couldn't see a thing. "What is that supposed to mean?"

"It means what it means," I told her. "It means it's about to get worse. Much worse."

First uncertainty, and then terror, spread across her face.

I felt quite calm, perfectly in control, practically blissful.

I finally had her right where I wanted her: at the top of the stairs frozen in her tracks. She had neither the power nor the opportunity to make an escape.

"Let's talk about the past for a few moments. Shall we, Evelyn?"

"The past? What about the past?"

"The past is a wonderful thing," I told her. "The way we can twist it and mold it and manipulate it to suit our needs. The way we can edit it to highlight the good and eradicate the bad. Tell me, Evelyn, do you think anyone ever tells the truth about their past?"

She swallowed hard. She was having a little trouble getting a good deep breath. "I don't know," she answered. "The truth is a sticky business."

I laughed. "Yes, I suppose it is. Very sticky." And then, "Do you remember the story I told you about my friend Russell?"

"The boy who fell in the river?"

"Yes, the very same." I felt so good, so light and airy. "Well, I left out a couple minor details when I first told you that story."

"Minor details?" Evelyn was pale, and completely subdued.

There would be no more trouble from Evelyn. All her cockiness had suddenly faded away.

"Yes," I said, "one or two. Russell and I did go skating that day. We did climb up on the bridge and discuss the possibility of jumping off. But the truth is: the ice was much too thin out there in the middle of the river. No way either of us would have dared to jump that day. We were young and stupid, but not *that* young and stupid."

Evelyn, her lips so dry she could barely part them, struggled to form a few words. "But . . . but . . . but you said—"

"Forget what I said, Evelyn," I told her. "I'm about to edit what I said. You see, that whole day, that whole week, my good buddy Russell had been bugging me about my mother. That's right: my mother! She had gone to California some weeks earlier, you may remember, to take care of her sick aunt. Or so I thought. Or so I wanted to think. Russell knew otherwise. Russell knew the truth. Russell knew what I knew but didn't want to know. He knew—"

"Sam—"

"Be quiet, Evelyn. I'm telling you about Russell. Russell kept needling me, the way kids will do, telling me my mother had run off with Dr. Blue. I kept telling him to shut up, but he wouldn't shut up. I warned him, Evelyn. I warned the little son of a bitch."

Evelyn tried to slip away. She tried to make a break down the hallway. But I easily slowed her down, kept her in place.

"Russell called my mother a whore, Evelyn. Right up there on the bridge my best friend called my mother a whore. So what did I do? I did what I had to do. I pushed the bastard off the bridge into the river. I just grabbed him by the collar and gave him a shove. Nothing to it. Easiest thing in the world."

"No!"

"Oh yes, Evelyn. Absolutely. No one saw me do it. And no one ever suspected me, either. We were best buddies, Russell and I. Inseparable. I cried at his funeral. In fact, I cried for days. For months. I cried not because I'd killed him, but because I missed him."

"You're sick." Her two little words barely squeaked out of her mouth. All the color had drained from her face.

"He should have kept his mouth shut," I told her.

Evelyn struggled to create some moisture in her mouth. "Sam, please. This is not right. This is—"

I put the palm of my hand over her lips. "Shut up, Evelyn. I want you to shut up. You have a big fucking mouth and I want you to keep it closed."

I took my hand away. She said not a word.

"Good," I told her. "Excellent. And now, story number two is going to get a little revision. The story of Ms. Karin Dodd. Do you remember me telling you about Ms. Dodd, Evelyn?"

She began once again to sob.

"Evelyn?"

She nodded. Oh yes, she remembered.

"Well then, I'll get straight to it. No need to mince words. Karin, it seems, had decided to quit on me. She wanted to leave me. She told me she no longer wanted us to be together after we graduated from Dartmouth. She wanted to go off into the big wide world and be her own woman. Free and independent. Loose as a fucking goose. I, of course, wanted us to remain a couple. I thought marriage was in our future. We talked and talked about the situation for weeks. It was, as you can easily imagine, Evelyn, a rather stressful time."

Evelyn could not stop shaking her head. Back and forth, back and forth. "No, Sam, no. I don't want to hear this."

"Oh, Evelyn, just relax. This won't take much longer. In fact, to make a long story short . . ." God, I felt so good, so powerful. ". . . I'll cut straight to the meat of the matter. Remember how I told you I'd invited Karin to go on a picnic. Cheese and bread and wine, the whole shebang. Well, she needed an awful lot of convincing, but eventually she agreed to go. Late in the afternoon we got out there in that field of wildflowers, just the way I told you before, and right away I started telling her I loved her. She thought that sounded pretty sweet, so I asked her to marry me, for like the fiftieth time. But Evelyn, Karin said no, not even maybe, just flat-out no. She did not even want to think about it. Well, that upset me, being rejected and all, but I didn't get mad. In fact, I stayed reasonably calm. I even—

"Sam, please—"

"Be quiet, Evelyn! I didn't want to hurt Karin. I really didn't. I loved her. God, I worshiped her. I didn't order those yellow jackets to attack. They did that on their own. Okay, so maybe I provoked them when I stirred their nest with a stick. And I suppose I didn't really do Karin much good when I poured some wine on her bare skin. Those yellow jackets went absolutely wild over that wine. It must have been the sweetness. They worked themselves into a frenzy. After that I just sort of stood off to the side. I guess I took a little too much time to fetch her shot of adrenaline. I guess I should have given her the shot instead of taunting her with the needle. I guess I should have gotten her to the hospital a little faster. I guess—"

That's when Evelyn snapped. She had heard enough. She began to pound me on the chest with her fists. "You bastard!" she screamed. "You murdering bastard!"

I grabbed her wrists. "Oh, come now, Evelyn. Let's not say things we don't mean."

She spit in my face. The bitch spit right in my face. Right in my eye. Not once but twice.

And then, to make matters worse, "You bastard! You psychopath! You should be behind bars! In a cage! You should—"

I chose not to listen to this verbal attack. I clamped my hand over her mouth.

She tried to fight back. She tried to break free.

I let her go. That's all I did. I simply let her go.

That's when she stepped back.

DECEMBER 8.

Yes, Evelyn stepped back. But too far.

Too far.

She hit that top step and lost her balance.

I reached out to grab her, to save her.

But too late.

Too late.

DECEMBER 9.

Another day at the hospital. Another long and depressing day. The news is not good. Or maybe it is good. Again, depending upon your point of view.

The doctors and nurses remain hopeful.

One nurse in particular. Molly Anderson. The overnight nurse. She perks me up when I am blue. She lights up the room when things seem darkest. Molly is a lifesaver. A real sweetheart.

DECEMBER 10.

It could so easily have been avoided. If only Evelyn had loved me. If only she had been honest with me, treated me like a man. We could have prevented all this pain and suffering.

She hit that top step, teetered there for just a moment, and then she went back on her heels. Her arms flew into the air. She began to fall, backward, down that steep flight of stairs. She screamed. Oh yes, I heard her scream. I think she screamed my name.

Or maybe it was the name of the Savior.

It took forever for her to reach the bottom. I stood at the top of the landing and watched her body somersaulting down those carpeted treads. I could only stare as she tried to grab hold of the mahogany banister as she struggled desperately to bring her fall to an end.

And then, all at once, she stopped falling.

A dead silence filled the house.

DECEMBER 11.

I stood there staring down at her. And all of a sudden I felt cheated. Cheated that she had fallen before I had the chance to tell her about Ellen. I had saved the best for last.

Oh well. You can't always get what you want.

Evelyn lay perfectly still at the bottom of the stairs. She looked small and pale and broken. Like some child's doll.

After a minute or two had passed, I called her name. "Evelyn?"

No response. Not a sound. Not the slightest movement.

I made my way slowly down the steps. And here is where I must be honest. Here is where I must not tell a lie. I had this thought: If my dear Evelyn is dead, I will just tell them I found her lying there when I came over to visit, when I stopped by to pay the rent, to shoot the breeze, to share a pot of coffee, to inquire about her injured son.

Yes, I took the time to create an alibi.

But my thoughts marched on, one step further. I decided if Evelyn was *not* dead, I would have to tote her back up to the top of the stairs and give her another ride.

After all, I could not have her walking around, spilling her guts, spreading lies and half-truths about me.

That simply would not do.

DECEMBER 12.

I bent down at Evelyn's side. She was all twisted and broken. Her neck was bent at a very unnatural angle. I felt for a pulse. I found one after a search, very weak but still working.

I started to pick her up, but stopped. I had this weird feeling that she was watching me, that she could suddenly see me. It gave me the willies. So I set off on a little tour around the house, just to get my bearings, just to take a few deep breaths. After that I took some time to pick up the pieces of that busted cello. I didn't want to leave behind any evidence of domestic violence.

Eventually I went back to her body. I did not look at her face. I checked again for a pulse. It was stronger now. She was definitely going to make it, unless I threw her down the stairs another time or two.

But right about then is when I panicked. I was just kneeling there at her side, minding my own business, trying to get up the nerve to throw her over my shoulder and haul her up the steps, when I heard someone down the hallway, out in the kitchen. Yes, I could have sworn I heard the back door open and footsteps on the kitchen floor.

I did not hesitate. Not for a second. I saw clearly what I had to do. I stood and went quickly into the study across the hall. In a flash, I swept the telephone up into my hand and dialed 911.

"Yes," I told the woman on the other end of the line, "I have an emergency!" I sounded scared, anxious, upset. "My friend has fallen down the stairs. She needs help. I don't know what to do!"

The woman asked for the address. Then she told me to stay calm, that help would be there as soon as possible.

I thanked her and hung up. Then I sighed heavily, the best sigh I could muster, and turned around. I fully expected to find someone, perhaps Miss Julie, standing there watching me, taking note of my SOS. I hoped I had sounded convincing.

But Julie was not there. No one was there. No one was in the house. No one had come through the back door. No one had been in the kitchen. No one except for Moxie. Fucking Moxie. My goddamn golden retriever.

She stood there wagging her tail and looking up at me with those big brown eyes. I wanted to kick her into the middle of next week. Of course, I didn't do it. I could never hurt one of my dogs.

I gave her a pat on the head. Then I raced through the house, made sure I'd done away with any evidence. Finally I went back once more to the body. Evelyn was still unconscious. Out cold. I decided I had to just leave her be. Keep my fingers crossed. Hope for the best. Nothing else I could do.

The ambulance arrived. I heard it pull up the driveway. I went outside and directed the two emergency medical technicians into the house. Two policemen came minutes later. The four of them hovered over the broken body of Evelyn Richmond, easily the town's most famous figure.

They could see she was in a very bad way. They debated for quite a while how best to proceed. It took them almost twenty minutes to place Evelyn on a stretcher and carry her out of the house.

Out in the driveway, I overheard the two policemen talking. "She's blind," one of them said.

"Yeah, I know."

"Must have fallen down the stairs."

"Looks like."

"I saw her on public television a month or so ago. Playing the cello."

"Yeah, well, doesn't look like she'll be playing that again anytime soon."

"No, she looks pretty busted up."

"A goddamn mess."

The emergency medical technicians loaded Evelyn carefully into the back of the ambulance.

One of the policeman turned his attention to me. "You're the one who called, sir?"

"Yes."

"Your name?"

"Adams. Sam Adams."

He wrote my name in his notebook. "You're the one who found her?"

I hesitated, but only for an instant. "Yes."

"Did you move the body? Touch it in any way?"

I nodded. "Just to feel for a pulse. To make sure she was alive."

He wrote that down. "Anything else you can tell me?"

I thought about it, even considered telling him the truth, a full confession. But then I said, "Not really. I live over there in the cottage. I stopped by to say hello, to see if she needed anything. I do that three or four times a week. Usually before I go to work. This time I found her lying at the bottom of the stairs."

He nodded, wrote it all down.

"God," I added, "it's horrible. I hope she'll be okay."

He shrugged, then closed his notebook.

DECEMBER 13.

For most of the next week I sat close by Evelyn's side. She lay there in her hospital bed, unmoving and unconscious. I barely slept, rarely ate, came home only to change my clothes and shave my face and walk the dogs.

To occupy myself while at her bedside, I always

brought along a manuscript and a pocketful of red pencils. I needed to keep busy, to occupy my thoughts. I edited my little fingers to the bone: shifting, cutting, rewriting.

Of course, I understood perfectly my true motives for spending so much time in Evelyn's hospital room. Yes, I was there out of concern, because I adored her and was deeply worried about her condition. But what really motivated me was the fear that Evelyn would wake up in my absence and start spreading rumors about me torturing her and attacking her and pushing her down the stairs.

I did not need that.

DECEMBER 14.

Both of Evelyn's wrists had been broken in the fall. "Her right wrist," the doctor told me, "is pretty well shattered."

His choice of words startled me. "Shattered?"

He nodded. "Mrs. Richmond's getting older," he explained. "As you get older, your bones begin to lose calcium. They become brittle. Instead of a bone simply fracturing, as it might in a younger person, it actually breaks, and in this case, even shatters."

"But she will be able to play the cello again?"

The good doctor gave me a look rife with pity. "I think it's best if we just wait and see, Mr. Adams. Time will tell."

Yes. Time will tell.

DECEMBER 15.

Two days after Evelyn fell down the stairs, Julie returned from California. She sensed immediately that I might be responsible for Evelyn's condition.

"How did this happen?" she demanded.

I shrugged. "She must have fallen."

"She never would have fallen."

I shrugged again, went straight for the change of subject. "How," I asked, "is Roger?"

But Julie was having none of it. Right there in Evelyn's hospital room, right there under Evelyn's nose, she confronted me. "What happened to the cello?"

"The cello?" I asked. "What do you mean, what happened to it?"

I had very carefully cleaned up the shattered cello. I had put the fractured pieces in a brown paper bag. The evidence had gone into the minivan and then into a trash can down the street.

"It's gone," she said.

For almost a year I had been putting up with Julie's bullshit. That was long enough. "Not there, huh? Strange. I don't know where it could be."

She glared at me. "I think you do know."

"Sorry," I said, "I don't."

I thought she was going to slap me, hard, right across the face. But she didn't. She just continued to glare at me with her cold, dark, English eyes.

I am not worried about Julie. She cannot touch me.

DECEMBER 16.

Then, on the third day after her fall, a man walked into Evelyn's hospital room. He was tall, broad, and handsome. And he looked very familiar.

I reluctantly made way as he approached Evelyn's bed. He stood over her, squeezed her hand, kissed her on the forehead and on the mouth.

Several minutes passed before he turned and acknowledged my presence. There were tears in his eyes.

"Sam Adams," I announced, bracing myself. "A friend of Evelyn's."

He wiped his tears away. We shook hands.

And then I remembered: it was the man I had seen that night through Evelyn's bedroom window. Her Swiss lover. Romeo.

I did my best not to scowl at him, not to punch him in the eye. This whole mess, I reasoned, was largely his fault.

"James Coddington," he said.

I nodded, my eyes narrowed.

"Evelyn's brother," he added.

Yes, that is correct: Evelyn's brother. James.

To cover my shock, and perhaps my shame, I put my head in my hand and rubbed my eyes.

James put his arm around me. He comforted me. Then he took me down to the cafeteria and bought me a cup of coffee, thanked me repeatedly for staying at his sister's side, for being such a good friend.

There was no lover up in Evelyn's bedroom.

Just as there was no lover up in Ellen's bedroom, no dweeb from the L.A. office.

Misunderstandings. Nothing but misunderstandings.

DECEMBER 17.

A day or two after that, while I was sitting there absorbed in a manuscript, Evelyn finally came around. She did some moaning and groaning, then her fingers and toes began to twitch.

I stood up so fast, the manuscript scattered across the floor. I quickly picked it up and raced to her side. I was the only one in the room. I undoubtedly hoped it would stay that way.

But no, the nurses had Evelyn on intercom out at their station at the end of the hallway. Before I could apologize, before I could explain, before I could find out what Evelyn had in store for me, two nurses and then a doctor rushed into the room. They pushed me aside.

"Roger," Evelyn kept mumbling, her voice slurred and barely audible, "where is Roger? I need Roger."

Too bad Roger was not with us. He was on the other side of the country in his own hospital room recovering from his own violent collision.

Evelyn's eyes flickered open.

I backed away, into a corner.

Not that I had to hide. Even with her eyes wide open, Evelyn could not see a thing.

The doctor turned to me. "Are you Roger?"

I did not want to use my voice. I did not want Evelyn to hear me, did not want her to know I was in the room.

The doctor grew impatient. "Are you Roger, dammit?"

I nervously shook my head. "No," I whispered, "I'm not. I'm just a friend." A friend? "Roger is her son."

The doctor turned back to his patient.

Evelyn had not heard my voice. No, she was too

busy moaning and groaning, calling for her boy. Roger. The love of her life.

One of the nurses rested a hand on her shoulder.

I stood there, in the shadows, rigid, more or less frozen in place. It was unpleasant not having control.

DECEMBER 18.

Evelyn moaned and groaned for maybe five minutes. Five endless minutes.

Then she slipped back into Never Never Land.

Where she has remained ever since.

DECEMBER 19.

It has been more than six weeks now since Evelyn took that terrible tumble down those stairs.

Six long and exhausting weeks.

I spend less and less time at the hospital, I feel quite safe. I am pretty much full-time again at work. Back on the job.

A novel I edited last spring just hit the bookstores: *The Seduction*. A title I suggested to the author. It is getting rave reviews. Everyone at Jackson, Jones & Reynolds is very pleased.

There is talk of a promotion. Perhaps associate publisher. Nice, but I think I prefer senior editor.

DECEMBER 20.

Last night I spent an hour at the hospital. I thought the time had come for me to have a little chat with Evelyn. She could not hear me, of course, but I still wanted to tell her about Ellen, about what had happened between us.

I thought she deserved to know.

It is really quite simple: Ellen wanted a divorce. She no longer wanted to be my wife. Not after I had struck her in the face and called her a whore the day I returned home from Switzerland. She said she no longer loved me. She insisted the bonds between us had been broken, the mutual trust so necessary in a decent marriage had been destroyed.

I, of course, thought differently. I thought we could make our marriage work. I thought we could fix what had been broken.

I absolutely did not want to get divorced.

DECEMBER 21.

Ellen and I talked about our little problem all the time. We discussed it morning, noon, and night. It became the sole topic of conversation between us.

I guess it would be safe to say that it all came to a head a month or so later in room 14 of Sloan's Motel.

Ellen informed me after Nicky had fallen asleep that she fully intended to hire a lawyer and file divorce papers as early as the following week. "I'm sorry, Sam, but I've had enough of the fighting and the bickering and the mistrust."

I stayed calm, gave her announcement a few moments to settle. Then, "Have you told anyone?"

"No one," she answered. "I've just made the decision. I think it's for the best."

I told her I thought she was making a mistake. A big mistake.

DECEMBER 22.

We started arguing. In the middle of the night. Right there in room 14 of Sloan's Motel.

Ellen told me she wanted the house and the kid.

I told her no goddamn way.

Then the kid woke up and we all started yelling and screaming. It quickly turned into a free-for-all. At one point the kid said he wanted to live with his mother, not with me.

That hurt my feelings. "We're all going to live together," I told them. "No one is abandoning anyone!"

Evelyn lay there in her hospital bed as I related my tale. She didn't say a word, not one word.

"I just wanted to keep my family together," I told her. "I just wanted the three of us to be together. Was that too much to ask?"

Well, then the creature rolled into our room. And that was that.

DECEMBER 23.

The main reason I go to the hospital now is to see Molly Anderson, Evelyn's overnight nurse. Molly and I have become fast friends.

She is young and pretty, a year or so out of nursing school. Last night she asked me if I wanted to spend Christmas with her and her son and her parents.

I said yes. Of course I said yes. My heart beats a little faster whenever I even think about Molly.

Molly got married at the tender age of nineteen. Divorced at twenty-two. In between she had a son. His name is Josh.

I met Josh the other day at the hospital. He is seven years old. A very pleasant young man. Full of energy and curiosity. I could easily learn to love him.

DECEMBER 24.

The doctors now say that Evelyn has suffered irreversible brain damage. She will never again have full use of her mental capacities.

Evelyn, I am so sorry. All I wanted to do was love you, trust you, feel your breasts against my chest.

So much tragedy in the world.

So much pain.

So much sorrow.

But let us not dwell in darkness. We have all suffered enough darkness.

Let us look on the bright side. It is Christmas Eve. Almost two thousand years since the baby Jesus came into the world to save the soul of man.

CHRISTMAS.

Yes, Christmas morning! Joy to the world!

I bought young Josh one of those remote-control cars. And his lovely mother a bottle of perfume and a cashmere sweater.

I hope they like their gifts.

DECEMBER 26.

They loved their gifts.

Josh played with that car until the batteries ran out of juice. Luckily, I had a spare set in my jacket pocket.

Molly disappeared soon after the gift giving, only to return a few minutes later wearing both the sweater and the perfume.

She gave me the sweetest smile. And then, a moment later, a kiss on the cheek.

I almost swooned.

Her mother served up a sumptuous meal; roast beef and gravy with all the trimmings.

Her father kept refilling my glass with red wine.

We laughed and told stories and laughed some more.

It was a fine Christmas.

And later, in the evening, after it had grown dark, after Josh had been sent to bed and the parents had retired to their end of the house, Molly and I took the bottle of wine into the living room. We built a fire in the fireplace. We sat on the sofa, our shoulders touching. The tiny white lights on the Christmas tree sparkled. A few snowflakes fell past the window.

I put my arm around her. She nestled in close against me.

A nice fit.

We watched the fire. The flames dancing. The wood crackling.

I kissed her on the mouth.

She kissed me back.

DECEMBER 27.

Molly and I spent the whole day together. We went ice skating on a pond near her house. She skates beautifully, like an angel. I could watch her glide around on those skates all day long.

I think, before long, we will lie naked together.

DECEMBER 31.

Beautiful days pass. Tenderness and the joys of lovemaking.

I think I have found myself a fine and pliable woman.

I will have to call and tell my mother.

ABOUT THE AUTHOR

THOMAS WILLIAM SIMPSON is the author of six previous novels, including *The Hancock Boys, The Caretaker,* and *This Way Madness Lies,* which has been optioned by Paramount Pictures.

Mr. Simpson lives in New Jersey, where he is at work on his next novel, *The Murderous Macbeths.*

BANTAM MYSTERY COLLECTION

____ 57204-0 **KILLER PANCAKE** Davidson • • • • • • • • • • • • • • • $6.50

____ 56860-4 **THE GRASS WIDOW** Holbrook • • • • • • • • • • • • • $5.50

____ 57235-0 **MURDER AT MONTICELLO** Brown • • • • • • • • • $6.99

____ 57300-4 **STUD RITES** Conant • • • • • • • • • • • • • • • • • $5.99

____ 29684-1 **FEMMES FATAL** Cannell • • • • • • • • • • • • • • $5.50

____ 56448-X **AND ONE TO DIE ON** Haddam • • • • • • • • • $5.99

____ 57192-3 **BREAKHEART HILL** Cook • • • • • • • • • • • • • • $5.99

____ 56020-4 **THE LESSON OF HER DEATH** Deaver • • • • • $6.50

____ 56239-8 **REST IN PIECES** Brown • • • • • • • • • • • • • • • $6.50

____ 57456-6 **MONSTROUS REGIMENT OF WOMEN** King • • • • • $6.50

____ 57458-2 **WITH CHILD** King • • • • • • • • • • • • • • • • • • $6.50

____ 57251-2 **PLAYING FOR THE ASHES** George • • • • • • • • • $6.99

____ 57173-7 **UNDER THE BEETLE'S CELLAR** Walker • • • • • • • $5.99

____ 56793-4 **THE LAST HOUSEWIFE** Katz • • • • • • • • • • • • $5.99

____ 57205-9 **THE MUSIC OF WHAT HAPPENS** Straley • • • • • $5.99

____ 57477-9 **DEATH AT SANDRINGHAM HOUSE** Benison • • • • $5.99

____ 57070-1 **THE KILLING OF MONDAY BROWN** Prowell • • • • • $5.99

____ 57533-3 **REVISION OF JUSTICE** Wilson • • • • • • • • • • • $5.99

____ 57579-1 **SIMEON'S BRIDE** Taylor • • • • • • • • • • • • • $5.99

____ 57858-8 **TRIPLE WITCH** Graves • • • • • • • • • • • • • • • $5.50

Ask for these books at your local bookstore or use this page to order.

Please send me the books I have checked above. I am enclosing $____ (add $2.50 to cover postage and handling). Send check or money order, no cash or C.O.D.'s, please.

Name _____

Address _____

City/State/Zip _____

Send order to: Bantam Books, Dept. MC, 400 Hahn Road, Westminster, MD 21157
Allow four to six weeks for delivery.
Prices and availability subject to change without notice.   MC 9/00